I0773223

RAVEN

SUZY VIVIAN

Copyright © 2025 by Suzy Vivian

Paperback: 978-1-969919-02-2
eBook: 978-1-969919-03-9
Library of Congress Control Number: 2025921311

All rights reserved. No part of this publication may be reproduced, distributed, or transmitted in any form or by any electronic or mechanical means, without the prior written permission of the publisher, except in the case of brief quotations embodied in critical reviews and certain other noncommercial uses permitted by copyright law.

This is a work of fiction.

Ordering Information:

Prime Seven Media
518 Landmann St.
Tomah City, WI 54660

Printed in the United States of America

Table of Contents

Chapter 1 1

Chapter 2 6

Chapter 3 16

Chapter 4 23

Chapter 5 30

Chapter 6 39

Chapter 7 44

Chapter 8 66

Chapter 9 75

Chapter 10 89

Chapter 11 97

Chapter 12 122

Chapter 13 135

Chapter 14 174

Chapter 15 179

Chapter 16 192

Chapter 17 223

Chapter 18 232

Chapter 19 236

Chapter 20 245

Chapter 21 254

Chapter 22 260

Chapter 23 265

Chapter 24 275

Chapter 25 291

Chapter 26 302

Chapter 27 312

Chapter 28 348

Chapter 29 354

Chapter 30 364

Chapter 31 372

Chapter 32 391

Chapter 33 397

Chapter 34 404

Chapter 35 419

Chapter 36 432

Chapter 37 455

Chapter 38 470

Aftermath 474

Chapter 1

The shapeshifter, who was also a large black cat, had escaped Neberon, an evil wizard who wanted to rule the world and destroy anyone who had magic. She didn't know it at the time. She had hidden in a cave where some humans had come to hide from Neberon. As a result, she had a very satisfying meal of fresh humans.

After eating, she had stopped not far from her cave when she felt something evil headed her way. She realized then that the reason the people had come into her cave so unwisely was because they were being chased by an evil thing.

Sensing the evil nearby, she crouched in the wooded area where she could not be seen and watched the evil wizard Neberon killing the other villagers. She also watched as one group, who had hidden in another cave, escape to the lake nearby. She knew that would be where they were headed.

She knew it was the closest place where they might be safe.

Neberon had stopped killing for a while and apparently rested for a bit. He didn't know that the other villagers had escaped. The cat shapeshifter decided it wouldn't be a good idea to stick around when he found that out. So she left and went deeper into the forest to hide.

Not long after she left, there was a powerful burst of magic that burned and leveled some of the trees where she had been. She was grateful that she left when she did. She might have been crispy otherwise.

Now she had no master or human to guide her. Her only master had been the assassin, Black Hawk. She heard about Black Hawk's death when she stayed at an inn in the next village. She found out later that he was killed at the hand of a female human by the name of Jasmine. The cat was shocked that a woman could kill Black Hawk. He was an expert assassin. For him to be killed by a female was impossible to understand. It just so happened that as Black Hawk was murdered, she wasn't able to help her master because there had been a large dog that had frightened her away from the area. The dog seemed to grow bigger as he got closer to her. She couldn't have known that the dog belonged to the wizard Zarcon. Someone she would seek later.

As time passed, she was getting used to the idea of being alone and it was starting to feel pretty good. She could now go wherever she wanted and do whatever she wanted to do. She had learned that she must be a bit careful, though. Some people hated her and wanted her dead like Black Hawk. But she knew how to avoid them now. She had learned a lot as she traveled.

This shapeshifter could change into a tall woman with long black hair and a slender body. She had unnaturally long fingernails and yellow slanted eyes. As a Shapeshifter, she could change from cat to human and back at will. She was a magical creature, only part human.

She decided that she must spend much more of her life as a human. And if she was going to travel as a human, she needed a human name. She chose the name Raven. It felt right. She had admired the birds for their beautiful black feathers and quiet flight. She wanted to be more like those birds as she moved quietly about as a human. So she would call herself Raven from that moment on.

She had an air of sensuality that drew a certain type of man to her like a fly to honey. She would lure them to her room, wherever it may be, and then just when the man thought she would be fun to molest, she changed into her true form as a large black cat with long claws and teeth to tear out his throat. She didn't allow time for the men to scream their last. It was over before they even knew what hit them. She had to leave as soon as she had her fill of the man because she left a really big bloody mess in her room. She knew there would be those looking for her to kill her.

Strangely, those men made a pretty good meal. In fact, that was how she had survived. But it also meant she couldn't stay in any village very long. Once a man was missing, and the mess discovered, she was the prime suspect of his disappearance. It was known among certain villages that she was the shapeshifter that killed at will. So she would leave in the night and move on to find a new place and a new life.

Gradually, rumors of her started to spread throughout the land. That is why she ended up in a cave in the forest. Now she must find another place to hide until her story grew cold. As a cat, she could hunt the animal life in the forest without suspicion. She would kill then eat everything. Someone walking along where she had killed would only see a bit of red mud and maybe a bit of animal hair on the path. She was a very efficient killing machine whether animal or human. So hunting in the forest became the preferred method of obtaining food. She was much safer there.

Parents began telling their children that if they weren't good, the big black cat would come for them in the night. The children didn't know whether to believe or not, but decided they didn't want to take the chance on it being true. Unfortunately, it was true.

She moved on and decided to try another larger town as a female. She headed north where more people lived. There was a town there called Synkana that she wanted to investigate. Surely there were men there looking for a female to harm. Her mouth started to water at the thought. It would be interesting to say the least.

As Raven, she decided to find an inn that was near the edge of town. That way she could escape much faster and cause more harm in the meantime. After living with Black Hawk, she had learned that many people were stupid and easy to kill. In her experience, it had proven true for the most part. She would rather chase the men through the forest, but so few men went there anymore that it was becoming almost impossible to find a likely victim.

So it was that our shapeshifter, Raven, moved toward Synkana to find entertainment and dinner. She was hoping she could stay there for a while. Synkana was one of the largest towns in the land. Maybe it would be easier to do what she did longer with more people and more space to do it in.

Chapter 2

Raven was traveling to Synkana as a cat. She would hide during the day deep in the forest and sleep. During the night hours, she would travel softly toward the town of Synkana. She stayed off the main roads to avoid anyone seeing her and trying to kill her. She was a large black cat that had been known to kill livestock and that was not allowed. If word got out among the ranchers, her life wouldn't be worth a pin. But she was good at hiding and going unnoticed if she chose.

The forest here was thick and easy to hide in during the day. But further ahead, it thinned out and would present a problem for Raven. If she remained a cat, it would be easier for the ranchers to find and kill her. So she decided to go on as a female human during the day now. She must decide, the forest was already thinning to just a few oak, aspen, and a few pine trees. There was only a bit of grass under the trees that was definitely no cover for daytime sleeping.

As Raven crouched under a pine tree as a cat, she also realized there were many more humans traveling to Synkana the closer she got to the town. This was a matter she had not considered when she decided to go there. There were carts of goods and farmer's wagons full of vegetables and fruit. There were others with animal pelts to sell. Raven very nearly attacked one such cart when she saw a pelt much like her own on the stack. She had to pull it all back in so that she wouldn't call attention to herself and end up dead. She wanted to tear that man's heart out right then. But that would be a huge mistake. Maybe she could get to him later in Synkana. She was hoping so. It was something to look forward to.

There were also families traveling together in wagons looking for a new place to live. The children ran around the other wagons looking for friends. There was much laughter, and singing among them. Raven did not understand that part. She never felt the need for any of it. In fact, she looked down on anyone who seemed to crave it in their life. It just seemed so silly to her. For Raven, life was a serious matter of life and death, no time for such things as singing and dancing.

After a large group of humans went by, she decided she needed to travel as a human woman and try to fit in as time went by. She was very beautiful and had pronounced canine teeth. When she smiled, it frightened the humans nearby. So she rarely smiled or showed her teeth, which were deadly to her victims. She always wore black dresses. They were all close fitting and made of velvet with long sleeves and high collar and low necklines to show off her cleavage. When she transformed from cat to human, she was automatically wearing one of her favorite dresses. It appeared as she needed it when she became human. It was the one with the slit above her knee. She had it on now.

Unfortunately, it was not appropriate for walking along the road alone. Another group of humans were coming up behind her. She didn't quite know what to do about her dress. She had to get other clothes and now. She noticed a farm house just off the road from where she stood. So she walked off the road toward the farm house. There was a path paved with flat river rocks that lead to the house. As she approached, she could see someone at the upstairs window. She knocked on the door and waited for someone to answer it.

Raven was waiting for quite some time when she knocked again. Finally, the woman from the window upstairs came to the door.

The woman was thin and looked exhausted and angry. She said, "What do you want?" After looking at how Raven was dressed, she said, "Why are you dressed like that? Who are you, anyway?"

"I'm Raven, I know I look strange dressed as I am. That is why I'm here. I would like to buy clothing more appropriate for walking on the road to Synkana."

"Well I got nothin' to sell. I only have a few dresses and I need them all for m'self. You understand I'm sure."

Raven was growing angry. She needed a change of clothes immediately. This woman was not helping her. She decided to smile at the woman and scare her into giving her at least one dress. She smiled and said, "I'm sorry, but I really don't understand. I really do need a dress to travel in and you're the only one who could possibly help me." As she smiled, she noticed that the woman's eyes grew very large in shock. She clutched at her chest in fear.

She said, "What's wrong with yer teeth? They're kind of frightening! Alright! I'll give ya one of my poor dresses. It's not purty, but you can have it. I don't want yer money."

Raven looked around and said, "I really appreciate your kindness. May I come in to change? I cannot change out here."

"Well, alright, but make it snappy! You scare me." She went into her bedroom and brought out a dress for Raven. The woman finally said, "Here's yer dress. I hope it fits ya."

Raven took the dress and stepped inside, away from the doorway. She pulled off her black dress and put on the one given to her. It was a bit loose, but Raven didn't care.

"Thank you for the dress. You've been very kind." She said. Then she left to continue on the way to Synkana.

She now felt like she could blend in with the other travelers even though she was alone. No matter what happened, however, she knew she could handle herself, whether other animals or evil-minded men. So it was that she moved on with confidence in her abilities.

The dress she was given was a plain blue with nothing of interest about it. It was gathered at the waist and hung to the floor. It had long sleeves, gathered at the wrists. It buttoned up the front and had a collar. Not exactly Raven's style, but it would do for her purposes. She just needed it long enough to get to Synkana and blend in until she could get something more to her liking. Such a small price to pay for such a short period of time.

She walked slow enough that the group that was behind her finally caught up. She blended in with a large family with many children. She stayed just far enough away that none of them questioned her or tried to have a conversation.

When the group finally stopped for the night, Raven decided to move off the road into the trees just off the road a bit. She took off her dress and transformed into the cat. She was able to sleep better that way. It was dark enough this night with no moon to speak of. She was not friends with any one she had been traveling with, so none of them would wonder where she went. At least, that was what she hoped.

However, there was one man who had seen her slip off into the trees. He had followed her very quietly and watched as she took off her dress and transformed. He was shocked. But now he knew her secret. He was pretty sure he could use it against her at some point. He quietly sneaked back to his own group and slept until dawn.

Raven was, of course, unaware of what had happened while she changed and slept. When she woke up, she transformed and put on the blue dress. She walked out of the trees and joined her group again. Something felt strange now, however. There was a man behind her that kept looking at her with an evil glint in his eye. She knew what that meant. He may have seen her go into the trees and maybe even saw her transform into the cat. If that were so, she would have some fun when she got to Synkana. He would not bother her for long whatever he was thinking to do.

She knew he would follow her there and try some kind of bargain or just try to hurt her, and move on. But she would be ready for him in any case. She had dealt with men like him many times and she would take care of this one too. She was hoping he was just as stupid as the others. She would find out soon enough. She never acknowledged him as they traveled, but he just kept looking at her, which was annoying.

There was a hint of possible rain as the afternoon approached. The group started to look for shelter as they moved along. They were just coming into a larger village by the name of Caprisio, when it started to sprinkle. They found the inn near the center of the village. It was called the Blue Falcon. They were getting close to Synkana. It was thought that they only had another half day of travel to get there.

The inn was large and all those in the group who chose to could have a room there. Raven decided to go to the inn farther up the road for more privacy. She slipped out the back door of the Blue Falcon and quickly moved up the back alley where it was less likely she would be seen. She found an inn called the Parrot. She was glad it was small. There were only a few rooms and they were all rented except one. She was able to get that room for herself. She felt pretty sure that the men did not know where she went.

She had a quick meal of roast pig and potatoes. She drank some red wine but did not eat the potatoes and asked for more pig. She never ate anything but meat. Other things upset her stomach. The innkeeper noticed her strange meal but credited it to a new way of eating for the already slim. He chuckled about it later.

It was getting late and Raven was tired from all the walking she had done the past few days. As a cat it would have been much easier to move faster and get where she wanted to be much quicker. But she knew that she had to travel as a human to stay alive with all the people around as she traveled to the city.

Raven was so glad that she was almost to Synkana. She could be herself once she was in a large city. She could blend in much easier and at night she could be a cat and find the food she really craved, fresh meat.

The roast pig had been good enough for the night. But it was cooked and she much preferred fresh. She thought about going out later that night, but decided against it just in case the men were out looking for her. It was inconvenient that one of them knew she could change into a cat. They would probably figure out that she would want to hunt at night. Luckily the innkeeper had prepared roast pig. Otherwise she might have had a problem. She couldn't go without meat for an entire day.

While at dinner, Raven had kept to herself. She didn't want to have any interaction this night that might bring attention on herself. In her plain dress, she wasn't really noticed anyway. She was very grateful for that. There would be plenty of time for attention when she got to Synkana. She knew that the bigger city would have many people and anything she might get up to wouldn't be noticed as much as it would in a small village.

Early the next morning, Raven decided to leave. She had eaten enough meat the night before to last until she got to Synkana. She paid the innkeeper and walked out the back door. He thought it odd, but let her go. It was none of his business anyway.

They were now several hours from Synkana. They would need to spend one more night on the road and get to Synkana later the next morning. The group walked along all that day only stopping to eat whatever they had. Water was a bit scares, but there was enough to keep going just a few more miles until they could call it a day and sleep. It had been a long, hot day of walking and everyone needed the rest before going on in the morning.

Raven decided not to change that night. It was now too risky. She could sense some sort of plot between the men behind her. So this time she stayed closer to the family and the children. She hoped it would foil any plans they might have made against her. She didn't sleep well, but got some rest for the last walk getting into Synkana.

Chapter 3

Raven was safe that night with the family nearby. The men left her alone. There would be more time later on to do their dirty work. Raven was likely seen as an easy target that they could have some fun with. Though one of them had seen her turn into a large cat, they discounted that as fantasy and ignored him.

They had heard of such things as shapeshifters, but had never really believed it to be possible. Anyway, they decided they could get to her before she had time to transform, if indeed she could.

As the sun came up, Raven walked along with the family some more. She did feel safer with them now that the men seemed to be out to get her. The children sensed something strange about her so they didn't come near. She was a bit frightening. Raven was glad they left her alone.

There was a bit of forest with pine trees and aspen that were thick enough close to the town that she could transform into being a cat. She made sure no one was around and changed. She left the plain blue dress there in a pile and left the area swiftly. Instead of taking half the day, Raven was nearing Synkana in an hour. She found a secluded spot close to the entrance gate and changed back into a human. As usual, she was wearing her black dress.

She walked up to the gate of the city and the guards were more than happy to watch her walk in. She headed for the inn closest to the farthest edge of the city as possible. She would need to get out of town to hunt at night and didn't want to have to go through town or the back alley to do so.

She found an inn named the Grey Owl. It had a large picture of an owl above the sign. It was perfect. It was at the end of the street and close to the forest trail leading out of town and deeper into the forest. She met the innkeeper whose name was Errole. He was thin with a potbelly. He might have been handsome in a rugged way when he was young, but now he was just a bald old man. He was nervous talking to Raven. She was the most beautiful woman he had ever seen. Her smile made him even more nervous. He told her how much rooms cost.

"Do you have a room on the main floor and near the back door? I am nervous being alone you see."

"It just so happens I do have such a room. I'll show it to you if you'd like."

"That would be kind."

He showed her to her room. "Will it do for you ma'am?"

She said, "It's perfect! Thank you so very much."

Errole left her and went back to his kitchen.

Her room really was on the main floor near the back door. This was so perfect.

She needed to eat now. So she went to her room opened the window, and transformed. She actually leaped out the window and headed for the forest. She ran deep into the forest and began hunting for something to kill and eat. She wandered close to a small stream running through the forest hoping she would catch a deer or other large animal coming for a drink. She didn't wait long. A few moments later a small deer came to drink from the stream. Raven prepared to pounce.

She was able to drag the deer down and break its neck. She was able to eat the deer quickly before any other animal could take it from her. She finished and washer her muzzle and paws with the stream water. She felt much better for having a full meal of fresh meat. She carefully moved through the forest until she was near her room. She leaped into her room and changed into her human self. She was worn out by then, so she fell asleep in her bed.

Her last thought as she went to sleep was that this was perfect for her. The room was close to the forest and she could come and go as she pleased. Being able to hunt so easily was also wonderful.

She got up near midday and headed for the common room. The innkeeper welcomed her to the dining area and asked if she would like something to eat. Raven smiled, which scared the poor man, and said she wasn't hungry. It was all she could do not to break up laughing. But she knew she must not. She didn't want anyone to suspect her real life, Raven was really smart, for a cat.

There were men in the common room. They all sat up a bit straighter when Raven walked into the room. She enjoyed the attention, but didn't want any trouble so soon. She wanted to stay at the inn for a few days if possible. She ignored the men and went to a table in the corner at the rear of the common room. She was hoping to avoid anyone coming over to her. She had a glass of red wine and asked the innkeeper for some jerky. He looked at her funny but brought her a plate of jerky. He shook his head as he walked away.

Raven noticed it and decided she needed to get used to some different types of food that were more normal for humans. She thought she would try some cheese next time. At least it wasn't a plant.

Later, Raven decided to go shopping for some dresses. Her favorite dress she was wearing was attracting too much attention. She didn't have the plain blue dress any more. So she found it difficult to come up with a disguise. She knew those men from the trail would be watching for her. She asked the innkeeper if he had a wife. He was confused but said that "Yes" he did. Raven then asked him if she could borrow one of her dresses. She was willing to pay for it.

"Well, let me ask her if she can spare one." He went to the back of the kitchen to find his wife, Gwenny. "Honey, would you be willing to let one of our guests borrow one of your dresses for the day?"

Gwenny answered, "I'm not sure I can spare one, it is washday tomorrow and I'm low on clothes just now."

"She said she would be willing to pay for it. What do you think?"

"If she'll really pay for it, I could give her one."

Gwenny went to her closet and brought out her best dress hoping to get more money for it.

Errole brought the dress out to show Raven. It was quite pretty, a little bit big, but it would do.

"I would be willing to pay ten gold coins for it. Will that do?"

"It will do nicely, thank you." He gave her the dress and took the money to Gwenny who was thrilled with it.

Raven took the dress into her room and put it on. It fit well-enough. It was also really nice. She hadn't expected to find something quite so pretty in this little inn. She was now ready to go shopping. She decided to stay close to the inn and not go into the main part of Synkana. She didn't want to take any chances of those men finding her unprotected.

She went out of the inn and turned left. It looked like there might be some dress shops not far up the street. She walked quickly to the closest one and hurried inside. The dresses there were nice and not terribly costly. She tried on a few of the dresses and decided to keep one that was black satin. It had long puffy sleeves and a tight bodice and full skirt. She loved it. It was also a bit low in the neckline. She knew she looked good in that dress. She also found a red dress she liked. It had slim sleeves and a low neck. The bodice was tight and fit perfectly. The skirt was not so full and showed off her slender hips. She did have the body of a cat in that respect.

The owner of the shop complimented her on both dresses. She was pleased to sell them to Raven who made her dresses look very nice indeed. Raven paid for the dresses and when they were boxed up, she left the shop and headed back to her room at the inn.

Raven got away with that shopping trip, but the men were looking for her in earnest. Would she dare go out again? It would certainly be risky. She could surely handle one man, but the four of them would be too dangerous to have to deal with at once.

She decided to stay in her room during the day and only go out to eat at night. She hoped she would be safer that way. Only time would tell.

Chapter 4

Raven was glad she bought the two beautiful dresses. She felt really good in them and knew she looked even better. But now she needed to go hunting. She was starving. The cat part of her needed fresh meat and soon.

So Raven put on the dress she had arrived in and climbed out the bedroom window. She took off the dress and laid it by the window on the ground below. She transformed into a cat and leaped into the forest. She went deeper into the forest hoping to find something bigger this time.

She was gone a fairly short period of time and went to the stream she had seen before. She was lucky. There before her was a large buck with horns drinking at the stream. Raven jumped on its back and attacked the animal's spine. She was able to bite its neck and drop the animal to the ground. She quickly gutted it and began to eat. She got most of it before she had to get back to her room. It was getting close to morning.

She decided to transform where she was so she could clean up at the stream. As she changed, she realized she wasn't alone. A man was watching her transform into her human form. It was too late to transform back into a cat. She had on her favorite dress after the change, but it gave her no protection from this man.

"What do you want?"

"I want you, obviously. Can we make a deal?"

"What sort of deal?"

"One that will make us both rich. What do you say?"

"I'm not interested."

"Then I'm afraid you will regret it." He drew out a knife with the intention of killing Raven.

But Raven was quick. She grabbed a dead branch off the ground and blocked his strikes. He missed her and she was able to hit him with the tree branch just enough to stun him. She had time to run deeper into the forest and hide in the brush.

He screamed and came after her. He thought he knew where she was and called to her, "Come on out, I won't hurt you. I was just having a little fun." He was getting angry because he couldn't see her anywhere.

It was dark and she was wearing black, so she blended in with the night.

He finally gave up looking and headed back to his own inn. But he was deeper in the forest than he realized and got lost. Finally, he found a likely place to sleep and spent the rest of the night there. Or planned on it.

Raven was terrified and had to stay where she was until she was sure she was safe. After an hour, when it was getting lighter, she transformed into a cat and went looking for the man. He was going to pay dearly. She was pretty sure she knew where he was. She had been watching him wander around. She could smell him. He had a rather foul order about him that she found offensive. She got close enough to him to attack. He was sleeping and stupid. She pounced on him and ripped him to shreds. He didn't even have time to realize what hit him and he was dead. She tried to hide what was left of his body with leaves.

Once again, she washed up in the stream after transforming again. She walked back to the inn and found her dress, climbed in the window and fell asleep as soon as her head hit the pillow. Using her magic to transform was very tiring besides. So she needed lots of rest. She slept soundly for the first four hours, but then she realized what had really happened. Luckily, she had eaten before the man came and ruined her night. He had paid for that.

It had been a terrible night. She thought she was going to die for sure. Raven now must decide what to do. She had hoped to stay in Synkana for at least a few days. Now she knew that since that man had found her, there must be others who now knew where she was.

She also knew that sooner or later someone would find the remains of that man she had killed. They would be looking for a big cat and she was it. The innkeeper would remember her strange eating habits and then someone would decide it might be her that did the deed. If caught, she would likely be hanged. The more she thought about it, the more she realized she had to leave right away. But if she left Synkana, where would she go? There must be someplace she could go and be safe. The city was not safe, obviously. So now she might have to go back to the small villages where her cave had been. She would have to be a cat most of the time. But maybe that was what her life was going to be.

So, she packed up her dresses into her travel bag and got ready to leave Synkana as soon as possible. She didn't even dare pay her bill at the inn for fear the innkeeper would make her stay for the officials to come and get her.

She slipped out the window again and walked through the forest until she was far enough to run. She wanted to keep her dresses, but if she had to, she would leave them and transform and run as a cat. She thought maybe she could steal a horse later on.

Raven slipped through the forest quietly. She was wearing her favorite black dress so she could hide in the forest better. With her black hair, she could remain unseen from the road, especially as she traveled at night. During the day, she found a place deep in the forest where she could safely hide and sleep. She used her pack for a pillow. It was nice to have it.

The forest was cool and dark. She liked it. She was thinking maybe she could just live in the forest and forget about life in a village. It was getting too dangerous for her now. Maybe killing men wasn't the answer. She would have to think about that for a while. She was changing into a cat to hunt for food. She was eating better than she had in a long time. Waiting for a human victim was too difficult. She couldn't count on getting enough to eat.

She finally decided to continue to the small villages where she lived before. She might even try to find her cave. She wasn't sure about that because she had enjoyed spending time at the inn in Synkana. A real bed was much more comfortable than the ground in her cave. She was safe there, but not comfortable, even as a cat.

She had heard about a wizard by the name of Zarcon, She hoped that he might be able to help her deal with her magic as a shapeshifter. She had heard that he was in the village of Anakik. It wasn't much farther now. She had come far in a short period of time. She had been able to run fast through the forest. The nights were long and she made great progress.

She only hoped Zarcon would be willing to talk to her and help her with her magic. If not, she just didn't know what she would do after that.

So she kept moving toward Anakik and traveling during the night and sleeping during the day. She was nearly there when she could see the village through the trees, she got really nervous. This would make or break her life. She would do the best she could to present Zarcon with her problem and hope he could give her some answers to what she could do about it.

She was close to the village and thought it best to enter during the day. So she slept a bit before morning so she could walk in rested. She hoped to be at her best when she met Zarcon. She found a small creek and washed off the grim of the days spent traveling through the forest as best she could. She decided to change into one of the dresses she had purchased in Synkana. She wanted to look her best, too. The dress fit her beautifully. It gave her the confidence she needed to move ahead.

Chapter 5

As Raven entered the village, there were those who saw her and wondered about her appearance. She was wearing a beautiful dress that drew the attention of all who saw her enter the main square. Jasmine, a friend of Zarcon, happened to see her coming and walked up to her and introduced herself.

"Hi, my name is Jasmine. Who are you?"

Raven was shocked. Could this be the Jasmine that had killed her master, Black Hawk? She steadied herself and replied, "My name is Raven. I would like to speak with Zarcon the wizard. Is he here?"

"He's here, but not doing well. May I help you?"

"Well, I need to talk with someone who has magic and can help me with mine. Can you do that?"

"Not exactly, but I know someone who can. Her name is Magg and she knows all about magic."

"Sounds like she might be just the person I need to talk to."

Jasmine led her to Magg's room in the inn and knocked on her door. Magg was just resting and came to the door. When she saw Raven, she was very curious about her. She was beautiful and elegant. Why would she be in Anakik?

Magg was short and a bit overweight with light brown hair that was hard to manage. She was very powerful in her magic and was learning more about it. So it was that she would be able to help Raven in her need to find out more about her magic.

Jasmine said, "Magg, this is Raven. She would like to talk to you about magic. Do you have the time?"

"Of course, I love talking about magic. Come on in Raven and let's talk."

Jasmine closed the door as she walked away. Magg was so curious to find out what Raven needed to talk about.

"Thank you Magg. I really need to talk to you about my magic. It's been causing me some trouble over the years and I need to find a solution to it all."

"Tell me more about your magic. What happens when you use it?"

"I should explain, I'm a shapeshifter. I can change into a big black cat. I need to eat meat as a cat. It's a problem for me. I have used men when they try to attack me. I also hunt animals in the forest. The problem comes when I go to a city and have the men after me. I seem to attract the wrong sort, if you know what I mean. But there is danger in that. When the bodies of the men are found, the officials come after me and I'm in danger of being hanged."

Magg was stunned. She hadn't heard of a shapeshifter before and she didn't know quite what to do or say. How could she help this beautiful woman? What could she tell her that could possibly help? If only Zarcon were up to helping Raven. He was more of a counselor than she was. Maybe she could talk to Zarcon herself and get back to Raven about his advice.

"Raven, I will be honest with you. I don't know what to say. I can help you with regular magic questions, but Zarcon would know more about what to tell you to solve your issues."

"Would I be able to come with you when you speak to Zarcon? I really need to see him and explain what's happening in my life."

"Well, let me go see Zarcon and ask if he might be up to it. I'll get back to you right away."

"That's fair. Where should I wait?"

"You can wait in the dining area. Are you hungry? Aribon cooks a terrific steak. He can leave it a bit raw if you like."

Raven smiled and said, "Perfect. You read my mind."

So Magg led her to the dining area and introduced her to Aribon. "Aribon, this is Raven. She needs a little something to eat. Do you by any chance have some fresh meat?"

"Really? Let me think. I believe I have a couple of steaks I could get for you Raven. Will that do?"

"Aribon, just warm them up please. I don't need them cooked at all, if that's alright with you?"

"Any way you want it is fine with me." Aribon smiled at that and winked at Raven. After he went to the kitchen, he felt a little odd about it. The grill was hot, so he just put the steaks on the grill long enough to get them a bit warm, took them off the grill and put them on a plate for Raven.

Alfias, Aribon's young assistant, was in a bit of a shock that someone would want a steak that rare. He wanted to see this woman who wanted raw steak. He peaked out the door and saw Raven. She was beautiful, but a bit scary. Her yellow eyes and long fingernails were strange. He moved back into the kitchen and was glad he could hide there. He was slender and tall. He had blond hair that was cut short for convenience when he worked in the kitchen. He was also a bit shy.

Aribon brought Raven her steaks and set them before her at the table.

Raven was so grateful for Aribon's kindness. "Aribon, thank you. I didn't realize how hungry I was until I smelled the steak. You are so kind."

Aribon blushed a little and said, "It's my pleasure to help you. Come to me anytime for more." He smiled at her then.

As soon as Aribon walked away, Raven dug into the steaks. She tried to use a fork and knife, but she was so hungry, she finally picked one up and ate it. The second steak she was able to use a fork and knife. It felt so good to have food in her stomach. She was grateful that she had come to Anakik. She believed she would have some answers to her problems.

Meanwhile, Magg had walked back to Zarcon's room. She was checking on him and how he was feeling. He was awake and Greta was holding him and comforting him. Magg could see that he was weak. Greta was an older woman who was still very attractive. She was slender and shapely. She loved Zarcon with all her heart. She had a special magic that made it possible for her to calm those around her. It was very important when situations called for cooler heads.

Magg said, "Zarcon, there's a woman here that needs your help. She says she's a shapeshifter…"

Zarcon stopped her from saying more, "Magg, are you serious? I've only heard of one before. It was a female that could transform into a black cat."

"That's her!"

"She's here? Now? What's her problem that she needs my help?"

"I'm not sure. She talked about her need for meat. She was killing men who planned to do her wrong. She's afraid of officials wanting to have her hanged for it. Can you give her any advice?"

"I can try, I suppose. I think I can handle it. I'm actually feeling pretty good this morning."

"Great, I'll bring her in now."

Magg went to the dining room to let Raven know she could see Zarcon. Raven had just finished her steaks so she was ready to talk with Zarcon. She was so glad she would actually get to talk to him. She had been worried that he would not want to talk to her.

"You can see Zarcon now, Raven. Try not to wear him out, he's not well right now. I'll be with you."

"I'll do my best and thank you for helping me."

Raven and Magg walked to Zarcon's room. Greta let them in and stepped outside to allow them privacy. They went in and sat in the chairs that were set beside his bed.

Zarcon spoke to Raven, "What can I do for you, Raven. I have heard of you and some of your history. You're a shapeshifter, is that correct? Tell me about what you've been going through."

"Zarcon, I have wanted to speak to you for a while now. I think you're the only person who can help me with this. As you probably know, I can transform into a black cat when I need or want to. I need fresh meat for the cat that is me. It gets me into trouble at times. For instance, if a man tries to attack me I change and kill him. To be honest, I actually lure him in so I can kill him. I look for men that are the wrong sort so I don't feel regret when they are dead. But when the body and blood are found, officials come after me and want to have me hanged. I would rather avoid that if you know what I mean?"

Zarcon did know what she meant and was at a loss. "What is your goal here? How can I help you?"

"I want to stop killing humans. I can live on the forest animals, but I need a place to stay where I can be safe. I've traveled a lot over the years and the only time I felt kind of safe was in the cave not far from here. I had to leave when the evil thing came. I knew he would kill me if he knew I was there. But I don't want to live in a cave any more. Can you help me?"

Zarcon thought for a few moments and finally said, "I think I can. Could you live here in a small cottage? You would be safe and no one would hurt you. The villagers here are very kind. You would have to promise to kill only forest animals. Could you do that forever? If you kill one human, you will be killed, understood?"

"I do understand and will follow your rules. I will only hunt at night, but I will need to sleep during the day. Would that be a problem at all?"

"I don't foresee it to be. We have a few cottages that were left vacant when we had a problem with some mist monsters that killed some of the villagers. It was terrible. But Magg could help you find a cottage on the edge of the village that would be yours. What do you say?"

Raven was so happy. She said, "Zarcon that is so much more than I could have expected coming here. I'm so glad I did. You and Magg are so kind. Thank you."

Magg smiled at that and said, "I'm so glad you could help Raven, Zarcon. We can help her as a village and keep her safe. Welcome to Anakik, Raven."

"Thank you Magg, I'm so happy."

Magg was happy to have been there with Raven to find out what Zarcon suggested she could do in

Anakik. She walked with Raven to the town main street. Magg pointed out the cottages that were vacant, there were only two now. The one on the far side of the village was small, but very nice. Raven liked it right away. "This is perfect, and there's a bed too. I can't wait to move in. Actually, all I have is my pack that I've traveled with. So I'm really grateful that it's mostly furnished. Is there a market here that I could get some linens and such?"

"There is, just in the middle of the village. I should have showed you where it was. Would you like to rest or come with me now to see it?"

"I would love to come with you now, but I think I would rather rest for awhile. Can we go see it later tonight?"

"Yes, we can. I'll come just after dark if that is alright?"

"Perfect, and thanks again." Raven was exhausted and really did need her rest. She normally slept during the day and was feeling it now. She said goodbye to Magg and went to her room and laid down on her bed and slept through the rest of the day.

Chapter 6

Raven spent the day sleeping. It took hours before she was rested enough to go with Magg to see where the only store in the village was located for future reference. She was grateful that Magg understood her need to rest. She had traveled all the way from Synkana and now she was going to have to remain a human, except when she needed to hunt for food. She had promised to only hunt animals and she would keep that promise. She really wanted to stay in Anakik where she would likely be safe. Much safer than in Synkana she was sure.

Magg was coming to take her on a tour of the village. She knocked on Raven's door to find out if she was awake and ready to go yet. It was near dark and they had agreed on the time. Raven came to the door ready to go with Magg. She was wearing one of her new dresses. It was the red one. Magg was a bit shocked by her low neckline, but said nothing about it. It was likely that once she got used to living in Anakik, she might decide to dress more appropriately for a small village.

Magg led her down the main road in the village. She showed Raven all the homes near the street and some of the small shops there. They came to the market and the owner let them in, even though it was after hours. Raven was impressed with the variety of items offered for sale. There were a few dresses for sale, but none of them interested Raven. Maybe she could find someone who would make her a dress more to her liking. As she thought about that she spoke to Magg about it.

"Magg, I was wondering if there's anyone who could make me some dresses. I would like to have some made to fit and more to my liking than what might be in the local store. What do you think?"

"It just so happens that we have a very talented young lady who does that very thing. I'm sure she would be honored to make some dresses for you. We can talk to her soon if you'd like."

"I would like that very much, Magg. I suppose we can discuss it later. I just had the thought and wondered if you could help me with that. I'm excited to talk with that young woman soon."

"We will do that. Also, here is the shop that will have some of the things you need now."

As they entered the shop, Raven did see bed linens that she needed and some other items to make her cottage more like what she would like it to be. She had an idea of what it should look like and this shop would likely provide what she wanted for that purpose. Her tastes were simple in that regard. She had been living in a cave for a few years, after all. She purchased a set of bed linens and a few other things. The shopkeeper put them in a cloth bag for her to take home.

Magg also showed Raven the rest of the village and took her inside the inn for a look around. She had been there before when she met Zarcon, but now she would have a closer look and see what it was really like. She talked with Raven about the new magic school they wanted to start and where the school would be built. Raven was excited at that. She really wanted help with her own magic and was hoping someone would be able to guide her as to how to use it wisely.

After their discussion, Magg showed Raven the way back to her cottage. She parted ways and let Raven do whatever she needed to do to find food for the night. Raven was grateful to get back to her cottage so she could transform into the cat and go hunting in the forest nearby.

She left her cottage as a cat and leaped into the forest. She went deep into the woods looking for an animal to eat. She found a small creek and hid in the bushes until a large elk came to drink. It was wary of predators, like Raven. The elk was very alert. It seemed to sense Raven's presence and leaped back into the forest before Raven could catch it.

Now she had to wait for her next opportunity for food. Finally, there was a rabbit that came to drink. Raven was so hungry, she decided it was better than nothing. She got ready and pounced. The rabbit was a fairly easy catch. She caught it before it could run away. It was a quick bite and satisfied her initial hunger. She would need more, so she decided to try waiting just a bit longer for something bigger.

It was about another hour before she finally saw a deer come to drink. She waited for it to get comfortable with drinking and showed no concern about her. She finally pounced and caught the deer. She was on its back and biting its neck before it knew what happened. She fed on the deer until she was full. It was enough to fill her and would likely last two days. She wouldn't need to go hunting for two more nights.

It was good that she could find enough to eat that she would be able to go an extra night before she would have to hunt again. If she could do this more of the time, she would be happier to live in Anakik.

It was the hunting she was nervous about. She felt safe here, but what would happen if someone saw her transform? Would she still be safe? Only time would tell.

When she finally got back to her cottage and before she went to sleep, she decided that she needed to get things settled better with Zarcon. But she would wait until he was strong enough to help her. He had been injured by a shard of magic glass in a battle with the evil entity, Neberon. There had been poison along with the magic of the shard. Zarcon was healing, but it was slow due to his advanced age. Raven was willing to wait however long it would take. Zarcon was a great wizard and knew so much about magic, she just knew he could help her with her problems.

In the meantime, she was happy and feeling safer than she ever had. She believed Anakik was the right place for her to finally be at rest and make a home for herself. She was truly grateful that Zarcon had been so welcoming to her. She felt ready to give up her traveling days and spend the rest of her life in this quiet village with so many kind people.

Chapter 7

A family was arriving from another village looking for Zarcon. They had adopted two young boys who had some magic. Their names were Kedron and Boren. They wanted to learn more, much as Raven did. The father's name was Karmine, and the mother's name was Roslin. There were actually four boys in the family now with the two adopted boys, Kedron and Boren. The other two boys, Mika and Lorin, were the sons of Roslin and Karmine. They were a very close family and had survived many horrific adventures in the recent past and finally found the time to seek Zarcon's help.

Just as they arrived in Anakik, a large creature attacked their wagon and almost killed Kedron. Luckily Magg and Jasmine were coming to see who was entering the village. She saw what was happening and Magg was able to destroy the creature before it could kill the boy. Magg also turned the animal to ashes so Kedron would know it couldn't come and get him in the night. It was a terrifying experience for all of them, especially Kedron.

Magg was especially shaken because she couldn't be sure this creature was the only one around. If not, it would mean serious problems later on she was sure. She needed to talk to Zarcon about it and get his advice right away.

Finally, when all were safe, Magg and Jasmine brought them into town. The two women took them to a cottage that was empty at the time. Jasmine and Magg helped them get settled. They had most of what they would need in their wagon. So with a little help unloading, they were able to get the beds set up for everyone. The family had come to go to the school of magic that was being built in Anakik. This was a happy time for their family. Karmine and Roslin were getting settled into their cottage that night. They would become very valuable assets to the community in a very short while.

It had been a few days since she talked to Magg about getting some new dresses made. So she went to Magg late one evening to talk to her about it. She went to Magg's room late one evening and knocked.

Magg opened the door and smiled at Raven, "What brings you here Raven? Is all well?"

"Yes, all is well. But I was wondering if there would be a time today or tomorrow that we could go talk to the young lady you told me about that makes pretty dresses."

"I do have time today for that. We can go to the family that lives close to your cottage and talk to a young lady by the name of Revinia. It appears she has magic and can create the most wonderful dresses. I know you'll find her to be very talented in that regard. Let's go see if she's home."

They walked up the main street to the cottage that Jarrone and his family lived. Magg knocked on the door and they waited a few moments for someone to answer. Jarrone finally came to the door.

He said, "Well, hello Magg. How are things in the village? What can I help you with today?"

Magg smiled and said, "This is Raven, she's new in the village. I think you met her a few days ago at the inn. She is needing some new dresses and we were wondering if your sister Revinia would be interested in making some for her."

"I'm sure she would love to. I'll go find her right now."

Jarrone went upstairs to another part of the house and found Revinia resting in her room. He said, "Hey, there's a pretty lady who would like you to make her some new dresses. Why don't you come and talk to her about it?"

"Really? I would love to!" Revinia had been known in the village as the girl who created beautiful dresses with the help of magic. She was popular with the younger women of the village and appreciated for her talent. Now she had the chance to create a dress for a beautiful woman new to the village. She was so excited.

They both went running down the stairs to see Raven and find out what she was wanting.

Raven said, "You must be Revinia. I'm Raven and I would very much like you to make me some pretty dresses to wear around Anakik. What do you think?"

Revinia said, "Raven, I would love to do that for you. Could we go to the shop in town and find some fabric that pleases you? That would be the place to start."

"I can go anytime either early morning or late afternoon. Would that work for you?"

"It would indeed. How about in the morning early? I can arrange to meet you there and have the owner open his store early for us."

Raven was thrilled, "I think that would be really good. I'm excited to see what you can do. Magg has told me so much about you. I'll see you in the morning then."

"Yes. I'll meet you at the store early tomorrow morning."

Magg and Raven said their goodbyes and went back to the inn. Raven expressed her excitement to meet with Revinia in the morning. She would have some new dresses. She was so happy to be in Anakik with such great and talented people. It was such a change in her life and she was enjoying every minute of it.

When she got back to her cottage and thanked Magg for her help, she went hunting. She transformed into the cat and headed deep into the forest. She had a successful hunt and fed on a large deer. It was very satisfying for her.

As she headed back to her cottage and transformed once inside, she dressed and got ready to meet Revinia at the fabric shop in the village. It was more exciting than she had expected. She was finally ready and walked out of her cottage and made her way to the shop.

Revinia was waiting at the entrance to the shop just as Raven walked up to her. They went inside and Raven was able to look over the fabrics available. She picked a blue one with small flowers printed overall.

There was another fabric that appeared to be velvet. It was a soft gray and was very beautiful. There were a few more fabrics that she picked that were made of a soft cotton. The colors were nice and they had a small print on them. She bought two that were plain.

Revinia was so happy to have so much to do. After being with Raven for the few moments they shared. She was getting an image of the kind of dresses Raven would enjoy. It was going to be fun to create them.

Raven delighted with the fabrics they had found at the shop that morning. She was looking forward to what Revinia would be able to create for her. This was something for her to look forward to.

A few nights later, Raven needed to go hunting again. She wanted to hunt on the south side of the village this time. As she left her cottage, she transformed into the large black cat. It was a quiet night and the wind was still. There was a bit of light from the full moon overhead. She crept toward the spring she knew about and had hunted before.

As she got closer to the spring, she noticed a large wolf drinking there. Raven crouched, ready to attack and destroy the wolf. But just before she jumped, she heard a man call to it to come to him. Then she knew the wolf was trained by someone, but to what purpose? She stayed where she was waiting to find out if the man would appear. This was the first time she had encountered anyone out hunting where she had been in Anakik.

It turned out to be two men talking about how to eliminate the "big black cat" that they had to share the hunting grounds with. Raven knew she could kill both men and stop their plot, but that would mean she would have to leave Anakik or be killed, and she didn't want that to happen if she could help it.

The men continued to talk about what the wolf was supposed to do to stop Raven from hunting in any area of the forest of Anakik. She also noticed that both men carried rifles. Even so, Raven knew she would be able to eliminate the wolf if she had a fair chance alone with it. But since the men had guns and would likely shoot her if they caught her killing the wolf she couldn't do anything just then. This was a really big problem especially since she was very hungry. It had been a few nights since she had had a nice meal. So she was getting desperate.

She decided to head deeper into the forest away from Anakik, at least for this night. She ran through the forest until she was sure she was well away from the men and their wolf. She would deal with them as soon as she got back to Anakik. She was fairly certain Magg would understand the problem and help her resolve it.

She finally found an area with deer and elk in a meadow. She hid in the brush nearby. The deer didn't see her in the dark. One of the deer ventured a bit closer. Close enough that she could get it easily. So she prepared to leap on the deer. Suddenly the deer seemed to sense her presence and started to run. Raven was faster and caught it just as it was about to get away. One bite on the neck and the deer was hers. She had a fine meal and felt much better after that.

She headed for her cottage now that her hunger was satisfied. She was a lot further from Anakik than she had thought. She had to creep along the underbrush as she approached the village, trying not to have an encounter with the two men and their wolf. She was able to transform and enter her cottage. She was exhausted from the fear and effort of the night. She would rest and then go talk to Magg about her problem. She knew that this situation must be resolved very soon. She had to feel safe to hunt.

Magg and her companion, Matton, had decided to visit Raven early in the morning, before the sun came up. Matton knocked on Raven's door and they waited a few minutes for Raven to answer.

Matton was just a bit taller than Magg. He was broadly built and had become close to Magg after he had been injured in a fight with thieves on the way to Anakik. He was a soldier and now stayed in a room close to Magg's. They appeared to be falling in love.

Raven, on seeing Magg and Matton, said, "I'm so glad to see both of you. I was wanting to come and find you this morning."

Magg responded, "I thought after a few days here, you would want to address any concerns you have had about living in Anakik. So what seems to be of concern to you, Raven?"

"I've been hunting at night, as you know. The trouble has come up when I see that some of the villagers are also hunting the same areas. I was thinking maybe we could set areas as mine and other areas that villagers can hunt away from mine. Would that be possible? I need to eat as do the others, but competing for the same game is risky."

"I see that, Raven. I'll check into having a village meeting to discuss this with everyone. You can present your case and explain why you need your own area to hunt in. I think the villagers will understand. They just don't quite get how important it is for you to find food in the forest. I'm sure if we make an area for you to hunt in and an area open to the villagers, they will see the value of it."

Raven replied, "Thank you Magg. I'm hoping to be able to stay here in this cottage for the rest of my life. I need to feel safe and that I will be able to have the food I need. I think anyone would understand that."

"I agree. I'll call a meeting for tonight and hopefully, we'll come to an agreement that benefits everyone. Matton and I will go get the meeting set up now and then we'll let you know what's going on."

"Thanks again, Magg. See you tonight?"

"Yes, as soon as things for the meeting are settled, I will come and tell you."

Magg and Matton left and talked together about the day and what they had learned.

"Magg, there's so much happening now. Zarcon is failing and that's a big concern for everyone. Then there's Raven and her needs. How are we going to take care of all that today?"

"I'm not sure. Let's get as many as we can to come to the meeting tonight first of all. We really need to keep Raven happy. She could be a very dangerous creature if she is not. Not to be afraid of her, but caution is something we all need to understand in regard to her needs."

"You're right, Magg. Now if we can just convince the villagers of how important this concern really is."

"Let's start with the general store where most of the villagers spend time during the day. Maybe we can make a poster and talk with the owner about letting people know about it. We don't have a lot of time, we have to get back to Zarcon."

"Great place to start. Let's go."

Magg and Matton walked to the general store and met with the owner, Toran. He was a tall man with wispy hair and a thin mustache. He was pleasant with everyone and enjoyed being the owner of his little store. He wasn't busy at the time, so Matton presented him with their idea to help Raven. Toran agreed to help them get the word out to the villagers. He even said he would post a notice on his front window for those just passing by.

"Great! Thanks for your help." Matton was so glad he listened to them.

Later that day, when word had gotten around the village for the meeting with everyone, there were those who were hunting anywhere they wanted, regardless of Raven and her needs. They were willing to come and talk, but they looked like they weren't about to give up their hunting grounds for anyone.

Their leader, a man by the name of Orshon, spoke first, "I know what you want to say. We've already told you how we feel about this hunting business with Raven. I don't see how we can give up any of our hunting areas just because some woman wants some of it to herself.'

Matton was shocked at his lack of understanding. He said dripping with sacasm, "I have a feeling you and your friends are missing the whole picture. Let me explain once more about this "hunting business" with Raven. We are trying to keep you and your friends ALIVE! Raven transforms into a very large black cat that can eat you for dinner before you would even know she was there. Now, Magg is going to ask you a few questions and I hope you'll be honest with us. "

Orshon just grunted his willingness to listen.

Magg began, "So, what is your very favorite hunting area? And don't say everywhere or this meeting is over and you will face hunting knowing Raven could be anywhere. Got it?"

Orshon answered after talking with his friends for a moment, "Alright, we like the area on the north side of the village the best. If we could have that area, we would be more willing to support the plan."

Magg was glad they came up with that so soon. Then she asked, "So, would you be willing then to give Raven the south side of the village for her hunting and hers alone?"

"Yes we could go along with that. We are also wondering if we could negotiate later on, if things change in some way."

"What are you saying Orshon? How would things change that we would need to renegotiate the terms of this agreement."

"Well, what if there gets to be more hunters and we need more space to hunt in? Then what do we do?"

"As I recall, the area to the north of the village is really a very large area. I don't see how that would happen in many years. And Anakik would have to grow much larger than it is now. So I don't understand the question. What are you really wanting?"

"We talked about this and decided that maybe if we could also have the area west of the village, we would be happier about it. Is that possible?"

"Orshon, you know that west of the village is another village where we helped the people with the mist monsters. I cannot allow you to use their land for your hunting. It wouldn't be right and those people would probably make your life miserable every time they saw you."

"Alright, it was just a thought. We're feeling hemmed in and thought maybe we could get more forest somehow.'

"This has gone on long enough. The north side of the village is plenty big for any number of hunters. You have the whole mountain and beyond to hunt in. You just have to be sure you don't accidentally cross over into Raven's portion of the forest. This is for your own safety, may I remind you? Don't take chances with your lives, that's all I'm asking. Raven needs to be able to eat and feel safe here. We will do all we can to make sure that happens. Do you understand the risks?"

"Yes, we see now that we need to keep to our own side of the forest or risk being eaten. I guess we didn't realize the seriousness of this proposal you've offered. We'll do our best to make sure Raven is safe and so are we."

"That's very wise of you Orshon. I'm grateful that you've agreed and will abide by the proposal as we have outlined it. I'm hoping sincerely that we won't need further discussion on this matter. It's far too important for you and for Raven. I have a paper I would like you and your friends to sign stating that you will abide by the rule of staying on the north side of the village for your own hunting. I insist that you all sign it."

"Oh, alright, we'll sign your paper. Come on guys, let's get this over with so we can go home and eat." Each of Orshon's friends signed the paper then Orshon finally signed it.

With that, the meeting was over. Orshon and his friends left without complaint and went to the saloon for a few drinks.

It was good that none of the other villagers were concerned about the hunting areas. It looked like Orshon and his group were the only ones that were.

Magg was glad they'd come to an agreement, but she was not so sure those men would really abide by it. They had been trouble in times past. She hoped they really did see the seriousness of the situation and not push their luck.

Matton was relieved once again. He kissed Magg and held her close as they walked back to the inn. Life had taken many turns since he met Magg and every day was an adventure.

Jasmine and Donavan, Jasmine's husband and also possessor of great magic, were following close behind. They had stayed near the meeting just in case. Donavan spoke up, "Magg that was great. I just hope those men are sincere about keeping to the agreement. It could go so badly if they don't. I really don't see a lot of combined brain power among them. That's what scares me."

Jasmine nodded her agreement. Only time would tell if things would work out as planned. She finally said, "I'm thinking it would be a good idea to have a couple of guards around her cottage for a while just in case. What do the rest of you think?"

Magg and Matton agreed wholeheartedly.

Donavan asked, "Who do you think would be willing to do that? I can help, but we'll need four or five more men to help. Maybe we could do shifts so no one would be stuck with the whole night every night."

Magg said, "The sounds like a good plan to me. What do you think Matton? Would some of the soldiers be willing to fill in on some shifts?"

"I'll ask them in the morning if they would want to help in that way. I'm pretty sure they will want to. They are concerned for Raven and her safety too. But I'll see if we can set up a schedule of some kind so everyone knows what is going on. Hopefully, Raven will be in agreement. I think it will help her to feel safer during the day when she's sleeping."

Magg agreed, "Let us know what you find out and we'll go from there."

"Of course.

Meanwhile, when Matton and Magg got back to Matton's room, he created a schedule for the soldiers to patrol Raven's cottage during the day and at night.

It was important that everyone was aware of the schedule and followed it for Raven's sake.

When Matton took the schedule to the barracks where the soldiers were getting ready for the day he talked to them about the reason for the schedule and why it was important for them to be sure to follow it for Raven.

The soldiers had all agreed that this was very important for all their sakes. Some people of the village suspected that half the soldiers were in love with Raven. She was a very beautiful woman after all, the cat part not withstanding.

It was obvious that the men looked forward to protecting her and feeling a part of something important in the quiet little village of Anakik. They didn't know that things could change very rapidly indeed.

A few nights later, Raven went out hunting in her usual places on the south side of the forest near Anakik. She decided to go near a small creek that she hadn't tried for a while. As she crept closer, she saw the same large wolf she had seen before. She really wanted to kill that wolf, but knew there were men protecting it, and they had guns. So once again, she stayed hidden and listened for the men.

After a few moments, she could hear them coming through the brush. They were mumbling about something she didn't understand. Then suddenly she did understand. They were once again plotting against her.

She could hear one of them saying, "I don't understand why we have to be so careful and can't hunt wherever we want." Even though the men had signed an agreement, it was still a matter of contention for them. As they continued talking it was as though they had already come up with a solution and were waiting for news of its conclusion.

Raven felt a stab of fear course through her. She had a pretty good idea what those men had plotted. Suddenly she didn't want to eat. She had lost her appetite. So, she immediately moved to her cottage to transform and get to Magg to warn her of their plot.

As she got near her cottage and was about to transform into her human self, she heard men talking just around the corner of her cottage by the door. She knew then that they were waiting for her to show up so they could kill her.

Raven decided to go to the inn and find Magg. She went along the back of the village and transformed at the door of the inn. No one saw her, so she entered the inn and knocked on Magg's door.

Magg opened the door, shocked to see Raven there dressed in a very tight fitting black dress. She was stunned, yet she knew that Raven would never come to her at night unless it was very important.

"What's wrong, Raven? I know by your face that things aren't right just now. Please come in and tell me about it."

Raven was on the verge of tears as she began her story. "Magg I was out hunting on the south forest when I saw the same large wolf drinking from the creek I had decided to hunt near. I was watching the wolf and listening for the men again. Then two men came near the wolf and talked about stopping the big black cat from hunting anywhere."

"Oh Raven I'm so sorry."

"I was terrified at that point so I left right then and headed for my cottage. Then, just before I was going to transform, two men were talking about me just around the corner of my cottage door. I couldn't go in, they would have killed me. So I crept along the back of the village and found you after I transformed, of course. I don't know what to do, can you help me?"

"Raven, we will get to the bottom of this right away. We are supposed to have men guarding your cottage, but it seems they weren't there when needed the most. I will find out who that was supposed to be and Donavan and I will find out what's going on. This cannot happen, EVER!"

"Thanks Magg, I'm really worried. I could have killed the men and their stupid wolf, but I want to stay here in Anakik, so I didn't do anything to them."

"I love that you're so smart Raven. I love you for your beauty and strength. We are going to help you with this right away. I will let you know about what is going on as soon as I know. Meanwhile, why don't you stay with me tonight? I don't want to take any chances with your safety tonight. I have an extra room with a door on it that you can use to sleep in until tomorrow night. Whatever makes you feel safe is what is important right now."

"I appreciate your offer, Magg. I will take you up on it. I don't dare go back to my cottage tonight. Thank you for being a good friend to me."

Magg showed Raven to her spare room and made sure she was comfortable before closing the door and heading over to Donavan's room. It was very late, but the matter needed immediate resolution. Magg had locked her room as she left it. At least Raven would be safe there.

She went straight to Donavan's door and hoped he would answer. She waited for a few minutes, then knocked again. She finally heard Donavan yelling.

"Alright, I'm coming!"

When he opened the door and it was Magg, he knew something important had happened.

"Come in Magg and tell me what's going on."

"I'm not sure you'll believe it. Raven was out hunting when two men with a large wolf came along and were discussing how to stop 'the big black cat' from hunting anywhere in their forest. She was headed back to her cottage when she discovered there were two more men waiting for her likely waiting to kill her when she came back. So she came to me for help. Where were the men who were supposed to be guarding her cottage? This is not going to happen again and we need to find out who left their post and put Raven in such danger."

"You're right Magg. We need to get to the bottom of this before it gets any bigger of a problem for all of us, but especially for Raven. She's counting on us to keep her safe. We can't let her down. I'll contact Matton to find out who is at fault for not guarding her cottage. Then we'll go from there to find out who is threatening her."

"I'm counting on you to do so, Donavan. Keep me informed of what you find out. I need to reassure

Raven that we're doing all we can. I'm going to my room to make sure she is safe."

"I'll let you know what I find out tomorrow morning at the latest."

"Thank you Donavan. Good night."

Magg went back to her room and tried to sleep a little before morning. She didn't. She was too worried about what they would find out.

Chapter 8

Donavan was very concerned about Raven's safety and comfort staying in Anakik. He wanted her to be a part of the community and enjoy living there. So he went to Matton, who was in charge of the schedule for those guarding Raven's cottage.

He went to Matton's room and knocked on the door early in the morning. He hadn't slept well and was a bit on edge. So when Matton came to the door, he was a bit harsh.

Matton was surprised to see Donavan at his door so early, but before he could say anything, Donavan started talking.

"Matton, I need to see the schedule for those guarding Raven's cottage last night. Something has happened and we need to get to the bottom of it."

"Good morning to you too, Donavan. Yes, I will find the schedule. Why don't you come on in and tell me what's happened while I get it for you."

"Sorry about that, but something happened to Raven last night and we need to find out how it happened and who did it." Donavan then went on the tell Matton what had happened and why he needed the schedule so badly.

Matton was astonished that anyone would dare do such a thing or think about doing it. He stepped over to his desk and found the schedule for those who had signed up to watch Raven's cottage that night. He returned to Donavan and said, "Donavan, here's the schedule. Let's see, it looks like Retin and Lucain were supposed to guard last night. Come with me and we'll question them about last night."

"That's what I was thinking, Matton. Let's go now and catch them before they start their day around the village."

Matton and Donavan left Matton's room right then and headed for the soldiers quarters not far from the inn. As they entered the building, they noticed the men were confused and upset. Matton called them to attention and started asking questions.

"Men, we have a problem that needs addressing this morning. Are Retin and Lucain around? We need to talk to them, now!"

There was more confusion. Then one of the men, Tenzi, spoke up, "We haven't seen Retin or Lucain since yesterday afternoon. We've tried to find them, but there's no trace of what happened to them. We found their boots, but that was all. We found them near Raven's cottage. So we know they were on duty at one point. That's why we're so upset. We were even suspecting that Raven may have had them for dinner. But that didn't make sense either. Now we don't know what to do."

Donavan and Matton were both in shock. Could there have been a murder in Anakik? Surely not!

Matton began asking questions, "So none of you saw them after yesterday afternoon?"

"No."

"When was it that you found their boots?"

"Later that evening. They were supposed to check in before nine last night. When we didn't hear from them, we started looking and found their boots. We haven't found anything else or any other sign of them at all." Tenzi said.

"Why didn't you come to us right away?"

"We were hoping they'd show up or we'd find something that made sense this morning. Then we were going to tell you about it."

"That was a mistake. Raven could have been killed. It appears that at least two men are after her to stop her from hunting in the Anakik forest. Do any of you know anything about that?"

That's when the men got really quiet. Finally, another of the men, Markos, stepped up and said, "There have been rumors for a few days now about a group of men who resent Raven getting to hunt the south side of the forest, which limits their ability to hunt wherever they want. I know you knew about that, so we let it go. We thought things were pretty much the same as it had been. We haven't heard of anything happening as a result of their resentment."

"Well, from now on, you must tell us of anything unusual happening even if it doesn't seem to be of much concern, got that?"

"Got it." They all shouted.

"So now we're going to organize a search for Retin and Lucain." Matton then divided the men into groups and assigned them to certain areas of the village and forest. "These men must be found or what happened to them must be known. Report to me or Donavan every half hour. Dismissed."

The soldiers moved out to their areas of search. It was getting desperate that they find the two men. They were afraid of what they might find. Those two men were liked and valued as really good soldiers and men. It was imperative that they be found, one way or another.

Matton went to Magg to tell her of their progress or lack of it. She was shocked to find out that the two soldiers assigned to guard Raven's cottage were now missing without a trace. Only their boots were evidence that they had been at the cottage last night. This was getting more and more concerning by the minute. Could the two soldiers have been murdered? They would find out soon.

As the day wore on and the men reported their findings every half hour to Matton, it was getting obvious that the two missing men were likely hidden somewhere in the forest. They kept searching for any evidence of what might have happened to them.

Finally, that afternoon, just as they were about to give up, there was a shout from two of the men searching. The others came running to see what was found. Deep under some leaves and dirt there appeared to be a shallow grave large enough for two bodies. Matton was called in to see what was found and identify the bodies if possible.

They used their hands to uncover the bodies. They had been torn up by what could have been a big cat or maybe a wolf. The bodies were identified as Retin and Lucain. It was a very sad moment for all of the men present. The two were well liked by everyone who knew them.

It was Lucain who had helped bring Zarcon to the village to save them from the mist monsters. His was a great loss. He had been the hero of Anakik ever since. Now he was gone. Such a brave young man. Whoever did this will pay very dearly.

Matton assigned the men to bury the two soldiers in a real grave and he would tell their families about what had happened. It wouldn't be easy. Losing two of the soldiers like this would upset the entire village.

There was concern about the level of anger and rage that would result from their deaths. They greatly feared that Raven would be blamed for it. It must be emphasized that she did not have anything to do with it. It would be a tough sell, but it must be done to protect her.

Now it was confirmed that they had been murdered. Matton would talk to Raven to find out if she knew anything about the two men and what had happened to them. It was decided that only Matton and Magg would speak to her privately. They didn't want anyone jumping to conclusions about their murders. Matton went to find Magg so they could speak with Raven.

He found her in her rooms waiting to hear from him. She jumped up when she saw him coming. He looked very solemn and worried. She was afraid to hear what he had found out.

"Magg we need to talk. We found the two soldiers, Lucain and Retin who were assigned to protect Raven's cabin. I have bad news, they've both been murdered last night some time. Their bodies were found in shallow graves in the forest where Raven likes to hunt."

Magg was horrified. "You don't think Raven did this do you?"

Matton quickly responded that he did not think Raven could have done such a thing. "Magg we have to talk to Raven and see if she remembers anything about the men with the big wolf. I have a suspicion that they may be at the bottom of it."

Magg agreed, "Raven did say she heard them talking by her door when she was trying to get home. I think it's a good idea to find out if she remembers anything more. Let's go, she's sleeping in my spare room right now."

Matton said, "That's good. It's important that we find out how Raven is doing. Hopefully she will have had time to rest enough for us to ask her a few questions about last night."

Magg and Matton went quietly to see Raven in Magg's spare room. Raven came to the door when Matton knocked, "Welcome you two, I'm so glad to see you. I have had a rough time sleeping after last night. I'm really concerned about what happened."

"That's why Matton and I are here. The two soldiers that were posted at your cottage door have been murdered. We were hoping to spend some time talking with you about what you remember about the men you saw with the big wolf. Would you recognize them if you saw them again?"

Raven was shocked to hear about the soldiers. She started to cry. She knew they had been killed because of her. "I'm so sad to hear that. I wondered why the soldiers weren't there. But I was so afraid of the men that it wasn't until later that I remembered about the soldiers not being there. As to your question, I'm sure I would recognize them if I saw them again. They were not the kind of men to come up against. They also had big rifles. I think they would have enjoyed killing not only me, but anyone who might have been in the way of their objective."

Magg gasped, "So you really believe those men would kill the soldiers?"

"Yes, I'm sure they would. The way they were talking about killing me was terrifying. It was like they were talking about what they would eat for lunch. They really hate me for hunting where they like to hunt."

Magg looked at Matton and said, "We're going to look into this and make sure we find the answers to these murders and why they want to hunt in the place you have been hunting for some time now. Maybe you should stay here in my spare room for a while so we can find those men and try to find out for sure what's going on."

"Actually, I would prefer to stay here. Those men know where I live and might come after me at some point. I don't want to be there just in case."

"My feelings exactly. We will keep you safe from whoever has killed those good men. They are bad men without any compassion or concern for other's lives. It feels like too much has happened already. The risk of you being harmed by those horrible men is more than I can bear. You will stay here for as long as is needed. We're not going to take any chances here."

Raven was so grateful to Magg for her concern for her safety. She would stay with Magg until it was safe to go back to her own cottage. No matter how long it was going to take.

Chapter 9

Later that day, Matton and Donavan went to see Magg in her room. They talked about the murders of the two soldiers and how Raven must be protected no matter what the outcome was. Those involved would be hanged for certain.

Magg was still horrified by what had happened to the soldiers. She was conscious of Raven in the other room, trying to sleep, and asked them if they would go into Donavan and Jasmine's room to talk about it further. They agreed and went there immediately.

Magg wanted Jasmine to know of everything that had happened. Donavan admitted that he had left her sleeping that morning and hadn't spoken to her since. So he called to Jasmine to talk to her about it. She was not happy to have been left out of the events of the day. But Donavan was able to calm her down when he explained the urgency of the situation and that they needed her now with the investigation.

When it was explained to her, she was terrified. "You're telling me we've had two murders here in Anakik? How can that be? And Lucain was killed? I love that young man. We must find the guilty parties and hang them all! I can't bear it!!"

Gradually Jasmine was able to calm down and participate in the discussion. It was a terrible time for each of them.

Magg was so sad and lost at this point. She asked, "So, Donavan, what do we do now? Investigating something like this will be difficult. Maybe we should ask Greta if she would help us try to keep everyone calm until we find out who's responsible."

"I agree, Greta has such power to calm and needs to feel part of what's going on. Jasmine, will you go talk to her, please?"

"I would be glad to. Also I'm thinking Jarrone should also help. He can tell the nature of a person by looking at their eyes. We will need that as we talk to the people who might know something, or who might be guilty."

Jarrone is a young man with powerful magic. He and his family came to Anakik when it was known that Neberon was after him for his magic. They had become a very important part of the village.

Donavan agreed, "Another great idea. We've tried too many times to get things done alone. That must stop right now. This is too big for us to do alone. We will only involve those we trust. So who talks to Jarrone? I think you, Magg, you're the one who rescued him and his family from Neberon. He will trust you above all."

"Alright, I'll go to Jarrone. We'll get going on this right away. Then Matton, will you round up that man, Orshon and his friends. They're the most likely suspects at this point."

"I would love too, Donavan. I would regret it if anything happened to them." His eyes betrayed his real feelings. He would like nothing better than for one of them to do something stupid so he could make sure they had an unfortunate accident.

"Not before we know for sure who's responsible, Matton. Don't get ahead of our investigation." Donavan was a bit worried about Matton after that remark.

"Ah, I was only joking around. We must follow the law." Matton rolled his eyes at that.

Magg said, "I'm going to go talk to Jarrone now. I'll let you know what he says when I get back."

"Agreed." Was Donavan's reply.

Magg headed for Jarrone and his family's cottage. Jarrone was practicing magic in the area at the back of the cottage, as usual. When he saw Magg coming toward him, he stopped and waited for her to come to him.

"Hello Magg, what brings you to my part of Anakik today?"

"I have a proposal for you. We need your special talent at this time. Have you heard anything about what happened last night?"

"I heard that two soldiers were missing, that was all. Why? What's happened?"

So Magg told him the story of what was going on and that the two soldiers were found buried in a shallow grave in the forest. It was a clear case of murder.

"We're investigating their murders now and need your help identifying those who might be lying. I know you can look at a person and know what kind of person they are and whether they are telling the truth or not. You also have other powers that might come in handy if things get out of hand. What do you say, are you willing to help us?"

"Wow, I'm so glad you've decided you need me for something important. I've been feeling left out lately. I would be honored to be a part of this investigation as you call it."

"Great! Can you come to the inn in about an hour to discuss what we're going to do?"

"I will be there."

In the meantime, Jasmine was meeting with Greta to ask her to help keep the villagers calm as their investigation continued. The people must not jump to the conclusion that it was Raven. Jasmine told her the whole story and let her decide if she wanted to be involved or not.

Greta thought about it for a few minutes, trying to decide if she could handle the magic required to influence the entire village. She knew if she didn't she would regret it. So she said, "Magg, I would like very much to help with this investigation. But if it becomes too tiring for me, will you allow me to rest at some point? I will also be checking on Zarcon periodically as the time goes by. Will that be all right with you?"

"Of course, Greta, we need you to be strong for us. We also need you to be able to make sure Zarcon is doing well. Both of you are so important to us. For now there is much to learn as we talk to those who may be involved. You will be an important part of what we learn. We need to keep Raven safe through all this. It will be natural for the people to suspect her first. So any calming influence you can offer will be very helpful. Can you come to a meeting here in the inn in about an hour to discuss what we will be doing?"

"Yes, I will be there after I have had a chance to tell Zarcon about it. He cares deeply about the village and its people. He will want to know what has happened."

Matton and Magg went to the homes of the families of the two men who were killed. They arrived at Lucain's mother's home and knocked on the door. Lucain's mother, Myra, answered Matton's knock. She looked at Matton's and Magg's faces and started to cry. She knew instinctively that something terrible had happened. Magg moved into the room and hugged Myra and held her while she cried. Myra finally calmed and invited Magg and Matton to come in and sit with her.

The room was small, but well kept. They sat on small chairs set near a longer couch. Magg sat next to Myra and held her hand as she told her about what happended to her son, Lucain. Lucain's father was killed by the monsters in the mist a few years ago. So Myra was living alone. She was now totally alone since Lucain was murdered. It was a terrible time for her as the reality of it hit her. Myra would need help now.

Magg finally said, "Myra, we will help you all we can as we get through this difficult time. You are welcome to come and talk to me any time you need to. We're so very sorry for your loss. His killers will be found and hanged."

Myra was sobbing as she said, "Thank you Magg. I feel that I'm going to need your support for awhile. This is too much for me to bear, especially now."

Magg and Matton stayed with Myra for another hour until she was able to calm down. She finally went to her room and slept. The exhaustion of grief finally helped her to relax and sleep.

Magg and Matton left her cottage softly. Magg left her a note telling her where she lived and that she was welcome any time to talk. Magg was crying softly as they left. Magg and the others had gotten close to Lucain when they had followed him to Anakik to destroy the mist monsters that were terrifying the people there.

Magg and Matton went to the home of Retin's parents next. Matton knocked on the door and Retin's father, Noran, answered. Once again, when Noran looked at Magg's and Matton's faces, he knew something bad had happened. He called to his wife before asking them in.

He raised his voice and said, "Layla, come quick, we have company."

Layla was in the kitchen and came into the room with Magg and Matton. Her tears were starting when she saw who was at the door. She too had a feeling of dread seeing Magg and Matton in their home. Noran and Layla sat together and held hands while Magg explained what had happened to Retin.

Layla started crying softly. Noran had tears in his eyes as they realized their brave son had been murdered. Noran said, "This is terrible news you bring us. What's to become of those murderers? Will they hang? Where will my son be buried? Has he been buried already?"

Matton spoke, "Retin has been buried in a beautiful clearing close to the forest. It's all we could do since he had been gone for several hours. We will be more than happy to show you where that is whenever you're ready to see it. Maybe we could move him later on if that suits you better;"

Noran said, "I appreciate that Matton. Maybe we could go in a few days. I'm sure we'll need a little time to grieve for our son. He's really all we had. There are no other children. But we will come to you when we are ready to see where he is laid. Thank you Matton and Magg for your kindness in bringing us this news."

Magg said, "We are so sorry for you loss. We will take you to the grave whenever you are ready. We'll leave for now. We're going to start on the investigation to find out all we can about the murders. We want to bring the guilty to justice as quickly as possible."

With that, the two of them quietly left their cottage and headed for the village and the meeting to start questioning any who might know something about the crimes committed in Anakik.

As those involved in the investigation arrived, it was clear that everyone was anxious to start the process. Murder had never happened in Anakik before and it was terrifying that it had happened now. Emotions were very high as they began discussing what they would do and where they would start.

Magg started the discussion, "What we do know is that there is a group of friends that have been unhappy with having to share the hunting areas near here. They did agree to abide by the rules, but now we're not sure they are doing so. We think they might be the ones who committed the crimes." She then explained what had happened, many had heard it already, but she was laying the groundwork for further discussion.

She continued, "I'm thinking that we should call them in one at a time and ask them some serious questions. Do they or anyone they know have a trained wolf in their possession? Do they know of anyone hunting in the area they are not allowed to be in? How do they feel about Raven? That's important because if they are hating her, we know they are probably interested in killing her or anyone who might be protecting her. Do you agree?"

Donavan spoke up, "I agree with everything you've said. I would add that with Jarrone there, he can assess their sincerity when they answer. He can judge whether they are telling the truth or what kind of person they are. Right, Jarrone?"

"That's right. I can do more than that. I have been practicing that skill and now I can feel their emotions as well. One of the strongest ones is anxiety or fear. Those two come through really strong, especially if they are lying."

Everyone grew very excited at that. Knowing Jarrone would be able to discern their emotions and their character to know if they were telling the truth would be invaluable. Anyone involved in this incident had to be evil and possibly narcissistic, one who only cares about their personal needs and wishes and no one else's.

It was agreed that they would start meeting with those they were pretty sure were involved in some way.

Donavan said, "So let's start with Orshon. He's the most likely suspect. Him and his friends haven't made it a secret that they resent Raven being able to hunt in a certain area that they liked hunting in, even though they had chosen the other side for themselves. As far as we know, Raven has honored that agreement. Who knows where to find this man?"

Matton said, "I have an idea where they are. There's a group of small cabins on the mountain east of here where it is said these hunters live with their families. I think it might be dangerous to go there alone. Remember, they are all armed and probably dangerous. How did we get them into town the first time?"

Magg said, "We saw them in town and asked them to come and talk. I really don't like the idea of waiting for them to come to town. But maybe that's the safest way. I don't want to send anyone up there and take a chance of them not coming back. Remember, they may have already committed murder here. What's to stop them from doing it again? Especially if they think they may have gotten away with it."

Jarrone spoke up. "Maybe we could give them a reason to come to town. What if we spread a rumor that food is getting scarce and everyone is buying up the food and there's not much left. Do you think they would come in a panic to buy food for their families?"

"Good idea. But it has to be believable. Let's see if Toran, who owns the store, will hide some of his supply just long enough for people to start complaining. Then when Orshon and his friends come to town looking for food, we can herd them into the inn to have a little talk. What do you think, Jarrone?" Magg asked.

"I think that might work. It will be hard when the villagers start complaining about the lack of their favorite foods. But it's for a really good cause, right?"

"So who wants to be the one to talk to Toran?"

Matton spoke up, "I think it might take all of us to really convince him of the importance of what we are asking him to do. Hopefully, it will only be for a few days. We don't want a food riot on our hands."

Jasmine agreed that they needed to do something like that. She said, "Can we buy some extra food ahead of time to make sure those who really need the food can get it from us? I don't want anyone to go hungry for very long, especially if they're struggling as it is."

Donavan agreed and so did the rest of the group. They must protect anyone who was really in need.

One more thing, said Jarrone, "If we are to arrest anyone in this crime, we need a place to put them where they can't get away. There's some space in the inn that is open and has no windows. Maybe we could built some sturdy cells for prisoners there. If we start right away, we could get the partitions up pretty quickly. They wouldn't need to be big, just big enough for one man to be able to lie down. Maybe between the soldiers and a few townspeople, we could have it done by tomorrow morning."

Donavan said, "Jarrone, that's brilliant. I hadn't thought of that. We do need someplace strong to keep these men in until we decide their guilt and punishment. Matton, can you see about that today?

Matton smiled, "Of course, I don't think there's even one soldier or villager who wouldn't want to help with that project. I'll get on it right away."

Donavan said, "While you do that, the rest of us will check with Toran and see if he'll agree to the plan to get those men into town."

At that Matton left to talk to everyone he could about building cells for those who might be found to be suspicious in the commission of these murders.

On that note, the meeting was over and everyone followed Magg and Matton to the village store. As they entered together, Toran felt in his heart that he wasn't going to like what they were going to say.

"Tell me what you want and get it over with."

"We want to make a proposal that you likely won't like. But it's really important." Magg began. She then explained what was needed and that they would be buying extra food for anyone who was suffering. They needed to get Orshon and his friends to come to town looking for food for their families. Then they would be brought into the inn for questioning regarding a recent set of murders in Anakik.

"Well, I don't like it, but I can see the reasoning behind it. As long as the truly needy are taken care of, I'm alright with it. I can give you a list of those most likely to need help. I will send them to you as needed. Will that do?"

Magg was grateful, "Yes that will do nicely and thank you for helping us with something as important as this."

The rest of the group thanked him as well. They left the store with much better feelings than they had had all day. Their plan was taking shape. Now if only Orshon and his group would show up for food in the next day or two.

Chapter 10

It didn't take long for Orshon and his friends to come to town demanding food for their families. It was exactly what Donavan and the rest of his friends were hoping for. Now they wouldn't be going up the mountain and facing Orshon and his guns. It was hoped that this would go as planned. If not, they had plenty of magic to change the outcome as needed.

As Orshon and those with him approached the village store, Donavan and his team of wizarads followed them in.

"We heard a rumor that the food supply was scarce right now. We need food to feed our families. The hunting has been limited for us, so we need more food from your store. I have a list of things we need right now. We will have them before we leave this useless village." Orshon was very angry.

Toran replied, "We can only give you what we have, sir. Everyone is limited right now. So I can give you some of the things on your list, but many things are out of stock. Sorry for the inconvenience."

Orshon yelled in anger, "INCONVENIENCE?? What are you talking about?! We must have what you have and now. Or there will be trouble for everyone in this godforsaken village. Do you understand me?" Orshon's face was close to purple as he raged at Toran. He was about to go for his rifle at that point.

It was then that Donavan stepped up and tried to calm the situation. "Orshon, what the store has is truly all it has. He can only give you those things in stock. Do you understand?"

"You're not listening to me are you? Our families need more food than you seem to have to sell us. Since our hunting grounds have been limited to the north side of town, we aren't getting enough meat for all of us. It's that witch Raven's fault."

Donavan was getting angry at this point in the discussion, "Raven's fault? REALLY?? And have any of you tried to do anything about it? We've had two of the guards killed and Raven nearly killed just two nights ago. Do you know anything about that, Orshon? Do any of your friends?"

Orshon turned a paler shade of purple, "What are you talking about? How would I know anything about what happened to Raven or anyone else in this village?"

"It would be because of your last few remarks about your hunting grounds and Raven herself that I suspect you might know something about what's happened."

Orshon's companions lined up behind Orshon in a threatening posture. Some of them had their knives drawn and guns at the ready. Donavan looked at Magg and Jarrone at that moment and said, "I'm thinking you don't realize what you're up against right now. Do we need to demonstrate what can happen if any of you decide to be stupid?"

Orshon looked at Magg and Jarrone and decided that maybe there was more here than he could guess. "What do you want from us anyway?"

"I would very much like to talk to each of you separately, starting with you, Orshon."

"Very well. But you won't find out anything from us. It must have been someone else who did all that to Raven and her guards." He said the last with a sneer.

"We'll see, won't we? Come with me now, Orshon."

Orshon followed Donavan to the inn where there was a room that had no windows. It was in the middle of the inn and served as a meeting room. Donavan showed Orshon to one of the chairs at the table. Orshon sat with a growl.

Donavan started questioning Orshon on his whereabouts on the night of the murders. "Where were you two nights ago around midnight?"

"I was home with my family sleeping."

"You know we will check on that, don't you?"

"Go ahead."

"Do you own a dog or one that looks like a wolf, by chance?"

"I do as a matter of fact. She's a wolf. She obeys me very well and hunts for game, too. Why do you ask?"

"The reason I ask is because it was a wolf that scared Raven that night. She had to go farther from Anakik than she normally did because of it. She was frightened by that wolf."

"Oh ain't that the saddest thing I've ever heard. Too bad for Raven."

"The other part of that is she couldn't get into her cottage because there were two men waiting for her near the front door. She went to another place to find help. When we checked on who was supposed to be guarding her, we found two men buried in the forest. They had been murdered by someone and buried in a shallow grave together. I see you have mud on your shoes. Can you explain that?"

"Don't be ridiculous! I live on the mountain where there's mud all over the place all the time."

"But this mud is a special color not found on the mountain and it is only on the south side of the forest that we have found it. It has dried on your boots where I can see it."

"Well, I think I'm done here." He drew out his knife and lunged for Donavan quick as a snake. Magg was waiting outside the room listening to the conversation. She opened the door when things were getting rough and in an instant cast a spell to stop Orshon from moving. Donavan also sent magic to cause the knife to melt.

Orshon was shocked, he couldn't move and dropped his knife screaming that it was too hot. Jarrone came in with some rope to tie him up and take him to the room that had been set aside for anyone who might be guilty of the murders. The room was partitioned off with bars for walls and locked from the outside. Orshon was ushered into one of the cells right then. He protested every step of the way. He was chained by the guards and cast into the cell none to gently and the door was locked. Orshon was screaming that he had done nothing wrong and demanded to be set free. He was ignored by all.

Donavan called the next member of Orshon's gang, Klerk, and asked him the same questions. The man was really nervous and confessed everything to Donavan.

"I was with Orshon when we were hunting on Raven's side of the forest. I knew we shouldn't be there. I also knew that something bad was going to happen. I saw the two guards at Raven's door, but I don't remember anything else from that night."

Donavan knew he was lying, but he would find out more later on. Klerk was also chained and taken to a cell in the room reserved for them.

As Donavan interviewed the gang, it became apparent that they were all guilty to one degree or another. When all five of them were in the room together, Donavan called Magg and Jarrone to meet with him as to what would be done about them all. It was decided that a court would be called so the town could attend and help judge them for their evil deeds.

It was also decided to have the men stay in their prison until morning. It didn't seem safe to let them out for the night. Magg and Donavan with Jarrone's help, would let the villagers know what was to happen in the morning. The villagers were concerned because they wanted not only Raven to be safe, but all of them and their families. Tomorrow would be very interesting.

Donavan, Jasmine, Magg, Matton, Jarrone, and Greta left the area to go to their own rooms for the night. Greta was excited to share all she knew with Zarcon who was resting. He wasn't feeling well and she wanted to take his mind off his health issues if only for a short while.

She walked into their room and saw Zarcon reading at his desk. She was glad he was out of bed. She said, "Zarcon, I have so much to tell you about today. Do you have the energy to listen?"

"Oh Greta, I would love to hear all you have to tell me."

"Well, you knew the men who are suspected of killing Lucain and Retin were brought in, right? They were indeed brought to Donavan and the others to be questioned about where they were on that terrible night. Zarcon, those men are so evil! It was frightening to me to listen to their attitudes toward killing others. I did all I could to calm the situation, but it was very difficult. Emotions are so high and understandably so. Anyway, the men are put into chains and cells have been built to house them while Donavan and the others try to find out what happened and who's guilty of murder."

Zarcon was shocked, but he was also proud of Greta for all she had seen and done to help with the awful situation. When Greta finished her story, Zarcon asked her if they might get to bed and spend the night together in peace.

Greta was happy to oblidge Zarcon in his wish. She was feeling so close to him lately. She loved him so very much. It was obvious that he loved her just the same.

Chapter 11

Morning came and the villagers were already filling up the square to find out what was going to happen to the men who had been arrested the day before. It was suspected that they had been involved in the murder of the two soldiers, Retin and Lucain. An air of excitement hung over the crowd. This had never happened in Anakik until today. Their village was normally very quiet and safe. Orshon and his gang had changed all that. Now it was hoped that they would pay.

Donavan and Magg came out of the inn to address the villagers. Donavan began, "We are going to hold a court to find out what exactly happened on the night that Retin and Lucain were so brutally killed. We are going to bring out the prisoners and question each one of them to find the truth. We ask that you remain calm and allow the court to find out what happened and how to respond to our findings."

Greta had agreed to be nearby to do what she could to calm the people as needed. It looked like it was going to be a difficult task. The hardest part would be trying to keep the prisoners from becoming violent. Greta truly had her work cut out for her. She would do all she had power to do while she was there.

The suspects, Orshon and his four gang members were brought out of their cells in chains. They were protesting everything from the food to the chains they were forced to wear.

Orshon was complaining the loudest, "This is ridiculous! We've done nothing worthy of chains and rotten food. Whatever you're planning, when we get free, we will make you all pay for it." He was so angry that his face was once again a bright purple.

Donavan laughed, "Keep talking Orshon, you're just putting the noose around your own neck. I'm sure your so called friends are not happy with what you're saying here. Threatening the village is not the way to make people like you."

"I don't want them to like me. I want them to see the ridiculousness of this entire situation. We've done nothing that you can prove."

"So say you."

All this was said as they walked to the front of the inn. The villagers weren't likely to hear what Orshon had been saying. Orshon and the others were led out of the inn and positioned in the chairs set by the steps for the purpose.

So now Donavan stepped up the steps that led into the inn. The front of the inn would be used for the temporary purpose of the court. The porch was large and would work nicely for the purpose. Chairs had been quickly set nearby for the witnesses as well as the prisoners. The sets of chairs were separated to prevent any violence from the prisoners.

Donavan started the proceedings by saying, "My fellow villagers, we are here to decide the fate of these men who are accused of murdering two soldiers here to protect you. We will ask questions of these men in an attempt to find the truth of the situation. We also have witnesses who have additional information.

"Orshon, please come and sit in the chair set aside for you while we ask you questions about the night the two soldiers were killed and buried in a shallow grave. Where were you on that night?"

Orshon was angry, "I told you I was home with my family! We didn't go out at all that night."

"I'm going to ask someone about that later. When you go hunting, did you not agree to hunt only on the north side of the village?"

"Yes, but it wasn't fair. We've hunted wherever we want for decades. Now you've let a freak live in town who needs the whole south side of the forest. You've divided our hunting area in half and we're not happy about it."

"But you agreed to the arrangement and signed a contract to the effect that you wouldn't hunt in the area given to Raven. I have the paper here."

"Ladies and gentlemen, you see the paper signed by Orshon himself that he agrees to only hunt in the forest on the north side of the village, leaving the south side for Raven to hunt."

"I would also state that the north side of the forest is much larger than the south side because there are no villages on that side of Anakik. So Orshon's remark about cutting his hunting grounds in half is irrelevant."

"That is all for now Orshon, please go back with your friends. I would like to call the man who lives just on the other side of Raven's cottage. Jarrone would you please take the chair while I ask you a few questions regarding the night in question?"

"Yes, I'd be glad to."

"Did you see anything strange on that night? Anyone around that was acting suspicious?"

"Yes I did, but I didn't think it was strange at the time. Earlier in the day, I saw Orshon walking slowly by Raven's cottage and trying to see in the windows. That's when Raven sleeps. I was a bit concerned, but when he kept walking past her cottage, I decided it was nothing to be concerned about."

"Do you think he was looking for anything or a way in that was not the front door?"

"I couldn't say for sure, but he was doing something strange and when there was so much trouble that night, I put the two together and wondered if he might have had something to do with it all. He was acting pretty suspicious."

"Thank you Jarrone, you've helped a lot."

"Now I'd like to call Raven herself to answer a few questions. Will you come and sit on the chair while I ask you some questions about the night of the murders?"

Raven had just arrived and agreed to sit in the chair for questions. She was nervous that there were so many people watching her. The worst part was when she saw Orshon and his friends chained and sitting so close to the chair she was supposed to sit in. They were looking at her with hatred in their eyes. She started shaking in fear.

Donavan noticed and asked her about it. "Raven why are you so frightened suddenly?

"Orshon and his friends are so close to me. They are looking at me with hatred and I'm feeling threatened."

"I'm sorry Raven. We've made sure they can't move or harm anyone here. I have just one question, can you tell me about the reason you're feeling threatened? Does it have anything to do with the night of the murders? Tell us about it."

"It does. The night I was going hunting in my side of the forest I had a bad experience. I had transformed into my cat when I saw a large wolf drinking from the creek I go to before I start hunting. This was the second time I had seen that animal. As I watched, a man called the wolf to come to him. I had known that the animal was trained and owned by a man from before. It was not wild. Then I saw two men come out of the forest and were talking to each other. One of them was talking about how to eliminate the "big black cat" that they had to share the hunting grounds with. I knew then that I could kill both of them, but I knew I would have to leave Anakik if I did. But I really want to stay here."

"What happened next?"

"I knew I would have to hunt farther south to avoid any problems with the two men and their wolf. I was able to find food farther from Anakik than I usually go. I was able to eat. But I was frightened by the two men so I crept back to my cottage. Then as I was approaching my cottage, I found that there were two men hiding on the side of the house by my front door. There was supposed to be a guard there to keep me safe, but that night there wasn't one. So I transformed as I walked quietly to the inn to seek Magg's help. She let me spend the rest of the night and next day in her spare room. I am so grateful for her help and concern."

"Thank you Raven. You may leave."

Raven left and went back to Magg's spare room. She was exhausted and needed to sleep the rest of the day. She also knew that Orshon and his friends couldn't get to her.

"Now I'd like to have Tenzi come and sit here for some questions. Will you come up, please?"

"My honor, Donavan."

"Alright, Tenzi, can you tell me what happened when I asked you about the men who were supposed to be guarding Raven's cottage that night?"

"You came to me and told me that no one had been guarding Raven's cottage. I told you that there were two men assigned to keep watch for Raven. I was concerned that Raven had not seen them anywhere and that two strange men were there watching her front door. We got very concerned about the two men and started a search. We finally found a shallow grave with two bodies in it. They were the two men we were looking for. We were angry that someone had murdered them in cold blood."

"Thank you Tenzi. I'll be asking you more questions later on."

"Orshon, will you please come to the chair again?"

"Why? I've already told you what I know."

"I would like to talk more about that night that you say you were home with your family. Isn't it true that you told me you had a big wolf?"

"I do indeed. But he's none of your business."

"I think he is. Raven told us that she couldn't hunt in her side of the forest because she saw a large wolf-like creature that was drinking at her usual drinking hole. She said the wolf belonged to at least one of the men that were talking about eliminating the big cat.

She made the choice to go farther south to hunt. She was able to find something to eat and then she was able to creep back to her cottage away from those men and their wolf/"

"So it's important that we determine whose animal it is. Would you please describe your wolf to us?"

"My wolf is large. He's obedient to me. I really like my big wolf."

"So the wolf is yours. Were you in the forest the night in question?"

"I told you I was not. Ask my friends. They'll tell you where I was."

"I intend to."

Donavan excused Orshon and called the friend that was the most nervous of the group, Tyri. This man was very thin and had a whiney voice. His small mustache was quivering when he spoke. His hair was thinning and his clothes were tattered. He looked the poorest of Orshon's men. As Tyri approached the chair, Orshon looked a bit sick. He got more nervous as Tyri sat down.

"Tyri, can you tell me about the night of the murders? Were you out hunting and if so, was anyone with you?"

Tyri took a deep breath and looked at Orshon like he was ready to cry. "I was out hunting that night."

"Who was with you?"

"I'd rather not say."

"Well, let me put it this way. If I say the name of the person with you, please blink twice. Do you understand?"

"Yes, alright."

"Was it one of Orshon's friends?"

"Yes. Well not exactly."

"Was it Orshon himself?"

Tyri blinked about a thousand times and didn't seem able to stop. Orshon jumped out of his chair at the side and was headed for Tyri to do him harm. The soldiers near him tripped him and held him down on the ground when he fell. He thrashed around and started screaming, "You're lying! Why would you say such a thing?"

Tyri calmly said, "Because it's true, Orshon. It was your wolf and you were talking about killing Raven."

The people erupted in rage. "Lock him up!" "Hang him and his friends!" "That man is evil!"

Greta sent out her calming magic and tried to settle the people down. It wouldn't do for them to rise up now. It seemed to be working as the crowd finally became quiet again and watched what was going to happen.

Donavan also tried to calm the people, "Quiet! These men are likely guilty, but we have to ask more questions. We need to find out who actually killed Retin and Lucain. It's looking like Orshon and Tyri were guilty of hunting in the wrong place and threatened Raven, but who was the killer?"

"I would like Tenzi to come back to the chair, please."

Tenzi quickly walked to the witness chair.

"Tenzi, when you were looking for Retin and Lucain, did you find anything that might lead you to the killer? Any footprints or personal items left near the grave?"

Tenzi thought for a moment, "Actually, I hadn't thought much about it, but one of the searchers found a button that had been torn off a jacket laying near the grave. Also, now that you mention it, the footprints were quite large around the area. Someone with bigger feet than mine."

"Do you or the other soldier still have that button?"

"I have it in my pocket. I kept it just in case it was important. It didn't come from either of the victims. So I kept it. Here it is if you'd like to see it. Maybe it will match someone here."

Donavan dismissed Tenzi and called for Orshon again. The soldier holding him down helped him up.

As Orshon got to his feet he started yelling, "This is getting really old and I'm getting very angry with all these questions. Now what do you want from me?"

"I would like to see the front of your jacket please."

"What if I say no?"

"Then we'll have to remove your jacket for you. Which do you prefer?"

"Alright, here it is. Check all you want."

As Donavan checked Orshon's jacket, all the buttons were there. It was disappointing, so he let Orshon sit back down with the others. Then Donavan called the other man, Tyri to come and sit in the witness chair.

"Tyri, may I have your jacket please?"

Tyri was shaking in fear. He kept looking at Orshon. He knew he was in trouble no matter what happened at this point. He finally took off his jacket and gave it to Donavan.

"Well, look here! There's a button missing and it just happens to match this one found near the grave. Can you explain how it got there, Tyri?"

"It must have fallen off my jacket one time when we were hunting a while ago."

"Tyri, do you expect all of us to believe that? You lost the button on the night of the murders didn't you? Maybe Lucain grabbed your jacket and the button came off in the struggle? This would be just before you killed him, right?"

Tyri started to cry, "I didn't kill anybody. It was Orshon. He killed them both because they knew about our plan to get rid of Raven and have the forest to ourselves again. I was trying to make Orshon stop, but he hit Lucain first with the butt of his rifle, then shot him as he lay on the ground. Retin was being held by another one of Orshon's friends, I think it was Klerk. While he held Retin, Orshon stabbed him with his hunting knife until he died. There was a lot of screaming and blood. I was amazed that no one came to investigate. We had dug a small grave and dropped them both into it and threw some dirt over them and made the area look like nothing had happened there." Tyri was sobbing as he finished his story.

Orshon jumped up and screamed, "It's all a lie!! I was home with my family all night that night."

Donavan was shocked that Orshon would continue to lie about the night of the murders. He finally said, "Orshon, you are not getting out of this so easily. We have another situation that needs to be solved and that is, who were the two men watching Raven's cottage while she was out hunting? I would call another one of Orshon's friends, Balko, to come to the witness chair."

Balko came reluctantly and sat down. Balko was a large man with a large belly. He looked strong and he had a scar on his upper lip that gave him a permanent scowl.

"Balko where were you the night of the murders?"

"I was with Orshon hunting."

"Really, and did you happen to be watching Raven's cottage while you were out that night?"

"Alright, I'll tell you. Shoner and I were assigned by Orshon to watch for Raven when she came back from hunting. If we caught her, we were to bring her to Orshon in the forest. I'm pretty sure he intended to kill her."

The crowd gasped in shock.

Donavan was also shocked at the evil of Orshon. "So you and Shoner were the two watching Raven's cottage that night?"

"I just told you so. Orshon was so angry at not having the entire forest to hunt in that he was willing to eliminate anyone who wanted to change it. He considered the rule to be taking away what was his."

"Did you agree with him?"

"No, in fact I was upset that he didn't want to just obey the rule and live in peace here in Anakik. Shoner and I had agreed that if we saw Raven going into her cottage that we wouldn't do anything about it. We were talking about what to tell Orshon. The good thing was that Raven never showed up."

"So you didn't have anything to do with what went on in the forest?"

"Absolutely not, we didn't know for sure what Orshon was going to do and when we found out, we kept our mouths shut because Orshon would have killed us if we had said anything to anyone."

"It appears Orshon is a violent man, am I right?"

"Yes."

Orshon started shouting curses and swearing revenge on Balko and Shoner. He swore he would kill them if he had the chance. Of course, none of that helped his case.

"Thank you Balko. You may go back to your chair."

"Really? With Orshon right there? He'll find a way to kill me if I'm anywhere near him."

"Maybe you'd better sit over here near the front, away from him.

"Thanks."

Shoner was also a large man like Balko. He was bald and had a long scruffy red beard. His clothes were a bit nicer than Balko's but that wasn't saying much. They looked like they had been worn for many years and had patches on the knees and elbows of his clothing. He could have been handsome if he were cleaned up and shaved. His beard gave him a dangerous look.

"Shoner, please come and sit here so I can ask you the same questions I asked Balko. Were you one of the men watching Raven's front door the night of the murders? If so, what was the plan if you caught her?"

"It's like Balko said, we were to take her to Orshon as soon as we caught her. I'm not really sure we would have let her go. Balko agreed with Orshon about having the entire forest to ourselves, no matter what Balko said. She was the one thing in the way of that. So it would have been easier to eliminate her right then and there. I was a bit disappointed that she got away that night."

Donavan was shocked at the casual way that Shoner said he was in favor of eliminating Raven. Donavan tried to maintain his composure as he said, "Shoner, you may join Balko. Next, I would have someone from Orshon's family come to the witness chair."

Orshon started screaming again, "You can't bring my family into this! They know I was home all night. Why would you ask them questions? They don't know anything."

Donavan dismissed Orshon's remarks and called his son, Orshon, Jr., to come to the chair. "Junior, was your father home the night of the murders?"

"I've been thinking about it ever since and all I can say is, he was not home that night. He said he was going hunting with his friends. I was afraid to come to you because my father is violent to us if we do anything he doesn't like. He can be brutal."

At that Orshon rose up and was about to charge his son in his rage. The soldiers near him tackled him and tied him so he couldn't move. They also tightened his chains. He thrashed his bonds and cursed and swore revenge on all of them. He remained on the ground at that point. No one wanted him loosened in any way.

The villagers started yelling again for his hanging.

Donavan was relieved. It appeared that the case was solved.

"Quiet everyone. We believe this case has been solved and the guilty parties found. I judge Orshon to be the killer and Tyri and Klerk to be his aids in this crime. In addition, we will judge Balko and Shoner as to their level of guilt in this crime. I will consult the rest of the team as to what will become of them and return as soon as we have made a decision. You may all wait here or return to your homes until the decision has been made. We will ring the chapel bell as soon as we do."

Many of the villagers left thinking it might be a while before the decision was made. Others decided to stay and wait. The prisoners were taken back to their cells to be held until the verdict was reached.

Donavan asked Jasmine, Magg, Matton, Greta, and Jarrone to come with him to the inn to decide what was to be done. They didn't talk as they walked to the inn.

When they got to the dining room inside the inn, they sat at one of the tables together. Donavan spoke up first, "I think the murders have been solved. What do the rest of you think?"

Jasmine said, "I agree, that terrible man, Orshon, is guilty as hell."

Magg and Matton both agreed.

Jarrone was hesitant, "I agree that it was Orshon who did the killing. But what about the two that were there helping him? I think Tyri is remorseful, but he still helped kill Lucain. The other man, Klerk, didn't seem to mind being involved. In fact, did you notice his smirk? It was like he enjoyed being a part of it. I don't know what all that might mean as far as the verdict goes, but maybe we could do something for Tyri."

Donavan said, "You have a point, Jarrone. But we have no way to keep a prisoner for long periods of time. We've never had a problem like this. Also, if Tyri is kept prisoner for a long time, we would have to take care of him. We can't do that long term. I could check with some of the closer villages and see if they could do it. But we can't decide until that happens. Magg, what's your opinion on this?"

"I see Jarrone's point as well, but all three of them were party to murder. We can't just keep them around not knowing if they would do it again. We have to protect the village above all else. I can sympathize with Tyri, but he was still a part of it and didn't come to us and turn himself in and tell us what happened that night. I say he's guilty and must be punished with the other two."

Donavan asked Matton what he thought.

"I have to agree with Magg. All three of them are guilty of murder. I don't believe the people of this village would think otherwise."

"Then let's take a vote, who believes them to be guilty of murder, raise your hand."

All raised their hands, even Jarrone. So the verdict was guilty for all three.

Donavan spoke, "Now we must decide the fate of the two not specifically involved in the murders. Balko and Shoner did as they were told, but didn't follow through, at least that is what Balko has claimed. Although Shoner seemed to think eliminating Raven was a good idea. Still we don't know if he was involved directly in the murders. What is your opinion Jarrone?"

Jarrone had been thinking of what would be appropriate punishment. "I've thought about it and decided that banishing them from the village might be appropriate. If they aren't here, we don't have to worry about them taking revenge on Raven for what Orshon and the others did. At least that's my opinion."

Magg spoke up, "I disagree. We don't really have anything to charge them with. They did hang out at Raven's cottage. But were they a part of the murders of the guards? Nothing was said about that. How did the two guards get to Orshon anyway? I'm feeling very suspicious about them and their actions that night."

Jasmine and Matton both agreed with Magg. Donavan was confused now. How could he have missed something as important as that? It was too late to bring everyone back to court. They must decide what was best as things were right now.

Magg had an idea, "What if we get Balko and Shoner back in here and ask them some more questions about that night? Surely that would be appropriate. What do you think Donavan?"

"I think that's a great idea. We'll just tell them we have a few more questions to ask them and bring them in here with a couple of guards."

It was agreed. Tenzi was called in and asked to go get Balko and Shoner for more questions. Tenzi was actually relieved. He had the same questions that Magg brought up. There was more to be learned from those two men.

Tenzi left and had two guards come with him to get Balko and Shoner. He found them in their cells.

"Balko and Shoner, you've been asked to come to the inn for a few more questions. Please follow me."

The two men acted nervous about the situation and didn't want to be asked any more questions. They got a little bit resistant when they entered the inn and saw Donavan and the others waiting for them.

Donavan began, "Thank you for coming. We just have a couple of questions that we were confused about. Balko, where were you and Shoner when the two guards were taken to Orshon?"

"Umm, well, we were hiding at Raven's cottage and um, Tyri and Klerk had already taken them to Orshon. So we didn't have anything to do with that."

"Really? Why would Orshon send Tyri and Klerk to get the two guards instead of having you two just bring them when you got to the cottage? It makes no sense. Can you explain that a bit better so I can believe your story?"

Balko was turning red and fidgeting in the chair. The heat had just been turned up on him. "Alright, Shoner and I did grab the two guards and tie their hands. We took them to Orshon and left them there with Tyri and Klerk. That's all we did! Then we returned to Raven's cottage and waited for her."

"I think that's a bit closer to the truth. But I'm thinking there was a bit more to your story than that. Tell us everything you did that night. We'll find out one way or another. It will go better for you if you tell us."

"Maybe Shoner should tell you the rest of the story. I can't go on just now." He was shaking like a leaf and looked about to faint.

Donavan sent Balko to the other chair and asked Shoner to come forward. Shoner was also a big man. He seemed on the verge of violence as well.

"Shoner will you please tell us the whole truth about what happened the night of the murders and how you and Balko were involved?"

Shoner was calm as he started his side of the story. "It was like Balko said. We went to Raven's cottage and tied up the guards and took them to Orshon. But that wasn't all. It was Balko and I that dug the grave for the men. We didn't have time to dig it very deep. So we left it kind of shallow hoping no one would find it. We watched Orshon murder those two men and then helped put them in the grave we had dug for them. We also helped Tyri and Klerk make it look like nothing had happened there before we went back to Raven's cottage."

Shoner was still calm as he finished his horrible story. He was really cold about the killings. Donavan and the others were shocked again to see how cold he was as he spoke of the murders of two fine men. Tenzi and the two guards took Balko and Shoner back to the cell none too kindly. It might be said that both men were limping a bit as their cell door slammed shut.

Donavan, with sorrow in his voice said, "It appears we have a bigger problem than we originally thought. I am more than grateful that Magg has a smarter brain than I have. I am so sorry that I didn't think of all that while they were being questioned the first time. Now it looks like they were as guilty as the rest of them. What shall be their punishment? They were definitely a part of the murders. Would you vote for hanging these two as well? Those in favor of hanging raise your hand."

Everyone raised their hands.

The verdict is guilty and hanging the punishment for all five, Orshon, Tyri, Klerk, Balko, and Shoner. Let's ring the bell and call the people back to hear what we've decided."

Aribon was sent to ring the bell. He had been waiting in the kitchen in case he could help with anything. Donavan had asked him if he would. He ran to the chapel and climbed the stairs to the bell. He rang it three times. The people came quickly to hear the verdict. There was an air of excitement to find out what would become of the criminals.

Donavan walked into the square. Orshon was still on the ground, guarded by four soldiers so he couldn't harm anyone, especially his son. He was still in a fit of rage. The other prisoners had been taken to their cells and were brought out for the verdict.

"We have come to a decision regarding the three men involved in the murders of Lucain and Retin. We find them guilty of murder. We have also decided on what is to become of Balko and Shoner who obeyed Orshon, but did no harm as far as we know."

The crowd cheered at that.

"Further, we have decided that the punishment for Orshon, Tyri, and Klerk. They are to be hanged by the neck until dead. As to the punishment for Balko and Shoner, we brought them into the inn to ask them more questions about that night. After learning of their involvement in the murders, we have determined that they are also guilty and will hang."

Tyri burst into tears. Orshon screamed in rage. Klerk just smirked. Balko and Shoner were upset, but knew it was coming. They had confessed and this would be their punishment.

The five of them were led to their prison cells and kept there until the hangings could be organized and a gallows built. There had never been a gallows in Anakik before. It was sad to have one now. It represented the deaths of two of their own.

The crowd was filled with sorrow over the loss of Lucain and Retin. They couldn't be brought back, but it was felt that at least some justice had been given to them and the village. People would feel safer now that the murders were solved and it was known who did it. The five of them would be kept away from everyone until the hanging.

Donavan and the others walked back to the inn quietly. It was finally over. It was difficult to realize what had happened and they had decided to kill the five men. But those men were guilty of something so horrific, that they must be eliminated to protect the innocent.

As to the funerals for Retin and Lucain, the parents of the two young men were planning a fitting ceremony to honor them. Their bodies were moved into the cemetary in the village. It would be held the next day with proper graves and prayers over them before they would be laid to rest properly. It would be hard for the people of Anakik to bury such fine young men. They would be sorely missed. The young men would be honored by the entire village. They were known by everyone as kind, brave young men.

Chapter 12

The noise of the gallows being built was heard by everyone. It was a sad sound for them all. Roslin and Karmine had witnessed the trial and the verdict. The boys had not been allowed to come. They stayed in their cottage playing games. It had been a terrible affair, but justice had been done and now the waiting for the hangings was getting hard to bear. The hangings were set to happen as soon as the gallows were finished. All five guilty men would be hanged at the same time. So the gallows was taking a bit longer to finish.

Roslin and Karmine walked slowly back to their cottage. It had been a horrific day for the entire village. Now they would try to process what had happened. It was also hard to understand how these men could be so evil. They thought of something no one else seemed to be concerned about. What about their families. It was surprising that none of them had come to the court except Orshon's son. Karmine decided he would bring it up with Donavan the next day. It was hoped that the families were nothing like their men.

As they got back to their cottage, they greeted the four boys and hugged them fiercely. The boys were surprised, but didn't mind. It had been a long day and it was almost time to get ready for bed. Roslin wanted to spend a few short hours loving her family and telling them so. Life was short and it wasn't often enough that they sat together and spoke of their love for one another. It felt so good to take the time now. After the day's events, neither Roslin nor Karmine had any interest in watching the hangings. They decided to stay away and spend the day with the boys.

Jasmine and Donavan spent that evening together, both worried about what would happen when the gallows was ready and the men hanged. Would there be trouble? Donavan urged Jasmine to stay at the inn until it was over. She readily agreed. She didn't want to witness the hangings. She also knew that Donavan could handle any problems that might come up.

Magg and Matton also spent the evening together. Magg tried to get Matton to stay in their room until it was over, but he refused. "What if you need help with the crowd? I'll be there to make sure you're safe."

Magg finally agreed to have him there with her. He gave her strength to get through the hangings. She knew it would be terrible.

It took three full days with men working throughout the day and into the night to finish the gallows and make them ready for the hangings. There were five nooses hanging from the top brace and looked very ominous. The entire company of soldiers were present to make sure nothing interfered with the verdicts being fulfilled. Most of the villagers were standing around waiting for the men to come out to the gallows. This was the day for the hangings.The tension was palpable.

The five men walked out of the inn where their cells were. The crowd started cursing them and shouting at them. There was one group, however, that was very quiet. Magg was observing the crowd and noticed them. She began to be concerned about them because there was a lot of anger in their eyes. She asked Matton to come with her as she gradually moved closer to them to see if she could find out what they were up to. As she got closer, she could hear them talking to each other.

"When do we act?" "It must be when our men are close to the gallows." "Did you bring your rifle?" "I sure did and I can't wait to use it." "Is everyone ready to act?" "Yes we are. We need to stop this from happening. So what if they killed a couple of stupid guards. There worthless anyway."

Both Magg and Matton were alarmed and moved away to alert Donavan and the others of their plans. It must not happen. Those men were guilty of murder and justice must be done. The crowd was so agitated there would be huge problems if that group acted out. She was sure there would be a lot of people killed or injured if a riot broke out.

Donavan asked her and Matton to help him alert the guards and bring Jarrone so that they could use magic, if necessary. Greta was also needed to help calm everyone. She was grateful she could help in some small way. The situation was looking a bit tense at this point.

Using magic on anyone wanting to cause trouble would be better than watching people get hurt or worse. Donavan decided that the ones with magic should be close to the gallows to prevent anyone coming after the men before the hangings. He sent some soldiers to go near that group to be ready to disarm anyone who threatened the bystanders or guards.

As the men drew near the gallows, it was apparent that the group was ready to cause trouble. Gradually they had moved closer to the gallows to try to rescue the men. However, with Magg, Donavan, and Jarrone standing at the foot of the stairs, they were prevented from doing anything in that direction. All three were ready to use magic to stop them. Greta was using all her strength to keep things calm and to prevent others from acting out in anger.

As those at the gallows watched, one of the women was getting ready to pull out her rifle and shoot them, but Magg sent a spell that heated her rifle hot enough that she dropped it on the ground. Matton was standing nearby and quickly moved in and held her so she couldn't pick it back up. Jarrone sent his freeze spell into the rest of the group. They couldn't move and were prevented from doing anything long enough for the hangings to take place.

The men were led to their positions and their nooses were put around their necks. Tyri started crying. The hangman put hoods over their heads and moved to pull the lever that would make the trapdoors fall away beneath their feet. They were given a long drop to be sure their necks were broken swiftly. None of them moved when they hit the end of the rope with an awful crack.

The local doctor was present and checked each one of the men and declared them all dead. There was no joy in his pronouncement. This was something he never expected to do. For him it was a terrible thing.

The crowd erupted in cheers of relief when it was announced by the doctor that all five were dead. The other group began sobbing. It was over, but they were left without their men. It was the families of those men that had tried to save them. Fortunately, they failed. Jasmine and Greta felt empathy for the families and friends of the men. What a horrible way to lose someone you loved, even if he was a really bad person.

Now that the hangings were over, the crowd began to leave and go back to their homes relieved that justice had been done for the men that were killed. The group of family members were about to leave when Donavan called to them. He was concerned about the future having these family members still around Anakik. Especially since they had been plotting to save those evil men.

"Wait just a moment all of you. I have a few words I need to say to you. Number one, you are under arrest for trying to stop a legal action by the court. However, if you agree to all of my provisions, you will not be detained. Number two, if you leave as soon as you get back to your cabins in the mountains, we will let you go. Number three, if you ever show your faces in this village again, you will be charged and put in jail, all of you. So, what will it be?"

The leader of the families, a rough looking woman of considerable size, and thought to be Orshon's wife, said with a smirk, "Oh, we'll leave alright. We don't want to stay in a town that kills its own men just because they were out having a little fun."

Donavan was shocked, "REALLY!!! So you're fine with killing innocent people, are you?? You say your men were out 'just having a little fun'? On second thought, I think we shouldn't allow you to go anywhere else. You are a danger to society and we will take care of you as soon as may be."

"What is that supposed to mean? You just told us we could leave!"

"Lady, you changed my mind with your attitude about what your men have done. There's a town not far from here that has a real sheriff and a real court. We're going to send you there, tied up, I might add. Once there you will face charges of attempting to cause a riot in our village and for attempting to kill one of our men with that rifle you happened to bring to the hangings. I'll be sending a runner to alert that village of what we will be sending to them. They have a really nasty jail that I'm sure you'll be miserable in.

"For now you will come to the inn and spend the time waiting in the same cell your husbands were in."

"You can't do that to us. We didn't do anything against the law. We were just trying to rescue our men from an unlawful hanging. You had no right to do that. They were supporting our family. Now what are we supposed to do?"

Donavan was almost speechless with shock. He finally said, "The fact that your husbands were all involved in killing two valuable young men makes their hanging legal. What you would have done to support yourselves is not my problem. What you are doing and saying now is my problem. Your days of freedom are sadly over."

The woman finally realized she wasn't getting anywhere with her anger. She calmed herself a bit and said, "Not all of us were part of the plan. Let them go."

"And who might those people be?"

"That would be the children. There are three of them with us and three that are back at the farm. One of the older children is watching the other two. Please take care of them while we're gone." The woman was actually close to tears. It looked like she might care about someone else after all.

Donavan was angry at her words, "I can't believe you brought children here to witness the hanging of their father. I think you better consider your children no longer yours. You'll be gone a fairly long time anyway."

Donavan then ordered the soldiers to take them to the inn and lock them in the cells. There were ten of them present. Three were small children and seven were adult women. The three children acted embarrassed to be with their mothers. They were separated and taken to the kitchen where they could be fed and watched until it was decided what was to become of them.

Just as they were being fed, a couple, Eskelon and Marva, came to Aribon and asked if they could take care of the children until it was decided what care they would need. Aribon was more than happy to let them take the three little ones. He knew them well and that they were wanting to have children of their own. It seemed like a good idea to have the children in a family situation rather than locked up in the kitchen.

"I'm so glad you are willing to take care of these little children. I didn't know what to do. I'm sure Magg will come and check on them and you in the morning."

The three children were brought out of the kitchen and given to the couple. They seemed happy to go with them. The adults were so happy to take them home. It was a good thing that they would be taken care of for at least one night.

As the women were led away, they were grumbling and cursing the guards. They were ignored and locked up anyway. The guards were happy to leave them in the cells. Two guards were assigned by Tenzi to keep watch on them. They were really tough women and it was likely they would attempt to escape.

Magg, Jarrone, Donavan, Jasmine, Greta, and Matton walked back to their rooms after the women were safely locked up. Magg asked Donavan if she and Jarrone could talk with him for a bit. He was agreeable and went to the dining area to talk while Jasmine and Greta stayed in the dining room to chat and discuss the morning's events.

Magg started off by saying, "Donavan, Jarrone and I need to talk to you about what you're planning for those women. We need to understand your reasoning for wanting them to go to prison when they have small children at home."

Donavan got a bit defensive and said, "Didn't you hear what that woman said about their men just out having a little fun? Are you really alright with talk like that? It scares me. With that attitude, they might be willing to do anything to get even with us for hanging their men. Don't you see that?"

Magg looked at Jarrone. "I guess I missed that part. I believe you're right. We can't allow thinking like that. Also, they're teaching their childern the same attitude. Then there's at least one more generation of very sick people. So, where is this town you're thinking of that has a sheriff and court? I don't know of one near here."

"I was hoping you might know of one. Magg, you know everything, or at least I thought you did." Donavan was grinning when he said the last.

"Very funny. But seriously, where would we send them? The only place I can think of that might have such things is Synkana. But that is too far away. They'd probably escape before we got them there."

"Not if someone with magic went with them to keep them in line."

"So who are you thinking to send?"

"I know, you're thinking it's me aren't you?" Jarrone asked.

"Well mostly."

"I'll go if there are plenty of guards going with me. Can we build a large wagon with bars for them so we don't have to watch them constantly? It will be hard enough if we have one."

Donavan thought about it for a few seconds, "You're right, of course. You and the soldiers will need to sleep at some point. We can't take the risk of them escaping, that's for sure. Do we have anything like that in town?"

Magg was thinking about it, "You know, it seems like we had a festival last year and had a pretend circus. We put some dogs dressed up like lions and pulled then through town in a rolling cage. We could check and see if it's big enough. I think we kept it in the barn just outside of town. Matton and I can check it tomorrow."

Jarrone spoke up, "I will want to see it for myself. It has to be very sturdy and large enough for seven women. What time do you want to meet there?"

"Let's get there after breakfast. What do you think?"

"Sounds good to me. I'll see you there right after breakfast."

They returned to the dining area and met with Jasmine and Greta. Then they all left for their rooms for the evening. It had been such a horrible day that they all needed lots of rest to recover physically and emotionally.

As Magg was relaxing for the night, she had a terrible thought. She suddenly realized they had not come up with a plan to take care of the children that would now be orphaned by the law. The fathers were all hanged and the mothers would soon be on their way to Synkana and prison. The thought terrified her. Where were the children even now? What could anyone do for them? She would speak with Donavan and the others first thing in the morning.

Chapter 13

The next morning, Magg called the team to her to talk about the children and what must be done for them. The wagon would have to wait until it was decided what they could do about the problem. Jasmine, Donavan, Matton, and Jarrone were there when the trial had taken place and they had decided to send the mothers away. They had not, however, decided what to do with those children.

Magg said, "I know we need to find a wagon to take the women to Synkana, but before we do that, we have to take care of the children. It's really important that they be taken care of before we do anything else. Do you agree?"

Jasmine spoke up, "Magg, I've been thinking the same thing since yesterday. There just wasn't time to say anything about it. I was wondering if we could gather the children together and find out what we're dealing with. Some of the families might be willing to adopt some of them. But if we find out that they're not really willing to stay here and be a part of our village, we might have a really big problem."

Donavan backed her up, "I agree Jasmine. I'm hoping they will be glad to be free of their parents and want a fresh start here. But if they're not, then what do we do?"

Magg listened intently, "All right, I think you're both right about what we need to do first. Let's get the children and find out what we're dealing with. Matton, would you be willing to take some of the soliers and see where the children are and if we can bring them here some time today?"

Matton hesitated, "I'm not sure how to handle that, Magg. The ones we know about are still up in the mountains without anyone to watch over them. If they're anything like their parents, we might need an army to bring them down. But I will see what I can do, today?"

"Yes, today. We have to get started on this problem right away. Does anyone know if any of the children are staying in town with any of our families?"

Jarrone spoke up, "I think there is one couple, Eskelon and Marva, willing to take the little ones left in town. It's the couple living next door to Karmine and his family. I haven't heard how that's going at all, however. They just took them last night."

"Will you go check on that for us, Jarrone?"

"I will as soon as we're finished here."

"Matton, when you are back from checking on the children living in their cabin, will you either bring them here, or let me know what you find, please? As far as I remember, there should only be three of them. One older one and two little ones."

"That I will. I'll leave now and get started with a couple of soldiers so we can finish sometime this afternoon."

She said, "It seems settled, let's go to it and see what we can find out. Thank you all for your willingness to work this out."

Magg was pleased by their progress. Matton would check on those children living in the mountains, Jarrone would check on the family that had taken three of the little children into their home. She would find a place to get them together and talk to them about their feelings and whether they would want to stay in town.

The others left and Magg headed for the dining area to talk to Aribon about a place to keep the children until they could decide what the long term plan would be. They would probably need a room for them until a solution could be reached. It would only be for the three that were still in their cabin in the forest. She was hoping the three being kept by Eskelon and Marva would be staying with them for at least a little while.

Matton went to talk to the soldiers and ask for voluteers to go bring the last three children into town. Tenzi and Markos spoke up and were willing to go with Matton. They saddled their horses and were soon on their way through the forest to find the three children left alone there.

After riding for an hour, the three men found the cabin the children were staying in. Matton hollered to the cabin, "Hello the cabin! We're here to talk with you if you're willing. May we approach and come in?"

The older boy called back, "Yes, we would like you to come and help me with my two brothers." He opened the door and came out with his two little brothers. They were dirty and looked really hungry. It was sad to see them like that.

Matton walked up to them and said, "We would like to take you back to town and get you some food and clean clothes if that's alright with you."

The boy's eyes lit up at the idea and he smiled at Matton. The three boys walked up to Matton and let him give them a hug. Each of the men took one of the boys and let them ride in front of them as they made their way back to town. The boys seemed really excited to be leaving their cabin and the memories they held there. It had been mentioned at the trial that their fathers were violent and brutal. The older boy had some bruising on his arms and back. He didn't have a shirt, just some old, jeans with holes in them.

Matton was so touched by the boy's excitement to leave that his eyes got a little bit moist. It hadn't turned out at all like he had feared. The boys seemed genuinely happy to be leaving their old life. Looking at the condition the boys were in made Matton glad he didn't have to go inside their cabin to see what it was like in there. There were a few other cabins in the area, but he wasn't curious about them either. Now he was in a hurry to get the boys away and to a safe place where they would be fed and cleaned up.

Tenzi and Markos were looking the same way Matton felt. They were also very glad to get the boys away from there. There seemed to be a feeling of evil about the place and they were all glad to leave it behind.

It only took them about half the time to get back to town since the trail was mostly downhill. They went straight to the inn. Magg heard them come into the inn and went to greet them. She was saddened by the boy's condition. They were just so thin. She helped the boys down from the horses and Matton, Tenzi, and Markos walked with them into the inn. The four adults decided the children needed to eat first, they looked like they were starving.

Aribon got them a bowl of his famous stew and some fresh bread to eat. They had apple juice to drink. They ate as if they really hadn't eaten for days. Matton asked them their names as they were eating their stew. The oldest boy was named Eagan, age 12; his brothers were Alden, 8, and Marron, 6. As the boys ate, they were smiling and laughing as if for joy. Matton was touched by their happiness. They looked completely different as they were happily eating good food.

Magg sat with them and talked with them about their lives with their families. They didn't want to say very much about it. They got really upset trying to explain what it had been like for them. So Magg let them finish eating and got them some clean clothes from the lost and found bin. She got a washcloth for each boy and had them clean off the worst of the dirt. Once they were dressed Magg turned them over to Aribon.

Aribon had set up a room for them near the kitchen so he could watch over them. Then he took them to their room. When they saw their beds, they ran for them and laid down to sleep. It seemed they hadn't slept well for awhile. It was an indication that they were feeling safe at the inn and with Matton and the others.

The adults left the boys and quietly left their room. Once they were away they could talk about the experience of finding them and bringing them to town.

Matton said, "Magg, they were glad to see us and even let me give them a hug. They did not smell good, I can tell you that. It was like they hadn't eaten or bathed in a very long while. It was so sad. But the boys were so glad to see us, it seemed. I'm so glad you remembered them, Magg, and to let us go get them. Who knew?"

Magg was so relieved to have them at the inn and safe. She was so grateful she had remembered about the children before the challenge of getting the wagon built and the women off to prison. Who could know what would have happened to them otherwise?

It wasn't long before Jarrone came in to tell them about the other three children that Eskelon and Marva had taken in. It was much like the story of the three boys brought in by Matton and his friends. They had been so glad to go home with Eskelon and Marva that it was as if they already knew them and were glad to be home at last. The couple was so glad to have them that they were wanting to just keep them. The three children were ages three, five, and seven. They were also too thin and dirty. Marva was able to get them cleaned up and fed that first night. Since then, things were going really well. Both Eskelon and Marva were very loving and kind. It seemed perfect for all those involved.

Only time would tell if that were true. But for now, it was a wonderful thing.

Aribon seemed happy to be taking care of the three boys that he was watching over until something could be resolved with them. He was in no hurry to be rid of them. They were so happy to be there. They were well behaved and appreciated whatever Aribon did for them. The older boy was even happy to help Aribon in the kitchen.

Now that the children were taken care of, at least for the next few weeks, Magg and the others could begin working on the wagon for transporting the women to Synkana. They were talking in the dining room after discussing the boys and where they would be staying for awhile.

Magg suggested they go look for the wagon they had discussed the day before. They decided to meet at the barn where the old wagon was being stored. They would meet in the morning right after breakfast to check it out.

Night time came and they were all settled in for the night. Another eventful day completed. Tomorrow would bring its own troubles. But they would not worry about that tonight.

The next morning, the group met for breakfast and once eaten they went to the barn to check on the wagon they might be able to use to take the women to Synkana. It looked to be a bit too small for what they needed. It wasn't sturdy enough either. They were disappointed, but it wasn't a surprise.

It was decided that they would have the carpenter in town create a new one that was not only bigger, but much stronger to hold those women for the long journey to Synkana. They walked around the inn and headed for the carpenters shop. They found the village carpenter and called to him, "Murdon, can we talk with you for a moment?"

"Sure, what's going on?"

Donavan said, "The wagon we found in the barn is too small to take Orshon's women to Synkana. We need something much bigger and stronger to keep them in until they get there. Would you be able to do that for us? We need it really soon, if at all possible."

Murdon thought for a moment, "Let me check my supply of wood and I'll let you know."

"Can we come back in an hour and get your answer?"

"Yes, that should give me plenty of time."

With that the others left to go back to the inn. It was about time for lunch, so they stopped in at the dining room to see if Aribon and Alfias were ready for lunch time. It smelled good enough to be time for lunch, so Jasmine peaked in the kitchen to see if Aribon was ready to feed them yet.

"How is lunch coming, Aribon? Can we eat now?" She asked sweetly.

Aribon made a funny face at her and said, "In a minute, alright?"

Jasmine laughed, made a face at him, and said, "Alright, alright."

So Magg, Matton, Jasmine, Donavan, and Jarrone sat down to eat lunch together. It was delicious after all. Aribon had made ham sandwiches, sliced tomatoes from his garden, and apple cider from the year before. After lunch, they decided it had been long enough to check on Murdon. As they approached the shop, they noticed that Murdon was laughing to himself.

Donavan stepped up to him and asked, "What's going on? What's so funny?"

Murdon looked at Donavan and smiled, "Well the thing is, I've just checked my wood supply and found a bunch of wood that I can use for your wagon. It's almost a miracle that I have so much. It just tickled me to find it, is all."

"So you'll be able to make the wagon really soon?"

"I will. I'll start on it first thing in the morning and should be able to finish it in about four days. Especially with my new helper, Oribon. He just started last week. He's a good worker and a quick learner, too."

Donavan was excited at that, "I'm so excited to have that wagon and be able to get those women out of here. They have been nothing but trouble since they were arrested."

"I understand your feelings. They were really nasty at the hanging. It will be a joy see their backs."

"Thank you Murdon. I'll be in touch. If you need anything just let me know."

"That I will."

The women were being kept in separate cells in the inn. They were given food and wash basins if they wanted to get a bit clean. There were always at least two guards watching them. The women were constantly yelling at them and making outrageous demands of them. They were ignored and treated like they were invisible. These women had been a party to the two soldiers who had been murdered by their husbands. There would be no mercy shown them, only the food they were given.

As time passed, each day brought them closer to the day the wagon would be finished and they would be taken to Synkana for imprisonment. Murdon was doing his best to get it built as promised. It was shaping up, but it would be really big and heavy. It was lucky that they had found four large work horses from the farms of the women to help pull the wagon. It was a wonderful irony.

Finally the day came when the wagon was ready to go. Murdon had done a great work making it strong and large enough for the women to fit in it with room for them to lie down. The horses were led to the wagon and were hitched up to pull it. The guards surrounded the women as they brought them up from their cells. They were very nasty to anyone who looked at them or said anything about them. They called back to the villagers and were so angry to be kept imprisoned for so long. Actually it was only a week and they had been fed the whole time. The villagers actually started to cheer as those women were loaded into the wagon. It was a good day for them to see those women leaving for good.

Two of the soldiers, Tenzi and Mikel were to drive the wagon part of the way. Jarrone was to ride alongside the wagon to maintain the peace. He could stop any disruption with his magic. The women were aware of his magic and respected it to a point. There were four other soldiers going with them. They would take turns driving the wagon when a change was needed. They also had a cook wagon following them with supplies for the journey to Synkana. It was hoped that they would be able to get more supplies as they traveled. Aribon had suggested that Alfias go with them and do the cooking. Everyone agreed that it was a great idea. Alfias was excited to get to travel with Jarrone and the soldiers.

Soon, Jarrone and the others were ready to leave. Magg was suddenly concerned about Jarrone and all those women. She decided at that moment to go with them and bring Matton with her. She still had her gypsy wagon and a horse, so it would be perfect for the trip. She ran to Matton,

"Matton, I think we need to go with them! I have a bad feeling if they go without us all of a sudden. Please come with me."

Matton was shocked but not really surprised by Magg's request. He'd been feeling the same way all morning. "Yes, let's get going. Is your wagon still working? Let's get it checked out and your horse hitched up and get moving."

"Oh Matton, you are my hero!"

So they ran to Magg's wagon and checked all the important parts and saw that they were good. They grabbed some clothes from the inn and let Greta and Aribon know they were leaving and to take care of Raven while they were away. Magg also needed to talk to Donavan about what she was going to do. She found him in his room with Jasmine.

Magg knocked on their door. Jasmne answered and called for Donavan. She could tell it was important by the look on Magg's face.

"Donavan, I've had a bad feeling all morning about Jarrone leaving with the women in that wagon. I feel that I must go with them just in case there's trouble, which seems likely. I'm concerned about leaving you here alone with the possibility of any of the creatures like the one that attacked Karmine's son as they entered Anakik. But how do you feel about it? We haven't seen or heard from one of them in all this time."

Donavan was shocked that Magg would want to leave now, there had only been the one creature that attacked Kedron and there didn't seem to be any more. The people that had been living on the mountain hadn't had any problems. So it seemed like a good time for Magg and Matton to leave and help get the women to Synkana.

"But Magg, you'll be gone for several days and we will likely need you here. I understand you concern, however. I believe I can hold down the fort for that long. But you've got to be quick. The gods only know how long the quiet will last. Even though we're not sure of any more of the creatures, I'm still concerned that there might be more. We'll get as prepared as we can while you're gone. But please come back as soon as you may."

"I will Donavan. I know you can take care of things while I'm gone. You have very powerful magic and can stop any of those monsters that might be around. I will get back as soon as I possibly can. Thank you Donavan for understanding."

"Just take care of yourself and hurry home, please."

"I will."

As soon as they left Donavan, they were able to pack up the wagon and head after the jail wagon on its way to Synkana. Magg was feeling much better as they headed out of Anakik. She was sure she and Matton would be needed on this dangerous journey.

Magg was driving for the first few miles and was able to catch up with the other wagon of women.

Their wagon was large and heavy and didn't make very fast going. Jarrone was pleased to see them arrive.

"What are you two doing? Aren't you supposed to stay in Anakik?"

Magg answered, "Well the truth is, I got this terrible feeling as you left the village that I needed to be with you. I'm not sure what that means, but I guess we'll find out."

"Well, you're more than welcome. I've been feeling like it would be good if you two were with us. These women are mean and vicious. It's like a wagon full of vipers, if you know what I mean?"

"I really do and I'm so glad we're here with you now. I feel so much better."

Jarrone said, "I'm thinking we can go another four hours and then stop for lunch. We'll figure out how to feed the ladies. I hope it won't be as bad as I fear."

Alfias happened to be nearby and said, "I feel the same way at this point. But they'll either eat what's given or starve is my feelings on the matter."

Jarrone agreed and so did Matton. When the soldiers heard about it, they laughed in agreement. There wasn't much the women in the wagon could do but eat or starve. After all they had done and their men had done, the soldiers were finished with caring about how they felt. They would feed them and care for them if they were hurt or sick, but that was all.

It was a long trip to Synkana, as everyone in the group knew it would be. Drivers of the wagon were traded occasionally so no one would be exhausted from it. It was difficult to keep the horses in line when the women in the wagon were making all kinds of noise and trying to tip over the wagon. They weren't the smartest of women.

Finally, Jarrone had to cast a spell on the bars of the wagon so that if the women touched them, they would get a nasty shock. Then he would change the spell to cause a burn if touched. It was working well enough that the women ceased trying to turn over the wagon or cause other kinds of problems with it. They finally seemed to settle down for the ride. Magic was very helpful in dealing with such horrible women.

Magg was hoping it would stay that way as they rode along in her gypsy wagon. She let Jarrone handle things as long as he could. She decided she would only step in if things got out of hand. Those women really did seem possessed by something evil. They were screaming at the soldiers most of the day. They tried to curse everyone, especially Jarrone. But he was able to counteract anything they tried to send at him. Magg was very concerned that they might get

Jarrone when he wasn't paying attention. That could mean disaster for all of them since Jarrone's magic was almost as strong as Magg's.

At first the women refused to eat the food given to them. No one was bothered by that since they were all so mean to everyone around them. It was understood that they would eat when they were hungery enough. The women were served the same food the rest of the group ate, so no changes were going to be made to the menu. In fact, every time the women threw their food out of the wagon, the soldiers couldn't help but laugh. They knew that the time would come when they would wish they had eaten that food.

Things continued much the same for another two days. Then it became apparent that they were getting low on supplies and unless they came to a fairly large village soon, they might very well run out.

Magg was worried about that happening. There was no way of knowing how those women would react if there was no food for them. She was sure it wouldn't be good. So she sent Tenzi, one of the soldiers to scout ahead for the next village to buy supplies. Tenzi left the group and headed up the road to see if he could find any town or village close enough to buy food for the group to last a few more days.

Tenzi was only gone about an hour when he came upon a bigger village. He rode into the the village on the main road and started asking the people if they had a store for his group to buy supplies.

One of the villagers replied, "We do in fact. There's the main store just down the road about a quarter mile. I believe he has about anything you might need."

"Thank you, sir."

Tenzi rode on until he found the store he was told about. It was quite large for such a small village, but Tenzi was happy to see it. He tied his horse and walked into the store. There were a lot of supplies available, including food. He was overjoyed since they needed a lot of things, but especially food.

He found the owner and said, "My name is Tenzi and I was wanting to buy some supplies for the group I'm with. Would you be willing to sell us the supplies we are in need of?"

The owner, a man by the name of Kyri who was about medium height and looked to be about forty years old. He was a bit rotund and balding. He wore brown work pants with a gray linen shirt under his tan work apron. He said, "I would be happy to sell you all you need. I carry enough to supply the smaller villages nearby. So I should have enough for your group, too. Where are you headed?"

"We're headed for Synkana and need to restock our supplies for the journey. My group is close by and will be here within an hour. We will have a list of things we need then. Will that suffice for now?"

"It will. You can wait here or on the bench outside if you prefer."

"Thanks, I'll be outside watching for my boss to come."

Tenzi left the store and waited on the bench just outside. It wasn't long before Magg and Matton rode into the village with the wagon looking for him. They had left the group in Jarrone's capable hands for the short time they would be gone. They were in Magg's wagon so they could pack up the supplies they needed for the rest of the group.

The three of them entered the store and told the owner the things they needed. Magg had a list and wanted to be sure they got everything on it. They still had a long way to go to Synkana.

The owner was more than happy to fill their order. Magg paid the owner for their supplies and she, Tenzi, and Matton began loading her wagon to get back to the others. There was barely room for all the supplies, but they made it all fit. When they got back to the group, they would unload her wagon into the main supply wagon. But they needed to get back quickly.

There was always the chance that those women would cause trouble if they knew there wasn't any food left in camp. It was fortunate that the three of them wouldn't be gone long.

Tenzi headed out first to make sure everything was alright back at their camp. Magg and Matton would come as quickly as possible with a wagon loaded with supplies. It would likely take them over an hour to get back and that's if all went well. Some curious villagers watched them leave. Magg worried that they knew there were so many supplies in her wagon. It didn't look like anyone was too interested, but she kept her eyes on everyone she could see.

One man in particular was watching them a little too closely for Magg's comfort. She whispered to Matton to get his gun out of the wagon just in case of need. Matton left Magg to drive the horses while he went back to find his gun. It was, unfortunately, beneath some of the supplies that he couldn't get to. When they were loading the wagon, he hadn't thought about his gun and that they might need it. He had always relied on Magg's magic. Now he was worried that without the gun, they wouldn't be able to scare the man away. Magg's magic was a bit too strong of a weapon in the small village. But he knew she would do what was necessary if needed.

Finally, Matton went to the front of the wagon and told Magg that he couldn't get to his gun. She frowned at that then said, "Well, I guess it's up to me to do something if necessary. I'm certainly hoping it won't be."

"I'm so sorry Magg. I wasn't paying attention as we loaded the wagon. It's under things I can't move."

"I suppose all we can do is keep our eyes and ears open for anything suspicious. The man that was watching us has gone into what looks like a bar over there. Would you please take over the reins in case I need to do something about him or his group? And will you help me watch for anyone coming back out of there that looks like trouble?"

"That I will, Magg." Matton quickly took the reins from Magg and increased his awareness of what was going on around them. He tried to increase the speed of the horses, but they were doing the best they could with the heavy load they were pulling. So Matton just kept them moving toward the end of town.

Suddenly, two men came out of the bar ready to take over the reins of the horses. Magg began chanting a spell immediately. The men could hear her chanting and decided to move away from the wagon. They took off their hats and waved them on. No action was needed. It appeared that they had some intelligence after all.

Magg and Matton both heaved a sigh of relief. It had been frightening for a moment and neither of them wanted to have to fight. They just wanted to be left alone to drive the wagon back to their camp.

Now they could keep moving. They remained aware of their surroundings just the same. Those men might not have been the only trouble makers in town. They were pretty much alone until they could get back to the group.

It was another hour before they were able to meet their group due to the load they had to carry. It was just passed time for lunch when they got there. Tenzi waved them down as they were getting close and stopped them. He needed to tell them what had happened while they were away.

He spoke quickly, "Magg, you need to come quick. The women found out we were out of food a while ago. They must have heard some of us talking about it. Anyway, they started screaming about being made to starve, we tried to ignore them. Then we heard something odd. One of the women is a witch. She cast a spell at the bars of their wagon and nearly took out a couple of them. Jarrone sensed she was up to something. He was about to cast a counter spell.

"As he cast his spell to try to counteract it, he was knocked down by a rock one of the women had hidden in her pocket, apparently. The witch's spell bent two of the bars large enough for the women to escape the wagon."

Magg was terrified at his words and jumped off the wagon and ran for the camp. She got there just as two of the women were making a run for it. She cast a spell without thinking and hit them hard so that they fell down and couldn't move. Two other women were about to escape, but when they saw what Magg could do to them they stopped. Tenzi and four other soldiers came to the rescue and caught the women trying to get away. The women were tied and none too gently pushed into their wagon. It was hoped that the women had learned another lesson about trying to escape.

Jarrone was just regaining consciousness and rubbed his head where he had been hit by the rock. He was angry and cast a spell that added more bars to the wagon all the way around. The women could barely see out of the wagon now. He saw Magg and realized she had just saved them all from certain disaster.

"Magg! You're just in time! We could all have been killed or wounded if you hadn't come when you did."

Magg was still shaking from the shock of what had just happened. "Jarrone, I'm so glad I got here in time, too. Now I know why I'm here." She was glad Matton was there to support her. The shock had used a lot of her magic and energy. She was feeling a bit weak and sick to her stomach. She didn't even know what spell she had cast at the women, but she was glad it had stopped them. She thought it must be a strong one for her to feel so tired all of a sudden.

Matton spoke to Magg softly, "Magg, you were right. We really do need to be here. I have been a bit worried about Anakik, but we really are needed here."

"Thank you Matton. I love you so much."

"Likewise my love." He kissed her lightly.

Jarrone ordered four of the soldiers to pick up the two women who had been hit with Magg's spell and put them in the wagon. The women were hurt, probably seriously. But they would be better sooner or later. Magg would watch them to see if they needed any medical help. She hoped they would not. She wanted them to appreciate what it had cost them to be so nasty. Consequences were no fun most of the time. But for these women it was going to be ugly.

Jarrone and Magg both watched the women to make sure they would do nothing to cause any more trouble. Once the women were back in the wagon, it was locked with even stronger bars on the door. With the extra bars Jarrone had put on the wagon, there would be no way the women could get out now. The only problem was that now the wagon was heavier and slower to pull. But the safety of the group was most important.

It was decided by Magg, Matton, Jarrone, and Tenzi that the women would only get gruel for the rest of the day. Alfias was more than happy to oblige. The women had been cruel to him too. Maybe they would think twice before doing anything else stupid.

The women looked at one another and started whispering. They knew that if they didn't get out of this wagon soon, they would be taken to prison in Synkana and there was no way of knowing how long they would be kept there. They had nearly escaped and that gave them the increased desire to try again soon. The new bars did complicate things, but they were sure there would be another opportunity. But they had learned to fear what magic could do to them and they were a bit afraid of it even so.

Magg suspected that they were plotting something when they suddenly became quiet and spoke in hushed tones to each other. She moved to speak with Jarrone and warned him of her suspicions. Jarrone said he had felt the same about what they were doing. He knew the women wouldn't give up with one attempt.

Meanwhile, Alfias was enjoying cooking for the group and was glad he had come with them. It was an adventure for him to be away from Anakik. He knew Aribon would find one of the young men to help until he got back. Those women scared him a lot. He'd never experienced such mean women. He hoped that when all of this was over, that he would never experience it again. But he had been taught that women like them were in the world.

Now that things had quieted down Matton went to the gypsy wagon to get it into place to unload the supplies as quickly as possible. Several of the soldiers came to help. Soon the wagon was unloaded and the supplies safely stored. It was such a relief they were all smiles knowing they had food and other supplies to get the rest of the way to Synkana.

Now that the women were afraid to cause any more trouble, the journey was mostly uneventful. It was another three days before they were actually there. As they approached the gates of the city, the women began to complain. They knew that this was their end. They would be imprisoned, hopefully for the rest of their days. Jarrone and Magg were on alert to stop any trouble they might want to cause to prevent them from getting to the government building that that would be their prison.

It got to be bad as they passed through the gates of Synkana. The women started begging passerby to help them, that they had been kidnapped and held prisoner. Some of the men looked up and acted like they might do something. Jarrone made sure to let them know what kind of women they really were. Just to be sure, Magg and Jarrone had cast a spell over the entire wagon to prevent anyone getting close enough to touch it. They would be shocked and knocked down if they did.

One man actually tried to pull on the bars and was knocked on his behind and in pain. When others saw that happen, no one else tried it. The women were pretty rough looking anyway. So any sympathy ended once they were really looked at. They were not a bunch of pretty virgins looking for their prince charming, quite the opposite.

They looked like what they were, some really rough women who had lived in the forest for years with men who were killers. They were as mean as their men, and looked it.

They finally made it to the government building and reined in in front of it. Jarrone walked up the steps to find someone in charge who could relieve them of the occupants of the wagon. As he walked into the front door, he was met by a man who seemed to be in charge. He was tall and slender with a thin mustache. He was wearing a pair of tight black pants and a red jacket with a double row of gold buttons down the front. He looked very official.

He sniffed at Jarrone and said with a nasaly voice, "How may I help you sir?"

Jarrone smiled and said, "I have a delivery for the prison in a wagon out front. Can you direct me to the person in charge of prisoners, please?"

"May I see your wagon? Have you notified anyone of your intentions?"

Jarrone was put off by his attitude, he said, "The wagon is just out front, if you would follow me, I would be glad to show you,"

The man didn't seem too thrilled to have to follow Jarrone, but he reluctantly did so.

Once outside, he took one look at the women and nearly fainted. He was obviously unaccustomed to seeing women in such rough conditions.

He said, "My, my, this doesn't look good. We need to get them into the prison as soon as possible."

"Yes, we do!" Jarrone was relieved that the man was agreeable.

The man quickly walked back into the building to find the prison warden. He couldn't get rid of the women soon enough. It took him only two minutes to send that person out to talk to Jarrone and to see the prisoners.

The man introduced himself as Derk, the prison warden. He was tall and broad with large muscles. He had a small scar on his chin from a prisoners attempt to cut off his head, but Derk ducked just in time. His chin was nearly cut off but the doctor was able to save it. The stitches were fine enough that there was only that small bit that was too bad to conceal. It did give him a dangerous appearance. It was obvious that no one was going to mess with him. Those women didn't have a chance of causing trouble now.

Jarrone greeted Derk, "Glad to meet you Derk. My name is Jarrone and I've been taking charge of the women in this wagon. They are yours as soon as you are able to take them off my hands. I would also let you know that I have magic to help with the women if needed."

Derk smiled after looking at the women in the wagon. He said, "Can you tell me what they have done to deserve prison?"

Jarrone told him about their husbands and how they had killed two of their soldiers in cold blood. He also mentioned the situation the day the men were hanged. They had been ready to cause trouble and refused to follow orders. They were very dangerous and wicked to all around them. There had been a court for all that and it was decided the women were too dangerous to let them be free in their small village and needed to be sent to Synkana and put into prison.

Derk smiled after he heard about what the women had done and what they were like. He said, "I would be more than happy to relieve you of those women. I'll get some of my guards to help move them into the prison. It will only be a moment."

Derek went back into the building and called several of his guards to follow him outside. They brought metal cuffs and chains with them to secure the prisoners. He could tell that they would be a problem if he didn't make sure they couldn't escape.

"Alright ladies, you are now under the custody of the Synkana Prison System. My men will take you out of the wagon one at a time and gently place these cuffs on you, unless you'd rather we do otherwise. You will then be chained together until we have a cell for each of you downstairs in the prison. Jarrone here will open the door to the wagon and be ready to use his powers on you if you decide not to cooperate with my men."

Jarrone walked over to the door of the wagon and used his key to unlock the metal clasp that secured the door. Immediately, one of the women decided it would be a good idea to lunge at Jarrone and try to get passed him. Jarrone was quicker and used a spell to "push" her back inside the wagon. She flew back into the wagon and landed on her behind cursing. The other women started to laugh at her. It was so funny to see her face as she fell. It was one of complete shock and embarrassment. She jumped up and ran for the door again. Apparently, it was difficult for her to learn a lesson. This time one of Derk's men was waiting at the door and pulled her out of the wagon using her momentum to get her all the way out and on the ground.

The guard was able to get the cuffs on her before she even realized what had happened. She started screaming in frustration, but no one cared. The next woman came out of the wagon without protest. She allowed the guard to put the cuffs on her without making any false moves.

Surprisingly, the rest of the women did the same. It was obvious that protesting was senseless and possibly dangerous. They even behaved while they were being chained together. Derk was able to lead them to the prison and lock them up downstairs in their cells. His guards were making sure that nothing happened until then.

When the women were all taken into the prison, Jarrone drove the wagon around to a stable close by.

The horses would be cared for and the wagon protected there. He joined the group once all was settled.

As Magg and Matton and the soldiers that had guarded them watched the women disappear into the prison building, they were so relieved they nearly started laughing hysterically. They regained control when they noticed the people around them watching suspiciously. So they settled down a bit. It had been a very difficult journey and one they were very happy to have an end.

Jarrone smiled and looked around at everyone and said, "Anyone want to celebrate our freedom now that the ordeal is over?"

There was general agreement among each member of their group. It really was time to celebrate a job completed. They all started laughing and decided to go to the nearest inn to relax and enjoy the end of the responsibility for those terrible women. They decided to book some rooms for everyone of their group so they could rest a day before heading back to Anakik. They knew the journey back would be made with speed.

They started their celebration by having mugs of ale all around. There was some delicious roast ham, potatoes, and some crusty bread to eat. After they had all had their fill and were getting sleepy they were ready go to their rooms for the night.

Magg and Matton were so glad to spend the night in a nice room with clean sheets and soft mattress. Magg's wagon was fine, but the mattress was a bit hard. So it was that they were able to snuggle and make love in privacy at last. It was exactly what they needed to strengthen the bond they felt for each other.

Jarrone had a room to himself and loved it. He was used to being with his family and having hardly any privacy, so for this night, he felt like he was in heaven. He was grateful for the opportunity to sleep in this room in this bed. He would thank Magg in the morning.

The soldiers were sharing a room with one other man. But since they were all friends and were used to the barricks where they were in a big room with several other men it was nice to only have one other person in their room. They had a really good night's sleep and woke the next morning well rested.

They had all agreed to get together for breakfast at nine in the morning. They did not want to get out of bed early. It was good to get to ease into the day. Magg and Matton were very happy to snuggle a bit longer before having to get out of bed. Magg washed up in the basin provided by the inn. She dressed in her brown leather pants and a sosft white cotton shirt. She was ready to face the day. Matton was up and getting dressed. He was wearing his blue denim pants and a black cotton shirt. He wore his work boots and Magg wore her soft moccasins. They were ready to go eat their breakfast with the others of their group.

The soldiers wore their uniforms and so did Jarrone. They looked really sharp. Their uniforms were dark blue with gold braid on the cuffs and down the front of their coats. They also had gold braid down the outside seam of their pants. Some had medals on their chests. All looked ready to eat breakfast and leave the city of Synkana.

As they finished eating, Magg spoke to the group, "I've been thinking that maybe we could sell the prison wagon and horses while we're in Synkana. Do you think it might be a good idea? We can save a lot of time on the way back home if we don't have that wagon to take with us."

Tenzi spoke up, "I think it's a good idea, though I feel a bit sad about losing all the work Murdon went to to build it. What do the rest of you think?"

Magg decided to save some time, "Let's take a vote. How many think we should sell the wagon here?"

All their hands went up. Magg said, "Looks like we're selling the thing. It's just so heavy and hard to move. We should include the horses in the sale. It will be nice not to have it to deal with, not to mention the memory attached to it."

A cheer went up when the decision was made. Jarrone was willing to shop around Synkana and see if they could find a buyer for it. In fact, he thought that the prison itself might have a use for such a well built wagon. So he went there first and spoke to Derk.

Jarrone found him just inside the door to the building that housed the prison. He was talking with the doorman at the time.

"So we have much to discuss with the mayor this morning. Don't you agree?"

The doorman said, "Yes, sir" and walked away.

Then Jarrone spoke up, "Derk, we have that big wagon that we used to bring those women here. Would you by any chance have a need for it? We're thinking of selling it before we leave Synkana. We would also include the horses."

Derk looked surprised and said, "I was just going to try to find you to see if you would be willing to sell it to us. We have to move prisoners sometimes but have no way to move more than a few at a time. That wagon would be really nice to have. What do you want for it?"

Jarrone thought a minute and said, "What will you offer?"

Derk smiled and gave him an offer he couldn't refuse. So the deal was done. Derk had the wagon and Jarrone had enough money to pay all the soldiers and some left over for Magg and Matton and himself. He could hardly wait to tell the others.

He almost ran to the inn where Magg and Matton were waiting to hear what had happened. He rushed into the inn and found them sitting in one corner of the dining area. He was so excited that he tripped on one of the chairs near them. Luckily he didn't fall, he caught himself on a nearby table just in time.

He laughed and quietly said, "I need to talk to you. But I can't discuss it here. Can we please go up to your room, Magg, and talk about it?"

Magg was so curious to find out what news Jarrone had that she jumped up out of her chair and grabbed Matton's hand saying, "Yes, good idea."

They tried to leave without haste, but it was difficult under the circumstances. They finally made it to Magg's room and shut the door when they were inside.

"So, Jarrone, tell us what happened. We're anxious to hear all about it."

Jarrone smiled and started at the beginning, "As you know I was trying to find a buyer for the wagon. Then I thought maybe the prison warden would be interested in it. As it turned out he was about to look for me to ask if he could buy it."

Magg and Matton gasped and started to laugh.

"He asked what I wanted for it. I thought for a moment and asked him what he could offer. He gave me an offer I could not refuse. It was so generous that I'm thinking maybe we could give everyone a bonus for helping us get those women here. What do you think?"

Magg smiled at Jarrone, "You are a genius, Jarrone. I love your idea of sharing the money with everyone. Let's count it out and divide it equally between us and the soldiers. It took all of us to get this job done. Should we bring the soldiers in now, or wait until we're on the road back home?"

Jarrone and Matton both said, "Let's wait."

Matton added, "I noticed some questionable men watching us downstairs. I don't want anything to make them think we should be robbed or worse. Do you agree?"

Magg agreed that it was the best idea for all concerned. They agreed to gather everyone together after they left Synkana and before they got to another town.

Magg was laughing as she said, "Well, well just think of the benefit that wagon has brought us all.

It helped us get those women here without so much trouble as we could have had and now we have extra money to reward everyone who helped. When we get home, we're going to celebrate like there's no tomorrow."

It was agreed that that would be a wonderful way to celebrate not only getting back home, but to be rid of the prisoners.

Chapter 14

They had eaten breakfast and were now ready to leave Synkana. It was a happy group indeed that walked out of the inn and collected their horses ready to leave. They were finally headed for Anakik. The day was sunny and warm as they left the inn and followed the road out of town. They cheered as they went through the gates and on to the open road.

Life was good at this point. They were on their way back to Anakik and they would make good time now without the wagon and the women that went with it. There was joy in their hearts after so much trouble and frustration.

The road was easy traveling now that it was just them and the horses. Alfias brought up the rear with the cook wagon. He was able to keep up with the others pretty well. The wagon wasn't as heavy as it had been when they were feeding themselves and those women. Alfias was so very grateful not to have to feed them now. They had been really terrible to deal with whenever he was trying to get food to them.

He had resigned himself to the fact that he couldn't make them eat. So he quit worrying about them and decided they would either eat what he fixed or not. It wasn't his problem either way. He was able to relax a bit after that.

They group was making good time as they rode along toward Anakik. There wasn't much traffic now. Although it made traveling faster and easier, concern began to build up when the traffic got less and less as they went.

Magg sensed something amiss after a few hours of being practically alone on the road that was normally very busy as it had been on the way to Synkana. Therefore, anything that was unusual was potentially cause for concern.

Finally, a small group of travelers came by. Magg asked them to stop and answer some questions. They were hesitant to do so, but since Magg looked nice enough, they agreed.

Magg asked, "Do you know why there are so few travelers on this road now?"

One of the men spoke up, "We know all right. People are nervous to leave their homes lately. There are rumours of some big hairy creatures that are attacking the villagers when they are alone out their homes. Many are being killed by them. But no one knows where they come from or what has caused them to start attacking people. They've taken some of the farm animals as well."

Magg was shocked. "Do you have an idea of how many of those creatures there are?"

"Ma'am, all I know is there are enough of them to keep people in their homes. We have to leave before it gets any worse. We have to keep moving so they won't come after us. It's really frightening I can tell you. Good luck in your travels." He said the last as he turned to move away from them. He was obviously in a hurry to protect his family.

Jarrone and Matton were listening to the conversation and became very concerned about Anakik and the villagers there.

Jarrone spoke first, "Could these creatures be the same ones we've had a bit of experience with in Anakik. Remember the one that attacked the little boy, Kedron? But it's odd that we haven't seen any since then. What if they're headed that way in a big mass?"

Magg said, "That's a terrible thought, but one that might be true. Maybe they're making their way through all the populated areas on their way to who knows where. We've got to get back to Anakik as quickly as possible. Poor Donavan is there alone and we don't know what he's dealing with while we're gone. Let's get going and move quickly. We will only stop to eat a bit and sleep a bit as we go. Let's hand out the food so that we all have something to eat on the road. I think we have enough for at least a few days. Alfias, will you check on that for me and let us know, please?"

Alfias had heard most of the conversation, too. He was now very anxious to get back to the inn in Anakik. He was really worried about Aribon. He got back into the cook wagon and took an inventory of the jerky and other dried food, such as raisins and dates. They also had some nuts and seeds to hand out. After taking inventory, Alfias went to Magg and told her all he had found out.

Magg said, "All right, we have enough snack food to get us by. Alfias will hand out what there is to all of you. I suggest you put it in your packs to eat as we go. We will stop one time a day for a regular meal, but the rest must be the dried food he's going to be giving you. The situation is critical now to get back to Anakik. Understood?"

It was agreed. They thought they might have enough of the dried food to get them all the way back to Anakik. Magg and Matton were pretty sure they were just three days away at the most. But they would try to shorten that time as they traveled.

As they moved along the road, they stayed close together to protect each other. There were a couple of times that frightened them all when the bushes near the road were shaking and they could hear growling and sometimes roaring from deep in the forest.

It was obvious that these creatures were very large. Magg had killed the one attacking Kedron and she knew how big they really were. They were also very fast. Magg made sure all the men kept their swords and knives at the ready. They would have no time to get them out of pockets or bags if attacked.

They stopped along the road in the afternoon each day to get a real meal. Alfias was happy to cook for them. He always made something that could be eaten in a hurry. He usually made sandwiches with meat or cheese and sometimes he made a quick soup that they could drink. It wasn't the best, but it was filling and easy to eat. So they were able to make much better time because of his efforts.

They were finally getting close to Anakik. They decided as a group to sleep as much as they could one more night and then push on to their home. They would probably arrive late in the evening, but they really had to get there quick. There was a sense that things weren't so great in Anakik.

Chapter 15

The next morning they woke early and had a quick bite to eat from their packs. They headed out as soon as they were ready and made for Anakik at a rapid pace. The horses were tiring at one point, so they had to slow down to a walk for an hour to rest them. Then it was off again to make as good a time as possible.

As the day wore on, it was obvious that they were all tiring. Just when they thought they could go no further that day, they saw a glimmer of light just around the next bend in the road. They were so relieved and happy to see that sign of home that they all urged their horses to a faster pace. They would be home in a matter of minutes.

As they rounded the bend, they could see that there weren't any villagers in the town square or near the inn. Magg got a terrible feeling then. She alerted the group to watch for the creatures as they approached their village.

Some of the villagers were looking out their windows as they rode into town. But no one ventured outside. The feeling was pretty grim at this point. Magg called Jarrone to her side. They would use whatever magic was needed in case they were attacked.

Alfias broke away from the group to put the cook wagon near the kitchen entrance. He was taking no chances. He jumped down from the wagon and ran inside the inn and slammed the heavy wooden door behind him.

The soldiers headed either for the barracks. It was getting dark and that meant trouble. It seemed an attack would be more likely in the dark, but they didn't know for sure yet. All they knew was that things had changed since they left Anakik and they were frightened.

Magg and Matton drove her gypsy wagon into the barn in back of the inn and ran into the inn as soon as they could get down and run. Jarrone came with them because he didn't want to ride all the way to his house alone. The three of them rushed in and saw several people inside eating a late meal.

Magg was surprised. She went to the kitchen to talk with Aribon about what was going on.

"Aribon, I'm home and so is Matton and Jarrone. Can you tell me what's going on here tonight? We've heard some really frightening rumors on the way back here."

Aribon was finishing up the meal he had prepared for those who were staying at the inn. He looked up at her words, but didn't smile at her. "Magg, welcome home. We've had a really bad couple of weeks since you all left us." There was a bit of accusation in his words.

Magg was very concerned, "Why? What on earth happened? Please tell me Aribon."

Aribon looked like he was ready to cry when he said, "Magg you shouldn't have left us. We've had some terrible creatures howling and seeming to move closer to the village every night. Donavan is terrified, as we all are. The monsters seemed to sense that you and Jarrone were gone and took advantage of your absence to try to take over the village. We've been living in fear since a few days after you left."

"Oh Aribon, this is terrible news! If only we'd had some idea these monsters were so close and ready to attack. I have to tell you, however, that we were needed to help Jarrone control those terrible women as we traveled to Synkana. I don't know what to say."

Aribon continued, "Not only that, but you need to know that Raven has continued to go hunting in the forest with those monsters so close to the village. Also, the villagers are acting more and more afraid.

Donavan has done all he could to try to calm them down. But it's like they need to know you're around too. You and Jarrone are really important to the sense of safety in the village.

"We nearly lost one of the children last week to one of them. He was saved by his father grabbing him just in time and getting him into the house before he was attacked. The monster crashed against the door just as it was slammed shut and barred. Please don't leave us again." With that Aribon was nearly crying.

Magg walked up to him and hugged him, "Aribon, I'm so glad I'm back. I worried about you all while I was gone. I was hoping things would have gone better. But now that I know how hard it was, I won't leave again. There should be no reason to now that the women are gone for good. I'm going to go find Donavan and find out what he's been through. I'm half afraid to ask him now."

Magg left Aribon and went with Matton looking for Donavan. They found him in his room with Jasmine after knocking on the door. Jasmine answered the door and let them in. They could hear Donavan crying in the other room.

Magg started to go to him to find out why he was so upset. Jasmine followed her and tried to stop her. She needed to tell her what had upset him so much. She was just able to stop her by putting her hand on Magg's shoulder before she could enter the room Donavan was in.

"Magg, listen to me. Donavan has reached the end of his ability to cope with all that has happened since you left. He had almost given up. It's a very good thing that you are back today. Can you come back a little later after I've had enough time to calm him down and let him know that you're back home?"

Magg did listen and agreed to wait until later to talk to Donavan. She was even more concerned and worried about the rest of the people in Anakik. There were no people walking around the village when they rode in and that was a very bad sign. She could see some of the villagers peaking out of their windows to see them coming. However, no one came out to greet them. The atmosphere of fear was almost palpable. It was time to find out all she could. She asked Matton to join her.

She decided that if Donavan couldn't talk about it just yet, she would find someone who could. Magg and Matton walked across the road to the store. They walked in and found the merchant cowering in a corner as if they were some kind of monster. There was true fear in his eyes as he looked up at them.

She spoke to the owner, Toran, "Hey, it's me, Magg. What's going on? I'm finally back to help you with the problems you've been having. Please come out and talk to me."

Toran was so shy that Magg couldn't believe it. He had never acted like that before. He finally came out to speak to Magg.

"Ahh, Magg, I'm so glad to see you again! It's been really intense around here since you left."

"Toran, can you start at the beginning, maybe the day Matton and I left town to help Jarrone with the prisoners?"

Toran had to gather his thoughts for a moment before he began the story. "It was almost as if the monsters watched you leave Anakik. You weren't gone long before they started howling again. They were moving in slowly. Donavan tried to make a show of his magic to scare them off. It worked for a few days. They still howled and screeched, but they didn't seem to come any closer.

"We got a bit complacent I must confess and some of the villagers started to wander a little close to the forest. We tried to warn them to stay away, but you know how some people are about rules and such. Well, you can probably imagine what happened next. One of their children, a boy, got too close to the forest. Close enough that one of the creatures moved to attack him. The father was aware and grabbed his son and ran for the house. He ran through the door just as the monster was about to grab his son. His wife slammed the door and he was able to hold it just as the monster hit it really hard. Fortunately, their door was made stronger when we had suggested it awhile ago. If they hadn't done so, I can't even think of what would have happened to that family.

"So the creature didn't get in. The whole village was alerted to the near-tragedy. From that time on, everyone was more fearful every day. It was becoming unbearable for many of us. Donavan kept trying to calm everyone down, but it was not possible at this point. As he was watching out the window, he saw a Monster in town lurking near one of the houses. He was so enraged that he ran out of the inn and started casting spells at it. He finally cast one that turned the monster into a puddle of green gel. He was delighted at the result. He shouted with joy and kind of danced around.

"But then another Monster creeped up behind him and almost got him. But Jasmine was watching him and screamed for him to run. He acted like he was frozen for just a moment, then turned and ran for the inn. He almost made it. The monster caught his pantleg and tried to pull him closer. Jasmine screamed again and hit the monster with a tree limb she found nearby.

"The monster looked up in shock and was going to go after Jasmine. While it was distracted, Donavan was able to get away and pull Jasmine into the inn with him. Most everyone was watching it all with terror in their eyes. It was like they felt that if Donavan could be caught, no one was safe. Of course, that is the truth and has always been the truth since those things showed up.

"Donavan had stopped the first monster, but then he almost got caught when he lost his concentration. I think his pride almost got the best of him. He has not been seen much since that happened."

Magg was in despair to think that Donavan had been in such danger. It was indeed very bad that she hadn't been there for him and the others. She was glad she had been with Jarrone when he needed her, but now she questioned her choice. She decided that her most important priority was this village and its people.

She finally said, "Toran, I'm so sorry I was gone. I was needed to be with Jarrone, but I may have been needed even more here. I will do my best to help Donavan heal from his scare. I'm thinking it will be awhile before he can heal from what happened, or nearly happened to him."

Toran said, "Well, now you're back and can set things right. I'm so glad to see you and Jarrone. It seemed like forever that you've been gone." He moved closer to Magg and gave her a little hug of welcome. Magg almost cried at the sign of affection.

She said, "Thank you Toran. You are very kind."

Magg and Matton left the store after looking around for any Monsters that might be lurking nearby. They half ran to the inn. Matton was concerned about Magg. He knew she was taking it hard that they had left the village. But he also knew that she would keep going no matter what. He was just grateful that he was here for her.

As they walked into the inn, they could hear Aribon arguing with Alfias.

"Alfias, I know I gave you permission to leave the village and run off with your friends, but I really did need you here. Most of sthe villagers eat here now. They need food and each other for comfort and strength. At least that's what I'm thinking. You must not do that ever again until those monsters are totally destroyed, got that?"

Alfias was feeling worthless at that point. Magg and Matton came in just in time to talk to him about what good he had done in cooking for everyone everyday. He was a kind of hero. Alfias was beginning to feel a bit better. No one could have known how things would happen ahead of time. They had prepared the best they could and found out that they needed to do much more. It wasn't Alfias' fault.

Magg finally said, "Alfias, you have to understand that Aribon has had a terrible time since we left town. He's on edge and probably scared. So don't let what he says hurt you. It's more about how he's feeling than who you are. He's just taking it out on you because you're here."

Alfias tried to smile, but he was understanding Aribon's anger better. It was just that things had been really rough while he was away from the kitchen.

Magg found Jarrone and asked him to follow her and Matton so they could talk about what had happened while they were gone. Jarrone was just getting ready to go back to his family when Magg called to him. So he followed her to her room where it would be more private.

When they got to her room with Matton, they sat down on the chair and bed to talk. Magg told Jarrone everything she knew about it. Jarrone was saddened by all of it. He was glad that Magg and Matton had come with him to deliver the prisoners, but now he felt sorry that things in the village had gone so badly.

He asked Magg, "What do we do now? Can we go talk to Donavan yet? Or should we wait until tomorrow? It sounds like he's having a hard time right now."

Magg said, "Would you like to go see if Donavan is ready for company, or would he prefer we come back tomorrow? Would you do that Jarrone? Please?"

Jarrone hesitated because he wasn't sure of the welcome he would get with Donavan. But he said, "I'll go. He can only tell me to leave, right?"

Magg smiled, "Right."

So Jarrone left the dining area and headed for Donavan's room to check on him. He quietly knocked on the door of his room. Jasmine came to the door and was surprised to see him.

"Jarrone, it's good to see you. What's going on?"

"Well, I'd like to know how Donavan is doing. Aribon said something about him not feeling well."

Jasmine hesitated, "Well, he hasn't been doing very good the past few days. But I'll go ask him if he would like to visit with you."

"Actually, if he'd rather wait until tomorrow, that would be fine, too."

"I'll let him know and come back to tell you his decision."

Jasmine walked back to their bedroom and spoke sofly to Donavan. "Jarrone is here and is wondering if you would like to visit now or maybe tomorrow?"

Donavan raised his head and looked at Jasmine as if he didn't know her for a moment. "Oh, well, I'm feeling really weak just now. I know I promised Magg we could visit later today, but I'm just not ready to see her right now. Maybe tomorrow would be better so I can prepare myself to face them."

"All right, I'll let Jarrone know that tomorrow would be better. Can you sleep a little my dear?"

"I'll try Jasmine. I'll try."

Jasmine left his side and went to talk to Jarrone. "I'm sorry Jarrone, but Donavan needs another day to recover. Maybe later in the day tomorrow would be better."

"That's fine, Jasmine. I'll tell Magg that we can see him tomorrow. We'll check in with you then, if that's all right."

Jasmine nodded her approval.

Jarrone left then and went back to Magg and Matton. He said, "Donavan is still having a hard time. Jasmine said it would be better if we went to see him later tomorrow. I'm really worried about him now."

Magg was sad, but understood. Donavan had had a really big shock and was worn out from all the drama. She felt a bit the same way. She was just grateful that she had Matton to lean on when she needed him. Donavan had Jasmine to help him get through it, but maybe he hadn't given her a chance to help. He was so very upset by all that had happened.

Magg was feeling like Donavan hadn't really realized how much power he had. He seemed to be holding back for some reason. She was definitely going to talk to him about it as soon as she could. He was very valuable to the success of destroying the monsters for him to be discounting what he could do to help.

It was getting late and everyone was feeling the effects of a rough ride to Anakik and the news that awaited them when they got there. It was time to call it a day and try to sleep. Magg and Matton went to her room for privacy. They slept in each other's arms for comfort.

Chapter 16

The next morning, the sun was shining and brought with it a sense that things might be better. Still no one came out of their houses. Magg knew that she had to do something and fast to make things better. She thought about what had happened to Donavan and how it had affected the villagers when he was nearly caught and killed by the monster. There had to be a way to bring hope back to the villagers. She also wanted to talk to Zarcon about what had been happening. He would surely have some wisdom to help her now.

Magg decided that it would be important for her to practice another one of the spells in Zarcon's Book of Spells. She needed more weapons to use against the Monsters. It was obvious that they were stronger than anyone had imagined before now. So she got out Zarcon's book and started leafing carefully through it. After a couple of hours, she finally found one that looked promising. It was supposed to send the target into another dimension. She had heard Donavan and Zarcon talking about how they had worked together to send the legendary Blue Orb out of this world and into another. Magg was thinking that would be a good solution to the Monsters. She would get Donavan to help her with the spell and how to use it. He could be very helpful with something like that. She had a few questions to ask Zarcon as well. She knew he could give her the advice she needed before she talked to Donavan about it.

Magg became excited when she thought about Donavan being the one to take charge of that particular spell. He would know what was needed to target the spell and how much more power he would need for it to be effective against the Monsters. The problem was that they were much bigger than the Orb had been. But he would know if it would work on them at all. It was surely worth a try.

Matton came to her about then to find out if he could help her with anything. She had been in their room for quite awhile.

He said, "Magg, what are you busy with? Can I help you with any of it?"

Magg looked up from the book and said, "Matton, I've decided to get Donavan to help with a spell they had used to send the legendary Blue Orb into another dimension. I'm wanting to talk to him about it to see if it might work on the Monsters. That way we wouldn't have to kill them all, we could just send them far, far away. What do you think?"

"Sounds great to me. That way they couldn't ever come back. I would just wonder what they might do in another dimension. Would they die on the way, or destroy another civilization that is unprepared for such terrible monsters? I realize either way, they'd be gone for good. So maybe when we talk to Donavan, we can find out more about it."

Magg sighed, "You know, Matton, those are things I've never thought about. You're right, maybe Donavan will know more about that. The thing is, I'm not really sure I care. We just need to have them gone."

Matton was a bit troubled by her attitude, but maybe she was right. Maybe it didn't matter where the Monsters went, as long as it was somewhere that they couldn't get back to their home here in Anakik or the world they were in.

One thing he did know, they really did need to talk to Donavan and soon. Maybe he would talk to them earlier in the morning. The situation was changing so fast that they needed all the help thay could get.

Magg decided to call on Zarcon to get his ideas as to what to do next. She also wanted to ask him about using the spell to cast the monsters into another dimension. He would know if it was possible.

So she asked Matton to go with her. They left their room and headed to Zarcon's room. Magg tapped on the door and Greta answered right away.

"Welcome you two! How can we help you this morning?"

Magg smiled and said, "I'd really like to talk to Zarcon about a spell he used with Donavan to destroy the old blue orb. Is he up to it?"

"I'll go ask him. He has been well the last few days."

She left them and went to Zarcon as he was studying in the other room. "Zarcon, Magg and Matton are here to ask you about a spell you used to get rid of the blue orb. Are you up to it this morning?"

"I certainly am, Greta. Send them in."

Greta motioned for Magg and Matton to come and see Zarcon to speak with him.

Magg spoke up, "Zarcon, I've been thinking about using the spell you used to send the orb into another dimension. Do you think we could use that on the monsters we have here?"

Zarcon was quiet for a moment. He finally said, "The power to do that to so many creatures would probably kill the person using it. I recommend against it. Even with help, it would still be much too dangerous. Have you looked at the spells I selected from my book yet?"

Magg looked down in a bit of shame because she had not done so in any serious way. She said, "No, Zarcon. I've been busy with so many other things. Did you hear that I went with Jarrone to take those evil women to Synkana?"

Zarcon was surprised, "No, I hadn't heard that. That explains why the village had been in such a state of fear. Tell me what's been happening?"

Magg started her tale, "You knew about the trials and the hangings, right?"

Zarcon said, "Yes, Greta told me about all that and how the women were so evil to back what their men had done. So you went with Jarrone and the soldiers to take the women to Synkana and prison. Is that what you're saying?"

Magg replied, "Yes, that's what happened to take Jarrone and I away from Anakik at a critical time, it turned out. It is my understanding that there are some nasty monsters terrifying the villagers. Donavan had nearly been killed by one just before we got back. I know now that I can't leave Anakik as long as those monsters are around. That's why I wanted to know if the spell to cast them to another dimension might work."

Zarcon looked up at Magg and said, "I know you meant well going along to help Jarrone. I'm glad you were able to help him. I just wish things had been better here. Greta has been afraid because of the stories she's hearing about the monsters and how close they seem to be getting to the village. But the spell you suggest is a quick fix, but far too dangerous to use on such a large group. I doubt that it would be possible to send even one of those things that way. My suggestion is to master the spells in my Book of Spells and use them wisely. You will succeed, Magg, I know it."

Magg felt much better. She said, "Zarcon, I'm so glad you've helped me with this. I would have likely killed myself and whoever would have helped me if I had tried to do what I thought might work. I'm going to practice one of the spells right away. There are two more that really sound effective. I'll let you know how they turn out."

"Please do, Magg. I want to hear of your progress. I only wish I could be of more help at a time like this."

Magg smiled and said, "You're far more help than you know, Zarcon."

She left Zarcon's room with renewed hope and desire to learn the two spells from Zarcon's book. She would master them and then teach them to Donavan and Jarrone.

Magg and Matton went to find Jarrone to see if they could go visit Donavan. They found Jarrone in the dining area eating his breakfast. They joined him and had a bite to eat with him.

When they were finished eating, Magg suggested they try to talk with Donavan and see what he was feeling.

He agreed and they headed for Donavan's room. Jasmine answered their knock and let them in.

Donavan was sitting at his desk and waiting for them. He was pale and had lost some weight. He said, "I'm so glad you came. I've been thinking a lot about the past few weeks and what has happened. But first, will you tell me about your trip to Synkana. I would like to hear how it went. I know you have to have had problems with those women."

She said, "Donavan, you know what I told you about why I was leaving. I had a terrible feeling that Jarrone and the others would need me at some point along the way. So Matton and I took my old gypsy wagon and followed them out of town. The women were really terrible the entire trip. We had to stop them with magic a few times. They were slow learners. They nearly escaped at one point, but I was able to help Jarrone stop them."

Jarrone broke in, "It's true, Donavan. If Magg hadn't been there, those women would have escaped and heaven only knows what they would have done in the small villages nearby. It was actually terrifying to me and the soldiers."

Magg continued, "We finally made it to Synkana and delivered them to the prison there. When we finished getting the women into the prison, we decided to sell the wagon. The prison warden wanted it and so we sold it to him. We spent that night at an inn and headed back to Anakik the next day. We were able to make much better time coming back without that big wagon."

Donavan said, "I'm glad to hear that you made it there and back home safely. We were all very worried about you. It's true the women were truly evil. We couldn't have kept them here any longer. Now I will tell you what went on here while you were gone. I wish I could tell you that all went well, but I cannot.

"The first couple of days weren't too bad. But we've been dealing with some truly nasty monsters. In fact it seemed that they could tell that both of you were gone. They started screeching and their screeches were getting louder and seemed to get closer every night. Then one day a child got too close to the forest and was nearly caught by a monster. His dad was able to save him, just barely.

The villagers have been much more cautious about going anywhere near the forest. That's one good thing. I was able to destroy one of the monster with a spell I used in a panic. I was so happy I danced around like at idiot and nearly got killed myself. There was a monster that saw me and about had me for dinner. I was able to escape with the help of Jasmine. I do have a wound on my leg from that adventure.

"I guess what I'm trying to say, now that I've had time to think straight, is that you couldn't know we'd have so many problems. I didn't know you had so many problems with the women and the wagon. So, I'm sorry I was so angry when you first got back. We need each other and we need to make a plan. So can we start today?"

Magg was stunned, she had expected to be yelled at, but Donavan's apology was a pleasant surprise. "Donavan, I honestly would not have left you if I'd had any idea what was going to happen. I now you did your best, and that's all that matters now. I do have some ideas as to how you can help us fight those monsters. I'm going to learn more spells from Zarcon's book and then I'll teach them to you and

Jarrone. We'll have enough power, together, to destoy the evil things."

Donavan smiled relieved that he would be playing an important part in the destruction of the monsters.

Magg, Jarrone, and Matton left Donavan to go to Magg's room so she could study the spells she would learn. Matton and Jarrone left her there to go about their business of the day trying to make sure the village was as secure as could be at the time.

Magg spent the day memorizing the first spell she wanted to use. It was a bit complicated and took the rest of the day to have it learned. She was proud of the progress she had made and was just finishing up and putting the book away when Matton came to her and suggested maybe it was time to go to bed and rest. She agreed and they got ready for bed.

But as they were ready to relax and great howl was heard. It sounded a bit too close to the village for comfort. But nothing could be done so late at night. Magg and Matton decided to worry about it in the morning. They were both too worn out to do anything tonight.

The rest of the villagers were upset by the sound. They turned out all their lights and got the children to bed quickly. They were all hoping that they wouldn't hear anything from the Monsters the rest of the night.

Indeed, the rest of the night passed quietly. That could be good, or it could be bad. They wouldn't know more until morning came.

Morning dawned bright and sunny. Magg and Matton were up and ready to head to the dining room for breakfast. Jarrone was actually just coming in the door of the inn when they saw him. He caught up with them and they went to breakfast together.

Aribon had fixed scrambled eggs and ham with fried potatoes from his garden. They sat down to eat and enjoyed the food and the company. Magg spoke to them of talking with Donavan and khow he had been so kind and apologetic.

Jarrone spoke up, "Magg, the thing to remember is that things were fairly quiet when we left Anakik. Also, those women had to go. I don't know if we'd have made it if you hadn't come with us. We all made our decisions based on what was happening and how we felt. Donavan did the best he could. I'm actually amazed that he took it so hard. Maybe it was just overwhelming to him. I can only guess. We can't blame ourselves for what we couldn't control or have foreknowledge of, right?"

Magg nodded in agreement. It was over and all seemed to be settled between them and Donavan. She was so grateful.

Matton said, "Magg, you did the best with what you knew and felt. We both thought that Donavan was strong enough to handle anything that might happen. I'm just glad he's seeing it that way now."

Donavan was up early and decided it would be a good idea to walk around the village and see what improvements they could make in securing Anakik and the people in it. So it was that the five of them, Donavan, Jasmine, Magg, Matton, and Jarrone left the inn and walked around the village keeping their eyes open for any potential trouble. There was a monster lurking near the back of the inn. Magg and Donavan sent a spell into it that froze it in place. It was basically stone at that point. It didn't even have time to screech.

That incident made them more aware of what was going on around them. They went near Jarrone's house and checked in on his family. Everyone was doing well. They had a plan for any attack that might come near their house or property. Magg and Donavan felt a lot better knowing that Jarrone's family was prepared as much as they could be.

As the day passed, they headed back to the inn in the hopes of getting some of Alfias' wonderful dinner. It was a bit of a walk, but it felt good to be out in the sunshine, even though they had to be cautious of the monsters.

As they walked back to the inn, they heard Raven weakly calling to them. Since it was late morning, it was unusual for Raven to be out looking for them.

Magg was surprised, she ran to the sound of Raven's voice and found her lying on the steps to the inn, she nearly screamed, "What's happened Raven?"

Magg could see that Raven had been wounded and was bleeding badly. It appeared that her side had been cut by some large claws. Raven was barely able to talk.

She said, her voice shaking from fear and pain, "I was hunting last night… I was about to get dinner by killing a small deer. As I prepared to pounce, I heard a loud roar and a monster came out of nowhere and attacked me. …I was barely able to escape before I was its dinner instead. You were right, Magg, (she groaned) these creatures are far more dangerous than I thought. It seemed to come out of nowhere when it attacked. It really hurts where it caught me. If I hadn't been faster than it was, I would have been dinner." She groaned in pain.

"That must have been the roar we all heard late last night as we were getting to bed. Let's get you to the inn and bandage your wounds. Aribon has some experience with wounds. You need to lie down and rest while we get him. I know there's some bandaging in the kitchen."

Magg called to Jarrone and Donavan to come and help with Raven. Magg was very concerned when she saw Raven's wound. It was deep enough to cause serious blood loss. Indeed, there was a lot of blood all over Raven and the amount of blood on the steps to the inn was really frightening.

Jarrone and Donavan helped Raven into the inn where they helped her lie down on one of the couches near the entrance. Aribon heard them come in and rushed to their aid. When he saw Raven's wound, he ran back to the kitchen to get his bandaging supplies. He also brought some whiskey for Raven to drink to numb the pain.

Jarrone found a cup and poured it for Raven and gave it to Aribon.

He held the cup close to Raven and said, "Here Raven drink a little of this. It will help numb the pain while I'm doing the stitching. What on earth happened to you?"

Raven was in a lot of pain by that time, so Magg answered for her, "Raven was out hunting when she was attacked by a monster in the forest."

"Oh, my." Aribon was busy trying to slow the bleeding as they were talking.

"It was one of those monsters that attacked Raven. They seem to come out of nowhere and attack to kill."

"This terrible. Raven I'm going to clean the wound in case there's some kind of nastiness from that creature in it that might cause problems. So take another drink and I'll get started."

Magg grew concerned at that and asked Raven if she could look into her blood to make sure there wasn't anything to cause an infection. Raven nodded. As Magg stepped closer to Raven, she cast the spell that would tell her if the wound was infected. After a thorough scan, she did find a bit of infection. She added a little magic to help with the pain and the bleeding. She was concerned about the infection that was getting stronger. She remembered a spell that killed the cause of infection right away and sent it into Raven to help her fight the infection and anything else that might attack her wound.

Magg was amazed that Raven had been able to walk to the inn. She wasn't aware that Raven had crawled in her cat form and then transformed when she fell on the steps to the inn.

Raven felt the spell taking effect. She took another drink from the glass of whiskey Aribon gave her anyway. She kind of liked it. He took the bottle of whiskey and poured it slowly over her wound to cleanse it. It stung Raven, but she didn't cry out. Magg's spell had numbed the pain enough that it wasn't too bad.

Aribon prepared his needle and thread that he kept just in case. He had sewed the wounds of many of the villagers for one reason or another. He knew what he was doing. He began to stitch the wound very carefully. He did his best to make it neat. He was very fussy about his work.

Alfias saw what was going on and came out to see if he could help. Aribon sent him back to the kitchen to get more bandaging. Raven's wound was bigger than he initially thought. He needed more to cover it after he had sewn it up. She was no longer bleeding, but her wound needed to be covered to keep it clean. Alfias came to the room just then with more bandages. Aribon was able to finish up the bandaging then. He thanked Alfias as he finished.

Aribon was worried that when she transformed, she needed to keep her wound covered. However, he didn't know if the bandages would stay on when she transformed. He wondered if it might be better if she didn't do that until all was healed.

Aribon decided to mention it to Magg, So he spoke to her softly, "Magg, maybe we should ask Raven not to transform until she is healed. I'm concerned about her wound opening up again if she's not careful."

Magg agreed to talk with Raven about it later. "I'm sure she'll agree. That wound is really deep and painful. She won't want to transform for quite a while, I'm sure."

Raven was feeling better after she drank a bit more whiskey. "Thank you Aribon. I do feel better now that my wound is clean and bandaged. And thank you Magg for your help. I need some help back to my cottage, if that's possible?"

"Raven, you really can't be alone until you are mostly healed. I'm worried about you getting into trouble at your cottage. You'll be awfully vulnerable in your current condition. You really must stay with me. Besides, your cottage is a bit too close to the forest for you to stay there."

"Magg, thank you."

"I'm really glad you're going to stay with me. I would like to take care of you until you're healed. Matton will be there to help, too."

Matton came in from outside and saw that things were a bit crazy just then. He asked what was needed.

Magg said, "Matton, Raven has been wounded by one of the monsters. Will you please help Raven to our room? She'll be staying with me while she heals. She's going to need plenty of rest. "

Matton was a bit shocked, but said, "I would be glad to. Will you come too, Magg? You will tell me the whole story later, right?"

"Right." Magg was so glad that Matton came in when he did. He was needed.

"Alright, Raven, let's get you to the room and get you settled so you can rest." Aribon was also there to help her. They half carried her to Magg's room.

Raven was very close to going unconscious at that point. The shock was finally catching up with her. She was also traumatized by the incident and would need to feel safe.

Matton and Aribon helped Raven to the room she would share with Magg. Both Magg and Matton helped her get settled. Raven fell asleep as soon as she was in the bed. She had truly been exhausted from lack of blood.

Magg told Matton she was going to spend some time making sure Raven was going to be able to sleep. She was also worried about the infection that she hoped she had destroyed. But she needed to be sure. Matton told Magg that he was going to stay with her as well.

It was a good thing she stayed because Raven started having problems right away. Her breathing stopped not long after she was settled in the bed.

Magg had to use magic to get her breathing again. She used that magic to clear Raven's lungs. Magg didn't dare leave her until she was sure she had done all she could to help her survive. Magg was really worried about her. Raven finally settled down and was able to sleep comfortably after Magg cleared her lungs and helped her fight the infection with a bit more magic.

Matton was glad he had stayed with Magg. She was looking very tired. Matton knew she had used a lot of magic to help Raven. So he called Alfias to come and stay with Raven until he and Magg could get something to eat and Magg could rest. Magg was so grateful. She needed to talk to the others to let them know how things were going with Raven.

They both went back to the dining area when Alfias arrived to relieve Magg. It was where the others were waiting.

Magg told them, "Raven is sleeping. She's been through a lot. I did find a bit of infection in her wound that I'm concerned about. I sent a spell that should destroy all of it, but only time will tell if I got it all. It took some time to make sure she would be all right for awhile."

Jasmine came in just then. She had been busy with other things. Then she saw the blood soaked cloths and Aribon's medical kit sitting on the floor, "What on earth happened here, Donavan?"

Donavan replied, "Raven was wounded by one of those monsters this morning. She just made it to the inn. Aribon was able to sew up her wound and Magg is letting her stay in her spare room for now. So it's been a bit eventful this morning."

"This is terrible! Poor Raven! Will she be alright? It's getting really frightening now."

Donavan tried to calm Jasmine, "Magg has done all she can for her right now. Aribon was able to sew up her wound. Now it's just a matter of time to see how she does."

Magg said, "I'm thinking it would be great if we could take turns staying with Raven while she heals. I don't want any one person to be responsible all the time."

Jasmine spoke up first, "I would really like to help with that, Magg. Would you like us to sign up for when we can help?"

Magg was delighted at the idea, "Great idea, Jasmine. Will you be in charge of that schedule, please?"

Jasmine was happy to do so. She wrote it up and started asking their friends who would like to help and when. It didn't take long to fill out a schedule that covered the first few days of Raven's recovery.

Greta and Zarcon had entered the room just as Magg was explaining what she had done to help Raven. Greta and Zarcon volunteered for a shift whenever they were needed. Matton wanted to help whenever Magg was there. He was very seriously in love with Magg.

Aribon volunteered if he could be with someone. He wasn't comfortable being alone with Raven. Apparently she scared him a bit. Jarrone said he would be there with Aribon any time.

So it was settled that they would take turns spending time with Raven to make sure she was not going to be left alone at any time. Her condition was much too fragile.

As the others went back to their rooms to get ready for breakfast, Magg stopped Jasmine and asked if she would take the first shift that day. Magg told her that she was too exhausted to do anything just now. It had been such a terrible morning. Jasmine was more than happy to do so. Donavan also volunteered to help Jasmine. They went to Magg's rooms and stayed with Raven until time for lunch when Aribon and Jarrone would take over.

When all their friends left, Matton took Magg by the hand and led her into his room. He was staying a few doors down the hall from Magg. Now that Raven would be staying in Magg's room, they needed a place more private for themselves. This was especially true when Magg was exhausted from the use of her magic, as now.

He knew she needed his company and comfort just then. It had been a long and terrifying morning trying to save Raven. When they were able to sit together and relax a bit, Magg told Matton all that had happened that morning with Raven.

Magg told him that she almost lost Raven a couple of times. The infection she had mentioned to the others was much worse than she had implied. Raven had stopped breathing for a minute or two. That's when Magg discovered the organism that was attacking her lungs. Magg had just barely been able to stop it in time. That experience scared Magg and made her realize that Raven was in more trouble that she had thought. That was why she had asked for help watching Raven.

Matton had been in the room with Magg and Raven at the time, but he didn't realize all that Magg was dealing with. Now he understood what she had been through while helping Raven. He understood then why she was so worn out. He had been with her when she had used powerful magic and knew what it took out of Magg to use it. She had been with Raven for quite a long while this morning and had used much of her magic in that time. It would be good for both of them to rest. Matton was always ready to comfort Magg. He wanted to be close to her as much as possible.

While it was still early, Alfias and Jarrone got together and decided it was time to clean off the steps to the inn. It was really terrifying to see all that blood. The villagers would soon be out and about and the sight of all that blood could cause a lot of children and adults nightmares. So they found the buckets in the kitchen and filled them with water from the pump in the square. They each had a bristle brush and scrubbed the steps until there was no sign of blood on them. It was difficult for them knowing it was Raven's blood they were removing. But it had to be done.

They finished just as the shops started opening around the village. The two men sat together on the steps to watch the village waking up for another day. They were hoping none of the villagers would hear about the terror of the morning until later in the day. There was enough concern about the monsters without having their fears confirmed first thing in the morning.

Alfias and Jarrone were becoming friends and congratulated each other on a job well done. Jarrone knew that he would check in on Raven's condition before he had his breakfast. Alfias needed to get going so he could help Aribon cook breakfast for the others. So they split up and went about the morning they had planned.

Jasmine and Donavan had quietly moved into the room reserved for Raven and saw how badly she was hurt, it brought tears to Jasmine's eyes. "Donavan, we must do all we can to destroy these creatures. They are far too dangerous to have them so close to the village. And now they've attacked and hurt Raven so badly, I'm not sure how she survived it at all."

"I know Jasmine. This is the point where we must act to defend the village and those we love. Maybe we could figure out some kind of alarm to warn us of their approach. The smell helps, but by the time you smell them, it's too late to run. I'm actually afraid now. I wasn't before, but seeing Raven like this is terrifying."

"Oh Donavan, I agree. We've seen people wounded by the Monsters in the Mist, but it was usually over before there was much blood. Did you see the steps to the inn this morning? They were covered with Raven's blood. I'm terrified too. Those monsters are pure evil."

"Indeed they are. Now to find out how to stop and destroy them."

The day continued and the friends took turns watching over Raven. She was so fragile that it frightened some of them. Raven was always so strong. That was probably what had saved her life. If what had happened to her happened to another person, it was a pretty good bet that they would not have survived.

The villagers were gradually becoming aware of what had happened to Raven and some came to the inn to ask if they could help in any way. Roslin and Karmine were among the first and they agreed that Roslin would come in the mornings after she got the boys ready for the day. They would come with her and play quietly in the dining area. They were good boys and would behave while Roslin stayed with Raven. Karmine would help with the boys and make sure they were given their dinner before they all went back home. So many were happy to help.

Later that evening, Zarcon and Greta were talking about what to do about the creatures. Zarcon was holding Greta close as he said, "You know, Greta, with so much magic here, you would think that a solution for destroying those evil things would be simple. But apparently, they are much more complicated than anything we've faced before.

"I'm thinking we need to have a counsel of those with magic to see if we can come up with anything that might work. When we happened to go outside for a short walk right after it happened, and saw the blood on the steps to the inn, it was shocking. Raven probably should have died out there. I'm so grateful that Magg came running and called for help right away. I hate to say it Greta, but I'm really afraid of those monsters."

Greta held Zarcon close and agreed with what he said. She had seen the blood too and was frightened by it. She knew that unless they could stop those monsters, tough times were surely ahead. She said, "Zarcon, we can only do what we are able to do and learn as we go. I'm so hoping a way will be found to stop them before anyone else is hurt or killed by them."

Zarcon kissed her as they held each other close and fell asleep. They hadn't slept much the night before from the noises the creatures were making, and it felt good to finally sleep.

The next morning at breakfast, Donavan and Jasmine were talking with Magg and the others.

Donavan said, "Maybe we should warn the villagers to keep watch for the monsters. They could warn us if they see anything."

Jasmine had an idea and said, "That sounds necessary to protect everyone. I wonder if we could ask Jarrone's sister, Lucintha to draw a picture of one and we could post some around the village to warn everyone about them. You know, she's a pretty good artist. She could possibly make it look enough like those creatures that the people in town would know what we're really up against."

"Good idea Jasmine."

Donavan turned to Magg and said, "We're going to ask Lucintha to draw some pictures of the monster and we'll post them around the village to warn everyone about them and what they might look like. We should be back before dark. Jarrone will you come with us? Maybe you could help describe the Skreecher to your sister better than we can. I know many of the villagers have seen the monsters, but a picture will warn the others."

Jarrone said, "Yes I will. I need to get back home anyway."

Magg agreed that it was a good idea. "Bring her picture to me when you get back. I'd love to see it."

Donavan, Jasmine, and Jarrone left the inn and went for a walk to talk to Lucintha about their plan.

She was a very talented artist as it turned out. They soon arrived at the cottage where Jarrone and his family lived.

Donavan was able to talk with Lucintha about the beast that they needed her to draw. She had some ideas and started to draw. She drew it as if she had seen it. Her drawing made Jarrone and the others fearful. It was so realistic.

When Lucintha finished, Donavan asked her, "Lucintha, have you seen this thing?"

"Not really, I just had a feeling about what it looked like. I heard it roar last night and this is what came to me about it. Now that I've drawn it, it scares me."

"I've seen it myself, and this is almost exactly what it looks like. Lucintha, you have magic and I can't wait to have you start at the school. No one could have caught the essence of that creature like you have. I'm thinking when we post this, the villagers will take watching for it even more seriously. I only hope they are not so frightened by it that they don't want to leave their homes."

Lucintha was astonished, "Donavan, are you serious? I have magic? This drawing is powerful enough to scare people? I just drew what was in my head."

"You have a lot of talent Lucintha. I believe your talent comes from the magic within you. We will be needing you for many things in the future. Once we can get you in the school, your talents will be more evident. You will be amazed at what you will find out about yourself."

Lucintha had to sit down, she was overcome with the possibilities of what her magic might mean.

Jarrone spoke up, "Lucintha, we're going to be in the school together and learn so much about magic. Aren't you excited to learn more?"

"I am! The future looks completely different than what I thought it might be."

Donavan held her drawing and told Lucintha that he would be posting this copy in the store window in town. "Would you draw three more so we can post them around the village?"

"I would be honored to Donavan. I'll have them finished by tomorrow morning early. It must be very important that we get the word to the villagers before it's too late. They've already come into the village. We must stop them somehow, right?"

"That's exactly the problem, Lucintha. I think your pictures will help with that. I think we'd better head back to the inn. It's starting to get dark. We'll come back tomorrow morning to pick up the other drawings. See you then."

"Good night."

Jasmine and Donavan walked back to the inn. It was a beautiful, cool, evening. The sun was just starting to set. As they walked, they talked about the drawing Lucintha had done.

Donavan said, "What a lot of talent Lucintha has. She seems to also be very intuitive. I think her magic is coming to maturity now. It will be most interesting to see how far she can go with it."

They arrived at the inn and stopped by Magg's room to tell her about Lucintha's drawing and show it to her and Matton. After Magg looked at the drawing for a few minutes she said, "This drawing is amazing, Donavan. How could she have captured that monster in so much detail, unless she has magic? Jarrone and his family are so interesting. Revinia makes beautiful dresses and uses magic to do it. Now Lucintha appears to have magic with her art. Of course, Jarrone is one very powerful wizard already. It just keeps getting better.'"

Donavan said, "We believe she has magic. This drawing is so good. I don't know anyone else that could do something so accurate without seeing it for themselves. We're going to go get the other three drawings Lucintha said she would make for us by morning. We're going to post them around the village. We're hoping it will sober the villagers to watch for anything strange in the area. Now that Raven won't be hunting for a while, we need to have everyone watching. With the magic Jarrone and I have learned, we should be able to take control of any of them that might cause trouble."

Magg thought for a moment, "It sounds good, Donavan. I'm wondering what we could call the thing. Let's give it a name. It will make it simpler when we're talking about it. Can you think of anything?"

"Let's think about it and maybe come together tomorrow and decide. Does that make sense?"

"Alright, Donavan. Let's meet in the morning and throw some names around until we find one that works."

"I think it's time for Jasmine and I to go to our room for the night. We'll see you in the morning. Let's meet in the dining room, alright?"

"Sounds good."

"Good night."

As they were getting settled in for the night, they heard a very loud roar from the forest. It seemed to be a bit closer than the previous night. Could that monster be coming closer and letting them know it was coming?

Was it coming?

Chapter 17

First thing in the morning, Donavan went to Jarrone's family home and knocked. Lucintha answered the door with a big smile on her face. "I've finished the drawings for you. Here they are. Do you need any help placing them in the village? I'd be glad to help."

Donavan smiled, "That would be great Lucintha. But don't go alone. Those monsters are around somewhere, so watch out and take Jarrone with you, please?"

"OK, I will. Jarrone needs something to do anyway." She smiled and went back inside to find Jarrone.

Donavan knew they would take care of the pictures in town. So he headed back to the inn to talk about naming the monsters.

As the group gathered to the dining area that morning to discuss what they should call the beast that was terrorizing them, there was a chill in the area that everyone realized the seriousness of the situation they were now in.

The first one to speak was Magg, "I couldn't sleep last night for worrying about the creature we now need to face. We've faced some terrible situations in the past. We've done well to conquer whatever we've faced. Now that Neberon is gone, we thought the creation of new monsters was over. What scares me about this new one is that it must come from the natural world. We know that we can destroy it with magic, but it takes a lot to do it. I believe with the magic we have now, that we will be able to conquer this one as well. Together, we can accomplish whatever must be done. Having said that, moving on to the purpose of this meeting, after much thought, I have to tell you, I have no idea what to call this new monster, have any of the rest of you come up with anything yet?"

Donavan spoke up, "Like the rest of you, I've thought long and hard about what this monster represents. It is, of course, really big. It also makes a lot of noise when it roars. It's a hairy beast, that's for sure. In addition, the thing smells really bad. The smell is actually a good thing because we can smell it coming from far enough away to get away, if we run really fast." Donavan grinned at the last, and the rest of the group chuckled for a moment, until they realized what he had just said. Some of the villagers weren't fast on their feet and might not be able to escape.

Jasmine looked at Donavan as if he had sprouted another head. "Donavan, that was not funny. I know we need to relax so we can think better, but try to be a bit more considerate, please."

Donavan looked at Jasmine with sad eyes. "I'm sorry everyone. It was just a sorry attempt at some humor. I will try to think of others before I speak."

Everyone laughed at that. They all knew that Donavan couldn't help himself most of the time. It was as if, he thought it, he said it. That was part of his charm. Yes, he got out of line sometimes, but that was just Donavan.

Jasmine looked at Donavan to say she was sorry. "What you said just hit me wrong. I'm sorry for jumping on you like that."

"It did startle me for a minute. But I forgive you. I know how serious the situation is. We really must get serious about not only what to call it, but how to stop it and all its friends."

Just then Jarrone, Revinia, and Lucintha walked in. They had finished posting the pictures Lucintha had drawn and wanted to be a part of naming the monster that was scaring everyone.

Jarrone couldn't help himself, he spoke up, "Let's call it Big Bad and Ugly."

Everyone did laugh at that.

Lucida said, as she was laughing, "That's not a bad idea. How about BBU, or BUB?"

Magg cut in, "Well maybe that would work, but I'd rather we kept trying and maybe we could come up with something a bit more in line with how we feel about it."

Revinia, Jarrone's other sister, spoke up, "OK how about Hairy Scary, or Scary Hairy?"

Magg spoke again, "How about a one word name?"

With a slight grin, Jarrone said, "How about the Stink Freak?"

Donavan chuckled, "Stink Freak? Really? How about the Ugly Shrieker? Maybe we could call it the Grisly Nightmare? Any of those catch your imagination?"

Jasmine got thinking, "How about the Grisly Abomination?"

Magg said, "Putrid Skreecher? Then we cover the smell and the noise of it?"

"Alright, let's vote on the favorites. I've asked Aribon to bring us papers to write our preferences on. As soon as you've picked your two favorites, hand your paper to Aribon, please." Donavan was a bit nervous about the voting, he didn't know why.

The various paper ballots were finally handed to Aribon. He stepped out of the room to count the votes. When he came back into the dining room, he had a funny look on his face.

Donavan noticed first and asked, "What's wrong Aribon? Was it that bad? Tell us what happened."

Aribon didn't quite know where to start. He said with a bit of fright in his tone, "For some reason, the Putrid Skreecher got all of the votes. The weird thing is, none of the votes were in any of your handwriting. I don't understand who has control of the vote, but it isn't us. I'm thinking that whatever this thing is, it wants to be called the Putrid Skreecher. Scares me, I can tell you that."

Everyone in the room turned white. Magg spoke up, "I'm feeling the same fear as you Aribon. I don't have an explanation for any of this. What about the rest of you? Any ideas?"

Jarrone nodded his head and said, "It's apparent we are up against more than we were prepared for. Can we possibly trace the trail of the magic used at this point?"

Magg agreed, "I think it might be worth a try, at least. Donavan, Jarrone and I will make a circle and recite the spell of power to find and follow another spell used recently. Let's hope we can find something helpful. Let's start here, then move to the forest if we don't find anything."

"Agreed"

As they started the spell, they began to feel a strange form of energy. It started in the ground at their feet and spread up their bodies. It was becoming frightening when Magg called a halt to the spell. "This is so much more powerful than I expected. I was hoping for a trace. But this is too much power for all of us together. I was actually afraid before we stopped the spell. Did the rest of you feel that?"

Donavan and Jarrone both looked terrified just then. Donavan finally spoke, "I've never felt anything like that before. What on earth do we do now?"

Magg replied, "A very good question, indeed. We'd better come up with something quick. Those things are getting closer and now that we know they have magic, it's even worse. I think we need Zarcon. He knows so much about magic. I'm hoping he'll know or have heard of this before in his long years with magic. I do hope he's up to it right now. Let's go to his room and see how he's doing."

It was decided that it would be best if only Magg and Jarrone went to him first. Donavan would come in if Zarcon was up to more visitors.

Magg knocked softly on Zarcon's door. Greta opened to them and told them to come on in. Zarcon was up and eating a small meal just then. He looked up in surprise and smiled. "I'm so glad to see you! It's been too long. I heard about all the trouble with those mountain people. I've been worried about Orshon and his friends for a while now. I'm grateful they won't be a problem anymore. Greta was glad to help with that.

"I can see by the look on your faces that that isn't what you came here for. What's going on that you need the advice of an old wizard like me?"

It was about a year ago that Jarrone had cured Zarcon of some poison from a shard of glass thrown by Neberon, an evil wizard. Zarcon was so well after that that he married Greta after so many years together. They had been more than great friends. Everyone who knew them was thrilled. So much had happened since then. However, over the last few months, age had started having its way with Zarcon and he was not feeling so great. His mind was still sharp, it was his body telling him he wasn't so young any more.

Magg smiled and said, "Zarcon, you're still the wonderful wizard you've always been. Now we need your wisdom on a question about those things in the forest, we are calling them the Putrid Skreechers. That is a story in itself. The thing is, we just tried to find the trail of some magic used at the naming of them and it scared us half to death. We're hoping you can tell us something about it."

Zarcon was troubled by the story so far. "I need more information, Magg. How did the spell reveal itself? What did you actually feel? How strong was it?"

Magg apologized for not explaining better, "Alright, Donavan, Jarrone, and I began the spell for tracing an unknown spell to its source. As we began saying the words, suddenly, power in the ground at our feet started to vibrate. The power went up our feet and into our bodies. I stopped the spell immediately at that point. None of us has ever experienced anything like it before. We are truly terrified by it."

When Magg finished, she looked at Zarcon. He was holding his chest and fighting back the terror that had suddenly possessed him. "I hoped never to hear of that spell again in my life," he cried. "You have no idea what is happening here!"

Greta ran to his side and held him until he could breathe again and the pain subsided. It was awful to see him so frightened. Magg and the others were even more fearful than they had been.

"Zarcon, can you tell us what you know? Would it be better if we let you rest and come back later? I can see that you're as frightened as we are, maybe more so.

Please tell us what to do." Magg was near tears now and feeling desperate.

Zarcon looked Magg in the eye and said, "I must rest. This has been a shock to me. I will send Greta to get you when I'm a bit stronger. Maybe tomorrow will be better."

"As you say, Zarcon. We will wait for Greta to come for us." Magg and Jarrone left and shut the door quietly. Donavan was waiting and wanted to know what happened. As Magg explained, Donavan, too, was even more concerned about what they were going to be able to do now. If Zarcon was that frightened what on earth could they do? It didn't bode well.

Chapter 18

When Magg told Zarcon about the magic that the Putrid Skreechers were using, it terrified him. He remembered it from long ago. He hadn't seen it in his lifetime. So, for it to come into his life now, when he was not at his strongest, was a shock and terrifying. The pain of it was surprising, too. He had not felt that from just hearing about a spell in his life. It showed how weak he was now. Greta had noticed the change in his appearance and went to him immediately. She held him and tried to give him of her strength. It seemed to help him a bit, but he was in bad shape for a while.

Zarcon knew of a few countermeasures for those powers, but to say that he was rusty, was a gross understatement. He would have to get out his Book of Spells and try to find the spells he needed. It would take time they didn't have from the sound of it. Raven had already been injured because of those horrible

Putrid Skreechers. He must find a way to stop them before anyone else was hurt or worse.

Zarcon spoke softly to Greta, "Greta my love, would you please find my Book of Spells? I believe it is in my pack in the closet. I'm going to need it for what is coming."

"You are seriously concerned about it, aren't you? I will find your book right away. This is truly a terrifying situation. I will do all I can to help."

"That is part of the reason I have loved you all these years. You are always ready to do all you can to help. You're special to me my dear."

"Zarcon, you are special to me too. No one is like you and that is something very special to me."

Greta left the room to find Zarcon's Book of Spells. She found it quickly in his pack, as he said it would be. She brought it to him and placed it on the table before him. The book was large and heavy. It was old and precious. The vellum pages were becoming fragile, so it was necessary to handle it with care. It would need to be recopied very soon.

Zarcon loved his book. It held all the spells the wizards had from the time of the university long ago. It was a priceless treasure. Now Zarcon needed it more than he ever had. He must find the spells to combat the Skreechers and fast.

Zarcon was feeling the pressure as he opened the book to begin the process of finding what would be effective against the power of the Skreechers. Magg had said the things could appear suddenly to attack. At least, that is what it felt like to Raven and others who had seen them and survived. This, of course, added another layer of power to deal with. It was becoming very complicated already.

As Zarcon searched his book, he spent hours and started writing down the spells he thought might be effective to put an end to the power of the Skreechers. He had to stop when he was becoming exhausted later that evening. Greta encouraged him to quit for the night. It was difficult for him, but he saw the wisdom of her words. He needed to have the strength to search more in the morning. He was becoming more hopeful with just the few things he had found so far. He was also trying to find out more about the spell that had affected Magg and the others. He needed to know what kind of spell would cause such fear in those with magic.

He was looking forward to showing Magg and the others what he had found and together they would find a way. They must.

Time was running out and they needed to know everything they could find out about the magic that the Skreechers had and how to counteract that on top of finding spells that would destroy them. How could something so complicated be his to deal with this late in his life? He could only hope Magg and the others were up to it. He hoped he could help, but time was not on his side just now.

Chapter 19

After spending time talking with Donavan and Jarrone about the magic they would need to overcome the Skreechers, Magg went to her room with Matton. She was so grateful for his strength just then. Matton held her close and reassured her that she was strong and would be able to take care of the villagers when the time came. As the evening grew late, they could hear the Skreechers in the not too distant forest seeming to remind the village that they were still around.

It can be said that the people of Anakik and the villagers nearby heard those howls and locked their doors and shuttered their windows at the sound. All of them had heard the stories of what the Skreechers had done to Raven. There were certain missing villagers that were never found to add to the nature of their fear.

Children were kept close at hand at all times and warned never to go into the forest at any time.

No one questioned the warnings, all could hear the things howling and heard the stories of what happened to those who disregarded them. It would be safe to say that most adults did not sleep well at night any longer. The fear was palpable day or night.

Roslin and Karmine heard the howling and did their best to comfort the four boys in their care. It was especially difficult for Kedron. It was Kedron that had been attacked by the Skreecher that came really close to Anakik. He had been dragged off their wagon and was about to be eaten, when Magg ran up and killed the thing on the spot. She had incinerated the body for Kedron so he wouldn't be afraid it might come back for him from the dead. That act distracted the family from the terror of the attack.

As Karmine and Roslin were in bed and trying to relax after a terrifying day, they started talking about their feelings and fears. Roslin spoke first, "Karmine, I really need you to hold me tonight. I need your comfort and strength or I won't be able to sleep at all. Can we talk about the Skreechers and what it means for the village, and for us and the boys? I'm wondering if we should move back to our old village away from all this terror. Maybe we'd be safer there. What do you think?"

Karmine held her close and tried to comfort her as best he could. "Roslin, there are some things we have no control over, as you know. So far in our marriage, we've been able to weather all the storms that have come our way. Things haven't always worked out as we thought they should, but we always relied on each other to get through them. That's what we're going to do now.

"One way or another, we will get through this one, too. I'm so blessed to have you in my life and I'm so grateful for those four boys we are raising. They are such a delight to me. I love this family we've created so very much. So let's stick together no matter what comes. We'll find a way. I was just thinking about that day when Magg came to our rescue and finally incinerated that Skreecher that had attacked Kedron. Remember?"

Roslin did manage to smile, "Yes I remember. It was so rewarding to see that horrible smelly thing getting incinerated. Magg sure saved the day, didn't she?"

"She sure did. But I still have nightmares about it once in a while. That had to be one of the worst experiences of our lives. I'm so grateful we still have Kedron with us. He's such an amazing young man."

As the two of them talked into the night, they found comfort in each other's arms and were finally able to fall asleep. Tomorrow would bring its own problems to solve and fears to deal with.

Now that the Skreechers were moving in again as a group, it seemed, the family was really getting afraid more than before. This was real and more frightening than ever. It was decided that Karmine would go to the inn and find out what was being done to destroy those terrible Skreechers. He slept with renewed hope. He would go first thing in the morning and talk to Magg or Zarcon, if he could.

Karmine had, of course, seen Kedron attacked by the Skreecher as they neared Anakik. He had tried to shoot it with his rifle, but it happened so fast that he couldn't get in a good shot. If Magg hadn't come running when she did…it didn't bear thinking about. It was much too painful, even now.

Roslin wanted to come with Karmine to talk with Magg or Zarcon, but she needed to stay with the four boys. They were just too frightened to leave now. They were really young, just under 10 years old. So it was not surprising that they were still too frightened to be left alone. Roslin felt so helpless and that was a terrible feeling for her. With Karmine's help, they had weathered many storms together. But this was different. This was so much more to deal with than ever before. She trusted Karmine, but he had no magic to stop those horrible things. She had seen the one that attacked Kedron and knew how terrible they really were.

Karmine and Roslin were pretty sure there were very few villagers who had any idea what they were up against. Yes, they heard the howling and some had seen what happened to Raven. But only a few of them had actually seen a Skreecher.

The poster the young sister of Jarrone had drawn was a wonderfully terrifying picture of the Skreechers. It was accurate to the detail. Unfortunately, the real thing would be much more terrifying. The villagers were acting a bit more cautious now that they had seen the picture. Reality was making its way into their minds.

Karmine believed that it was time to band together as villagers to protect each other and especially the vulnerable among them. There were a large number of children in the village and some of the villagers were getting older and needed a little help with everyday things at home. If a town meeting could be called to address all the needs, maybe they would have a better chance against the Skreechers.

He would talk with Magg or Zarcon about his ideas in the morning.

As the night grew quiet, and it seemed all in the village has settled down for the night, suddenly there was a roaring and howling that seemed to go on forever. This had never been heard up to now. It also sounded much closer than any of the previous nights. Zarcon was alert immediately. Magg jumped out of bed, sending Matton to the floor in his shock. They both dressed hurriedly and ran to Zarcon's room.

As soon as they knocked, Greta let them in. "Come in, Zarcon is awake too. I haven't slept for a couple of days either."

Zarcon heard them come in and called to them to come and talk with him. "Magg, I know that's you. We really need to talk about what's happening. That sound tonight was worse than we've heard yet. I'm sure the villagers are ready to take up arms and get the Skreechers themselves. The children are horrified and hiding under beds now. I have some news, however. I've found some spells in my Book of Spells that I'm hoping will be effective against the Skreechers. Magg, will you look them over and let me know what you think. I know you understand magic at least as well as I do. I've marked the locations of the ones I've found so far. The only thing I haven't looked into is the magic you felt when you were tracing it. I know of its history, but I need to be stronger to tell you about it"

"Zarcon, I'm so grateful you have this Book of Spells. You've taken such good care of it all these years. I would be honored to look at the spells you've found and do my best to understand their meaning. Can I talk with you when I have questions? And when you're ready, we can talk about that other spell."

"Certainly. There is much to learn there. It is the collected knowledge of hundreds of wizards going back several hundred years, to the days of Neberon and Xyrene. They were the two most powerful wizards of all time. Xyrene tried to do good things. But Neberon did everything he knew to do evil. I refused to copy the evil that Neberon had created. I didn't want another wizard like him in this world."

Magg was shocked that so much information was in Zarcon's Book of Spells. "Zarcon, I'm amazed! I'm also very honored that you would trust me with it. Thank you. I will let you know my feelings about the spells you chose first thing."

Zarcon was feeling better now that Magg would also be working on the spells against the Skreechers.

She had great power. He was almost afraid of her power. Maybe it was good that she didn't realize how powerful she really was. At least not until she was a bit more mature in the magic. Time would tell and he had bigger things to worry about just now.

Magg said before she left Zarcon's room, "I'm pretty sure we can do no more tonight. I'll keep your book safe and study the spells you've selected. It will be such a challenge for me to do so. I will see you in the morning as soon as I finish studying."

"Thank you Magg. I look forward to hearing from you and what you find. Good night."

Greta closed the door as Magg and Matton left the room.

Zarcone continued, "I'm feeling a sense of hope with Magg looking into the spells. She'll figure them out and hopefully she can teach Jarrone and Donavan how to do them. It's going to be interesting, don't you think, my dear?"

Before Greta could answer, Zarcon was asleep. Greta smiled and made sure he was covered with a blanket as she climbed into bed next to him. It felt so good to finally be married to this wonderful man. They had been close friends for so many years that Greta didn't think they would ever take their relationship any further. Then when that evil Neberon had come and wounded Zarcon, it was a bad time for all. Zarcon seemed on the edge of death for a long while.

Jarrone had come to him and asked if he could help. Zarcon was doubtful, but let him try anyway. Jarrone had actually healed him. Zarcon was feeling so great that he proposed to Greta on the spot. They were finally married in just a few short days after that.

It had truly been a miracle that Jarrone could heal him so quickly. He was so strong in his magic that it seemed anything was possible now. Zarcon and Greta had been very happy since that day. Life was great for them both.

Jarrone had become the village hero for a long time. Many felt that he was almost as strong as Magg. There was still some difference between their maturities in the magic, but the power was great in them both. It was good that they were such good people. So much power in someone not so good would be very dangerous, indeed.

Chapter 20

After another night of horrible noises and screeching from the forest that seemed to go on far too long, Karmine reluctantly left his bed and dressed to go find Magg. If she couldn't see him, he would try to get to Zarcon's room to talk with him about his ideas. He felt so strongly about it that he felt urgency in talking to someone in a position to help get it started.

Magic was good for so many things, but sometimes other means could be used to make a difference as well. If they could do both at the same time with everyone helping, they had a better chance of success. At least, that's what Karmine was hoping for.

Karmine left their cottage just as the sun was coming up over the mountains. He quietly walked to the inn to find Magg. When he arrived at the inn, all was quiet. He could hear Aribon in the kitchen starting to cook the morning's breakfast. Karmine stepped to the kitchen door and knocked on the doorjamb. Aribon was a bit startled. He was usually alone this early in the morning.

"Sorry Aribon, I didn't mean to startle you. I was wondering if you could tell me which room Magg is in."

Aribon recognized Karmine as the father of the new family in the village. He asked Karmine, "What do you need? I'm sure Magg is sleeping at this hour. Would you like to have some breakfast while you wait? Magg is really fond of her mornings and likes to sleep just a bit later."

Karmine was a bit disappointed. But he decided that if he had to wait, he might as well eat something. Aribon was a great cook, after all. "Thanks, Aribon, I would like to eat some breakfast. I guess I wasn't taking into account other people's sleeping habits when I took off from my cottage so early. I have an idea I really want to share with Magg and maybe even Zarcon. I'm hoping that she'll like my idea for fighting the Skreechers."

Aribon was very interested in what Karmine was thinking. "What's your idea Karmine?"

"Well, I think if we all work together to help and protect each other, we could be much further ahead as a village. I don't want to sit in my cottage just waiting for those with magic to take care of things while I hide at home. I'm pretty sure I'm not the only one that feels that way. What do you think, Aribon?"

Aribon thought about it for a moment. "You know, Karmine, I'm thinking it's a great idea! Like you said, there are those who don't want to just sit and wait for things to happen. They want to be a part of the solution. I'll be very interested in what Magg has to say about it."

"I'll let you know after I talk to her. I'm really excited to share my idea."

Aribon finished cooking breakfast for himself and Karmine. He put it on plates and served their breakfasts on the table. As they ate they talked some more about Karmine's ideas.

Just as they finished eating, Magg and Matton walked into the dining room for their breakfast. When they saw Karmine talking with Aribon, they walked over to them to see what was going on.

"Good morning Karmine, what's going on, my friend?" Magg was very curious as to why Karmine would be here so early in the morning.

"I was looking for you to talk to you about some ideas I have to help the villagers fight the Skreechers. Do you have a few minutes to listen to my ideas?'

Magg was intrigued, "I do have plenty of time to listen to your ideas. Go ahead and tell me what you're thinking."

Karmine was thrilled that Magg wanted to hear his ideas. "I will start by saying that I've wanted to tell you about it for a few weeks now. I've been planning and working out my ideas for that long. What I'm suggesting is that we get together to support each other in the village to protect and provide security as we watch for the Skreechers and what they're doing when they get near the village. The reason I feel so strongly about this idea is that I can't sit home and wait for it all to end. I don't believe I'm alone in this either. I appreciate magic and its effect in protecting us from all the problems we've had to face so far. I believe this situation is a bit different. It feels to me that we need more involvement from all of us. What do you think, Magg? Could we work together to make new plans?"

Magg was impressed with the thought Karmine had given the situation they were currently in. "Karmine, I would be delighted to talk with you and solidify your ideas. We can work out some details and then present them to all the others. Will that work for you, Karmine? We'll take all the time we need to decide how each part of your ideas will come together."

Karmine was a bit concerned when Magg suggested they take all the time they needed. The whole idea was that they could get started right away. The danger of the Skreechers was getting graver by the day. So after thinking for a minute how to express his feelings, he finally said, "Magg, my ideas are simple and won't require much planning. I'm feeling the pressure of the Skreechers and their increased activity near the village to want to put off getting started on my ideas any longer. I haven't slept much the past couple of nights because of the noise of those horrid beasts. I'm sure most villagers are having the same problem. I think the sooner we get going on gathering up the villagers and getting them involved, the better. Do you agree, Magg?"

Magg was stunned. She had apparently fallen into a state of complacency regarding the danger of the Skreechers. For some reason, she was thinking they had plenty of time. With Karmine's help, she realized it really was an urgent matter to address right away.

"I'm sorry Karmine. I don't know what came over me just then. You are so right. We must get working on this immediately. Those Skreechers are getting closer every night. The howling is driving everyone crazy. It really can't go on much longer. Can you come to my room as soon as Matton and I are finished eating? I know Matton will also have some good ideas to add to your own. Then, hopefully, later today we can call a village meeting and let everyone know what we're planning. If you need to go home for a few minutes and talk to your family, now is a good time."

Karmne decided that was a good idea. So he left the inn and walked back home to explain to Roslin what had happened this morning. As he walked in the door, Roslin greeted him with concern. "Karmne, what's going on? You've been gone most of the morning. Is it about the Skreechers? Do you have a plan to fight them? I sure hope all the villagers who are able will want to help."

Karmine smiled, "That's exactly what we're planning. Magg and Matton will be helping to decide how to work it out so we can talk to the villagers this afternoon. Roslin, I finally feel hope that things will work out. Until now, I thought we were all going to be eaten alive. Now there is hope."

"Karmine, don't ever say that again! You're scaring me. I know the Skreechers are very dangerous and seem to have some sort of magic, but don't ever suggest we might be eaten alive! NEVER AGAIN!" Roslin started crying, she had kept much of her emotions inside. But now she let it all come out. It was so overwhelming that Karmine's casual remark about being eaten alive broke the dam.

Karmine immediately pulled Roslin into his arms and held her until she quieted. He hadn't realized how all the stress had affected her. "I'm so sorry. I didn't realize how much you were holding in until now. It's been at least as hard on you as it has on me, maybe more so. I can see that now. I've been foolish not to keep you informed of my ideas. You've been in the dark and I haven't helped in any way. I will do better. Since Magg's friend Matton is coming to the meeting, would you like to be there also? We can see if your friend, Ruby, can watch the boys for a little while."

"Oh, Karmine, I would like nothing better than to be included in that meeting. I've wanted to be involved for a very long time. The boys have come first and I love them so much. It's just been hard for me to always be on the outside looking in. I know it was my choice to stay with them, but now that they're older, maybe I can leave them with Ruby once in a while and be more involved. I love you Karmine. You are my friend and sweetheart and always will be. I'm so glad you thought of me."

"Roslin, you are so precious to me. I didn't want to tell you everything because I didn't want to scare you. Now I see that keeping things quiet had the opposite effect. You must be part of the team that is us from now on. You must know all that I know, no secrets or hidden feelings. I will be much more open to you so you won't get so scared again. Please let me know if you ever start feeling left out. I promise to do better."

"Karmine that is all I needed to hear from you. You have set my heart at ease and I feel I can ask you questions now. It's such a relief to me to know how you feel and will try to keep me informed. I love you so much, my darling."

Just then the four boys came running into the house chasing each other around the room and around Roslin and Karmine shouting, "I got you first!"

"Boys, what's going on? Settle down and tell us what you've been doing, right now!" Karmine was very upset with them for disturbing the tenderness between himself and Roslin just then.

"We were playing Skreechers and villagers just now with some of the other kids. It got a little scary, so we decided to come home to just chase each other. It's not as scary that way."

"Kedron, I know you're all trying to be brave, but it really isn't a good idea to scare each other about a very real monster. Do you understand what I'm trying to say?"

Kedron nodded and so did the other boys. It had been a little too scary for them to play as they had been. All the boys knew very well that the Skreechers were real. They listened to them nearly every night making such noise that they could hardly sleep at all now. Playing had seemed like a good idea at the time, but it turned out not to be.

Kedron spoke for the other boys, "Mom, can we stay in the rest of the day? I think we're too afraid to play outside now."

Roslin was concerned, "Of course you can stay inside. I'd feel better if you did not go out now, anyway."

The boys cheered and went off to their bedroom to play a quieter game.

Karmine and Roslin looked at each other with deep concern. It was affecting the boys more than they had thought. It seemed there were emotions at play that were just now being discovered. It was time to be more aware of each other now that the Skreechers were more active and closer to the village. Something had to be done and quick.

Chapter 21

Raven had been staying with Magg for two weeks healing from the damage done to her by the Skreechers when she was out hunting one night. She had mostly slept while her body healed. She woke a few times a day to eat some meaty soup and drink water or juice. This day she woke up and stayed awake for several hours.

"Magg," she called out finding herself alone. "Where are you?"

Magg was just in the room next to hers and hurried in to see what Raven needed. It was good to hear her voice and know that she was awake and talking. Magg entered Raven's room, "Raven, you must be feeling better. Are you hungry this morning? What can I get you?"

Raven smiled to see Magg and finally feel like talking and eating. Raven had spent the first week unresponsive and trying to heal. She had been in shock the day she was injured and was so weak from loss of blood that she was unconscious for a few days. She had had nightmares while she lay in bed. The Skreecher that attacked her had been huge and she was barely able to escape and survive. She kept dreaming about the attack and would sometimes wake up screaming and fall back into unconsciousness.

Magg had stayed close to her through the first two weeks and had watched her regain some of her strength. She was very concerned about Raven's survival. She had deep wounds on her side and it was taking a long time to fully heal.

It had been difficult for Magg to help her heal with the magic she used. She was able to help with the pain, but the nightmares had a life of their own. Now that Raven was conscious and needing to talk, Magg was relieved. It was a good sign of healing.

Raven smiled and asked Magg if she could have some of the meat that Aribon kept in the icehouse nearby. Magg was surprised that Raven would want meat so soon after becoming conscious.

"Raven, do you really want to eat meat now? You've barely become conscious after all this time."

"Yes, Magg, I really feel the need for some fresh meat. I haven't really had much since the attack. I'm feeling a bit weak without it. Do you think Aribon would have some in the icehouse? He's been so kind to feed me when I couldn't go out to hunt."

"I will go ask him right now and see if he can heat some up a bit for you, just the way you like it. I'll be right back." Magg smiled as she left Raven's room. She was so happy that Raven was improving.

She was smiling as she headed for the kitchen. It had been a good thing for her to be able to watch over Raven. She was healing nicely and would be able to get out of bed and start walkig soon. But she was also sure that Raven did not realize how weak she would be when that happened. Magg had noticed that her muscle tone was fading and her legs were very thin. She would need to get her strength back slowly so that she would be able to get back to her life before the Skreechers.

When Magg entered the kitchen, Aribon was busy making breakfast for everyone. When he saw Magg, he made a funny face at her and asked, "What do you want now Miss Magg?" He chuckled.

Magg made a face back at him and said, "Well, you know my friend Raven? She is needing some fresh meat this morning. What do you think of that?"

Aribon laughed, "How can that be? She's still sleeping, right?"

"Wrong, she's up and hungry. So you'd best be getting her what she wants, or you'll likely regret it. I don't want her to hurt you."

Aribon laughed again, "Yes ma'am! I'm with you there. Barely warm meat coming right up."

It took about two minutes for Aribon to heat up the steak for Raven. He put it on a plate and handed it to Magg. "There you go! And she'd better eat all of it!"

Magg started laughing and walked out of the kitchen to take the steak to Raven. When she got there, Raven was up and waiting. Magg handed her the steak and watched her devour it. She truly had been very hungry indeed.

"I'm so glad you're that hungry and eating so well, Raven. It gives me joy to see you getting better."

Raven smiled as she wiped her mouth with her napkin. "That was delicious! I feel better already. Aribon is so kind to me. Give him my thanks, please."

"I surely will, Raven." Magg stayed with Raven and talked with her for a while before she had to leave to find Matton and the others. Alfias was due to come and sit with Raven in just a few minutes. Magg waited until Alfias arrived, then took the plate from Raven's steak to return it to the kitchen.

Magg said, "Alfias, it's so nice of you to come and spend time with Raven. She just ate a steak that

Aribon cooked for her. She is doing so much better today. Maybe you could discuss how you can help her get her strength back."

Alfias was surprised that Magg wanted him to help Raven get stronger, but he was more than happy to do so. He said, "Magg, I would really like to help her get stronger. Maybe as she eats more and gets stronger inside, we can work on getting her body stronger on the outside. It's something I've never done before. Maybe we could go for short walks at first. What do you think?"

"I think that's a great idea, Alfias. What do you think Raven? You would probably get stronger faster with someone to help you along the way."

Raven was pleased to think that Alfias was willing to help her and said so, "I'm not ready for that yet, but when I am, it would be great to walk with you. I'm getting to the point that I'm going a bit crazy staying in this room all the time."

So it was settled that Magg had Alfias helping her watch over Raven and willing to help her get her strength back. Magg knew she couldn't do it by herself and was relieved to have his interest in helping both her and Raven.

Magg finally said her goodbyes to Alfias and Raven and left them to find Matton and the others.

There was so much that needed to be done to eliminate the Skreechers. She was feeling the strain lately.

Magg headed for the kitchen where she knew Matton was waiting. She spotted him near the door to the dining area and moved toward him. When he saw her, he smiled and reached out his arms to hug her close. He could see that Magg was tired from all that was happening. It was good to go in to breakfast together and spend time with the others to discuss what they would do next.

Chapter 22

Aribon was busy getting breakfast out for those staying at the inn. He decided it would be better if he made something easy to digest and would provide energy for what the morning might bring. So, he prepared pancakes with plenty of fruit and syrup. There was juice to drink and bacon to add flavor. The kitchen was smelling really wonderful. Soon those in the inn began to file in for their breakfast. The smell was irresistible. The first ones in were Magg and Matton. Donavan and Jasmine were close behind. Zarcon and Greta came in with Greta holding Zarcon's arm.

There were a lot of hugs and chatter as they entered the room. Everyone voiced concern for Raven and her recovery. Magg had visited her for a few minutes before coming in to breakfast. She reported that Raven was doing better and healing slowly. Her wounds were very deep and would need extra time to completely heal. There was a bit of sadness in the room at the thought that Raven had been through such a difficult and terrifying experience.

There was a bit of conversation regarding what must be done to stop the Skreechers from their rampage of killing and terrifying the villagers. It was becoming more and more difficult to sleep at night. The Skreechers had started doing their loudest howling and didn't stop until the sun started coming up. It was so difficult to sleep that some of the villagers had started sleeping during the day when it was much quieter. This led to problems of getting what was needed from the shops during the day time.

The general feeling in the village was one of fear and anxiety. No one knew what the Skreechers would do next. Inside the inn, Magg called everyone to consider what might be done to prevent the Skreechers from destroying their lives and the village. She wanted the others to think about what might be done. She told them that she wanted to have a meeting with everyone interested or who might have some ideas. Anyone could come and contribute if they wished.

There was general agreement that it was a good idea to get more input on solutions to the problem. It was hoped that with more minds working on a solution, they would have a better chance of ending the terror of the Skreechers in a shorter period of time.

After eating the delicious breakfast prepared by Aribon, everyone went back to their rooms and talked about what might work. Magg asked for help in getting the word out that anyone could come to the meeting with any ideas they had to stop the destruction and death caused by the monsters.

Matton, Donavan, Jasmine, and Aribon were happy to help. The village was still small, so it wouldn't take long to get the word out. They would meet that afternoon in the inn. Aribon offered to have snacks ready for the people. Magg was grateful that her friends would come through for her like that.

As the volunteers left the inn, they agreed to the areas of the village they would work on. So they split up and talk to everyone they came into contact with. They also went door to door to those that were not out yet.

Magg went to Jarron's house to talk to him and his family about the meeting. Magg knocked on the door and waited until Lucintha opened it and greeted her.

"Hello, Magg. How are you this morning? What's going on?"

Magg smiled and said, "I'm fine, actually. I came to let you and your family know that we've decided to hold a meeting this afternoon to talk about what we can do about the Skreechers."

Just then, Jarron walked into the room. Seeing Magg at the door, he grew concerned. "Is anything wrong? What's happening? Is Raven doing alright?"

Magg told Jarron about the meeting and that Raven was doing better. "We need to find a solution to what the Skreechers have been doing. Can all of you come to the meeting to help us find a solution?"

Jarron was excited to be invited, along with his family, to have a chance to discuss what might be done to stop the destruction done by the monsters. "I will bring my family to the meeting. I sure hope we can come up with a solution, maybe even more than one."

Magg agreed, "Jarron, I really appreciate your enthusiasm and interest in helping. It will also be great to see everyone again. Thank you, see you tonight." At that Magg left them and headed back to the inn.

Matton had walked through the village a decided to stop at the home of Roslin and Karmine. He knocked on the door and it wasn't long before Karmine answered. He was a bit surprised to see Matton on his doorstep. They had never really spoken to one another much.

"Well, hello Matton. What brings you to my humble home this morning?"

Matton was glad to meet and talk with Karmine. He had heard some great stories about his family and wanted to spend some time getting to know them. "Karmine, I am here to invite you and your family to a meeting we're having in the village this afternoon. We want to discuss ways to stop the Skreechers. We believe that the more input we get, the better chance we will have of finding answers. Can you come and join us?"

Karmine was delighted and told Matton so. "We would be honored to come and help. My wife and I have been thinking of ways to defend the village and those we love. Yes, I do have some ideas and so does Roslin. We'll be there."

Matton was pleased to hear that. "Great! I look forward to seeing you all there. I have really good feelings about this meeting. See you then."

Matton walked away with a smile on his face. This meeting was going to be great and he was sure a solution would come out of it. There were a lot of smart people in the village who had helped fight the monsters in the mist. They had pulled together and accomplished what needed to be done. The monsters were no more. Now it was time to do the same with the Skreechers. There had to be a way to accomplish that and soon.

Chapter 23

The town meeting was about to start and many of the villagers were already gathering to discuss a solution to the terror of the Skreechers. The people were in open conversations about what could be done. Many opinions were expressed, some loudly. Before the level of emotions got any higher, Magg stepped into the dining area to start the meeting.

"Welcome everyone, it's so good to see so many of you here to help figure out a way to get rid of the curse of these monsters we call the Skreechers. I would like to start with some rules for those who wish to contribute to the conversation.

First, there will be no insults to any members of this group.

Second, keep all comments kind and civil.

Third, please make your comments thoughtful and helpful to the cause we seek to solve.

I would like to start with Karmine who has an idea for us to consider. Karmine?"

"Thanks for giving me the chance to speak. I have some ideas that I hope will start us thinking of ways to work together to protect our village and especially our children. I've thought about this for many weeks and I would like to share what I have learned.

"I noticed from the conversations I've had with many of you, the thing that helped the most, besides the magic, was that you all worked together. I'm hoping we can do that again. I suggest that we divide into teams to keep watch on the forest and what the Skreechers are doing, whenever safely possible. This way, we can be working together for the benefit of everyone. We would know more about what the Skreechers are doing if we can all work together to warn the village when necessary if there's going to be trouble from the monsters. We can even decide on a place to meet for protection of all. If we decide to use my ideas, we would just need to decide what the groups would consist of and how they would work together. Thanks for listening."

The villagers erupted in applause and cheers for Karmine. Shouts of "great idea, let's get started, you're so smart Karmine, hooray!!"

Magg stepped forward and said, "Great ideas Karmine! Is there anyone else who would like to add to Karmine's suggestion or maybe there's another idea to propose?"

Roslin, Karmine's wife, stepped forward. "I have a suggestion. I'm thinking we need to decide what we'll do with the children when the time comes to fight the Skreechers. There are so many factors involved. What if they attack someone's home, or the inn, or even the barn where the horses are kept? I'm thinking we need to make sure there are more than one exit in each home. That way the children can get out no matter which way the Skreechers try to get in."

Magg hadn't thought of that. "Roslin, that's so important. We must take care of the little ones. They are so important! I can't believe we didn't think of that before."

Magg asked if there were any more suggestions. When there weren't any she said, "Let's have a vote. Those who like this idea, raise your hands. Those who want to have other ideas or add to Karmine's ideas, raise your hands."

No one spoke up, so the vote was taken on both suggestions from Karmine and Roslin. After the vote, it seemed that most of the villagers were ready to use Karmine's and Roslin's ideas and work together to solve the problem of the Skreechers. It was time to get started. The monsters were becoming more aggressive and moving closer to the village. The fear was palpable even now. It was really necessary to start acting on plans for destroying them.

Magg continued, "I suggest that we put villagers close to each together, maybe four homes together, that you get together and discuss what you will do to be watchful of the monsters. Will you get into groups and decide who will be in charge of the assignments we just talked about? Any questions?"

The villagers began talking to their neighbors and tried to decide who would be in each group. It seemed to be going well. The people all seemed excited to be able to do something against the Skreechers. It was good to feel less helpless against the threat.

Just as things were going well, there was a terrible roar from the forest. This was closer than ever. The people panicked. The children started to cry and the adults were fearful of what it could mean that the Skreechers were so much closer to the village.

Magg was just able to quiet everyone down. "Find a place to sit, if you can and let's talk about the situation we have now. Obviously, the Skreechers are moving closer than ever. It's good that we've met together this afternoon so we can think of what to do to stop them.

How do you feel about what we've accomplished so far? Do you have any questions?"

One of the villagers raised his hand to speak. It was Karmine. "I feel like this meeting has brought us together as a village like never before. I'm hoping it means that we will fight for each other and have the courage we all need to stand firm against these monsters."

A cheer went up for Karmine and shouts of "I finally feel like there might be hope for us. You really made us feel like we can do something to protect ourselves, I'm not as afraid as I was before, thank you Karmine."

Another one of the villagers spoke up, "I don't know about the rest of you, but I'm not going to go home tonight. The Skreechers are much too close for comfort. It's getting late and I'm hoping it will be all right for us to stay here in the inn until morning."

The rest of the villagers agreed. It was terrifying with the monsters so close. It was getting late and no one wanted to be out, especially with their families on such a night.

Magg spoke up, "Then let's agree that all of us will spend the night here in the inn. I'm sure we can find a space for everyone. Thanks for the suggestion. It really is a good idea to stay together tonight with the Skreechers so close. It will be better to see what's going on in the morning."

Zarcon and Greta came into the dining hall just then. Zarcon spoke, "I heard the roar of the Skreechers and came to see what was going on here."

Magg said, "Zarcon, we've met to try to find a way to protect each other from the Skreechers. It was going really well until we heard that roar so close to the village."

"We've decided to spend the night together for protection. Everyone is too upset to go home tonight."

"It sounds like you've made good plans. Tell me more about it later. I was just getting ready to retire for the evening. I came to get a snack before bed. Greta needs something too. I'm so glad you've decided to do something as a village. With the Skreechers so active, and apparently getting closer to the village, it will be better to fight than to hide in your homes alone. Courage is something we will all need from here on. If I can help in any way, please let me know. I would rather be a part of the solution."

Magg replied, "Thank you Zarcon for coming to see what was happening. Please stay a while and visit with us. We don't see as much of you as we'd like."

"I think I can stay a bit longer with Greta here. We will sit and talk for a short while."

"I'm so glad. We're right over here at this table." Magg led them to the one in the middle of the room. They all sat down and had just started talking about what needed to be done. Each group was working out what their members could be counted on if there was trouble.

Just then another roar was heard from the forest. Everyone grew quiet. The children started crying again. As they were being comforted, Aribon came out of the kitchen. "I've made a large pot of stew and fresh bread. There's plenty for everyone. It will comfort us all in this time of trouble. What do you say?"

The villagers were in need of comfort and stew was just the thing to help. Everyone found a place to sit near a table. Magg, Donavan, Jasmine, Jarrone, and Matton helped Aribon serve the stew to the villagers. It took their minds off their fears for a while. The children were comforted, too. This bit of normal was good for everyone. The village leaders ate last, when they were sure everyone else got plenty to eat.

Zarcon spoke with Magg quietly at the table, "How are you doing with the spells you found in my Book of Spells?"

"Zarcon, I found three that would work, I'm pretty sure. I haven't practiced them because we've been so busy. Raven still needs care. She's doing much better, but still can't take care of herself completely. That's been a major worry, though others have helped with her care. I was thinking we had to fight the Skreechers only with magic. But, one of the men, Karmine, came to me with an idea to have the villagers help. Zarcon, I can't tell you how that eased my mind. I was thinking it was all on me for a while there."

Zarcon tried to comfort Magg, "You can't do it alone. There are others with powerful magic to help. You can also give some of the villager's assignments to help you with the things they can do. Then work on the spells. That is your most important task right now. The people can only do so much, you must figure out the magic right away. Do you understand what I'm saying?"

"Oh Zarcon, I do. I've been putting off the most important thing. Now it's almost too late. I'll make assignments tomorrow so I can concentrate on the spells. Thank you for the reminder."

"Magg, you can do it. You're much more powerful than you realize. I have every confidence that you will succeed in destroying those Skreechers."

Magg had tears in her eyes as she hugged Zarcon, "Thank you Zarcon for your faith in me. It has restored my confidence immensely."

Zarcon yawned, "I've got to get to bed. It's late for me. Remember what I said."

Greta said, "It's been so good to see you all again. We seem to be living in our own little world a lot of the time. If you need Zarcon, or if I can help with anything, just let us know, please."

"We will do that for sure. You are missed when we don't see you."

After eating some of the stew and talking with their friends, Zarcon and Greta stood from the table and walked toward their room together.

When everyone was finished eating, they were assigned rooms or spaces to spend the night as families. Blankets were placed on the floor for the children and their parents were close by. Soon most of the people were sleeping soundly.

Magg was worried. She needed to start practicing the spells she had found in Zarcon's Book of Spells. Not only that, she needed to make them work and then teach Jarrone and Donavan how to use them. There wasn't time for all that now, but it had to be done, just much faster than she had thought. She was grateful for Zarcon's warning.

Magg and Matton headed to Matton's room for the night. Raven had friends to help her if she needed it. So they could leave and stay in their own little world for a few hours. As Magg was finally able to sleep, Matton stayed awake beside her, knowing how she would worry. He couldn't sleep. The near future was becoming a bit terrifying. He was hoping they would all get through the night safely. But it didn't look very good. The Skreechers were close and they weren't prepared as they should have been. When he did finally sleep, it was with one eye open.

The Skreechers made no more sounds during the night. Most of the villagers woke to a sunny day and birds singing in the trees. It was a good sign that this day might be a good one to prepare as families in their groups to decide the assignments of each member of the group. Even the children would be involved in watching out for each other. It would not be allowed for any of them to go near the forest. They were all aware of how close the Skreechers were to the village. But they didn't know how close the monsters really were. If they knew, they would not leave the inn.

So it seemed good to be naïve as far as knowledge of the monsters whereabouts. They would find out soon enough. Hopefully, they would have enough time to prepare somewhat and Magg would be able to learn her spells well enough to teach them to Donavan and Jarrone. Only time would tell. Time was a very scarce commodity at this moment.

Chapter 24

As the morning progressed and the villagers were spending time together deciding how they would deal with the Skreechers, It was noted that the Skreechers hadn't made any more noise during the night. It was as if they had done enough to scare the people of the village for that night and would begin again later on.

Magg finally had slept since the night was so quiet. Matton woke next to her and was so glad to see her sleeping. He loved her with all his heart. But he was worried about the strain the situation with the monsters was having on her. It had begun to show in her eyes and how she moved a little slower from the weight of all she needed to do in the next few days. Matton was feeling it too. He wanted to train his soldiers in tactics to distract the Skreechers and work with Magg so they could be destroyed with magic. At least, that was his plan. He would have to discuss it with Magg today.

It wasn't long til Magg woke up and was surprised to see Matton watching her. She smiled and kissed him. She was so happy to have found him. He gave her strength to go on when things got too hard for her. It didn't happen often, but when it did, he was there for her, watching her back.

"Matton, I'm going to spend most of the day working on the spells from Zarcon's Book of Spells. I'll just be beside the inn, near the stables. I don't want to take a chance on hurting anyone. Would you mind watching me from a distance in case I get in trouble with the spells? I'm not quite sure how they'll come out or what they'll really do."

"Magg, I would love to do that. I would actually feel better if I could watch out for you. Thanks for asking me. Did you want to start right after breakfast?"

"Yes, the sooner the better. I'm not really sure how much time I have to get the spells right. It will be challenging, I'm sure."

Magg decided to check on Raven before she went to breakfast with Matton. Raven was using the extra room Magg had, so it didn't take any time at all to visit with her for just a moment.

"Raven, it's me, Magg. How are you feeling today? Any better?"

Raven was glad to see Magg. She wanted to talk to her about what was going on with the Skreechers. She said, "Magg, I'm so glad you came to my room. I was wondering how things are going with the monsters. What can I do to help? I'm feeling much better. I would like to start walking around the inn a bit, if you think that would be all right."

Magg smiled at that, "Raven, I'm so glad to hear it! You are more than welcome to move about the inn as you can. Just don't do too much, please. Your wounds are healing nicely, but too much movement might open them up again. You might ask someone to walk with you."

"Great, thanks Magg. I won't be doing much for a while, but I would like to get moving a little. I've been laying around a bit too long for my own sanity."

"You know that you've needed that time to heal, right? No one even thought for a minute that you were being lazy. You don't realize how much the villagers care about you and your welfare. So just relax and concentrate on continued healing. I am glad you want to move around a bit. That's a very good sign of your recovery. I'll let a few of the people here at the inn know that it would be good for them to help you with that. Would that be all right with you?"

"I would really appreciate it, Magg. Thanks for your help."

Magg smiled and left Raven to go eat with Matton. She told Aribon that Raven was ready for some food as well. Aribon knew that meant fresh meat, barely warmed. So he got right to it.

Magg and Matton enjoyed their breakfast practically alone. It was still early and Magg wanted to get started on the spells as soon as she could.

After finishing breakfast, they both went out by the stables so Magg could practice her spells. She had the first spell written on a small piece of paper and kept it in her pocket. She drew it out and read it carefully so she could remember exactly how it went. She had spent some time trying to memorize it over the past two days. She just hadn't had the time to try it out.

She decided to practice on a large rock several feet away. She began the enchantment and focused on the rock. She cast the spell at the rock. Nothing happened for a second or two. Then suddenly the rock started to melt. It slowly grew flatter and spread out as it did so. It began to bubble near the end and started on fire. Matton grabbed a pail of water that he had filled just in case. When he threw it on the melted rock, it became solid again. Only it was flat and smooth, unlike it was originally.

Magg was shocked, she wasn't sure the spell was supposed to do that. Matton was so excited by the result that he was practically jumping up and down. "Magg, look what you've done!"

Magg smiled and said, "Yes, I did didn't I? I'm going to practice that a bit more and then teach it to Jarrone and Donavan. It is exciting isn't it?"

"It sure is!!!"

Next, Magg found an old dead tree to practice on. After casting the spell at the tree it simply flew apart. That one was a bit too dangerous. So Magg decided not to use the spell on living things just yet. Even though the tree was dead, it was still an example of what might happen to a living tree. Her third attempt was on an old metal can that was laying on the ground near the stables.

She cast the spell and as with the rock, the can melted nicely. Matton was ready with a pail of water again and threw it on the can. This time, it sides rose up and formed what looked sort of like a crown. It was actually interesting how it turned out. Both Magg and Matton were pleased with that one. The question was, what would it do to a living thing?

It was time to get Donavan and Jarrone to come and learn this spell with her. Fortunately, both men were in the inn at that time eating breakfast. Matton entered the inn and called to them to come outside. They both hurriedly finished their breakfast and joined Matton in the yard.

Magg spoke, "I'm so glad both of you were close by. I've just learned a spell that I think will be one that will stop the Skreechers in their tracks. Let me show you how it works. See that rock over by the trees there?"

"Yes, we do."

Magg began to say the spell and focused again on the new rock. She cast the spell at the rock and it hit the rock squarely in the middle. It must have been a different kind of rock. Instead of melting, this one expanded until it was twice its normal size. Then suddenly, it collapsed into itself and was half its normal size. Once again, Matton threw water on it. It burst into flames this time. There was some kind of reaction within the rock when water was thrown on it. So Matton, Donavan, and Jarrone kicked dirt on the flames and finally put out the fire.

Donavan yelled, "Well done!"

Jarrone shouted, "I want to do that!!"

Magg told them about how the spell had worked on the other two objects and showed them the result. They were astonished at the flat rock and the thing that looked like a crown.

"So we don't really know how the spell will work on each individual thing, do we?" was Jarrone's concern.

"That's true, but at least we know that it works." Magg tried to calm Jarrone down.

Donavan spoke up, "I guess we'll have to be careful of what we use it on is all."

Jarrone was quiet for a moment, then said, "I still want to learn it. I'm just thinking we need to be a bit cautious with it. I don't want to hit a bunch of innocent people with flying pieces. That would be a major disaster."

Magg understood and said, "You're right Jarrone. We must practice and make sure we have a good idea of what will happen when we use this spell. So now let me teach it to both of you and we'll see what we can figure out together. Does that make sense Jarrone? I want us all to be as comfortable with this spell as we can be."

"That seems reasonable to me now. Thanks Magg for helping me through this issue. I was worried there for a bit that we wouldn't be able to control it as we should."

"Good thinking Jarrone. I probably wouldn't have thought of that." Donavan could see the logic in learning the spell in such a way that they would have a pretty good idea of what would happen when they used it.

Magg wanted to get started teaching. So she said, "Now that that is settled, let's get to work. Are you both ready?"

Jarrone and Donavan both said, "Yes indeed."

Magg was pleased as she started the incantation that both men were very attentive and ready to learn the spell. It didn't take long for them to have it memorized. Now it was time for them to try it out on something stable.

Jarrone picked another rock from just inside the forest and brought it to the side of the stable. Donavan picked an old rusty barrel that he had seen on the way to the stable. It was pretty large, so he was going to have to be careful as he used the spell on it. He brought it to a place near the stable to practice on.

Donavan was the first to try the spell. Magg watched him closely. He said the spell correctly and used the right hand motions. She told him to go ahead and cast the spell to the barrel.

As Donavan cast the spell to the barrel, it hit it with a bang. The metal screamed in protest and began to shrink. At the end of the spell, it flattened and the sides rose up to create a spiral of points that looked like some kind of artwork. It was kind of pretty, actually.

"Wow! That was different than I expected!" Donavan laughed. Jarrone and Magg joined him in the laughter.

"That was a surprise!" Magg was amazed. "I guess you never know what you'll get with this spell."

Now it was Jarrone's turn to try with his rock. He said the spell and used the hand movements and cast the spell to the rock.

As the spell hit the rock, it acted much like the one Magg had tried. It immediately started to melt. But being a larger rock, it swelled up and burst in the middle. The middle expanded and formed what looked like a spire. It was several feet high and came to a point at the top. It was very impressive.

Jarrone stood with his mouth open trying to comprehend what had just happened. The rock still glowed from the heat of the spell. But looking at it made Jarrone almost cry. It was so perfect and straight that no person could have formed it. The magic had done its own work.

Jarrone finally spoke, "Magg, do you see what happened? How could that be? It's a work of art, truly."

Magg smiled at his enthusiasm, "You're right Jarrone. It is a work of art, magic art. This spell is amazing. You both are amazing. Your magic is so creative! I'm impressed with what you each have done here. Now that you've both learned the spell, I'm going to study the other two spells I've selected. I'm going to practice them to see what happens with them as well. I will let you know when I'm ready to show you and teach you each of them. Will that be alright with you?"

"Whatever you think, Magg. We'll be ready anytime you are." Donavan spoke for Jarrone as well. So it was agreed.

As they broke up to go do other things, Magg was excited to think of the progress they had made already. She was ready to start working on the next spell and learn its effects. This was more exciting that she had hoped.

When she got back to her rooms at the inn, she looked in on Raven.

"How are you doing this morning Raven? I've been worrying about you."

"I'm much better today. Aribon took me for a short walk around the inn. It was more difficult than I had expected, though. Some of my stitches are pulling a bit. Some of them itch, which is good. I know I'm healing, but it sure takes a long time. Patience never was one of my virtues. Isn't it amazing how your body can teach patience, whether you want to learn it or not?"

"I have found that to be true myself. You're still young, you will heal much faster than the body does as it ages. Unfortunately, it takes time and all we can do is wait. I'm so glad you are doing so much better, Raven. Did your walk wear you out?"

"I hate to say it, but it did. I've been resting for a while now. But I still want to walk again later today. Aribon said he would go whenever he could get away from the kitchen."

Magg thought for a minute, "Raven would you be comfortable if Greta walked with you?

She's very patient and would be happy to help. I know she's been feeling a bit bored lately. Do you want me to talk to her about it?"

"You know, I never thought about Greta, but that is a perfect suggestion. She doesn't move really fast, so I know she'll be patient with me. If she wants to do it, will you have her come to me so we can talk about what I would like to do?"

"Sounds like a great idea. I'll speak to her later today. Well, I'm really glad you are doing so much better. It was touch and go there for quite a while. You were so very badly hurt."

"And I am so grateful for your good care and all those who have helped me through it. I know I would have died without it. Thank you so much.

I'm feeling the love of the people in this village now."

"That really is something. The people here are very kind, overall. Those who have stepped up to help really do care about you. I'll stop in later today to see how you're doing after your second walk. Just don't overdo it and you'll heal faster."

"Magg, I will try to do as you say. It's just difficult for me to lay around for so many weeks. Now that I'm feeling better, it's even harder. But I will try. Greta is probably the best option for me. She's patient and doesn't move as fast as some of the younger people. And thanks so much for caring about me all this time."

With that Magg left Raven to go speak with Matton. He had left after Jarrone and Donavan were finished practicing the spell. She found him in the garden picking weeds. Aribon was with him and they were having a fun time of it.

Matton looked up and saw Magg watching them. He smiled and stood up from his gardening.

"Hey Aribon, Magg wants to see me. I will come back if possible. It's been great getting the garden in shape.

"Magg! What's going on, my love?"

"Matton, I just realized I haven't seen you since we finished practicing the spell. I spoke with Raven to be sure she's doing well. I'm so glad I found you. Can we go to the inn and talk?"

"I would really like that, Magg. Where should we go?"

"How about the small dining room? No one goes there much. With Raven in the room next to mine, I don't feel like there's really much privacy for serious talks."

"Serious, huh? I can hardly wait to hear what you have to tell me."

They headed for the inn and went to the small dining room together. They sat at the table across from each other. Magg wanted to hold Matton's hands while she spoke to him.

"Matton, I wanted to spend this time with you to talk about something that's been on my mind for a while now. You do know that I love you right?"

"Of course I do. What's this all about?"

"The thing is, I don't want to lose you. I have come to rely on you in so many ways. I really need you because I love you so much. What if we got married really soon?"

"WHAT? Married? Are you sure about that? The thing is, I was hoping to ask you first. I've been feeling so close to you lately that I can't imagine my life without you in it. Of course I'll marry you! Anytime, anywhere, my dear."

Magg was worried there for a minute. Now she just giggled. "Matton, you really are something else. I was afraid at first that you were going to say NO! I'm so relieved that you said yes and that I can make the plans. You did say anytime, anywhere, right?"

"Yes I did. And I meant it too. I would like nothing more than for you to be happy and have a wedding day that you desire. Oh, and I want to help with the preparations, if you don't mind my lady."

Magg and Matton both laughed at that. They were so happy to finally have decided to seal their love officially. It was true that no one was going to be surprised, just relieved that the suspense was over.

Matton thought for a moment, "Magg, this doesn't have anything to do with the Skreechers does it?"

"Well, sort of. I want to be your official wife before all the danger really gets started. Life is too short to just let it go on when there are important things to be done. I feel that this is one of those really important things. Don't you?"

Matton smiled, "Of course I do. I was just checking is all."

Magg moved close to Matton and they held each other for a long while. It felt good to be so close to the one they loved. Things were going to move in a strange direction from this moment on. But for now, they were both very happy, and that's what was important just then.

Magg pulled away and kissed Matton with serious passion. "Magg, what do you want?"

Magg laughed and pulled him into the little room just off the dining area where there was a couch for the staff. She pulled him down and kissed him again. He was on her before she could take a breath. He made love to her with the same passion she had used to kiss him. Magg was panting before Matton could get their clothes off. They enjoyed each other's bodies in a special way that made the promise of marriage even more delicious to think about.

They lay in each other's arms for a while caught in the glow of their love. Magg looked Matton in the eye and said, "Can we do that again?"

"I thought you'd never ask." This time their lovemaking was slower and gentler. There was a lot of moaning going on in that room.

When they finally had enough of lovemaking, they dressed and left the room with knowing smiles and a certain warmth between them. Aribon happened to walk by at that moment and took one look at their faces and started to giggle. There was no hiding what had been going on in that little room. Magg and Matton started to giggle, too. It was their little secret. But maybe not such a secret. Anyone looking at the two of them would know what was going on between them.

Chapter 25

Magg and Matton went to her room so that Magg could study the next spell to learn and teach to Donavan and Jarrone. She had a good feeling about this one. She was sure it would destroy the Skreechers quicker than the last one she had learned.

So Matton decided to go back out to the garden to work with Aribon, if he was still wanting to do so. Matton caught Aribon in the hall.

"Hey, Aribon, are you still wanting to work on the garden this morning? I think there's still enough daylight to get something done."

Aribon smiled and said, "I would in fact like to get some more weeding done on the garden. It will be needed really soon, I'm sure. We need the plants to produce as much as possible before the fight starts, you know?"

"Good thinking, Aribon. Let's get working. We probably don't have a lot of time."

Meanwhile, Magg was reading up on the new spell. She was memorizing the steps involved and it was looking like an extremely complicated and powerful spell. As she studied it, she was becoming more and more wary of using it. If not done properly, it could potentially burn down the entire forest. Magg debated learning it at all. She was also concerned about teaching it to Donavan and Jarrone. She decided to talk to Zarcon about it before she took any further action on it. So she went straight to Zarcon and Greta's room.

She knocked on Zarcon's door. It was only a few seconds before Greta answered with a smile. "What's going on Magg? Come on in and relax a while."

Magg smiled back and responded, "I came to talk to Zarcon about the new spell I've been studying. Is he good to talk with me?

"Actually, he would like nothing better. Come and sit down. I'll go get him for you."

Greta left the room and went to the bedroom to get Zarcon. He was reading at his desk, but was glad of the interruption. He thanked Greta and went to greet Magg.

"Magg, you came to see me about one of the spells you found in my Book of Spells?"

"Yes. I found one that seems a bit too powerful for us right now, but I need your input about it."

"Which spell is it, Magg?"

"It's the one called "the Bomb". It struck me as funny at first, but after studying the spell itself, I decided maybe that was accurate. I fear if we use it incorrectly, we might start the whole forest on fire."

"Can you explain the spell to me? What is the spell exactly?"

"It starts with humming and it's very strange. I started with the humming and the floor started to shake. I stopped immediately because it scared me so much. The rest of the spell was using very powerful words and motions that I've never used before."

"Show me the motions, please."

After a quick demonstration, Zarcon called a halt to it. He could faintly remember one of the wizards using it long ago. It was indeed dangerous. That wizard had done something wrong and had burned his castle to the ground and everyone in it. He told Magg about it and told her he was confident that she could do it properly.

But Magg was terrified after hearing about the use of it. Even by an experienced wizard, the spell was extremely dangerous as she had feared.

"Zarcon how can I use something that dangerous? Should I even try its use? I'm not comfortable with anyone else trying it."

Zarcon thought for a minute, "I think you are right not to teach it to anyone else. But if you learn it and can do it well, it could be the one spell we'll need if things get really bad. It will be our secret weapon when all else fails. I'm assuming we won't need it, but if we do…"

"Oh Zarcon, do you really think I can handle it safely and not burn the whole village and forest to the ground?"

"As I have told you many times, Magg. You are far more powerful than you realize. I totally believe in your ability with this powerful spell. If done properly, it could destroy all the Skreechers at once. But that would only be in a case of extreme need. I want you to learn this spell and try to rein it in so that it will have a controlled effect. We don't want others to see how powerful you really are just yet."

Magg sighed, "I understand Zarcon. I appreciate the warning and support. There's a clearing just down the road a bit. I'll go there to practice. I'll have Matton come with me to provide help if I get into trouble with it. What do you think?"

For the first time Zarcon smiled and said "You are wise, Magg. I think having Matton close by is a good idea. He'll keep you safe. Come back and tell me about it when you've learned more. I would love to be involved."

"Thank you Zarcon. I think I'll get on it today. I've memorized the spell, so it would be a good time to work on it. I know Matton will help me. I'll keep you informed as my progress moves forward."

Magg gave Zarcon and Greta a hug and left to practice the Bomb.

She found in the garden helping Aribon pull weeds and plant more seeedlings.

Magg called to him, "Matton, can you come with me while I practice this new spell I've learned?"

Matton looked up from the garden at her. He was always glad to see Magg. "Sounds interesting. Aribon, would you mind if I went with Magg now? I kind of hate to leave you when we just got started."

Aribon was a bit disappointed that they would have to stop working in the garden now, but he understood that Magg needed his help. "Go ahead Matton. I can finish up here."

"Thanks Aribon. So, Magg tell me a little about this spell you want to practice."

"Well, I've studied it and it's dangerous, so I need you to be there in case I get into trouble."

"You know I love to watch you practice. Now is a good time to go try it out."

They headed for the clearing where Magg wanted to practice. They walked toward the end of the village, then turned to go down the road. They were very careful to watch for any Skreechers that might be roaming around the area. They could be anywhere. As they drew closer to the clearing, Magg spotted one of the Skreechers in the forest near the clearing. The Skreecher saw them and started running toward them. Magg was still thinking about the new spell and without further thought, started to hum. The ground started shaking as the humming grew stronger. Magg began the motions to cast the spell quickly. The Skreecher was nearly on top of them when she cast the spell at it.

She yelled at Matton to get down. The spell hit the Skreecher in the chest.

Magg and Matton watched in horror as the Skreecher blew up in a huge ball of blue flame. It started with a hole in his chest and opened up with fire. The fire finally consumed the Skreecher and the last they heard was a scream like no other. It was a horrible experience.

Matton looked up as the Skreecher was consumed by the blue fire. "All he could do was shout Hallelujah! He had been so frightened that when it was over he started to laugh. Then Magg joined him. They looked at each other and kept laughing. It was a release from all the terror of the Skreecher running at them. They had been very close to death at that moment. Magg's quick thinking saved them just in time. So it was either laugh or cry, they laughed.

Magg went to Matton and clung to him. She was trembling from the shock of what had happened. Matton held her until they could both stop laughing. But then they were holding each other and crying. It had been such a terrible experience for both of them.

There was only one downside. When the Skreecher was turned to ash, there was a terrible smell. Magg and Matton started running from the spot and made it to the center of the clearing. The shock of being alive and whole, was too much. They both fell to the ground and lay there for a while so they could recover from it all. Matton finally looked over at Magg and stroked her hair. She opened her eyes and looked up at Matton.

"Magg, you are amazing! That Skreecher had us! You saved us from a horrible death. I'm so glad you had that new spell handy."

They both started laughing again. Magg said, "I'm really glad I did it right! Otherwise we would be as crispy as the Skreecher. The whole area might have been charred."

Matton then realized how close they truly had been to death. He was sweating and started trembling again. Magg noticed and held him. They finally calmed down and were able to get back up and return to the village. Magg didn't want to practice the spell any longer. Once was more than enough experience.

It became obvious to Magg and Matton that the new spell would definitely be effective against the Skreechers. The problem once again, was the power and fear to use it. It would have to be something of a desperate situation to make Magg use it again. It was fortunate that she cast the spell in a controlled manner. She only killed the Skreecher. She didn't start any big forest fires. Neither Magg nor Matton realized that fact until much later in the day.

Magg and Matton finally got back to the village and decided it would be a good time to report to Zarcon how it went that morning. They walked to Zarcon's room and knocked on the door. Greta once again opened the door with a smile.

"Welcome you two! I assume you want to see Zarcon. I'll go get him right now."

Magg replied, "Thank you Greta."

Greta stepped away to find Zarcon. He was resting on his bed, but not asleep. When Greta walked in and Zarcon turned his head and smiled at her. "What is it Greta, my love?"

"Magg and Matton are here to talk to you. Magg looked anxious to see you."

"Oh, yes, she did want to tell me about a spell she was working on. I assume that's what it's all about. Let's go see."

As Zarcon and Greta walked back into the entry room, Magg's face lit up in a smile of relief. "Zarcon, you won't believe what happened today!"

"Oh my! Tell me all about it, Magg. I've been waiting to hear from you."

"Well, Matton and I went out to the clearing I told you about. We were just getting to the clearing when we saw a Skreecher running toward us from the edge of the forest. We were entirely shocked. All I knew was the new spell. I automatically started humming. As I hummed louder the ground started shaking. I started the motions and sent the spell to the Skreecher just in time. He was so close to us, we could see his red eyes.

"The spell flew to his chest and burned a hole in it. The flames were a bright blue. The Skreecher's chest burned a moment, then he was burned to ash. There was a terrible smell at that point."

Matton spoke up, "Magg was wonderful. She cast that spell as if she did it all the time. The horror of that Skreecher coming at us so fast was more than I could deal with. When it was over, I just started to laugh. I think I was in shock and didn't know how to react. When I looked at Magg, she started laughing too. It took us a while to recover from that experience. The smell sent us running away, but when we got away, we fell over in exhaustion. We just rested for quite a while. We finally got up and headed back to the inn."

Magg added, "Zarcon, I could hardly wait to tell you about our experience. The important thing is, the spell worked wonderfully. But as we talked about before, it will be saved for an extreme situation. We can't allow anything to go wrong with it. I really think that I should be the only one to use it. If that changes I will teach it to Donavan and Jarrone. What do you think about all this Zarcon?"

Zarcon was stunned by her tale. He was impressed, and said so.

"Magg, this is truly good news for the most part. I'm so very grateful that you performed the spell with such accuracy. I do agree that the fewer hands that know that particular spell right now, the better. I think you are very strong to have done such a complicated spell in the face of such a dangerous situation. It proves what I've been saying for so long. You are special, my friend."

Magg blushed at the compliment. "Thank you Zarcon. I will not disappoint you, I promise."

"Of that I am certain, Magg. You continue to impress me. We will talk again in the morning." With that, Zarcon and Greta sent them on their way.

Zarcon was encouraged by Magg's control of the spell she just used. He was still a bit concerned about the Skreechers and what they might be up to. He was sure it was nothing good.

Of that we can be sure...

Chapter 26

Raven had started walking with Greta the past few days. Greta seemed to know just how fast to walk with her. Raven could feel herself getting stronger. It was a slow process, but she was glad to be feeling better. Greta was always so kind and patient with her. Raven had never had anyone treat her so kind in her life.

As they walked this day, Raven said, "Greta, you are so kind to me and patient. I very much appreciate our walks. I'm feeling so much stronger now. Your kindness is part of why I'm doing so much better. I don't feel threatened by you and that is such a relief to my soul."

Greta had tears in her eyes as she responded, "Raven, it has meant a lot to me to be needed by you. I do enjoy getting to know you as well. It gets me out of our room and out from under Zarcon's studies. He's always trying to find another way to defeat the Skreechers. I'm so glad you survived the attack. Everyone in the village has been so worried about you. I'm glad I can report that you're doing well now. I think it will only be a few more days and you'll be needing to walk with Aribon again. You're getting stronger than I can keep up with."

Greta smiled as she spoke that last bit. She really had enjoyed being with Raven. She was so different from anyone else she had known in her life. She would miss their chats and the nice walks they had had.

Raven and Greta both knew that it was very important that Raven get well and strong. She would be needed to help fight the Skreechers very soon. Hopefully not too soon, however.

As they walked around the village, they enjoyed stopping and visiting the other villagers as they passed. They also enjoyed looking in the stores that lined the village square. They expecially enjoyed the dress shop. Jarrone's sister Revinia was working there now making some very pretty dresses. She had started working there after she made Raven's dresses. They had turned out so nice that the other women in the village were interested in them now. The shop was very popular among the villagers as a result of her talent. As Raven and Greta walked near the shop, they decided to look inside and shop for a few minutes.

They both loved the dresses there and wanted to come back when Raven was stronger.

Raven began to feel tired after shopping so Greta walked her back to her room with Magg. Greta helped her to her bed so she could lay down for a rest.

"Thank you Greta for your help and patience. We went a bit farther this time, didn't we? I think the little bit of shopping we did really wore me out."

Greta smiled, "We did indeed. I hope it didn't tire you too much. I think it's good to push ourselves a little. What do you think?"

"I enjoyed making myself walk a bit farther. It did wear me out, but in a good way. I think if we do that once a week, just so I can adjust to it, would be great for me."

"Well, I shall be going back to Zarcon now. Do you want to go again later today?"

"I'll let you know if I'm up to it. Will that be alright?"

"Absolutely, just send someone to get me. Bye for now."

On the way out the door, Magg came walking in. "Hello, Greta, how are things going with Raven's progress?"

"She's doing really well. We went a bit farther than usual today and she's a bit tired, but she did well. She may want to go again later on. Will you let me know if she does?"

"I will, Greta. And thank you for helping with Raven. I know she really appreciates it."

"Truthfully, I'm so grateful to have the chance to help her. It's given me purpose and I enjoy her company. We've become friends through it all. Thanks for asking me to help."

"Greta, you are invaluable around here, as is Zarcon. We really need both of you to feel whole as a community and friends. So, I thank you once again."

Greta smiled in gratitude as she walked out of the room. She was very happy to be able to do something worthwhile;

When she got back to the room she shared with Zarcon, she noticed the silence and became concerned about Zarcon. She called his name and ran to his office door. As she opened the door, she saw that Zarcon was slumped over his desk and didn't look good.

"Zarcon, can you hear me? Zarcon answer me!"

Zarcon moved a bit and turned his head to look at Greta. "Who are you?" he said.

Grets's heart broke in two. "Zarcon, it's me, Greta. What's wrong? What happened?"

Zarcon started coming to himself and realized it was Greta asking about him. "Oh Greta, I'm so sorry.

I was working here on finding some other spells for Magg when I suddenly felt a terrible pressure in my head. I guess I passed out from the pain. I think I'm alright now."

Greta held him for a moment then said, "I'm going to go get Magg. She'll know what to do."

"I hate to bother Magg, she's got so much on her mind right now."

"Zarcon, you know she would be upset if I didn't tell her we need her. So come and lay on the bed while I go get her."

So Greta helped Zarcon to the bed and made sure he was comfortable before she left to find Magg. She rushed to Magg's room and knocked on the door. Magg had just been talking with Matton. She got up from her chair and answered the door.

"Greta, what is it?"

"It's Zarcon, I found him hunched over his desk just now. He said he had a bad headache and must have passed out from the pain. The worst part is, he didn't know me at first. It broke my heart. Can you come now?"

"Of course, maybe Matton should come too. He's stronger and can help if he's needed."

They all three headed for Greta and Zarcon's room in a hurry. When they got there, Zarcon was asleep on the bed. He didn't react when they called his name. Magg stepped close to the bed and shook Zarcon gently.

"Zarcon, can you hear me? Please, just say yes."

Zarcon finally opened his eyes and looked around like he didn't know where he was. Greta came closer and said, "Zarcon, it's me, Greta. What happened? Are you alright?"

Zarcon opened his mouth to speak, but nothing came out. He started to panic and looked around wildly for help. When he saw Greta and Magg, he calmed down a little.

Magg felt his forehead for fever, but there was none. Greta tried to comfort him as best she could. She got a damp cloth to wipe his face and spoke to him softly. Zarcon looked at Greta with so much love. It was almost like he was saying goodbye to her. Greta burst into tears and held him in her arms. This could not be happening. They had been through so much together. She sent calming magic to him. He seemed to respond by relaxing his body.

Magg was greatly concerned. She used a bit of magic to see if she could do anything to heal whatever it was that caused the problem. She found a broken blood vessel in his brain that could not be fixed. It had already done its damage. There was nothing she could do but make him comfortable. She sent Matton to get Donavan and Jasmine, Jarrone and his sisters, Aribon, and Raven came when everyone left in such a hurry. She knew something bad had happened.

Soon everyone was there in Zarcon's room wishing him well and hoping he would recover. Magg finally told them quietly that he would not recover and he might not last the night. Soon everyone was crying quietly. Zarcon was so valuable to them all. They could not imagine not having him around. Greta kept holding Zarcon and talking to him softly about their life together and how much she loved him all those years. He looked at her with tears in his eyes and lay still.

Zarcon was gone.

Greta held him and rocked back and forth. "No Zarcon, you cannot leave me like this. No! Please, no!" She was sobbing as she continued to hold Zarcon.

Magg came to Greta and held her close and rocked her. It was terrible for all of them. Her grief was beyond anything they had witnessed before. It was as if with Zarcon's death, part of Greta was gone as well. They stayed with her until she could regain some control of her grief. It was so hard for her to do so.

She finally pulled away from Magg and let Zarcon go as well. Donavan helped her lay him carefully on the bed and cover him with his blanket. She let Magg hold her again for comfort she desperately needed. Jasmine joined Magg, then the others gathered around Greta and they held each other in sorrow.

Donavan took it especially hard. He had known Zarcon since before the Wolf Wars and the witches and the Blue Orb. He had been Donavan's friend and mentor for so long that he couldn't fathom not having him around to talk with and share life's adventures with. They all knew Zarcon was aging and was getting weaker all the time. It's just that he wasn't supposed to die this day! How could that be?

Donavan was overcome and stepped out of the room to cry on his own. He didn't want the others to see him break down like this. Jasmine saw him walk out and waited a few minutes before she joined him. When she found him, she just held him close and let him cry on her shoulder until he was able to calm down. It was a long while before that happened. Donavan had truly loved Zarcon.

Magg and Matton also stepped out of the room to ask Aribon if he would get a couple of the soldiers to come and move Zarcon's body to one of the empty rooms in the inn. He would be wrapped in a sheet and laid to rest for a day or two so the villagers would be able to say their goodbyes.

As the rest of the group began to leave for the evening, Raven went to Greta and said, "Greta, would it be alright if I stay with you for a few days? I don't want you to be alone now. I know it will be really hard for a while and I want to be here for you."

Greta started crying again at Raven's kindness. "Oh Raven, it would be so nice if you stayed with me. I fear being alone just now."

So Raven went to her room and brought her clothes and a few things so she could spend time with Greta. Losing Zarcon was a terrible shock and she shouldn't be alone.

Magg learned of Raven's plan and was happy that she had stepped up to help Greta. It was such a good thing that she and Greta had become such good friends in the past few days.

Magg and Matton made sure that Zarcon's body was taken care of and that Greta was going to be alright before they went back to Magg's room for the night. It had been a very eventful day and they were glad to call an end to it for now. Zarcon's death was going to make it difficult to sleep. His wisdom and experience would be badly missed. Magg had grown to depend on him when any question came to mind. Right now she was feeling at a loss.

She could not guess what tomorrow might bring. It would likely be even more eventful. With the Skreechers, you never knew.

That night, as the villagers tried to sleep, the Skreechers were howling and making so much noise that it was really difficult to sleep for anyone. The monsters did sound a bit closer and that made the people even more nervous and upset by their noise. Knowing that Zarcon was gone was another reason sleep did not come for most of them.

Chapter 27

Morning came with an angry gray sky and a feeling of sorrow as word of Zarcon's death was learned by the villagers. Jarrone and his family were affected badly. They had come to the village to meet Zarcon and his friends. Now Zarcon was gone and it left a hole in the fabric of their lives.

Zarcon had truly been a vital part of the life of the village and its people. He had been instrumental in helping to eliminate the Mist Monsters and the Black Wind from the world. He had nearly died from poison thrown at him from the monster Neberon. If it hadn't been for Jarrone and his magic, he would have surely died then.

Zarcon had spent most of his life with Greta. The people of the village were also worried about Greta and how she would survive without Zarcon. They had been inseparable most of their lives. So the sorrow was felt for Greta as well. She must be included even more in what goes on in the village so she would continue to feel a part of it.

When Magg was awake, she felt lost. Without Zarcon, she didn't know for sure where to start. She knew she needed to learn the last spell against the Skreechers, but she struggled to begin the process. Her grief was overwhelming just now. But she also knew that she couldn't take a day to grieve. The Skreechers were moving in so fast now. She must be certain that the villagers were following the plan set forth by Karmine.

She decided that going to the families in the village would be a good place to start. She would talk to as many as she could to see what the progress was. They were asked to work together in small groups to work out a plan of defense for their section of the village. Each family would be responsible for an aspect of that defense. It would be good to know what was being planned. She knew Matton would help. She would also ask Jasmine and Donavan to canvas another part of the village. It shouldn't take long to canvas the whole village this morning.

Now that she had a plan, she felt better about moving forward with the day. She got out of bed and woke Matton so she could talk to him about her plans. She didn't have any trouble waking him. She just kissed his face and ear. He moaned and opened his eyes. He smiled brightly and reached for her to hold her close. Magg let him hold her for a few minutes before starting the conversation of the morning.

"Matton, can we talk about what I would like us to do today? I would rather stay here with you and snuggle, but there is much to be done before we have to face the Skreechers."

At the mention of the Skreechers, Matton grew serious and knew he must listen to what she was thinking. It would be even more important to know how to deal with the monsters now that they were getting closer and more aggressive all the time.

"Matton, what I want to do this morning is to talk to the villagers and find out about their plans for defending the village from the Skreechers. I'm hoping they are using the plans set out by Karmine at our meeting. They must be ready to defend their homes and families as a group. We can't do it all with magic, that's for certain. Can you help me with that?"

Matton didn't even have to think about it, "Of course Magg, when do you want to start and are there others we need to have help us?"

"Yes, I want to talk with Jasmine and Donavan and also see if Jarrone can help. I think we can cover the villagers in the course of this morning. What do you think?"

"I like the idea, Magg. Where should we start? Should we talk to Jasmine and Donavan first? Then we can head for Jarrone's home to get him involved, too. Will that work, my darling?"

"Good thinking, Matton. Let's do that. Jasmine and Donavan are just down the hall from here."

Once Magg and Matton were dressed and ready to go, they headed out to Jasmine and Donavan's room. Matton knocked on the door.

Jasmine answered the door and smiled when she saw Magg and Matton. "It's good to see you two! What brings you here this morning? Is everything all right?"

Magg spoke up, "Actually, we're going to talk to the people in town to find out how the plans Karmine talked about at our meeting are going. We were wondering if you and Donavan would mind helping us with it. I've been thinking we need to see what the villagers are doing and maybe suggest some things to help them. Can you go this morning?"

"Let me go ask Donavan what he thinks. Come in and I'll go find him. He's probably in the next room studying."

Jasmine called out to Donavan and asked him to come talk with Magg and Matton. He came into the room immediately. "What's going on Magg? Can we help you with something?"

"As a matter of fact, you can. Would you and Jasmine help us talk with the villagers about their plans for defending their homes and families? We need to know if they need any help with planning."

"Sounds good to me. Do we start now?"

"If we can, that's the plan." Magg smiled in gratitude for their willingness to help. But truth be told, she knew they would. Jasmine and Donavan were always ready to get involved.

The four of them discussed which part of town to start their enquiries. Once decided, they left the inn and began their questioning of fellow villagers.

Raven was with Greta to help her through her grief. She loved Greta and didn't want her to be alone. She was really glad she had decided to help. Greta cried all night and was still tearful in the morning. Raven had been able to hold her and comfort her as much as she could.

"Raven, I'm so glad you stayed with me. I can't believe Zarcon is gone. I'm in such pain at his loss. It feels like half of my heart has been ripped out of my chest. Zarcon has been my whole life and reason for living. How do I carry on without him?"

Raven had been crying, too. She said, "Greta, I can't imagine such a loss. I've always stayed away from men because they usually want to hurt me. I'm not sure I will ever find that kind of love. You and Zarcon were so lucky to have had each other for so many years."

Greta said, "Raven, you're young, there is still a really good chance that you'll find a good man to love you. Just remember, if it's to be, it will be in its own time. I do want you to know that you really are a good friend to me, Raven. I'm so glad you can stay with me. I would hate to be left alone at a time like this. And I am so exhausted from all that's happened. I'm going to lie down for a while. Will you please stay close by in case I need you?"

"Greta, I wouldn't leave you. I can be here to help you for as long as you need me." Greta smiled and went into her bedroom to rest. She fell asleep from exhaustion right away. It had been a terrible shock to lose Zarcon so suddenly. She didn't know how she would be able to cope now that he was gone. She didn't realize how strong she really was.

Raven was able to sit quietly and rest. She was nearly as tired as Greta. It had been a long night. The night was not as bad as it could have been since Raven was mostly nocturnal. Her days and nights had been switched around since her injuries. But she still had a hard time staying up all day long. She was hoping that soon her wounds would be healed and she could venture out at night. Yet she realized it would be very dangerous to do so. The Skreechers wouldn't let her off so easy next time. She would be killed immediately. She had learned a few things about them from her experience fighting them. She knew she would have to tell Magg about that very soon. But for now, she would rest.

Magg and Matton and Jasmine and Donavan were making great progress interviewing the villagers. Jarrone had joined them and started talking with the villagers on the end of town that he lived in. He had stopped at Karmine's house to see if he had time to help. Karmine had been happy to join him. Since they both lived closest to the forest end of town, it was doubly important for them to be sure the other villagers were prepared to defend their homes and families. Everyone had a job to do.

Jarrone told Karmine about Zarcon as they walked through the village. He was devastated to learn of Zarcon's death. He and his family had come to Anakik to meet Zarcon and find out if the two boys they had adopted had magic. There was a school of magic being set up just on the edge of town, but with the Skreechers, no one had dared go there. It was just too risky. So some of the important things in the area were halted until the monsters could be stopped or destroyed.

No one knew when that would happen, but it had to happen. If they didn't get rid of the Skreechers, those monsters would eventually kill everyone in town. There was also the very real danger of the Skreechers spreading to the rest of the world. So, right now things were looking pretty grim. Whatever they could do as a village, they had to do immediately. The Skreechers could not be allowed to spread to other villages.

Magg and Jarrone were aware that the Skreechers had come from other parts of the area. But it was looking like they were gathering around Anakik. There seemed to be more of them now. It was hoped that when they were destroyed here that they would be gone forever. At least that is what they were hoping.

Jarrone and Karmine were checking with each of the houses along the edge of the village. All the families they checked were doing really well with their plans and working together with their neighbors.

As Karmine was walking to the next house, he noticed a woman and some children leaving in the wagon in a big hurry. Karmine wondered what that was all about.

When he got to one of the homes close to the forest, Karmine knocked on the door. The door slowly opened and he found a large man with terrible wounds all over his body laying on the floor. He was bleeding badly and obviously needed help. Karmine shrank back in shock on seeing him in such a state. Blood seemed to be everywhere.

"Sir, what has happened to you and why have you not asked for help? You're pretty close to the village. We have ways of healing such wounds. Are you the only one hurt in this house?"

The man was laying on his back near the door and could hardly answer the questions. He finally said in a raspy whisper, "I went out this mornin' to hunt some food for ma family. One of those Skreechers caught me just as I was walkin' back home. He caught ma leg and ripped it badly before I could get away. He scratched me up really bad. I finally hit him with a tree branch that was close at hand. I guess I hit him hard enough to make him unconscious or at least so he would let go of me.

"I was able to hobble home after that. I have no other family here now. As soon as ma wife saw me limp in the door, she screamed and packed up the kids and went to Synkana. She said she'd be there until the Skreechers were all dead and not before. She just left, but she wouldn't even get help for me first. I think it was too much for her. She's been terrified for a long while. So I'm here alone and wounded with no help. I'm too hurt to go anywhere anyway."

Karmine was appalled. "I'm so sorry sir. I may have seen her leaving just now. How long have you been like this? Never mind, I'll call my friend Jarrone and we'll get you help right now." Karmine left the man just long enough to call to Jarrone.

"Jarrone, come quick! We have a wounded man here that needs help right now!"

Jarrone was just at the house next door and came running. He also brought the town carpenter, Murdon, who lived in the house he was visiting. They got to the door and saw the poor man with blood all over him and laying on the floor.

Jarrone went to the man and touched him with his magic to see if he could do anything to stop or slow the bleeding. "Karmine, I need some clean water and cloths to wipe up the blood. I can't tell where the blood ends and his wounds begin. He's lost a lot of blood as it is. I've started the healing of the worst of his wounds, but it's going to take more magic than I have to do it all. We need Magg or Donavan to come quickly."

Karmine brought some clean water and cloths for Jarrone, then he left to find Donavan if he could.

Jarrone stayed and wiped the blood off the man's body as best he could. It was difficult because he was still bleeding. Jarrone also kept working on him with his magic trying to stop the bleeding. He also sent a spell that would ease the pain. The man seemed to relax after a bit of time.

Karmine was able to catch Donavan and Jasmine who were not far away. They both came running as soon as Karmine told them what they had found.

"How long ago was he injured? Do you have any idea? Is he bleeding badly still? What has Jarrone done to help him?" Donavan was almost panicking from worry.

Karmine answered with all he knew about the man, "It's kind of crazy, as I walked up to the house, I saw a woman and some children in a wagon rushing out of town. Then, I knocked on the door just a few minutes ago. The door was open and I could see that he was in big trouble. He said one of the Skreechers had caught him just as he was returning home from hunting for food for his family. But he said his wife took one look at him and left with the kids and wouldn't even get help for him. I guess she was not thinking clearly. It's a sad case for sure."

Jasmine was shocked to hear that his family left him injured and didn't even try to get help. "The poor man. It's a miracle that you and Jarrone were there when he needed you most."

Donavan ran ahead to see what he could do to help Jarrone. As he walked in the door, he could see that the man was in very bad shape. "Jarrone, what can I do to help?"

Jarrone beckoned him over and asked him to help him heal the man. "His wounds are too many and too deep for me to heal them all alone. If we work together, we can surely save his life."

"I'm sure between the two of us, we can heal the man. Jarrone, start the healing spell, and I'll be ready to start working when you do."

So they both put their hands on the man's body as Jarrone spoke a healing spell over the man. The magic of both Jarrone and Donavan was really powerful. They finally had to stop because the man was heating up from the work of the magic. It did become clear that the magic was working. His wounds were closing up and he was no longer bleeding. They still needed to put bandaging on a couple of his really deep wounds to be sure they would not open up again. Donavan realized that more magic might be required later on if things didn't heal properly. He was fairly confident that it wouldn't be necessary, but he wanted to be sure.

Jasmine had followed Donavan and stood beside the man when she saw him and how badly he was injured. She was able to watch the magic working on him. As the magic took effect, she was so excited to see it work so quickly. She was holding the man's hand as the magic took effect. When it was obvious that the magic had done its work, she said, "Sir, how are you feeling? Can I get you anything? And what is your name?"

The man finally opened his eyes and smiled. "I feel much better, thank you. What a horrible experience that was! I hurt so bad, I didn't think I'd survive it, to feeling so much better in just a couple of minutes. I'm still a bit sore and weak from losing all that blood. I could use a glass of water. And, ma name is Horan. I've lived here in Anakik all ma life. Ma family and I never did much with the village. We just kept to ourselves. Maybe that was a mistake. Ma wife didn't have any friends, neither did the kids. We have two boys and three girls. But they're all gone now. Ma wife took them away when she saw me so injured by the Skreecher. She was very afraid and being alone here was not helping. I should have done more to help her feel part of things here."

Jasmine tried to comfort him, "I'm so sorry this has happened to you. I know looking back sometimes we can see how we could have done things differently. But it isn't comforting right now. What will help now, I think, is to rest and heal up from the shock of it all. Would you like to come to the inn so that others can help you if you need anything?"

Horan said, "I think that might be a good idea for a little while. I'm not comfortable in ma home just now. I'm feeling a bit fearful of the Skreechers coming for me in the night."

"That could happen, I'm afraid." Jarrone was thinking of what had happened to Raven. "What we can do is take you to the inn for a while until things settle down a little. We'll make sure there's a room available for you when we get there. Does that work for you right now?"

Horan thought about it for a few seconds. He was nervous to go into town. He had lived in Anakik all his life and had stayed away. Finally, he said, "I'm nervous about being in town. I've not spent a lot of time there. But I would rather go there than to stay here in ma cabin alone."

Jarrone smiled, "I'm glad you decided to come. I would feel much better with you at the inn where there is help for you, than to leave you here in danger."

So Karmine, Donavan, and Jarrone helped him stand and try to walk to the door. It soon became apparent that Horan was not able to make it to the inn without more help. Donavan stepped up and suggested they make a travois for him.

Karmine and Murdon went out to the yard and found some rather long, straight tree limbs. They removed the twigs and any rough spots from the limbs. Then they brought them inside and tied the top ends together. They realized they needed a lot more support between the poles. Horan told them there was some rope in the shed outside his house.

Murdon went out to look for the rope in the shed and he found it by the door. Just as he was leaving the shed, he heard some rustling in the bushes a few yards away. He ran for the house as fast as he could, running for his life. He just made it to the door when one of the Skreechers burst out of the forest and was after him. He started screaming for Donavan to open the door. Murdon made it inside just as the Skreecher was about to grab him. The Skreecher hit the door and almost broke it down. The monster seemed to detect the use of powerful magic from inside the house. He looked around and ran back to the forest in fear. Everyone gave a huge sigh of relief that it was gone.

Murdon was terrified. "That was way too close for me. It's the first time I've been so terrified. Here's the rope." At that, he grew very pale and passed out on the floor before anyone could catch him.

Jasmine and Jarrone ran to him and helped him come back to consciousness. Jasmine brought him a glass of water when he seemed to regain consciousness and said, "Murdon, you're safe now. We've got to get the travois ready for Horan and get him to the inn before anything else happens here. Do you need to rest a few minutes while we get Horan ready to go?"

Murdon opened his eyes while Jasmine was talking to him. He felt a bit embarrassed that he had fainted. He thought himself to be stronger than that. "Did I just pass out? I'm so embarrassed! I feel pretty well now. I'd like to lay here for a few minutes to get my blood flowing properly again."

"That's fine. We'll make sure you're ready when we are about to leave with Horan. So relax until then."

Murdon was a slim man with broad shoulders and a thick black hair and a beard that came almost to his belly. He seemed to be really strong, but he was so frightened by the Skreecher that his mind couldn't cope with the threat. He had just seen Horan and how badly he was wounded and that was what started him down the road to passing out.

Karmine made sure that Murdon was going to be fine, then he began to lash the rope to make the travois secure. He worked quickly and soon it was ready to carry Horan. Karmine asked him if he was ready to leave.

Horan said he was very happy to be leaving his home of so many years. The effect of recent events had convinced him that he needed to leave it and the memories behind. He was carefully helped to the travois and covered with a heavy blanket. There was another blanket under him. He seemed fairly comfortable as Karmine and Donavan pulled him out the door and headed for the inn.

As the group moved out of the house, they were all watching for the Skreechers or any chance of more trouble. Jasmine was especially observant since she wasn't helping with the travois. Jarrone made sure the path to the inn was as clear as it could be as they moved closer to town. The tension was thick as they left the house. They all seemed jumpy at any sound nearby.

Things seemed to have quieted down since the attacks. Murdon had joined them just as they were about to go out the door. Jasmine had made sure he was ready to walk to the inn. He followed the travois in case he was needed to help pull it. Horan was a large man, after all. Donavan and Karmine were going fairly fast as they needed to escape the area of the attacks. They were both strong men and fairly young.

Jarrone decided to help by adding a bit of magic to the travois to make it easier to pull. He may have over projected his spell because Karmine and Donavan nearly fell down when the travois was suddenly much easier to pull.

"What happened? Jarrone, did you do some kind of magic just now? You could have warned us first! We both about fell down! It could have hurt Horan besides! Next time you think it's a good idea to make things easier, please advise us so we can be prepared!! Donavan was very upset and angry.

Jarrone turned red in the face from embarrassment. "I'm so sorry, Donavan. I wasn't thinking it through as well as I should have. It's just that it looked so heavy and I wanted to help. I'll be more careful from now on, I promise."

"See that you do. That was a close one, my friend."

Karmine and Donavan began pulling the travois again and it was plain that Jarrone's spell had made it much easier to pull. They were able to get to the inn much faster than they would have otherwise.

Donavan thought about it after they were safely at the inn. "Jarrone, what you did was a great idea. It helped so much to get here quicker. I was just upset because we came so close to falling down. I'm sorry I was after you so hard."

Jarrone looked at Donavan with a slight smile, "I understand. I'm sorry I didn't ask about the idea before I did it. I know that I'm just a bit impetuous at times."

Jasmine laughed, "At times? You're really funny Jarrone. We have to watch you every minute." She kept laughing until all of them were laughing, even Jarrone.

Murdon was looking at all of them laughing and wondered what the joke was all about. Finally, Donavan explained about Jarrone and how he was always up to something with his magic. The scary thing was, Jarrone was very powerful. He was probably much more powerful than he even knew. Murdon smiled at that. It was good to be in on the group humor.

Horan had been laying quietly and now he was starting to feel his wounds. He moaned and said, "What now? Will I be able to stay at the inn? Is there a room for me here? I'm bleeding again. Please do something." Horan was getting weaker and needed to be stable and resting.

Jasmine stopped laughing and said, "Horan, I'm going to go find out right now. Aribon will be able to tell us what's available." She left them at the steps into the inn and went to find Aribon.

He was in the kitchen preparing lunch when she found him. "Aribon, we have an injured man who needs a room to recover in. He's been badly wounded by one of the Skreechers. Do you have anything right now we can use for him?"

Aribon thought a moment, "There is a small room on the other side of Greta's room you can use. It is pretty small, but I think it will do while he's recovering. Let me show you where it is and you can let me know if it will work."

They went down one of the halls and passed Greta's room. At the end of the hall was a room, just as small as Aribon had said. But there was a nice window and a fairly large bed that would be a good size for Horan.

Jasmine was pleased, "This will do nicely. Now we need to get the men to bring him here and get him settled. He doesn't have anything with him yet. So there's plenty of room until he brings some things from his house."

Aribon followed Jasmine to the front of the inn where the men were waiting with Horan. When Aribon saw Horan and how badly he was wounded, he almost fainted. Horan's injuries had started bleeding again from all the movement and he looked terrible from loss of blood.

Murdon could see that Donavan and Karmine were tiring and so he stepped forward and offered to help lift the travois into the inn. There were only three steps, but they were a bit high. Donavan was especially grateful for the offer.

He said, "Murdon, it would be great if you could help. Can you come to the front and help pull this slowly and carefully up the steps? Horan is in enough pain and bleeding again. We must be careful of any more jarring."

Murdon was more than happy to help. He got in front of the bar and the three men were able to carefully pull Horan up the steps. He moaned a bit, but he was in a lot of pain. Once inside the inn, they were able to take him to the small room Aribon led them to.

The three men were able to carefully lift Horan from the travois and carry him to the bed. As soon as they laid him on the bed, Donavan and Jarrone began healing spells to stop the bleeding and ease his pain once again. It was exhausting because Horan was so badly injured.

Jasmine ran to get Magg. She was needed at a time like this. Her magic was much stronger and she knew more spells for healing. She knew Magg was out with Matton visiting with the people in town. Fortunately, she was close by. But both Magg and Matton were inside one of the cottages just then and didn't see the men bringing Horan in on the travois.

Jasmine saw Magg leaving the cottage and she called to her, "Magg can you come? We have an injured man in the room next to Greta's. He was badly injured by one of the Skreechers and needs extra help with healing and pain. Can you come and see for yourself if he needs more than Donavan and Jarrone can do for him?"

"When did this happen and why wasn't I alerted immediately?"

"We just got here with him a few minutes ago. He was brought in on a travois. We were able to get him to a room. We didn't realize how much magic would be needed to help him. It's really bad and we did what we thought was best until now. We try not to bother you unless we must."

"Alright, I understand. Please show me the way to the room he's in."

Jasmine and Magg hurried to Horan's room. Magg was shocked at the appearance of Horan. He really was in bad shape. Magg could see that she needed to scan his injuries and determine what else needed to be done to ease his pain.

Donavan and Jarrone looked up when Magg came in. Donavan said, "Magg, I'm so glad you're here. We were thinking we could handle this ourselves, but there's something here that neither of us understands. We can't detect what's happening to Horan. We're hoping you can figure it out before it's too late."

Magg stepped up to the bed and put her hands on Horan's chest. She sent a tendril of magic into his body searching for what might be causing his resistance to healing. It took a few moments, but she did find a deadly poison hiding in his wounds. It was gaining strength as time passed.

"There's a poison in his blood that is very powerful. I need both of you to help me with this one."

Magg quickly started a spell that she was hoping would counteract the poison. Donavan and Jarrone joined her to increase the effectiveness of her spell. As she chanted the spell, she could feel the power leave her body. She could see the magic coursing through Horan's body. The poison reacted immediately and mutated to avoid the spell. Magg had to increase the intensity of the spell and make some changes to it as she worked. The poison was being defeated a little at a time. She needed Jarrone and Donavan's help to keep going. Finally, the poison was removed from Horan and he began to feel better.

Magg then sent a healing spell with the aid of Donavan and Jarrone. Between the three of them,

Horan began to heal quickly. His wounds stopped bleeding and the redness was diminishing. Even so, it was apparent that it would be some time before Horan would be able to leave his bed.

Magg sighed heavily and said, "That was very difficult. The Skreechers are becoming more powerful. This was exhausting for me. I'm sure you felt the same way. It should not have taken so much magic to heal Horan's wounds. I know they were really bad and he has lost a lot of blood. It's just that if it weren't for the two of you, I would not have been able to heal him. That poison was very powerful. We have to do all we can to avoid anyone getting it in the future."

Donavan replied, "Magg, I think I speak for Jarrone as well when I say that this was one of the most difficult situations we've faced since we got here. I'm so glad we were all three here to help this man. He could so easily have died today. I feel strongly that we must warn all the villagers about the poison and the wounds the Skreechers are inflicting now."

"I agree Donavan. For now, I need to rest and so do you and Jarrone. It took far too much magic to do the work that needed doing. Jasmine, will you get Greta, and can you both watch Horan while we rest? If anything happens while we're resting, don't be afraid to wake one or all of us. We'll see you when we are rested and we will check on Horan at that time."

Jasmine spoke up, "Magg, the three of you are so amazing. I'm sure that Greta will be more than happy to watch over Horan with me. We'll keep him company and make sure he continues to heal." At that, Jasmine went to get Greta.

Horan was just barely able to say a few words, "Thank you all… for saving my life… I thought I was about to die today. Now… I feel like I might just live. I too will rest now… It's been a terrible day…for me."

When Jasmine knocked on Greta's door, Greta answered quickly. She had heard the noises next door and was about to go check on it when Jasmine knocked.

"Jasmine, what's going on? I could hear all the noise next door and I was about to go see if I could help with anything."

Jasmine explained what had happened and asked Greta if she would be willing to help watch Horan with her. Jasmine explained that his injuries had been very serious. His body would need time to overcome all that he had been through both physically as well as emotionally.

Greta was happy to be involved in something so important. She had a caring heart and could calm people down when things got stressful or dangerous. She could calm Horan when he became anxious about his injuries or problems he would be facing as he healed.

Jasmine asked Greta to come with her into the hall so she could tell her about what had happened to Horan that day.

"Greta, Horan has had a terrible day today. He was injured badly by one of the Skreechers while trying to get food for his family. He was barely able to escape and make it back to his home. It was a miracle that he made it at all. But when his wife took one look at him, she panicked and gathered up the children and left Horan without getting him any help.

"Horan did mention that she had been very worried about the Skreechers and when he came through the door with such terrible wounds, she panicked and left with the kids and anything she could pack. She must have been terrified.

"Anyway, luckily, Jarrone and Karmine were close by. Karmine found Horan and called to Jarrone to come quick. Horan's neighbor, Murdon, came with him to help. Jarrone was barely able to slow the bleeding, it was so bad. So he had Karmine go find Donavan. I was there too. Both Jarrone and Donavan tried more magic to save Horan.

They were able to help, but not completely stop the bleeding. That's when they decided to build a travois to get Horan to the inn. They were able to get him here just a little while ago. Magg was called and she was able to work with Jarrone and Donavan to stop the bleeding and ease the pain for Horan. Together we can make sure Horan continues to heal. I know you can help to keep him calm. He must rest so he can heal. He will need lots of water and fluid to make up for all his blood loss. What do you think, Greta?"

Greta was crying quietly by that time. "Jasmine, I'm so sad to hear all that Horan has been through. I'm so glad to be able to help keep him calm and rested. We really do need to be with him for a while. He will need all the compassion we can give him. We can't let him feel like no one cares about him. Should we work together day and night, or take shifts? I'd like to work together for a while. Then when we know more about what he needs from us, we could try shifts. How do you feel about it, Jasmine?"

"Greta, I agree with you. Let's work together until we can be sure that he is stable. I would like to wait until he can take care of himself a little bit. When the pain is under control and his wounds are healing nicely, then we can do shifts. Do you agree?"

"Sounds good to me. Let's go in and see what he needs."

As Greta and Jasmine went back into Horan's room, he smiled. He said, "I'm so glad you're back. I'm feeling a bit stronger. The thing is, I'm so weak. Would you bring me a pitcher of water and a glass? I'm so thirsty right now."

Just then, Magg walked in with a full pitcher of water and a clean glass. "I'll bring a pitcher of wine for you in a few minutes."

Greta filled the glass with water and gave it to Horan. He gulped it down and asked for more. After three glassfuls, Horan was satisfied for a while.

Magg said, "I'm so glad to see you drink that water. Now I need to see how your wounds are doing Horan. Can you remove the blanket for a few minutes while a check you over?"

Horan carefully moved the blanket off himself and let Magg check his wounds and make sure he was healing properly.

"You're doing pretty well Horan. I would like you to drink this pitcher of water today and half the pitcher of wine I will bring you in just a moment. Can you do that Horan?"

"I'll do ma best Magg. Thanks for being here for me. I really appreciate it. I honestly thought I was going to die several times this day. My heart also hurts since ma wife left me. I'm in a lot of pain."

Magg was glad Horan mentioned his pain. She asked if she could help him with the pain.

Horan was more than happy to have Magg ease his pain, both physical and emotional.

Magg placed her hands on Horan once again and sent a spell that would ease the pain he was experiencing. It worked really well because Horan was able to go to sleep almost immediately.

When Magg was satisfied that Horan was going to be all right for a while, she walked out and motioned for Greta and Jasmine to follow.

"Have the two of you decided how you're going to take care of Horan?"

Jasmine said, "Yes, we decided to work together and then take shifts later when he has healed more."

Magg replied, "I'm so glad. I know the two of you will take great care of him. Be sure to let me know if anything changes please. I will come anytime you need me. He's been through a lot today and we need to make sure he lives. His wounds are every bit as bad as Raven's were. I don't really want a lot of people to see him or visit him until he is better. He's just so weak right now. Make sure he drinks that water and half of the wine today. He needs it. I will be right back with the wine."

Magg left and went straight to the kitchen to get some wine from Aribon. As she walked in, Aribon could see that she needed something. "What is it Magg?"

"Hello Aribon, I need to take a pitcher of wine to Horan, the man who is wounded. He lost so much blood that he needs lots of fluids to replace it. Do you have enough to spare?"

"Of course I do! I'll get it for you right now." Aribon went to the cupboard and found a large pitcher and went down the steps to the cellar and filled it with wine."

He came back upstairs and carried the pitcher for Magg to take toHoran. They walked together to Horan's room and Aribon set the wine on the table for him.

"Thank you Aribon. It will help him mend with plenty of fluids. Would you be so kind as to bring a pitcher of water every day and maybe bring wine tomorrow afternoon?"

"I will do it for you Magg. We'll get poor Horan well in no time."

"Thank you Aribon, I know I can count on you."

Aribon and Magg left the room to do other things while Greta and Jasmine sat with Horan. He was able to sleep for an hour since Magg had helped him with his pain.

The two women were able to spend some time catching up on what was going on in the village. After only an hour of rest, Horan began to stir. He woke up moaning in pain.

Jasmine asked him, "Horan are you in pain again? Should we get Magg to come and help you with that now?"

Horan moaned a bit and whispered, "Yes, please. It's getting pretty intense all of a sudden."

Jasmine and Greta were both thinking he shouldn't need pain relief so soon after Magg had helped him. So Jasmine turned to Greta and said, "I'm going to go talk to Magg about his request for more pain relief. I'm sure he needs it, but there might be something more going on here causing the pain to come back so soon."

"I think that's a good idea, Jasmine. Magg can find out what's going on with his injuries that we can't see."

Jasmine left the room and went to find Magg. Fortunately, she was in her room with Matton. Jasmine knocked on the door and when Magg answered, she said, "Magg, Horan is in pain again and is requesting relief from it. But, Greta and I were thinking it was a bit soon. Will you please come and check into it in case there's something else going on that we don't know about?"

Magg was very surprised that Jasmine had come to her room already. It had been a very short while since she had helped Horan. She said, "Jasmine, this is worrisome. I gave him enough magic to keep him pain free for several hours. If he's in pain already, there is a problem we don't yet understand. Lead on." As she walked out the door, she gave Matton a quick kiss and left their room.

Jasmine and Magg walked to Horan's room quickly. When they got there, Horan was genuinely suffering. Where his wounds had been clean and pink, they were now red and hot again. They looked like they might be getting infected.

Magg went to Horan and asked, "What's going on here Horan? It looks like a lot of nastiness has begun to work on your injuries. Where do you hurt the most?"

Horan groaned and whispered, "I'm not sure. I just hurt all over. Maybe ma chest hurts the worst. Can you help me? I feel like I'm on fire everywhere."

Magg was shocked to hear that. "Can I touch you to see if I can find anything that might be causing all this pain?"

"Please do. I don't know how much more I can take of it."

Magg put her hands on Horan's chest and sent a tendril of magic into his system. She found another organism she hadn't seen the last time she looked. It had started eating his organs a bit at a time. This was causing his wounds to inflame and increase the pain he was feeling. As Magg analyzed the organism, she became a bit uneasy. It would take a lot of magic to kill it and even more to heal the places that the organism had been destroying Horan's organs.

Magg pulled back from Horan and said, "Jasmine, will you please find Donavan and ask him to come and help me with the magic I need to heal Horan once again?"

"Yes." Jasmine immediately left the room. She knew Donavan wouldn't be far away, not with Horan in such bad shape. She finally found him talking with Aribon in the dining room.

"Donavan, come quick, Horan is needing more magic. Magg found something that troubles her and she needs your help."

"All right, let's go." And Donavan headed straight for Horan's room, right behind Jasmine.

It only took a moment to get to Horan. Magg was visibly upset by then. Horan was in big trouble. Magg spoke quickly to Donavan, "Please put your hands on Horan's abdomen and let's work together to heal him. We need to eliminate a very dangerous organism that has invaded his body. I'm not sure if it was there all along since he was attacked by the Skreecher or not. But it is fast working and we must stop it now."

"I'm ready," said Donavan

Magg began her spell and with Donavan's added magic, they were able to find the organism and destroy it. Magg pulled out of Horan and signaled to Donavan to do the same.

"Now that we've found and eliminated the organism, we need to heal the damage it has done to his organs. Are you ready to help heal him?"

"Yes, let's get this poor man healed."

They both put their hands on Horan and sent healing magic into his ravaged body. It took a lot of magic and time to heal everything damaged in Horan's body. Sweat was pouring off both Magg and Donavan by the time they were finished. There was much more damage than either of them had imagined.

Magg finally motioned for Donavan to stop. They had done all they could for Horan. Both of them were exhausted and in need of a lot of rest.

Magg looked over Horan's body and could see that his wounds were once again healing as they should. Horan was resting peacefully now. Greta had been holding his hand to help him stay calm and relaxed while the magic was taking place. She was worn out from her own efforts by the time Magg and Donavan were finished healing him. It had been a hard won battle with the unknown.

Magg sighed and said, "I think we've done all we can for now. I for one am more tired than I can remember. Next time, if there is a next time, we'll have to ask Jarrone to help. How are you doing, Donavan?"

"I'm really worn out as well. Let's call it a night and get some rest. Who knows what tomorrow will bring?"

Jasmine groaned, "Don't say that Donavan! It's bad enough thinking it, but don't say it."

Donavan was surprised by Jasmine's remark. "I'm sorry, I guess it's the exhaustion talking. Let's get to bed, my sweet wife."

Jasmine hesitated leaving Greta alone with Horan. Greta looked every bit as tired as the rest of them. But she said, "Don't worry about me you two. I wouldn't be able to sleep anyway. I'd rather sit by him and make sure he doesn't need anything between now and morning."

"Call if you need anything, please."

"I will."

When the others were gone, Greta was thinking that maybe it would be a good thing for Raven to help with his time alone. Greta knew she was doing much better. She also knew that having been through what Horan was going through would help him have hope for his own healing. She went to sleep in the chair next to Horan's bed thinking tomorrow would be interesting indeed.

Chapter 28

Raven had been walking with Aribon twice a day. She was regaining her strength quickly now. She had been resting in her room when she heard some noise at the entrance to the inn. It sounded like someone had been injured. She had decided to check on the others to find out what it was.

Raven found Aribon in the kitchen, as usual, and asked him about it, "What's been happening today? Was someone hurt or something?"

Aribon smiled when Raven walked in. He had grown fond of her since they had started walking together. "Yes, indeed. A man in the village in one of the homes close to the forest had gone out hunting for his family. While he was out hunting food for his family, he was attacked by a Skreecher. It was really bad, he nearly bled to death, from what they're saying. Donavan and Jarrone brought him in and tried to heal him, but it was too bad. They were able to do a little healing, but some of his wounds were still bleeding. Some were really deep.

"They sent Jasmine to find Magg to help them with her magic. If the three of them couldn't heal him, it was hopeless. Fortunately Magg was able to find a poison from the Skreecher and was able to stop its effect with the help of Jarrone and Donavan. He seemed to be doing a lot better when they finished with the spells. Horan was able to sleep for a bit. Greta and Jasmine decided to stay with him in case he needed something.

"From what I've seen recently, it's a good thing they did. Horan started being in pain again and Jasmine went to get Magg again to help with that. I understand that she needed to have Donavan come and help because there was more to the problem than Magg had thought. Anyway, Horan is doing much better, according to what I'm hearing. So do you need anything Miss Raven? I suspect you're a bit hungry by now."

Raven smiled, "You know me too well Aribon. Do you happen to have any raw meat around that you could warm up a bit for me?"

"As a matter of fact, I do. Coming right up for you miss." Aribon went directly to the kitchen to warm up a bit of meat he had ready for Raven. He seared it on both sides and put it on a plate for Raven.

Raven had come to the doorway of the kitchen and said, "Aribon, that meat smells too good I can hardly wait to eat it. You are amazing to always be ready for me to eat what I crave. Not being able to go hunting for so long has been difficult for me. But more than that is the real fear of those monsters. And now we know they can put poison into your body and maybe even other things to kill you later on. So I'm more than grateful for your help in getting me meat to eat every day. Thank you, my friend." Raven started eating her serving of meat right away. She was much hungrier than she thought.

Aribon said, "Raven, you are so welcome. I'm so glad I can help you while you need it. I am kind of hoping it will be a while before you are able to go hunting. It's just so nice to have you here."

Raven actually blushed at Aribon' words. She hadn't even liked a man before now. But there was something about Aribon that was so comfortable and kind. She felt a strange sensation that might be friendship bordering on, dare we say, love? Naw!

When Raven finally finished her meal, she decided it would be good to go and visit the new patient. She had heard that his name was Horan. It was time she let him know that he could heal, if he was careful and rested properly. She would speak from experience as no one else in the village could.

She thanked Aribon for the meal and said, "I'm going to go check on the new guy, Horan. Want to come with me or are you too busy right now with dinner?"

Aribon was surprised that Raven would invite him to go with her. So, he jumped at the chance and said, "Absolutely."

Aribon and Raven left the dining room and headed for Horan's room. They didn't meet anyone on the way there, so they made quick progress. At Horan's door, Raven knocked softly in case Horan was sleeping.

Greta came to the door. She was happy to see Raven and Aribon. "Come on in. Horan is resting quietly right now. I think he would like to have someone else to visit with. He wants to know what's happening in the village and with the Skreechers if possible."

Raven stepped up to Horan's bed and said, "Hello Horan. I'm Raven and the man with me is Aribon. He's the one who cooks your food."

Aribon spoke up, "Horan, it's good to meet you. I was at the door when they brought you in. I helped get you into your room. It's good to see that you're doing better. We were all very concerned about your survival."

Raven said, "I understand you've been through a lot recently. How are you feeling today? Any better than yesterday?"

Horan was a bit groggy, but he was feeling much better and said so. "I am feeling better than yesterday. I've been through more than I had ever thought to go through in my lifetime. I'm so grateful for the people here with such powerful magic. The magic has been able to heal me and cure some bad organism that was attacking ma organs. But other than that, things are looking pretty good."

Raven chuckled, "I know how you feel. I went through much the same thing a while ago. If you would like to talk about any of it, I'm more than happy to discuss it with you. When you're ready, let me know. I'm not far from your room."

Horan was so pleased to meet Raven. Not only was she beautiful, but she had been through the same kind of thing. He was going to enjoy talking to her about his experience, he was sure.

He said, "Raven, I look forward to talking about what has happened to both of us when I'm stronger. I will let you know when ah'm ready to do that. Right now ah'm really tired. But I would like it if you two would come and see me tomorrow."

Raven smiled, "We will do that. It's good to meet you Horan."

Aribon added, "I am so glad to see how much better you are doing. We'll see you tomorrow."

Aribon and Raven left Horan, saying goodbye to Greta on the way out. "We'll see you tomorrow too, Greta. Let us know if you need a break."

"I will and thank you."

Raven and Aribon walked to Raven's room together. Aribon knew she was tiring and left her to rest. It was getting late. Raven was having to sleep when everyone else did now. She didn't even want to go hunting in the forest. The Skreechers had taken it over. She hoped she could help in the elimination of them. They were becoming too powerful and dangerous. As Aribon left, she smiled to herself. He was such a good man and had been helping her in so many ways. She was curious to see where their friendship went from here.

Chapter 29

Raven was glad to be back in her own part of Magg's room. She noticed that Magg and Matton were already asleep. Raven had learned from Aribon that Magg had used a lot of magic with Donavan trying to help Horan. Raven knew that the use of so much magic really drained Magg's energy and she needed to rest afterwards.

Though Raven wanted to talk to Magg about stopping the Skreechers, she knew that it would have to wait until morning. She was hoping she could have a part in the process of eliminating them. She wanted revenge for the damage they had done to her and others.

Now that it was known that the Skreechers had some form of magic, she was beginning to suspect that they may have been created by Neberon, the evil wizard, before he was sent into the ether by Magg, Jarrone, and Donavan. It made sense to her that there would be something terrible left behind by him. It didn't seem like a coincidence that they showed up not long after Neberon was sent away, never to be heard from again.

She was thinking that the Skreechers might be sent to the same place when the time came to get rid of them forever. Raven was sure that Magg was going to find a spell that would accomplish that, but it would be a matter of time before they would all be ready with their own part in the destruction of the Skreechers.

She sat on her bed and wondered what part she might be able to play in the coming battle with the Skreechers. She finally relaxed and was able to change into her night gown and get ready for sleeping. As she crawled under her blankets, she was able to put all those thoughts out of her mind and sleep. She would talk with Magg in the morning.

Magg was finally sleeping next to Matton and felt safe and protected. She went to sleep quickly and knew no more until morning. Matton was so happy to have Magg sleeping next to him. He was happier when she was near. He could feel her power and intelligence as she lay next to him. He fell asleep one of the happiest men in the village.

Morning arrived with a roar from the Skreechers. Everyone in the village bolted out of bed and ran to the window to see if they could find out what was going on. They were terrified, but were afraid to go outside to investigate. Most of the villagers knew what had happened to Horan just a few days ago. It had been so bad that the level of fear had sky rocketed throughout the village. No one was willing to take a chance on it happening to them, and understandably so.

Raven heard the roar and jumped out of bed to find Magg and see if she knew what was happening. It was obvious that the Skreechers were moving in not a good way. She found Magg up and getting dressed. Matton was doing the same.

Raven spoke up, "Magg, do you have any idea what's going on out there? I really want to help with the destruction of those evil things. Can I do anything right now?"

Magg smiled when Raven came into her room. "I don't know yet what has happened or is happening. If you would like to come with Matton and me, we could check around the area and see if we can figure out what the noise is all about. But we must be extremely careful and move quietly to see if we can understand what's going on."

Raven nodded her head and said, "I would like to come with you. I want to know what it's all about."

Magg and Matton were pleased that Raven wanted to help. More eyes on the problem would be a good thing right now. So the three of them walked out of Magg's room to start an effort to understand what the noise was about outside. It was hoped that the Skreechers were still outside the village and not entering it to attack the people. They would soon find out.

As they approached the entrance to the inn, they carefully opened the door a crack to see if there was anything going on outside just then. There were villagers looking out their windows, but no one was out in the street. That was a good thing. So they left the inn together and looked up and down the village streets. There didn't seem to be any Skreechers lurking in the village that they could see. But they knew that the Skreechers could hide very well indeed.

One good thing about the monsters was that they really reeked. If one of them was near, they could smell them right away. There was no trace of the smell just then. So the three of them walked up the main street with their heads on the swivel so they could see any movement before they might be attacked. Nothing moved. It was also a bit too quiet just then.

The dogs were all inside their owner's homes and so were the cats. The thing that bothered them was that the birds were not singing. The hair on the back of Magg's neck began to stand up. Matton grabbed her and Raven's hands.

Suddenly, there was another big roar and two of the Skreechers jumped out from some bushes near them and started chasing them. Matton held Magg and Raven's hands as he pulled them into one of the houses nearby. The family had seen what was happening and opened their front door to let them inside before the Skreechers could get to them.

"Oh, thank you so much. That was way too close! Karmine, you saved our lives!"

Karmine and Roslin had heard the roars of the Skreechers and were watching the street in case someone needed help. It was very fortunate that they had done so.

"I'm so glad we were watching the street just then. I just had a feeling something was going wrong. Come and sit down. You must be terrified after that near encounter."

"We are. Thank you Karmine and Roslin. We may have been Skreecher meals if not for you two." Magg was very grateful for Karmine's quick thinking. All three of them were very pale and shaking from the terror they had just experienced. Matton held Magg close, grateful for their safety. Raven had to sit down on one of the chairs to steady herself. The horror of her encounter of a few months ago came rushing back to her. She was thinking maybe she wasn't ready for this kind of situation after all.

"Magg, I'm not sure I can do anything to help now. This has set me back remembering the attack I survived a while ago. I think I should stay at the inn and look after Horan. Would that be alright with you?"

Magg could see that Raven was about to faint from shock and fear. She went to her and sat by her to try to comfort her. She said, "Raven, I totally understand. I was actually amazed that you offered to come with us. It hasn't been that long since you were attacked. So please do stay inside the inn and help with Horan until this is over. It will end soon, of that I am sure."

Raven started to calm down a bit. Karmine and Roslin were there and offered them something warm to drink. It was a tea Roslin made that was calming and helped heal the spirit.

All three of them had a cup of the tea and felt better for having it. "That's really good Roslin. Thank you. It surely is helping me calm down."

"That's what it's for. My mother used to give it to us kids when we were young. It helped us heal after a fight or a scare. I have used it ever since."

"If I have any feelings at all about what is to come, I would say that we'll probably need a lot more of this tea in the coming days. Can you keep up with that just in case?"

Roslin thought for a minute, "I believe I can. It would be nice to feel needed in this effort to get rid of those nasty Skreechers."

The group agreed with that. They chatted for a bit and finally were able to relax. Karmine kept checking out the window to be sure of where the Skreechers were. He tried not to show it, but he could sense that the Skreechers had not left the area.

It appeared that Magg, Matton, and Raven might be with them for a while. He also feared that the monsters might hang around or try to break into his home. He went to check on their boys and found them sitting on the floor together, too frightened to move into the kitchen where the others were.

Karmine sat close to them and said, "I know this a scary, boys. But the thing is, we've got to be brave and do our best to keep each other safe. We have Magg here with us for a bit. Remember that she has very powerful magic and can help us if the Skreechers try anything nasty. So, will you come out and talk with the rest of us and tell Magg what's bothering you?"

The boys stood up and said, "OK dad. We'll try to be brave."

"That's all I ask of you. I know you are brave. You've been through a lot in your lives so far. We'll get through this. There are a lot of people who want to help and we have a plan to fight the monsters. So, we all need to be brave until the monsters are gone for good."

Karmine and the four boys walked out of the bedroom together and greeted the others.

Boren, the oldest boy, said, "We're scared and we were hiding in our room together. Maybe we can be brave now and help with the fight. We don't want to be afraid all the time. We want to be able to help get rid of all of the Skreechers."

The adults had tears in their eyes at that statement. It was plain to see that they were really frightened by all the noise and trouble the Skreechers had brought into their lives. It was hoped that it would soon end. But no one knew how it would happen. It was going to depend on what magic Magg could use against them. Donavan and Jarrone were also strong in the magic and between the three of them, much could be done.

For Magg it was a realization that she had to work on the spells more than she had been. Their lives depended on it. She was suddenly remembering Zarcon's warning of a few weeks ago. She was sternly told to get the spells and practice them right away. She had no time left to play around with them. It was mandatory that she prepare. Well, she had not done as Zarcon warned and now she was paying the price.

If she had learned the most powerful spell, she could have stopped those Skreechers before they could get so close to them. She was ashamed of herself. But now she knew what she must do.

Matton sensed her sadness and moved to her to comfort her. He loved her so much. He held her for a few moments and said, "Magg, you're doing the best you can. There's just so much going on right now. Don't be hard on yourself, we need you to be strong and smart. You can do whatever you must to get us through this. Understand?"

Magg looked up at Matton and tried to smile. His words really did help her to feel better about what she had been doing. There really had been a lot of things to deal with, but now she must concentrate on doing what she could do best to help the village survive that Skreechers.

The three of them, Magg, Matton, and Raven stayed with Karmine and Roslin for a few hours just to be sure the Skreechers were gone from the area. When it seemed that all was clear and safe to go back to the inn, it was with a bit of sorrow that they realized the monsters had been able to get into the village and cause so much fear. It seemed they needed a better early warning system in place. The roar of the Skreechers was much too late. If they hadn't roared and just attacked instead, who knew what the consequence would have been? It didn't bear thinking about.

It was obvious that their time had rum out for preparations. They were either ready now, or they weren't and would pay the price of it. Everyone was feeling the terror of the morning. Magg was especially feeling it. She knew that if they were to survive, they must work together and warn each other of the dangerous times ahead.

Chapter 30

Magg, Matton, and Raven finally made it back to the inn safely. The attack had been too close for comfort. All three of them might have been killed if Karmine and Roslin hadn't been on the alert when needed most. Magg realized she needed to work on the spells to destroy the monsters and learn them before it was too late. After what happened that morning, it was obvious that she needed to prepare as soon as possible. Her fears had been realized and now it was almost too late.

She immediately got out the Book of Spells that Zarcon had given her. She had just started on the most powerful spell and knew that she would be the only one with the knowledge and power to use it and control it. She was aware that if more people knew about it, there would be a good chance of a disaster happening from the use of it.

She started by memorizing the spell. She would go outside the inn to practice it. She didn't want anyone to see what it could do. She was fearful that if someone saw her practicing, they might pressure her to use it before it was necessary. She wanted it to be a secret weapon and reserve it for desperate times, which to be honest, were very close indeed.

The memorization of the spell took some time. It was a bit complicated and she knew she had to learn it perfectly, no doubt in her mind what she needed to do. Even the slightest misstep could bring disaster to the village and its people.

As time passed, she was able to remember the spell perfectly. She was feeling good about it when Matton came to her and asked her to come with him to eat something. Magg had been so consumed with the spell that she had not realized how hungry she was. She was glad that Matton had come to get her to eat.

So, they left her room to go to the dining room to see if Aribon had anything left from lunch. As it happened, he did in fact have some very delicious shredded pork roast and some fresh baked rolls to make a sandwich out of. He also had some of his wonderful sauce to go with it. There were also some fresh vegetables and baked potatoes cut into pieces.

"This is delicious, Aribon. Thank you so much for your efforts every day to feed all of us."

Aribon smiled and said, "It is genuinely my pleasure to do so, Magg. Thanks for the appreciation. It means a lot to me."

When the two of them finished eating, Magg asked Matton to come with her to practice the new spell she had learned. She felt that she needed him to be with her in case something went wrong and she needed his help.

Matton was always happy to help her with her spells. He was glad she trusted him to be there watching her practice. He would have been very nervous to not be there. There was no guarantee that things would always go well.

Magg said, "Matton, I want to go someplace away from the villagers, but not anywhere near the Skreechers. Although, I'm kind of afraid they will sense the magic and come to me. Will you please watch for me in case they do?"

"Absolutely!"

"I'm so glad you're in my life! I don't know what I'd do without you, my darling man."

Matton just smiled as he turned a bit red in the face at the complement.

So Magg found a spot near the road, away from the village. She thought about the spell she was about to use and for some reason, she became very nervous about it. It was so powerful that she wasn't sure she wanted to see the results of its use. But she began the incantation anyway. She had to know.

There were also hand signals to go with the words of the spell. She carefully began both. She was going to aim the spell at the big tree on the other side of the road. As she said the spell, blue fire shot out from her fingertips. It struck the tree and vaporized it and the two trees not far from it. The ground around where the trees had been was scorched earth.

Magg immediately sank to the ground in a faint. Matton ran to her and sat her up in his arms. It took some time but Magg slowly opened her eyes. "Matton, what happened? Did the spell work? Why am I on the ground? Wasn't there a couple of trees over there? Where are they now?"

Matton gave a little chuckle even though it really wasn't funny, "Magg you used that spell. Do you remember that?"

"Yes."

"Well, it hit the tree you were aiming at and vaporized it and the two near it. It was so powerful that it took all your strength to do it and you fainted."

"WHAT??!!"

"Yes, you fainted. I know that seems impossible, but it's true. I'm so glad you decided not to teach anyone else how to do it. I hope we can let Donavan and Jarrone know that they will need to be near you if you need to use it. Maybe they can either hold you up, or add their strength to yours somehow."

"Matton, this spell is indeed too powerful. I was hoping it would be, actually. Now we know not to use it unless there is nothing else we can do. Call it the Last Resort Spell. What do you think?"

Matton smiled, "Sounds good to me. I'm just hoping Donavan and Jarrone will be alright not getting to learn it once we tell them about it. This is a serious game-changer."

Magg thought about it for a moment and said, "I am glad that neither Donavan nor Jarrone are the type of wizard to be jealous of this spell. They may very well be grateful that they are not going to have to learn it, at least for now. I may have to change my mind as time goes by. I just hope not."

"I feel the same way, my love. Time will tell if we need to include anyone else. What concerns me is the fact that it was so powerful that it took all your strength to use it. You probably will need to discuss it with both of them before long."

"I see what you mean, Matton. I would like to practice it a bit more, but I fear the consequences. Really, Matton, if once can drain me to the point of fainting, how can I know when to use it knowing I can only do it once? Let's see if we can meet with Donavan and Jarrone today some time."

"Good idea, Magg. Maybe until then we should rest up. After you've rested awhile, we can see about talking to the others. What do you think?"

"I like the idea. I'm needing some rest and possibly to sleep just now. After that I'm pretty sure I'll need something to eat. I will probably need to replenish my energy after using that spell. It was shocking to me that it was more than I could support on my own. Maybe we could figure out a way to have the other two give me some of their power to help with the spell without them actually using the spell."

"I'm hoping that will be the answer to the problem. You can't risk fainting in the middle of some battle with the Skreechers."

"That's for sure."

It turned out that Magg needed to have Matton support her on the way back to the inn. She was weaker than she thought when she got up to walk. She really must talk with Donavan and Jarrone today.

When they arrived at the inn, they went directly to Magg's room so she could rest awhile before dinner. Matton was glad he could be there with her while she slept. That new spell actually frightened him, especially when Magg fainted. That had never happened before and he was shocked. Magg was able to sleep for a couple of hours. She needed that rest desperately.

When Magg woke up, she was hungry. Matton suggested they go straight to the dining hall and get something to eat. They were able to get some stew that Aribon was making for dinner. It was ready to eat, so the two of them had a bowl and some of his sourdough bread to go with it. It was a perfect meal to help Magg regain her strength. When they finished eating, Magg felt much better.

Just as they were ready to leave the dining hall, Donavan walked in with Jasmine. Magg motioned them over and they went to a corner of the inn to talk. Magg began explaining what had happened with the spell she had tried. Donavan was shocked that it was so powerful that Magg had fainted using it.

Jasmine was speechless. This was unheard of. All of them realized that it was a good thing Neberon hadn't had that spell when he was trying to kill everyone. He would likely have succeeded, a terrible thought. Everyone was grateful that Magg was the one who had control of it.

So it was that Donavan supported Magg. He would supply some of his energy if she ever needed to use the spell. He promised he would stay by Magg if the battle became so serious that she would need to use it.

Jarrone and his family came in a bit later. Before he could sit down, Magg called him over to talk about the day's adventure with the spell. They went to the same corner with Donavan to talk.

Magg began, "Jarrone, I tried a new spell this morning. It is very effective. I was able to destroy some trees growing nearby. But the bad part was that I fainted after using it. It was a good thing Matton was with me. I've never had that reaction from the use of a spell before."

"Wow! That's really powerful magic. What would you like me to do?"

"Well, Jarrone, I would like you to stay with me when we're using magic on the Skreechers. That way, if I do have to use that spell, you could add some of your power to it so that I don't have to use all of mine. Is that a possibility?"

"That spell sounds dangerous to me. I sure hope we don't have to use it. But if we do, I will be beside you and do whatever is necessary to protect you."

"Thank you, Jarrone. I knew I could count on you."

Chapter 31

Raven was helping Greta with Horan. He needed his bandages changed every day and Magg had made a salve to put on his wounds to help them heal and to help with the pain. Horan seemed to be doing better every day.

Raven went to the dining room to get Greta and Horan some food. When she walked in, she noticed Magg and three or four others in a corner talking. She was really curious about it and walked over to ask Magg what had happened. As she drew near, she could sense that something had happened indeed.

"Magg what's going on? I sense something has happened today. Are you well? You look a bit pale."

Magg tried to smile, "Raven, I have had a rough morning. I tried a new spell and it proved to be a bit more than I had expected when I used it. I actually fainted as soon as I spoke it. I took all of my energy. Matton was there, but I'm just a bit fearful of using it again. Jarrone and Donavan have offered to help give me more strength if I have to use it. That's comforting, but what if they're not there when I have to use it?"

Raven was shocked, "Magg you can't worry about it now. It's hoped that you won't need to use it at all. You'll be stronger than ever for using it. I have a feeling this is the beginning of your power in a new way. Be careful from now on that you don't do more than you expect with your other spells."

Matton turned pale at Raven's words. "I hadn't thought of it like that, Raven. You have magic of your own, aside from transforming that is. Have you always been able to feel things like this? I'm surprised that you could be so in tune to such things. I've only ever heard of one other person who could do that and he was in Synkana doing tricks. He could scare people sometimes with his talent."

Raven thought for a moment and said, "You know, I don't think I've had these feelings before. I was just looking at Magg and it came to me that her power was growing immensely. It shocked me a bit, too."

"Magg, this is something new for Raven. Did it shock you that she could see such things in you?"

Magg replied, "It really did surprise me. I've never heard anything like that from Raven before. Raven, would you mind if we tested your magic a bit to find out what it means and what you can do with it?"

Raven smiled, "I would be delighted to test this new talent I have. Maybe I can be more help with the battle against the Skreechers. This is exciting for me."

"Great, let's start right away. If this will help with our battle, it could be very significant. I can't wait to test your talent. Let's go try it out on Greta and Horan. Maybe you can tell us what's going on, especially with Horan."

"Sounds good to me. I'm really curious about this."

So it was that all four of them went to visit Greta and Horan in his room. They were hoping Raven's new talent would help them see how Horan was really doing mentally. He seldom said anything and kept his feelings to himself. It would be good to know if he was still struggling with the departure of his wife and children.

As they knocked on Horan's door, they could hear him talking with Greta. He was saying, "Ah'm feeling better today. Ah'm hoping to be able to get out of this bed sometime soon."

Magg knocked on the door to Horan's room just then. Greta hurried to answer their knock. "Welcome my friends, it's so good to see you! I've missed our visits. Horan just told me he's feeling better today and would like to soon get out of his bed. What do you think, Magg?"

Magg looked at Horan closely and saw that he was still a bit pale and sickly from all he'd been through. She finally said, "Horan, I would like to wait a few more days. You need to get your strength back before we dare have you up and around the inn. We'll keep bringing you food and helping you when you do need to get out of bed. But, for now, let's let you heal. Do you understand the need right now?"

"Unfortunately, Ah do. Ah am still a bit weaker than Ah feel Ah should be b' now. So, Ah'll follow whatever you think Ah need."

"Are you needing anything right now that we can get for you?"

"No, Greta brought me something to drink and Ah've just eaten some lunch. Ah'm fine for now. Greta is an angel. She has stayed with me the entire time. She brings us both something to eat, it's great."

Magg was glad to hear that. She said, "Horan, I'm so glad you're getting better and we're so grateful for Greta's kind help. Thank you Greta. When you need a break, let me know and I'll either come myself, or send someone else to help."

Greta had been feeling a bit tired and bored with her job of being with Horan. She just didn't dare say so. Now she felt it necessary to ask for the help she needed. She finally spoke up for herself, "Magg can I talk to you in the hall for a minute, please?"

"Of course."

The group walked out into the hall, but Raven decided to stay with Horan while they were gone. She had become worried about his condition. She had seen something in Horan that didn't seem right.

"Horan, how are you really doing? I sense something amiss and would like you to tell me what it is."

Horan blushed a bright red, "Raven, there's a place on ma back that is hurting more all the time. Ah've faked it for too long and now Ah'm scared. How could ya tell?"

Raven sighed, "Horan, please don't do that. We need to be aware of what you're going through so we can help you heal properly. Roll over and let me see what's going on."

So Horan rolled over for her to see where it was hurting him. When she saw what it was, she let out a scream. "This is terrible, Horan!"

Just then Magg came running into the room to see what had happened. She could see Horan's back where he was hurting and she groaned, "Oh no!"

Horan flinched at that. He had an idea that what was causing him pain was a bad thing. He just hadn't realized how bad it really was until that moment. Magg's reaction shocked him. He knew then that he was most likely in trouble because of his wound. His eyes begged Magg to help him. He was terrified at this point. He began to fear, not for the first time, that he might be dying. The Skreechers were more powerful than he had realized, and maybe the others hadn't realized either.

Magg came close to him to look at his wound to see what was going on with it. It was bright red and had a large white spot in the middle of it. The worst part was that there were black edges around it. She was so shocked at the appearance of it that she didn't know where to begin to help him. She was fearful that once again she might be in deeper than she wanted to go. After fainting from the use of the spell, she was concerned that this would be difficult for her too.

Magg was so concerned that she asked Matton to go find Donavan and if possible, Jarrone as well. He left the room immediately.

Matton went directly to Donavan and Jasmine's room and knocked. Finally, Jasmine came to the door.

Matton asked Jasmine, "Is Donavan here? He's needed to help Magg with something that is going on with Haron."

Jasmine simply turned and spoke loudly, "Donavan, you're needed in Haron's room."

Donavan came immediately and said, "What is it Matton?"

"Magg needs your help with healing Haron. He has another problem with his wound that looks pretty bad. Can you come now?"

"Yes, let's go. Jasmine, I love you, bye."

The two of them left and made it to Horan's room in just seconds. Donavan hurried into the room asking Magg, "What is going on, Magg? How can I help you?"

Magg breathed a sigh of relief when he walked in. "Donavan, I'm so glad you could come. Take a look at Horan's back. What do you see?"

When Donavan looked at the wound on Horan's back, he nearly fainted from shock. It was the worst he had seen in all his life. It wasn't really big yet, but it was going to grow.

"Magg, what is it?"

She motioned for him to follow her out of the room. Once in the hallway, she said, "It looks to me like an infection that is caused by the poison from the Skreecher wounds he had before. I think this one has been hiding and has finally decided to come out where we can see it. It's obviously causing Horan a lot of pain. It angers me that he didn't say something sooner."

"What can we do about it? Do you think we'll need Jarrone to help with this one?"

"That's exactly what I'm wondering. The only thing about that is that I'm not sure we can wait until he gets here."

Just then they could hear Jarrone's voice in the dining area. He was ordering something to eat for himself and his family. Matton heard it too and ran out the door to go get Jarrone to come help.

Matton was in the dining hall quickly and called to Jarrone, "Jarrone, we need your help with a wound that has appeared on Horan's back. Can you come right now? They're in Horan's room."

Jarrone nodded and followed Matton to Horan's room. He was glad to see Magg again. Donavan was also there. Magg told him to see the wound for himself. He was also shocked when he saw the wound on Horan's back. Jarrone looked closer to see if he could figure out what he was looking at.

Jarrone looked over at Magg and asked, "What am I looking at?"

Magg spoke to Jarrone quietly and told him what she suspected. "It's pretty scary looking isn't it? That black ring must mean that his flesh is either dying or gangrene is setting in. Either way, it's deadly. I think we should clean up the outside of the wound the best we can before casting the spell to heal it. I would like Aribon to come and do that. He's been able to help a lot with wounds. Matton would you mind getting Aribon in here to help with this wound? I'm feeling that if we clean out as much of the infection as possible and then try the spell, it might go much better."

Matton found Aribon in the kitchen preparing dinner, "Aribon, we need you and your skills with wounds to come and clean a nasty one on Horan's back. Can you come now?"

Aribon was pleased to be asked to help. He found his medical bag and followed Matton to Horan's room. As they arrived, Aribon noticed the horrible infection on Horan's back.

"This is nasty Horan. I'm going to have to lance the infection and clean it out. It will be a bit uncomfortable for you, but must be done. I'm going to pray to god that I can do this properly." Aribon took a couple of minutes to pray over Horan before he started working on cleaning the wound.

A soon as Aribon was finished praying, he took out his knife he used for such things and cut the area of the infection. Horan yelled, "Um, this is a bit too much for me right now. Can somebody ease the pain for me?"

Magg blushed at not thinking of that. So she hurriedly put her hand on Horan's head and put a slight amount of magic to ease the pain for him.

"Ahh, much better. Thanks Magg."

Aribon began again to lance the infection. There was a lot of pus in it. Aribon was able to clean it all up with the clean cloths he had in his bag. He also had some ointment that would kill what infection remained on the surface. He had to use something like scissors to cut all the blackened areas off the wound. He didn't bandage it because magic was going to be used and he would bandage it afterward. There wasn't a lot of blood, which was a good thing. But just in case, Aribon left some clean bandages to mop up what might happen later.

Meanwhile, Magg was so happy that Aribon had come and done such good work on Horan's back, she said, "Aribon, I had no idea you were so handy with emergencies. You've done very well. Now it won't take quite so much magic to finish the cleanup. At least that's what I'm hoping. Thank you so much."

Aribon was a bit embarrassed at the compliment, but he just smiled and went back to the kitchen.

Horan had fallen asleep from the spell Magg had done to ease the pain. She was grateful for that as well. She would try to make sure he stayed asleep until the spell was cast. He would likely be in a great deal of pain otherwise. He may wake up in pain, and likely would, but she could deal with that when necessary.

Donavan asked, "Now what do we do? What spell are you thinking of, Magg?

Magg suggested a spell that was a simple healing spell, but with the three of them it would be much more powerful. Magg believed that the organism causing the infection was very powerful and would take a lot to kill it completely. She was grateful that Aribon had started the healing process by cleaning out the surface infection. She knew this went really deep into Horan's body.

Raven looked at Magg and said, "Be careful Magg. Your power is much stronger. Don't use too much please."

Magg nodded to confirm what Raven told her as she continued with the spell. "Now, let's put our hands on Horan's back." Magg began to cast the spell. The three of them directed the spell to the infection on Horan's back. Magg directed it carefully and watched Horan's reaction as they applied the spell to his wound. As soon as Horan began to show discomfort as he slept, Magg pulled back on the spell until she could see that he was handling it better.

Magg began following the spell to find out what it was that was causing the problem for Horan. As she looked deeper, she found the organism. It was larger than any she had seen before. It had sharp teeth and there were a lot of them chewing on Horan's tissues. Magg was outraged and sent a special tendril to the organism and his minions. With the help of Donavan and Jarrone, Magg was able to up the spell to destroy all the organisms.

As the spell hit them, they began to shatter into pieces. She then used another spell to burn the pieces into powder. They would not come back. As Magg pulled back out of Horan and brought Donavan and Jarrone with her, she was sure they had destroyed the organisms completely. Horan should be able to heal fully now that there were no more of them in his body.

As all three of them finished the spell and withdrew from Horan's wound, they could see that the wound was getting better. It would be awhile before it was completely healed, but at least now there was hope. Magg had cauterized the wound as they pulled out and prevented any unnecessary bleeding.

Magg had used so much of her magic that she almost fainted again. Donavan noticed she was having a hard time standing up. So he caught her and had her sit on the chair Greta had left for her. Matton went to her immediately and as they left the room, Magg said, "I'm so glad the spell worked. I'm sorry I'm so exhausted from it. I must get back to my room and sleep. I'll see you tomorrow."

Donavan was also worn out from the experience and needed to rest. Jasmine had been waiting in the hall until the magic was finished. She came into the room and helped Donavan go back to their room.

Donavan said as he left the room, "That was one powerful spell Miss Magg. I'm glad I was able to help." He was just able to get back to their room leaning on Jasmine before he collapsed on their bed.

As Jarrone was leaving, he said, "I'm going to go get the food for my family now. I am also grateful I could help with something so important."

Jarron, being much younger, was just a bit tired from the effort. But he was still surprised. No other spell had affected him like that before. He left to get the food he had ordered for his family. He found that he had to rest a bit while he waited for the food. As soon as he got the food, he left for home. Once there, he was glad to eat and rest for the evening.

Meanwhile, Raven and Greta were left to watch Horan the rest of the day. They were glad to do so and also grateful that the spell was finished and Haron was doing so much better so soon. Greta smiled at Raven and was glad she was staying.

Horan started to wake up. The spell for pain was wearing off. He was doing much better and said, "Ah'm so grateful to everyone for helping me. The magic was something else. It felt really warm and even hot at one point, but then it cooled off a bit. I could tell when the organism was destroyed, I could feel them no longer chewing on me inside. What a relief that was. Ah think our wizards were drained from the effort. Ah'm sorry about that, but Ah couldn't do anything about it."

Greta smiled and said, "Horan, they were glad to help you. It was shocking how bad your infection really was. I was so worried about you and whether they could help you with it. How did you feel, Raven?"

Raven moved closer and sat on Horan's bed beside him, "Horan, it was scary how bad that infection looked, but it's looking so much better now. Can you lay on your back now that the magic has done its job?"

"Ah can, Raven. It hardly hurts now. Ah'm feeling like there's hope for me after all. Ah think Ah need to sleep some more. The pain was exhausting for me. Now that it's gone, I need to sleep all of a sudden. Will you stay with me while I sleep? Ah'm feeling the need for company even now."

"Greta and I will both stay with you while you sleep. One of us will be here when you wake up. So don't worry about being alone all right?"

"All right, thanks both of you." Horan promptly fell back to sleep.

Raven was glad he was able to sleep. He had slept during the spell, but only briefly.

Greta had spent a lot of time with Horan, so she asked Raven, "Would you mind if I take a break? It's been a really long day and I'm really tired."

Raven realized then that Greta really had been there most of the day. She said, "Greta, not a problem, you go rest all you need. Take a walk or get some food. I'll stay and watch Horan tonight. If you need to take the night off, it would be fine with me. I know that Horan really appreciates all that you do for him. It's your turn for a night off."

"Thank you Raven. I'm so tired. I really do need a full night off. But come and get me if you need me for anything. Good night." With that, Greta left Horan's room and went to her own room to sleep.

Raven was actually grateful to be alone with Horan. She had been around too many people for her own nerves to handle. She liked the people well enough, she just needed to have them around for short periods of time. For some reason other people were exhausting to her after a certain amount of time. Sitting quietly with Horan was just what she needed after the excitement of the day. She could relax and enjoy the quiet.

Horan was able to sleep for about four hours before he woke up with a start. He said he had been dreaming of the Skreechers attacking him. He was very relieved to see Raven sitting in the chair beside him. It helped to calm him down to know that he was not alone.

"Thank you Raven for staying while ah slept. Ah'm still a bit nervous about waking up alone. After ma wife left with the kids, Ah was wounded and lay on the floor for just a few minutes before Karmine found me. It was like a miracle that he came along when he did. Ah would have died for sure otherwise. Now Ah'm here being cared for by wonderful people like you, Raven. Then when the wizards came and helped my body heal and continue to help me. This has really been such a terrible experience for me. Ah'm still having horrible nightmares from all of it. Do you still have nightmares after your experience?"

"Horan, I do have nightmares still. It's been awhile since the attack, but, like you said, you can't forget the horror of those Skreechers and how they attack you so viciously. They really do seem to come out of nowhere. That's part of why it's so terrifying."

"Yes! That's it! It was so shocking to be attacked so suddenly without warning. You know it could happen at any moment. So now Ah'm afraid to go out of this inn. Do you still feel that way?"

"I sure do, Horan. Looking all around for any danger is not enough to feel safe. We must destroy them all or we will never be safe. Magg is practicing spells to defeat them. I'm so hoping with all of us helping, that those Skreechers will be gone forever and soon."

"Ah wish Ah could be able to help with that. Ah lost so much blood that it will be awhile before Ah have any strength at all. Ah'm trying to drink lots of water to build it back up. It just takes so long."

"That's the hard thing about being injured. It takes so much patience to let our bodies heal on their own. We're truly blessed to have the wizards to help the process. Magg is such a wonderful person and has so much magic. She has made all the difference in the healing process for you and for me. So we have a lot to be grateful for. Are you feeling better since Magg helped your healing? One unsettling thing is that you continue to be attacked by strange organisms. That was the third time she's healed you and the second time she's had to destroy those organisms. I'm sure it has taken a toll on your body and mind. I'm so glad you continue to fight. Don't let all the terrible things that have happened discourage you. You will survive, but you do have to continue the fight."

"Ah really do, Raven. Ah'm feeling stronger every day. But it's still a slow process. Is that what you have experienced?"

Raven sighed remembering how long it was before she was even able to walk slowly with Greta. "Horan, it does take quite a while to heal and get your strength back. So what you really need to do right now is rest and eat healthy and drink lots of water and juice. Does that make sense, Horan?"

Horan smiled and said, "It sure does, Raven. Ah'm so glad Ah have you to talk to about all this. It's good to know another person has been through it too. Thanks for caring and spending time with me while Ah heal."

With that, Horan closed his eyes and slept a bit more. It seemed that talking wore him out. So Raven stayed with him through the night and slept a little in the chair beside him. It was comforting that she could be there for him.

He was the first man she spent a long time alone with and didn't necessarily want to kill. He was so kind to her and the others. Maybe she would be able to stay in Anakik awhile longer.

Chapter 32

A new day dawned with a different darkness and feeling of dread. There were no howls from the Skreeckers during the night. Most of the villagers were concerned about that. When they howled, the people got an idea of how close they were to the village. Now they didn't know. Thinking about the Skreechers and not knowing where they were was unsettling. There seemed to be a dark shadow over the village that morning. A bit of fear was forming in the minds of the people of the village.

Magg woke up next to Matton and felt the darkness. Matton woke up then as well and when he looked at Magg he knew that she was feeling the same darkness he was feeling.

Magg spoke, "Matton, I can see that you are feeling the same thing I am. There seems to be a darkness over all of us. I'm so glad I have used the spell that will be our last resort if things get out of hand with the

Skreechers. I'm feeling like we need to be ready for an attack, maybe even today. We must warn the others. I'm hoping they feel the urgency as we do."

"It really does feel as though we're about to have something terrible happen today. Let's get going and let everyone know that we must be ready today for anything the Skreechers might plan against us."

"Great, let's go!

So it was that Magg and Matton left their room to find and warn all their friends and then send them out to warn the village. It is hoped that their planning would pay off now that they needed it.

Magg and Matton found Jasmine and Donavan in their room and warned them of the trouble that they felt was upon them.

Donavan said, "I was feeling the same way this morning. When the Skreechers didn't howl, it felt like a darkness had descended on us all. I believe we really do need to talk to all the others about being prepared for anything today."

Jasmine agreed, "I feel the same way, too. It feels so different from the other days we've dealt with. It's much more oppressive. Where should we start with warning all the others? We don't know for sure where the Skreechers are right now. They could be anywhere. We might have a real problem trying to get the word to all the villagers. I sure hope Jarrone is feeling the change. I wish we could get word to him without having to risk going all the way to their house at the other end of town. What do you think, Magg?"

Magg had been silent through the discussion and finally spoke up, "I am also worried about Jarrone and all those at his end of the village. I'm wishing we could have set up a signal for them to know what's going on here. Too bad we don't have anything set up. We surely should have. Zarcon tried to warn me to get everything done quickly. But I have simply put it off and now we're possibly in trouble.

"I guess we could start by warning everyone here at the inn and the soldiers in the barracks close by. I'm not sure what to do beyond that. Anyone have any idea of how to get word to the others in the village?"

Just then several of the villagers came running into the inn to find Magg and the others. They were saying, "We're afraid that the Skreechers are about to attack. We have a terrible feeling about what is going on today. What should we do? How do we warn those closer to the forest? What do you want us to do first?"

It was overwhelming to Magg and the others. The villagers were saying the very things that they had been concerned about just moments before.

Magg stood taller and spoke with the power she possessed, "We have felt the same things that you have felt this morning. This is something we knew would come sooner or later. We had all hoped it would be much later, but here we are. Have any of you seen any of the Skreechers yet?"

One little boy, who was hiding behind his mother's skirt shyly raised his hand. Magg called on him to speak, "What's your name young man?"

"I'm Robyn." He said, very shyly.

"Have you seen a Skreecher this morning?"

"Yes I did. It was sneaking around the house across the square. I saw it as I was looking out the window in the front of our house. I didn't expect to see one, but it was there. I'm really glad it didn't look at me."

Magg was shocked, "Did you just see the one, or were there others sneaking around?"

Robyn thought for a moment and said, "Well, I only saw the one, but I had a feeling that there might be more. I noticed that it kept looking around and waving its arms like it was signaling to other Skreechers."

"Are you sure my dear one? This is very important."

"Yes, I'm sure. I really did see the one for sure."

The people in the inn were shocked at what the boy said. Then they started muttering to each other about what it would mean. As they thought more about it, they became more terrified. The Skreechers were in the village? Now what do they do? What could they do? They had planned for this, but now it seemed very inadequate for the situation. It was then that the people realized they had no way of getting word to the others near the forest.

Magg noticed the discussion about the other villagers and became very anxious. She was feeling the stress of what she could do. This was very important and needed to be taken care of. But at the moment she had no idea of how to handle it. Right now she was missing Zarcon and his wisdom and knowledge. He had told her many times that she was ready to be a leader and help the village and everyone in it. But she was having doubts about her ability and this was the worst time for that.

She knew she must protect everyone as much as she possibly could. She had practiced the spells meant for a time like this, but she was almost fearful of using them. She realized in that moment that she needed to call the others to help her decide what the next move should be.

Magg beckoned to Donavan and Jasmine to follow her to the small dining room where they could talk out of earshot of the others. Magg was really worried about what to do to stop the Skreechers for good. She really needed their advice. The time had finally come for action and it had to be swift and powerful if they were to survive. She would find a way to make their attack a complete surprise for the Skreechers. They must be off guard if it were to be successful. But how?

Chapter 33

Magg was so concerned about the next step in survival that she hadn't slept much, but she had rested. The Skreechers still hadn't howled during the night or this morning and that caused much concern for all of those in the village. After they heard from the boy Robyn that the Skreechers were in the village, Magg was almost on the verge of panic. She knew two spells that would cause harm to the monsters, but then what? The townspeople were willing to help and had planned for their defense, but was it enough?

She knew they must do something and that it had to start this day! There was no more putting off the inevitable. She knew she was as prepared as she could be at this time. The darkness seemed to be part of what the Skreechers were planning. They wanted the people to be afraid and not fight back when they chose to attack the village. But Magg was feeling ready now to face whatever she needed to do to overcome the Skreechers. She knew that it wouldn't happen in one day or maybe even in a week, but today was the day to start.

Matton was feeling ready to fight with Magg. They would fight together to free the village of Anakik from the monsters that wanted them all dead. It was time.

Both Magg and Matton had left their room early. They found that Aribon was ready for them with a breakfast of fried eggs, ham, coffee and toast. He had kept it simple because he knew there would be war this day. The others would be coming in soon enough. Magg and Matton ate heartily not knowing when they would have time to eat again.

As they were finishing up their meal, Donavan and Jasmine walked in for their breakfast. They stopped at the counter and picked up their meals. Then they walked over and sat with Magg and Matton. There wasn't much conversation at this point. All four of them were very worried about what this day would bring and what their part in it would be.

Magg was really glad to see them and said, "We need to talk about what we're going to do today, from start to finish if possible. Do either of you have an idea of what we need to do to start this war with the Skreechers? We know they're here in the village. I haven't heard of any attacks by them yet. I'm hoping we can come up with some way to surprise them and take them off guard if possible. Any suggestions?"

They sat and thought about it for a few minutes. All of them had been thinking about what to do all this time, but they hadn't come up with anything of value yet. It was a very difficult situation they were in and there wasn't an easy answer to the problem.

Donavan spoke up finally. "I wonder if we could use the first new spell we learned in the yard not too long ago. Remember how each of us cast a new spell at something and we each had a different reaction to it. Maybe we could use it on the Skreechers and as we hit them, they would become something else. What do you think Magg? We could startle them and maybe even scare them away for a short while."

Magg smiled at the thought and said, "That's a great idea Donavan. Since we had different reactions, the Skreechers wouldn't know how to react. If we could position ourselves randomly around the village and hide and move around, maybe we could even do a lot of damage to them. I suggest we try that right away. I want to save the most powerful spells until we are in great danger. What do you say, Jasmine? Any other ideas?"

Jasmine remembered something the villagers had come up with for signaling each other. They had made red flags to hang out their upper windows when there was a Skreecher nearby. There was another color of flag, yellow, to let the people living at the other end of town know what was going on in town. It was hoped that they would know right away regardless since they were at the end of town where the Skreechers were most likely to attack first. That end of town was watched carefully for any color of flag that might show. So far there had been none. That fact was actually a worry. Were they still alive? Had they been attacked already? Terrible thoughts.

Those with magic began to watch for the flags from the windows of the inn. Suddenly, there was a red one just across the road from the inn. Magg was watching and saw a Skreecher creep around the house there. She decided to act. She quietly opened the door of the inn and began the spell. She said each word of the spell very carefully and used her arms to form it. She cast the spell at the Skreecher and watched to see what would happen to it.

It took a moment to affect the Skreecher, but then it appeared to melt into a puddle of greenish slime. It bubbled for a few seconds then fell quiet. Then there was a smell that defied all description. It burned the eyes, along with coughing and nose running. It was terrible. But at the same time, it made smiles appear in spite of it all. The thing was dead for sure. Magg had used the easiest spell for them that she had learned from Zarcon's Book of Spells. The same one she had taught both Donavan and Jarrone.

As Magg thought about her spell, she began to wonder what Donavan and Jarrone's spells would do to the Skreechers. Each one of them had had a different outcome when they practiced in the yard a while back.

As Magg was thinking about those things she finally realized that she could hear some cheering and hand clapping in the village. She finally looked up to see a group of people outside the inn cheering for what she had just done to the Skreecher. She smiled and waved at them in acknowledgement. It was fun to be appreciated like that once in a while. She shyly went back into the inn and shut the door.

The important thing about the episode was that it had worked great. The red flag told her she needed to do something about a monster lurking in the village and she had taken care of it. She called Donavan and when he came to her, she told him about how the red flag had helped and she had killed a Skreecher as a result.

"Magg, that's amazing! We know now that we have got to watch at all times and be ready to act when needed. We need to let Jarrone know about it, too."

"Yes we do."

Just at that moment, Jarrone had seen the red flag in town. It had surprised him since there had been no sightings near his end of town. He decided to alert the neighbors near him that things were getting very dangerous indeed. He was cautious to look all around his house through the windows before he ventured outside. It seemed that all was clear for a moment. He was sure Magg had killed the Skreecher that had been in town, but there were more than likely others of them lurking nearby. He decided that the safest thing to do would be to fly the yellow flag to alert the other neighbors that a Skreecher had been spotted in town. That was really all he dared do just then. He would watch for the monsters at all times.

Jarrone went to the others of his family to alert them to what had happened. He gathered his father, Revinia, Lucintha, and Hoskins to talk to them about what he knew about the Skreechers.

"I'm so glad you are all here. I know I haven't shared enough about the monsters that hide in the forest and attack people. One was just seen in the village and Magg was able to kill it. She taught me a spell to kill the monsters. I'm so grateful that I have that spell. I'm not sure what it will do to the Skreechers, but I know it will kill them.

"What I'm asking is for all of us to be on the lookout for them and holler if you see anything move nearby. I can kill it before it can harm any of us or our neighbors, but only if we see it first. So as you walk around the house, keep an eye on what's going on around us. We have to be aware at all times so we can save ourselves and everyone else close by. Got it?"

The family smiled and as one said, "GOT IT!"

And so it was that they were all ready to fight the Skreechers and watch out for their neighbors.

Would it be enough?

Chapter 34

As Jarrone and his family began watching for the Skreechers even more than they had been, some of their neighbors opened the curtains of their windows to wave at them for letting them know there was trouble when they raised the yellow flag for them. Soon all of their neighbors were watching for Skreechers anywhere near them or the village. All of them were so grateful that they had Jarrone close by to help fight them. They would do all they could, but there was nothing like having a little magic close by.

Even so, they all knew that it was going to take more than Jarrone's magic to destroy the Skreechers. Each of the families had been preparing what they could do if they had to do something on their own. A few of the men had rifles and ammunition. The problem was that they didn't know if it would be enough to kill a Skreecher. It had never been tried.

The villagers had gotten complacent about having magic to do the fighting for them. It was becoming obvious at this point that the magic just might not be enough.

As Karmine had suggested a few weeks before, they each needed to decide what they could do to help with the fight to survive and defend themselves and their families. They all knew that all their lives would depend on the courage of each person. The Skreechers were too powerful and aggressive to think that the three people with magic could do it all themselves. When Karmine suggested each of them needed to decide what they could do, it hit home and made them think more seriously about protecting each other as a village family.

Realizing that the Skreechers were now in town and moving in, the men with guns decided to get ready for that kind of fight. If it worked, great! If it didn't work, at least they would know to try something else. The men would not go outside and act as a target, but they would fight from inside looking out the windows, guns ready. It was time to try.

After a bit, one of the Skreechers was sneaking up on Karmine's house. He was ready with his gun and opened the window a crack ready to shoot. As the Skreecher rounded the side of his house, Karmine shot it in the head at close range. He shut the window immediately.

The Skreecher fell backwards onto the road and didn't move. Karmine had shot most of his head off, a sure sign of death. Karmine and Roslin cheered and got ready for the next chance to shoot a Skreecher.

But apparently, the fact that one of their own had been shot so suddenly seemed to enrage the Skreechers. Two of them came out of the forest and carried their fellow monster away. Karmine was getting ready to shoot one of them, but thought better of it. He wasn't sure that making them even angrier was a good idea. So Karmine decided that he wouldn't kill any more of them unless they were threatened. Maybe a good idea, maybe not.

Jarrone had watched what happened. He was proud of Karmine for acting on his own. Now he knew that the villagers really could help in the fight.

Karmine put up a red flag to let the town know that a Skreecher had been nearby. The alert was noted and now the town was focused on elimination of the monsters. They also knew that guns could help in the fight.

No one had thought of guns before because they had always used magic. That meant that those with magic were totally depended on for the safety of everyone else. It was just the way things were done in the past. Now with the possibility of new weapons of war, the villagers were feeling a sense of hope that they had not felt before.

So with care, a new plan was being discussed among the people of Anakik. They couldn't communicate with those with magic easily, but they could send messages to those close by.

Karmine decided they could write on large sheets of fabric, such as their bedsheets, the messages they must send. His was the first one. He wrote, "Guns are able to kill the Skreechers. Get yours ready and loaded. Be sure you have ammunition to last a long while."

The neighbors were able to write back, "We have guns and ammunition we thought we wouldn't need until now. We are ready to use what we have to destroy Skreechers."

The sense of foreboding that had enveloped the village to this point was lifting. It was as though the people gave a heavy sigh of relief to think there was even more they could do to fight these terrible monsters that had invaded their town.

Back at the inn, Magg and Matton had heard the gunshot from Jarrone's end of town and were wondering what it could mean. They could also sense some form of joy and pride coming from that end of town. They reasoned it must be that the gunshot had killed one of the Skreechers. If so, it was cause for celebration. The villagers had more power than ever before and would be helping with the fight on a very real level.

Magg called Donavan and Jasmine to come and see what had happened. They were on their way when the shooting had started.

Magg decided to call a meeting of all those in and near the inn who could come. It was dangerous to ask the people to risk the monsters to come. But it would be so much better if more were there to hear what Magg was thinking.

Magg put a yellow flag out for all to see, hoping the right message would be sent. It wasn't long before several of the villagers risked crossing the village square to find out what was going on.

Magg had also called Greta, and Raven to come to the meeting. Some of the villagers were also coming, Murdon, Eskelon, Marva, Toran, and a couple of other village members came. Magg called them to the dining room to sit while she talked to them about what had happened on the other end of the village.

She began, "I'm so glad so many of you could come. I have some important news to share with you all. From the sound of things a bit ago, it appears that guns are also effective against the Skreechers. How many of you have rifles and ammunition?"

All of the villager's hands went up. It used to be a village of hunters after all. They had gotten out of the habit of hunting when the risk to Raven became obvious because of Orshon and his friends.

Now they would be very much needed.

Magg continued, "This is so important to our survival. With the help of all those with guns, we can fight together to destroy the monsters. I've been concerned about having to take on fighting them with just Donavan, Jarrone, and me. Now we can be even more effective with all of you being able to stop the individual monsters as they approache your homes. I'm hoping to use a very powerful spell to take on more of them at once. But I only want to use it when nothing else will.

"Here I have a map of the village on this table. Would each of you with guns and ammunition please mark on the map where you live? Then we can see what the coverage of the village will be."

Those present took turns marking the map for Magg. It appeared that the village would have pretty good overall protection with the people who had guns. They were scattered randomly around the village square. All were feeling a bit more hopeful now. They had a plan and the villagers were going to be able to make a significant difference in the outcome of the day.

Alfias saw what was happening and offered to feed everyone before they headed back to their homes. Magg agreed and they all found a table to sit together and enjoy the roast chicken and potatoes Alfias had prepared for them. It was amazing how much the time spent planning with the others had made in the spirit now. The gloom of the morning was ended and now they were all looking forward to what they could do to stop the Skreechers and even destroy them.

After their meal, it was decided that they should get back to their own homes and do all they could to protect them. The Skreechers had been quiet for awhile now. So Magg and Matton went to the door of the inn and cautiously looked up and down the square and the road that led to the other end of town. They could see no monsters and the birds were back singing again.

It seemed safe enough for the people to leave the inn at that moment. Eskelon and Marva were first out. They were concerned that they had left their adopted boys home alone. So they grabbed each other's hands and ran home. They made it easily.

Murdon, the carpenter, was next. He made a dash for it and got to his shop just in time. One of the Skreechers was close to his building and ran at him just as he was able to close the door and bolt it. It was a close one. He went to get his rifle and loaded it. He wanted badly to kill that one. He looked out the front window when he was ready. The monster had made the mistake of hanging around the front of Murdon's shop. So Murdon took aim and shot the thing in the middle of its chest. His rifle was very powerful and blew a hole in its chest, killing it instantly. Murdon was so pleased with himself that he jumped up and down for joy.

Toran decided that he would rather spend the rest of the day at the inn. The Skreechers were too close to take the chance just now. Magg agreed that he should wait til later in the day. It was hoped that the Skreechers would find a different place to hang out than so close to the center of the village.

They heard Murdon's gunshot just then and looked out the window in time to see the Skreecher fall over with a big hole in its chest. They also heard Murdon laughing and jumping up and down for joy. Then Magg, Matton, and Toran did the same. It was a beautiful thing.

Meanwhile, Eskelon and Marva both got their guns out and were ready to use them. They hadn't quite been ready when the one tried to attack Murdon. But they would be watching now. In fact the oldest boy, Eagan, that they had adopted, was actually a good shot and wanted to help out. So Eskelon gave him one of the rifles and he was ready to defend their home as well. They each took one side of the house to guard and were prepared to shoot.

Just then, those in the inn heard a gunshot from Eskelon and Marva's house. One of the monsters had tried to climb in the side bedroom window that had accidently been left open. Eagan had seen it coming and had shot it just as it was starting to climb in. He had been able to blow a hole it its head and send it back through the window and into the yard. He was shaken by it, but he was also proud that he had stopped that thing. Eskelon hugged him and told him how proud he was of him. He was so brave to do such a thing.

Things were looking up indeed. But it was still just one at a time being destroyed. Donavan wanted to talk to Magg about using the spells they had practiced.

He said, "Magg, when would you like us to start using the spells we've been practicing? We could start hunting the monsters instead of just waiting for them to attack the village. What do you think?"

Magg had been so excited that the people of Anakik could help that she wasn't thinking about how they could start using their magic to cause more problems for the Skrecchers. Now was the time.

She said, "Donavan, you're right! We need to be hunting the monster ourselves. Waiting for them to come to us is a waste of time when we could actually be taking them out before they can attack."

Donavan thought for a moment and said, "It will be very dangerous to do this. We'll need to be close to each other so we can watch the area as we go. But we don't want to be so close that one Skreecher could get to two of us at once."

Magg spoke up, "I know we need to be the ones on the attack. But we must be very careful not to put each other at risk of being caught alone. We would have to be sure to have a spell ready to go at any moment so we can act quickly. There must be no time to think about it. So we each need to pick a spell and be ready to use it in an instant. Does that make sense? The monsters are not going to give us a chance to think before they attack us. Can we work together to decide what spells we want to use and have ready in any emergency?"

Jarrone had been thinking about all this and finally said, "I would really like to use the new spell you taught us awhile ago. Not only because it will be very effective, but because I am very curious to see what happens when we use it. Any other suggestions, Donavan?"

"I agree. I would like to start with that spell and then if we must, we can move on to others that we have known for a long time. Most of those would work if we use them together. Also, let's not forget that we need to be able to get to Magg in case she has to use one of her really powerful spells to destroy more of the monsters at one time. So we can't be spread very thin in order to protect each other as we go."

Magg agreed, "I think we're on the right track now. When and where do we want to start this battle? I'm feeling that our time has run out and we must start right away."

Donavan said, "Magg, you're right about starting right away. Do you think we should go after them during the day when they might be less active, or at sunset when they are coming into town? I'm thinking the sooner the better."

Magg agreed, "I also agree that the sooner we start the better for all concerned. Should we warn the villagers that we're going to be out in the village looking for Skreechers and to be careful with their rifles that they don't mistake one of us for one of those?"

Donavan said, "That is an important consideration. We can't risk the villagers shooting at us when we're out trying to destroy the Skreechers."

Just then, there was a volley of gunshots near the inn. Everyone ran to the windows to see what was happening. As they watched, there were five Skreechers moving into the village in a group looking for someone to eat. Several of the villagers had their guns out their windows and started shooting them. All four were shot and killed on the spot.

Magg was very happy to note that those who fired on the Skreechers were very careful to shoot only when they knew what they were shooting at. No windows were broken and only the Skreechers were killed.

But before anyone could celebrate, more of the Skreechers came running out of the forest. It was a massive attack. Magg and Donavan, went out of the inn together and started using their spells on them.

Donavan hit one of them using the new spell, the Skreecher folded in on himself and melted into a blob of brown ooze. Flames started licking at the edges of his body and he was consumed by the flames.

Magg cast the spell and hit two of the Skreechers at the same time. They both reached for each other as they collapsed into a large pool of ooze. The ground beneath them seemed to open up and swallow them before they caught on fire. It was like a grave had been formed for them. They were completely gone.

The villagers were screaming and shouting for joy as the Skreechers were being destroyed. Further up the village gunshots could be heard from the area of Karmine and Jarrone's family. The battle was joined by all who were able to help.

Meanwhile, Jarrone and his family were ready for battle as well. Jarrone's brother, Hoskins, knew how to shoot a rifle and so did his father. So between the three of them, they wree able to keep the Skreechers from getting into any of the homes nearby.

Karmine and Roslin were ready and started shooting the monsters as soon as they came near to their home. The boys were told to stay in the room with them so they knew where they were. The boys helped with the ammunition and making sure their parents had what they needed. It was going well for them.

Murdon was home and was using his rifle on the monsters. He shot several of them as they ran out of the forest. It gave him great satisfaction to do so. He was thinking of Horan as he was shooting. He kept saying, "That's for Horan you filthy beast."

Jarrone decided that he needed to start using the spell he knew and get rid of some of those Skreechers himself. He moved to the back door and was ready to use the new spell just as one was almost on him. He cast the spell just in time to burn a hole through the middle of it. It looked up in surprise and screamed a horrible sound as he burned up and melted into the ground. The mess was disgusting and smelled terrible. But the thing was dead.

The battle continued through most of the rest of the day as everyone who could destroy the monsters was working hard. Finally, the Skreechers seemed to sense the fight was much harder than they had thought and some started to go back to the forest. They were be gone at least for a time.

Jarrone's brother and father had killed many of the Skreechers themselves and were feeling very proud of their efforts. Jarrone was so happy that Hoskins had stepped up and helped that he hugged him when the fighting finally seemed to be over for a time.

He said, "Hoskins, you're amazing! I'm so glad you decided to help. I didn't know you could shoot like that. It was almost magic that everything you shot at, you hit and killed. You seem to have some form of magic of your own that we wouldn't have seen without the Skreechers."

Hoskins was embarrassed. He wasn't used to so much attention. He had spent his life in Anakik being a loner and doing his own thing for years. No one seemed to notice him most of the time. But now those days were over. He had finally stepped into the light and was a hero.

Jarrone's father was also a loner and kept to himself most of the time. As with Hoskins, he had come into his own when he was truly needed in the battle with the Skreechers. Revinia and Lucintha had made sure the men had ammunition ready as they were needed. The whole family had come together in this time of great need. They were very proud of each other and themselves for what they had accompolished so far in this battle.

The other neighbors were having much the same realization. They were able to do hard things when they worked together. Karmine and Roslin and their boys, and Murdon had all come through with pride and a sense of accomplishement. Now they all knew that come what may, they could fight and kill the monsters together.

Back at the inn, there was a celebration for the work everyone had done that day. They knew the war wasn't over, but they had fought and won the battle. The Skreechers were stopped for a time.

Chapter 35

The next day, the people of Anakik spent a large part of it burying the bodies of the Skreechers killed by gunshots. They could have been burned with magic, but it seemed a waste of energy to do so.

There were about fifteen bodies. It was a gruesome task, but couldn't be avoided. The bodies of the Skreechers would soon rot in the sun and the smell would be enough to drive out the people of Anakik. The men started digging a large hole and made sure it would be big enough for all of the Skreecher bodies. It was also deep enough to eliminate any smell of rotting flesh from coming up out of the grave and too deep for any predators to dig them up.

Finally, the hole was deep and wide enough to push the bodies inside. The hole was quickly filled in and stamped down. Nearly everyone in that end of the village joined in. They made a sort of dance about it as they stomped the earth. The area was guarded by those with guns and magic just in case the monsters decided to seek revenge on those who had killed their kind.

Fortunately, none of the Skreechers showed up then, but it was only a temporary reprieve at best. All were aware that more was coming sooner than later. So everyone stayed alert and ready for action if needed. It was a very tense situation.

Just then, a prolonged howl ripped the air and caused all the villagers to head for their homes. The sound repeated three more times and was held for several seconds. Gradually, they people realized it was most likely the sound of the Skreechers mourning their dead. It caused a chill in the air and a feeling of great sorrow to fill everyone's heart. The children burst into tears and clung to their parent's legs for comfort. It was obvious that when the Skreechers mourned their losses, they emitted s very deep sorrow to anyone near enough to hear it.

Magg sensed how the sorrow as being felt by everyone. She knew that she must do something right away or all might be lost to the sorrow that would be difficult to overcome. She feared that all the village would be paralyzed by this sorrow. They might not be able to defend themselves, or even care to. She was having a difficult time fighting the feeling herself.

Magg called to Donavan to come to her so they could plan a way to prevent complete loss of the will to live. She could sense that part of the emotions of the howling was a lethargy that might become permanent. She sensed some form of magic involved.

Donavan came to her and they spoke about a plan to combat the Skreechers death mourning.

Magg said, "Donavan, we've got to prevent the people from getting caught up in the magic of the howling. I'm convinced there is magic involved in the sound. Do you feel it?"

"I have noticed that there seems to be much more to the howling than simple sorrow. It is likely that magic is involved in the tone used for the howls. What do you think we can do about it?"

"I'm thinking we could hum tones and see which ones cancel the tone used by the Skreechers. Let's get Jasmine and Greta to help. What do you think?"

"I'm going to go find Jasmine and Greta and see if they will help. They both can sing, so it might just work. If it does, we can recruit the villagers and make the tone that works really loud."

Donavan left and headed for the rooms where Jasmine and Greta were staying. He called them to him saying, "We need the two of you to help with a quick plan to fight the sound being made by the monsters. We're wondering if it contains some form of magic. Please come with me to talk with Magg about her plan. Will you come with me now?"

Jasmine and Greta looked at each other and nodded. Jasmine said, "Let's go."

Donavan led the way to the dining area where Magg was waiting. As they joined Magg, it was plain that she was really worried. She said, "I'm so glad you both could come. I'm thinking we could hum a tone to fight the sound of the Skreecher's howls and see what happens. It's my feeling that the howls of the monsters is of a certain tone designed to stop any opposition to their attacks. I'm thinking they really want to destroy all of us because we were able to defend ourselves against their first attack. I'm also concerned that they are using some strange form of magic to add to the effect.

"When we try a tone, if nothing happens, then we try another one. We keep trying until we find one that cancels the tones in the Skreecher's howls. We'll need to work quickly before the sound cripples everyone in the village with sorrow such that they can't move. I really think that's the goal of the monsters.

Are you willing to try it with me? I know both of you have some talent with singing and can hold a note. What do you say Jasmine?"

Jasmine smiled and said, "I am more than willing. What if it works and we find that singing can stop the Skreechers in some way?"

Greta agreed with Jasmine and told Magg she was all in.

So Magg hummed a note and Greta and Jasmine joined in. It didn't seem to have an effect. Magg hummed the next tone and Greta and Jasmine joined in. There seemed to be a slight effect, but nothing of value. So Magg tried another tone and the two women joined in. This time the air seemed to shimmer for a moment. This tone had an effect, but not quite enough to stop what the Skreechers were doing.

Magg tried one more tone slightly higher than the last one. But this time she added a touch of magic. When Jasmine and Greta joined in, it was magical. Not only did the air shimmer, it flashed and broke the spell of the monster's howls. Suddenly, it was as if everyone in the village woke up and started laughing. It was such a relief that the effect of the howls was broken.

Magg decided to teach more of the people of Anakik the same tone. She decided to invite anyone who could sing to join them in the dining room to be trained. She sent some of the men to get the word out to the villagers.

It took a few minutes to get everyone who wanted to participate to file into the dining room. There were about twenty people who came to help. Word had even gotten to the other end of town to Jarrone and his family. Karmine and Roslin heard about it too. They decided to join the group at the inn.

Jarrone's sisters and even Hoskins wanted to help. So the group of them with Karmine and Roslin with their four boys all hurried down to the inn. It appeared that the monsters were quiet for a moment or two after the tone Magg had found to stop their torment.

So it was that they all made it to the inn without incident. Magg was delighted to see them all walk into the inn. She said as she laughted with joy, "You're here! I didn't dare to hope that you would get the word about what we're doing. We have a big enough group to make a huge difference in the volume of the tone we need to use to fight what the monsters are trying to do to us. Thank you for coming."

Karmine spoke up, "We want to do all we can to fight against what the Skreechers are doing. If we have to sing to do it, we're in no matter what."

"This is going to be almost fun. I can hardly wait to see what we can do with this tonal weapon." Donavan was excited to start.

Magg said, "This won't stop the Skreechers, but at least it will stop one of their weapons from doing the damage they've designed it to do."

The tone Magg had found gave them hope that they really could fight the monsters in many different ways. It was looking good right now. It was time to find a way to put them all together as a line of defense.

They practiced as a group for over an hour to make certain that they all had the right tone. Each time they hummed the tone, it seemed to grow in strength. With that much accomplished, it was decided that it was time for dinner.

Magg had sent Donavan to check on Aribon to see if there would be enough dinner for everyone. When Donavan left, he hurried to the kitchen to find Aribon cooking an especially large meal as if it were a celebration or something.

Donavan said, "Aribon, I see you've already figured out that Magg would feed everyone dinner today. When do you think it will be ready for everyone to come and get it?"

Aribon smiled, "I suppose any time now would be fine. I've made plenty of roast turkey and potatoes and gravy for an army. So I've been hoping all of you would want to eat. The soldiers are coming as well. So bring them in and let's feed them!"

Donavan left the kitchen laughing. Aribon was really amazing. He was so generous with his food and time it almost made Donavan weep with gratitude. He hurried on to the dining area and told everyone that dinner was actually ready and all were invited to eat. It turned out that there really was plenty for everyone. The turkey was delicious and the potatoes and gravy were wonderful. Aribon included some vegetables from his garden and fresh water from the spring he had plumbed into the kitchen.

Everyone sat where they wished and stayed in family groups. Jarrone and his siblings were having a wonderful time. Jarrone's father came down to the inn when it looked like the monsters were staying away for awhile. So the whole family was together for dinner.

Jarrone's father had been seeing a widow that lived closer to the center of town and so they met for the dinner that day. Things were looking up for his father. He had found that pretending to be helpless hadn't really worked well for him. So now, he was trying to do new things, such as getting to know new people. He really liked the widow. Her name was Helza. They really hit it off and were becoming great friends.

Another change was that Hoskins was coming out of his shell. He hadn't had anything to do with the town or even his family for a long time. He had finally decided to try living and it was feeling pretty good.

Jarrrone's sisters, Lucintha and Revinia were enjoying the time away from their home. Both girls were pretty and the boys in town were trying to be a part of their lives as well. The girls were picky, and wouldn't let anyone in who didn't seem to be a good person.

Raven and Horan were spending a lot of time together. Raven liked Horan, but not as anything more than a friend. She was mostly liking Aribon. He had done so much for her and had been so kind that she couldn't help but think of him in a very kindly way.

Raven had heard the Skreecher's howling and felt its effect like the other villagers. She also felt it when Magg and the other's stopped the effects of it. She decided it was time to investigate what was happening in the inn just then.

Raven assured Horan that she would be back in just a few minutes while she went to check on what was going on.

She walked out of Horan's room and headed for the dining area. When she got there and saw so many people there, she was shocked. She went to Magg to find out what had happened.

"Magg, I've felt some powerful magic the past few minutes and wondered what might be happening. Can you tell me?"

Magg looked up at Raven and smiled, "Raven, it's been a really eventful morning. Sit here and I'll tell you all about it." So while she finished up her dinner, Magg explained what had been going on all day. She finished by telling Raven about the group of those who could sing and what that meant for the Skreecher's howlings.

"Magg, that is so exciting that you've found a way to stop the effect of that awful sound. I could feel it in my bones. It was so very sorrowful and yet seemed to want to control my feelings. Is that what you mean?"

"It is exactly what I mean. We've found another way to fight the magic that the monsters use against us. It's giving us even more hope of defending ourselves against their attacks."

"I did feel when the noise stopped. It was such a relief. It felt like I could breathe again. It's a wonderful thing to have magic to help in all this."

"I feel like it's a wonderful thing that so many are willing to help right now. It's going to take the whole village to combat and hopefully destroy those horrible Skreechers. By the way, how is Horan doing right now?"

Raven smiled, "He's doing remarkably well. I was actually wondering if he could get out of his bed and walk around the inn a little. What do you think?"

Magg said, "Let's go have a look at how Horan is doing. I've meant to check on him for a few days now."

Raven was delighted, "I would love it if you would come and see him. He's really doing well since the last time he was healed. The pain isn't bothering him much and he's getting itchy. I think his wounds are healing nicely too. But do you think we could bring him a plate of food while we're at it?"

So the two of them went to Aribon and requested a plate of food for Horan. It was freely given. They left the dining area with food and headed for Horan's room. Raven opened the door and let Magg enter. Horan was sitting up on his bed and was studying a book Raven had given him.

He said, "Well it sure is good to see ya Miss Magg. Ah've been feeling really good the past two days and wondering if Ah might get to stretch ma legs a bit. What do ya think?"

Magg said, "We brought you some food to help you get your strength back. Eat your food then let me check you over. She looked at him while he ate and saw that he really was looking much better since she had last seen him. Then she asked if she could put her hands on his chest to see for herself if he really was doing better.

Horan said, "Of course ya may. Ah need to know if Ah'm really doing as well as Ah think Ah am."

Magg put her hands on Horan's chest and listened to his heart and body. She was amazed that he sounded so well. He showed no signs of the illness he had fought against for so long. His body was healing really fast now. It was amazing that the magic could work such a miracle in him.

She said, "Horan, you really are doing amazingly well for all that you've been through. I'm thinking you could get out of that bed and walk down the hall once a day. Let's see how you do after a week. What do you think?"

Horan was so pleased, he said, "Magg those are the sweetest words Ah've heard in a long while. Thanks for all you've done for me. And thanks for the food. It was delicious"

"I'm just so glad you're doing so well. Just remember to take it slow for this first week, please."

"Oh, Ah will do that for sure."

Raven was so pleased to know that Horan could now get out of his bed and move around a bit. She was smiling ear to ear.

"Well, I need to get back to the others. Here, I'll take his plate with me. Be sure to take it easy now. I'll check back in a few days to see how it's going."

Raven followed Magg to the door and closed it after she left. "I'm so happy for you Horan. It will be a great thing for you to be able to get out and walk a little now. I know how I felt when I could finally leave my bed. It was beginning to feel like a prison. Is that how you've been feeling?"

Horan laughed, "It sure is. Nothin' like a sick body to put you in a prison you cannot escape."

Back at the dining area, people were leaving to go back home. But it was with joyful hearts this time. Hope had returned to the village at least for a time. They were still being very watchful of the Skreechers. They could still be anywhere ready to attack. But this night everyone got home safely. But tomorrow would be a new day of the war.

Chapter 36

The day had ended in a quiet peace. It seemed that the Skreechers might be resting, but to what end? Everyone knew the end was not yet. But since all was quiet, they could use that time to get rested for whatever was to come next.

Magg and the other leaders of the village had learned a great deal that day. Not only were the Skreechers vicious and destructive, they also had magic of a different kind. The first sign of their magic was when something had attacked Magg, Donavan, and Jarrone the day they had decided to name the monsters. In trying to track the magic used to choose the name by which they would be called, they found that the magic was extremely dangerous. Something had come up through the earth itself and had moved up their bodies before they could stop the spell they were using. Fortunately, they had stopped the spell before they were injured by it. But when Zarcon had heard about it, he had been frightened more than anyone realized.

It also seemed to be magic the way the monsters could appear suddenly and attack to kill. They also seemed to carry some kind of organisms that attacked those they had injured and caused terrible infections that nearly killed the person. Most recently, they had found that the monsters could use sound to cause emotions in those they wished to destroy.

This very morning, the howling of the Skreechers had caused what felt like gloom had descended on the entire village. People were so sorrowful that they could barely think. It was so severe that Magg was fearful that the Skreechers would be able to walk into the village and kill everyone without a fight.

It was very fortunate that Magg had decided to try her own tones to combat the feeling sent by the Skreechers. She knew that sound could change mood and energy on a small scale. She thought that what the Skreechers were doing might be connected to that, only on a much larger scale. As she thought about it, she realized that she was likely on to some way of combating the sound being made by the monsters. She had finally found a way to stop the horrible oppressive cloud of depression that had descended that morning. With the help of Greta and Jasmine, she was able to find the right tone to break the spell the monsters were trying to cast on them.

However, Magg was realistic enough to know that what she had done would most likely cause greater anger in the Skreechers. Their spell had been neutralized and they were bound to try something new, probably even more deadly.

Magg was feeling a bit confident that whatever the Skreechers tried, she and those with her would be able to combat it. It would be a time of reckoning for all of the people of Anakik.

It is hoped that Magg wasn't feeling overconfident at this very critical time.

That morning, Jarrone had come to the inn with his family to have breakfast together. It was good to get out of the house for a few hours. Jarrone also had a feeling Magg would want to have a meeting today after what had happened the day before.

Karmne and Roslin came a bit late with their sons. They wanted to be a part of whatever was discussed regarding the monsters. And they were there ready to participate.

The Skreechers were far more powerful than was suspected. It also seemed that they were getting smarter in their own use of magic. They may have been far more intelligent than they had appeared to be at first. The first law of warfare is to never underestimate your opponent. It was time to reevaluate what was thought of the monsters now, before it was too late.

So Magg had decided to call her companions together to discuss what must be done to stay current with whatever the Skreechers would attempt this new day. Magg had the intense feeling that something big was going to happen and very soon.

Magg called Donavan, Jasmine, Greta, Jarrone, Karmine and Roslin, and her love, Matton, to come and meet her in the dining area as they had the day before. It would be important to also include Aribon in their plans. He was playing a very important part in keeping everyone fed and calm. He was a very kind person and had the ability to see things before they were needed. It was especially true when it came time to feed everyone. As soon as everyone was present and ready to listen, Magg began explaining her thoughts.

She said, "You all know what we're up against. The Skreechers seem to have been able to add new magic to their fight against us. So far we've been able to adapt to those new changes. But we must move ahead faster to put a stop to whatever new thing they plan to use against us. I'm not sure how we'll be able to do that, but we must find a way. Does anyone have any ideas to help us with that?"

Karmine spoke up first, "I've been thinking about the tone used yesterday to stop the dread caused by the monsters. I would really like to ensure that the tone used by the villagers was always the same one. Could some kind of device be made to hand out to everyone who wanted to help that would be the same for all?"

Magg and the others were surprised that he was the only one to think of that.

Magg said, "Karmine, you are a genious! We surely can do that. It will be very important that we all have the same tone if it's to be effective. Jasmine, would you be willing to talk to the blacksmith about creating something like that for us? Something that can be tapped to make the right sound. I'm hoping it won't be very difficult. You know the tone we need the best."

Jasmine replied, "I would be honored to help with that. I'm not sure the blacksmith can do something so fine, but I will find out for you today."

Jarrone spoke up, "Maybe it could be something like a whistle. Does anyone know how to carve whistles of a certain pitch? That might be easier. I'll look into that area myself. We can surely come up with something soon."

Karmine spoke up, "Actually, I know how to make whistles. I could make up a few and we could decide which tone is the one we need. May I do that? I can have them ready by this evening."

Magg said, "Karmine, maybe it would save time if Jasmine went with you instead. She can help you find the right tone faster that way. I agree with the whistle idea. I'm not sure the blacksmith would even know where to start. It would have to be pretty exact to work, right? So let's get back together later today. Karmine will bring his whistles and we will test them to see what happens. Does that make sense?"

The rest of the group agreed that they would meet after dinner that day.

Karmine, Roslin, Jasmine, and the four boys headed back to Karmine's house to get started on the whistles. Donavan went along to protect them just in case a Skreecher happened along the way.

Everything was going well for the first few minutes. But as they approached the main road to the other end of town, they could smell something that was off. Donavan braced himself and started a spell knowing they were not alone. Just when he was ready to cast the spell, a Skreecher came out of nowhere and was about to attack the group. It was coming in fast on their left side.

Donavan let his spell fly into the Skreecher. It hit it just as it was about to pounce. It flew at them but the spell stopped it and knocked it backward onto the the road. It wasn't dead yet, but it was stunned and disoriented. Donavan prepared another, more powerful spell and sent it into the Skreecher's chest just as it was rising to attack again.

This time the spell hit the Skreecher and as it went deep into its chest, it exploded and blew the Skreecher apart. Some of the monsters body parts got on the groups clothing. The blood splattered everyone, but the monster was definitely dead.

Karmine and Roslin had sheltered the boy's bodies from the Skreecher even as it was trying to attack them. When it was over, they all cried and gagged at the smell and gore that was on them. Donavan kept calm as he hurried them into Karmine and Roslin's home jujst a few yards ahead. The boys were untouched and because their parents sheltered them, they didn't have much gore on them. But they were greatly traumatized by the experience. Jasmine was unhurt, but had a lot of gore on her clothing. She was very shaken by the experience as well. It was her first experience up close to one of the Skreechers and she was terrified.

As the group entered their home, they began removing their clothing and putting it in the can reserved for burning waste. They got some clean clothes on. Roslin found a dress that would cover Jasmine. It was a bit large, but covered her body until she could get something back in her room at the inn.

Karmine was able to take the can outside the back door and burn the contents. Donavan was able to start the fire that would completely destroy the contents of the can.

Donavan was so very glad that he had accompanied them to their home. But he knew that the Skreechers were still around and wanting revenge. He had a bad feeling all day that he hadn't mentioned to anyone. But he was very grateful that he had paid attention to it and followed the others to their home, especially since Jasmine had gone with them.

Once all was disposed of and cleaned up and burned, Karmine and Roslin were able to realize what had nearly happened to them all. It didn't bear thinking about what might have happened if Donavan hadn't followed them. He was their hero and saved all their lives.

Donavan decided to stay with them for a few hours to make sure the Skreechers didn't come back after the killing of another one of their kin. The rest of the day was spent talking about what had happened and letting the boys express their feelings and fears.

Kedron spoke first, "I've had some really scary experiences in my life, but this one made me think I was about to die for sure. I'm so grateful to mom and dad for protecting us as the monster came at us. But seeing Donavan cast those spells at it, was really exciting. Watching that Skreecher die made me very happy. I hated the stuff all over us, but it was worth it just to see it destroyed with magic. I hope we can destroy them all just the same."

Donavan said, "Kedron, I am also very glad that I was with you all today. I've had a bad feeling all morning and when you decided to go start on the whistles, I knew I had to go with you. We learn more about the Skreechers as time goes by and we're getting better at protecting each other. But I really worry about the affect all this is having on you children. I'm hoping more children will feel as you do about destroying them and saving each other from them."

Karmine listened to what was being said and spoke up, "Those monsters are so unpredictable. Everything seemed so quiet and then suddenly we're being attacked by one. I'm so grateful that you were ready with a spell to stop that evil thing. Without you, we were helpless."

Roslin was very near tears when she said, "Donavan, we owe you our lives. Please stay for awhile until we feel safe here in our house. I'm fearful that they might decide to attack us here after you leave. I know you need to get back to the inn with Jasmine, but maybe you could help us make our home a bit more secure. Those things are just so strong and powerful. We just aren't as prepared as I thought we were."

Donavan had a hard time answering Roslin. He knew what she was saying was true. He needed to speak with Magg and the others about a way to keep everyone together while they fought the Skreechers.

He finally said, "I'm thinking we may need to decide what the best thing to do might be. This attack has made me much more aware of the threat we're facing. It took a lot of magic to destroy just that one Skreecher. They are stronger than we thought. But for now, I will stay with you until we can decide how to be safer in our homes. Since we decided to make whistles for protection, let's do that and then take them to the inn. We can do that right now. I'm thinking we need to be busy and take our minds off what has happened today. We'll talk about it later when the others are with us. They will need to know what happened here."

Karmine and Roslin agreed. Karmine went about collecting what he needed to make the whistles and started showing Roslin and the boys how to make them. It wasn't long until they had several whistles made and ready for Jasmine to test them for the tone they made to be sure it was the right one. When Karmine finished the first one, she blew on it to test the tone. She was very surprised that it seemed to be the right one. She suggested one small change. When Karmine was finished, she tried it again. It was perfect this time.

"Karmine this sounds perfect. Can you make the rest of them just the same?"

"I'm sure we can. The wood I chose is very hard and will hold its shape for a very long time. I'll show the boys how to do them and with Roslin's help, we can finish them very quickly. "

Roslin and the boys were careful to follow Karmine's instructions carefully as well. They knew how important these whistles were to the survival of the town. The whisles they made were made with pride and attention to detail.

Jasmine and Donavan watched as the family made the whistles and let Jasmine test them to make sure they were all alike. She was very pleased with the results they had created in such a short time. They had a dozen whistles to hand out to those willing to use them.

Now they were ready to take the whistles back to the inn. Donavan knew that Magg would test each one before they were given out to the villagers. Karmine was very good at making whistles that were the same in construction as needed. It was absolutely necessary that these whistle be exactly the same and make the same tones. Karmine had designed them to be big enough to make a very loud noise when used. Hopefully, it would be loud enough to warn everyone who lived nearby. They were easy to use and would help warn the villagers of any attack the Skreechers might start.

Donavan was watching the road back to the inn and tried to find any danger from Skreechers so they could get back to the inn with the whistles the family had made. It was getting late in the afternoon when Donavan decided they needed to get back to the inn. If they waited any longer, the monsters might move in and attack them before they could get back.

The whistles were bagged up and Karmine carried them for the run back to the inn. The boys were ready to make a run for it too. Donavan opened the door and looked around for signs of danger. He didn't see anything just then, so he motioned for the family to follow him out the door. As they got passed the front of their house, they started to run for the inn. The boys were kept in the middle of the group for safety.

They ran faster than they ever had and were terrified that the monsters would see them and chase after them. They were getting really close to the inn when they heard a loud screech coming from the left side of the village. Donavan and Karmine each picked up two boys and ran even faster for the inn. Roslin and Jasmine were keeping up with them as they ran.

Suddenly they heard a Skreecher coming for them from behind. Magg and Matton had been watching for them and opened the inn door just as they ran through safely. The door was slammed shut and the crossbar added just as the Skreecher hit the door really hard and almost cracked it when it hit. If not for the crossbar, it might have done some real damage.

The boys were even more terrified and clung to Karmine and Roslin as they cried and trembled in fear. This was another close call for Karmine's family in the same day.

Karmine spoke up, "We've had two really bad scares today. I don't want to risk another one. May we please stay here at the inn until this is resolved? The boys are really terrified now. They've been able to cope all this time, but today brought it all home. Now they realize how dangerous things are here in the village. I can't risk them any more. There must be a place we can stay as a family."

Magg was thinking the same thing as they all came running into the inn. She said, "This cannot happen again. You've done so much to help the village, the least we can do is protect you from further danger. I'll speak with Aribon about what we can do for you all. I'll let you know later today."

Karmine was so grateful that Magg understood what they had just been through. He said, "Magg, I really do appreciate your help in keeping my family safe. We just can't face anther attack like we've had today. I'm glad you understand."

Magg smiled and went back to the kitchen to talk to Aribon about finding a large enough room for Karmine's family to stay in for a while.

Aribon said, "Magg you know I'm almost booked solid right now. But I think there might be a large room upstairs they can have. Remember when we rebuilt the inn and decided to add an upstairs? We haven't actually used it. It's ready for use, but it's never been used. Let's have the family move up there. Will that work for now?"

"Oh, Aribon, you are such a great person to think of that. Are there beds up there?"

"Magg, I'm pretty sure there is everything that could be needed. It's been awhile since we furnished it, but we can check it out if you'd like."

"Sounds good, let's take Roslin up there and see if she would need anything for her and the boys to be comfortable."

"Great. Do you want to check it out now, or later?"

"I'll go get Roslin and see if she's willing to go now."

So Magg left the kitchen and went back to Karmine and Roslin to tell them the good news and take Roslin upstairs to see what was there for her family.

"Roslin, we have a big room upstairs that we haven't really needed to use for a long while. Would you like to come upstairs with us and take a look? See if there's anything you might need beyond what is up there."

Roslin was excited to find out what Magg and Aribon were suggesting. So the three of them went to the hallway next to the kitchen and went up the stairs to the room. As they entered, they saw that there were several beds with feather mattresses and windows at each end of the room for ventilation. It took up all of the attic area. There was a stand for a washbasin and a large table in the middle of the room with benches on both sides. It was plenty big for Roslin's family.

She asked Magg, "Would there be linens for the beds and dishes for eating if we decided to eat up here?"

Magg looked at Aribon who said, "We have extra bedding and dishes for you to use. We can help you set up the beds, if you'd like."

"I think I would like to have Karmine and the boys bring up the bedding and dishes so we can fix it up ourselves. Would that be alright?"

Aribon smiled, "I think that would be great! Let's get back to the family and tell them about their new place to stay."

The three of them walked back down the stairs and found Karmine and the boys talking with Donavan and Matton about their day.

Karmine went to Roslin as soon as he saw her enter the room. "What did you find out?"

Roslin was smiling and told Karmine about the room that Aribon had given them. "We need to get some bedding and dishes from Aribon and we can set it up how we want. What do you think?"

"I think we need to get started right now."

So Karmine and Roslin took the boys to the kitchen and Aribon gave them the bedding and dishes they needed. They were so excited that the boys ran up the steps to their new room and picked the bed they wanted to sleep on right then. However there was some disagreement between Kedron and his brother Boren. Boren insisted that since he was the oldest, he should get first pick. Kedron disagreed on the principle of first come, first served.

Roslin and Karmine came up a bit slower with their arms full of bedding. They would go back for the dishes later. They laughed when they saw their boys fighting over who got which bed. It was easily settled when Karmine took control of the situation and told them who got what bed. They were each given bedding and told to make up their own bed. They were happy to do so for once in this new place.

Roslin started on the bigger bed on the other side of the room. It was separated a bit from the other beds and had a screen set beside it likely for privacy. Karmine went back downstairs to get the few dishes they needed. When he got back he noticed a small cupboard in the corner that was just the right size for their dishes. He organized them in a very short time.

Once the beds were made and they settled in, the boys were really tired. It had been a very scarey day for all of them. So it was that they decided to go to bed early and get the rest they very much needed. It was hoped that they would indeed be able to sleep after all the trauma they had experienced that day.

Karmine and Roslin went back downstairs to talk with the others about the whistles they had made and to see if Magg approved of their size and tone.

Karmine had left the sack of whistles with Magg when they arrived in such a hurry trying to escape the Skreecher chasing them.

Magg had actually been testing them while Karmine and Roslin were getting settled upstairs. She was impressed with the quality of them and the tones were perfect. How Karmine and his family could have done such a thing in such a short time was amazing.

While she was talking to Donavan and Jasmine about their day and experiences with Karmine's family. She found out how terrible their day had really been. No wonder they were terrified. The poor boys were almost in shock from it all.

Donavan explained the spells he'd had to use to kill the one monster and how difficult it was to do so. Magg was not happy to hear that. These monsters were getting to be a bigger problem all the time. Now they were harder to kill. She was wishing Zarcon were here to help her figure things out better. She felt almost alone in the problems she was facing now.

Donavan on the other hand was feeling a renewed confidence in his ability to destroy the monsters. He had invented the spell that finally killed the Skreecher. He was coming into his own power now. He had cast aside his doubts and began to feel the strength of his magic. It was about time. Magg had been hoping for this day for years. But as yet, she was unaware of his progress.

So things were developing in a positive way now, at least for Donavan, but also for the sake of the defense of the town of Anakik against the Skreechers and the terror they instilled in everyone in the village.

Magg started testing the whistles quietly at first. Greta and Jasmine were with her to make sure the tone was correct. As they blew on each whistle, they found that it seemed to lighten the mood of those around them. The gloom of the Skreechers was being driven back.

Magg was thrilled with the effect so far. Greta and Jasmine were excited to try the whistles and make them as loud as possible. Karmine had made them larger than expected and that made it possible for the whistles to be really loud when needed. Combined with the right tone, they would be a great weapon against the gloom cast by the monsters.

Magg went to Karmine and said, "Karmine, you've made these whistles exactly right. The tone is perfect. Have you noticed any lessening of the gloom cast by the Skreechers?"

"I actually did just now. It's amazing that my little whistles could do such a good thing. We can now protect ourselves from the mood that the monsters cast on us. I'm pretty excited to realize that we can stop worrying about that part of their power."

Jasmine and Greta were excited about the workmanship of the whistles. Karmine and his family had only been working on them for a few hours and they turned out not only the right tone, but were also made with great care.

Greta went to Karmine and Roslin and said, "These whistles that you have made are perfect in every way. I'm very impressed with the care you took to make them so perfect and in such a short time. We're all very proud of you and your family."

Roslin replied, "Thank you Greta, the boys caught on really fast when we were making them. They knew how important it was that they be made correctly so that they would work properly. I'm proud of the work we did as well."

The night was coming on fast and they were all worn out by the excitement of the day. Jasmine took Donavan by the hand and they went to their room for the night. Magg found Matton in the kitchen talking with Aribon about what the day had brought and what had been learned.

Magg went to him and listened to their conversation for a few minutes. They were aware of all that had happened and how Donavan had saved Karmine's family and Jasmine from the Skreecher.

Matton was saying, "I'm thinking Donavan is gaining control and understanding of the power he actually possesses. He had a different look about him when they came running into the inn. Yes, he was scared, but it seemed that he knew he could handle it if necessary. He hasn't had that look before. His confidence is increasing, and might I add, just in time."

Magg cleared her throat as she entered the kitchen, "So you've seen that Donavan is gaining confidence in his magic?"

"Yes, Magg, he's a bit different now. It's subtle, but you can see it in his eyes. I think he may have discovered something when he killed that Skreecher protecting Karmine's family."

Magg was thoughtful, then said, "I will have to pay more attention to him now. I'm so glad to hear what you say. It's about time he got things figured out. It's been a long time coming. Matton, will you come with me now? I'm really tired and need you to give me strength tonight. Tomorrow might be a crazy day with all that's happened with the Skreechers."

Matton smiled, "Of course, my love, lets get to bed and rest for tomorrow. We don't know what we'll face so it's vital that we at least get our rest." As they left, Matton gave Aribon a little wink and smile. It was not likely that much sleep would be part of the night for them.

It's actually incredible the power that lovemaking has over the body when two people really love each other as Matton and Magg do. They would need this night to bond and reassure each other of their love.

They were holding hands when they went down the hall to Matton's room. Raven was still in Magg's room for her safety's sake. They needed their privacy this night. As they entered Matton's room, they held each other tight for a few moments. Matton kissed Magg with soft passion. Magg was melting into his arms when they were removing each other's clothing. They took their time and felt the passion build. When they finally got into the bed and covered themselves up, it was a night of slow passion and gentle caresses. They each expressed their love for the other in sweet words and soft touches. Finally, the passion took over and they couldn't get enough of each other. In the end, they lay in each others arms in the glow of their lovemaking and the closeness they felt. In that moment, tomorrow seemed very far away indeed.

They both slept soundly and with smiles on their faces, holding each other close as they slept. They really needed this time alone to reaffirm their love and concern for each other. It would help them through whatever the next day would bring.

Jasmine and Donavan had much the same sort of night together. Donavan did express his renewed confidence in his powers. Jasmine was so proud of him and told him of her pride in being his wife and loving him for who he was. Their bond renewed, they were able to sleep close together and find comfort and strength there.

Karmine and Roslin went up the stairs quietly and found the boys sleeping soundly in their new beds. The two of them were exhausted by the events of the day and the fear they had dealt with protecting the boys. They had survived two encounters with the Skreechers that day and were feeling grateful to be alive. They made ready for bed and slept holding each other close for comfort and strength as the others were that night. Tomorrow would come when it would and they would be ready for it.

Jarrone and his family decided to stay at the inn as well. They had rooms that were reserved for them any time they were needed. So when all the excitement settled down, they went to their rooms for the night. It was far too late to try to make it back to their home in safety. It turned out to be a good thing they were all together for this night.

Chapter 37

Morning came with a crash and a scream. One of the Skreechers had tried to get into the inn through one of the windows near the front of the inn. It had broken the window and was just climbing in when Greta, who was getting some tea for herself, saw it and screamed bloody murder.

The Skreecher was caught off guard and hesitated as it was trying to enter. Aribon heard the racket and grabbed his rifle and came running to Greta. He saw the Skreecher coming in the window and fired at it. He hit the thing in the head and blew most of it off. The Skreecher fell backwards into the street from the force of the gunshot. It was dead before it could cause any more trouble.

Jarrone ran into the dining area just as Aribon shot the Skreecher. Magg and Matton came running next with Donavan and Jasmine close behind. Greta was shaking and weeping from the shock of it all. Jasmine went to her to comfort her.

Jarrone was ready with a powerful spell in case it was needed. He wanted to be prepared. He had watched Aribon kill the Skreecher that was trying to enter through the window. He was alarmed that one of the monsters would be aggressive enough to try such a thing. He found Magg and Matton and asked what had happened.

Aribon was just loading his rifle again just in case more of the things decided to do the same thing. He stood next to the window that had been broken and watched what was happening outside. It looked like the Skreechers had left the area. They must have known that it would be death to them if they tried anything more at that time.

The noise had brought many of the villagers to their windows and many had their rifles ready to shoot if necessary. Seeing the dead Skreecher in the street was a terrible way to wake up in the morning. But in fact it was a sign of success for those in the inn that were trying to protect them all. Success with the Skreechers was death to them and victory for the village.

Aribon was hailed as the hero of the day. Greta was comforted and led back to her room. Raven came running in to see what had happened and was hoping to help in some way. She did lead Greta back to her room and stayed with her that morning.

Horan was concerned and Raven had promised to come to his room to tell him all about the past couple of days' events. He felt helpless and alone. He knew a lot had happened recently, but he had no idea what it was. He was hoping Raven would come and talk to him soon. He was afraid that she was too busy to care about his lonliness.

In fact, Raven had been worrying about Horan and knew she needed to let him know what had happened. She really had been busy with helping everyone prepare for the final battle with the Skreechers. She knew that she had to get to Horan soon. But Greta needed her right then. Greta was settling down from the shock of the Skreecher's attack.

Raven asked Greta if she would like to come with her to inform Horan about recent events. She was hoping to help Greta think about something else and help her help Horan, too. She said, "Greta, are you up to talking with Horan about what's been going on the past few days? He's been alone all this time and I'm getting worried about him."

"Raven, that's a great idea. I really do need to get out of my room and talk with other people about the things we've been through. Can we go now?"

Raven was so happy that Greta wanted to go talk with Horan that she said, "Greta, let's go now. I'm sure Horan will be really happy to see us."

They left Greta's room and went straight to Horan. He was awake and looking sad when they walked into his room.

"Raven, Greta, it's so very good to see the two of you. Ah've been feeling lonely lately. Ah'm so glad you could stop by today. Please tell me what' been goin' on."

So it was that Raven was able to tell Horan all that had happened the last week. There had been so much that it took a while to tell him about it all, but Horan enjoyed every minute of it. He really liked these two women who had done so much to help him through the really bad time he had had.

Magg was very concerned about the attack and saw it as a sign that the Skreechers were getting more aggressive and willing to risk more to get revenge for those monsters that had been killed in the last few days. It was time to up the fight and finally end the terror of the Skreechers for good.

Karmine and Roslin came down to see what had happened. They were glad they had been upstairs at the time. But that was small comfort for the shock Greta had just had. It was obvious that the whistles must be given to the villagers so others could be warned of the presence of a Skreecher in the area. It also looked like their windows really were a weak spot in their defences.

When Karmine came to Magg he could see that something must be done. He had been thinking of the problem for a while, but hadn't thought it would be so important yet. Now he saw that he was wrong. The problem had become very real just this morning. He must talk to Magg about his idea to fix it.

He spoke to Magg, "Magg, I have an idea that will help with protecting the windows, but I'm not sure we have the materials we will need to do anything. What if we could put bars on the windows. Maybe if we could use magic we could do it without risking anyone's life outside where the Skreechers can attack at any time. What do you think?"

Magg suddenly remembered something that Jarrone had done to prevent the women they were taking to prison from escaping the wagon on the way to Sykana.

He had actually been able to add iron bars to the wagon so they couldn't get out or cause other problems.

She said, "Karmine! You've done it again! I'm so glad you thought of that. When we were taking those women to prison in Synkana, Jarrone had been able to use magic to put more iron bars on the wagon to protect us from the women. I'll bet he could do something like that with the windows of the village. I know he's around the inn someplace. I'll find him and mention your idea. I'll let you know what he says as soon as I know."

Magg left Karmine and went to find Jarrone. She did find him talking with Aribon about what had happened that morning. She walked up to him and said, "Jarrone, can we talk for a minute?"

Jarrone gave Aribon a nod and turned to Magg. "What is it, Magg?"

Magg guided him to the corner of the dining area and said, "Jarrone I was wondering about the spell you used to put more bars on the prison wagon. Do you think it might be possible to repeat that spell?"

Jarrone paused, then asked her, "Why do you ask?"

"Karmine had a great idea for protecting the villagers and the windows in every home. Do you think you could somehow use magic to create the same bars on the homes in Anakik?"

Jarrone thought about it. He knew it would take a lot of magic and he wasn't sure he could do it. He finally said, "Magg, it would take a lot of magic and I'm pretty sure I can't do it alone. Would you and Donavan like to learn how I did it?"

Magg was thrilled. She said, "Jarrone, we would be more than happy to help you with that spell. Donavan is finally feeling how powerful he is. We can do it together, absolutely. When can we start?"

Jarrone smiled, "Any time, how about after lunch?"

"That sounds great. I'll talk to Donavan right away."

Magg knew they could do it if they did it together. She found Donavan talking with Jasmine and Aribon. She motioned him over.

"Donavan, I've been talking to Jarrone about putting bars on the windows using magic. Can you meet with us after lunch so we can learn the spell we need to do it?"

Donavan said, "That sounds great! I'm excited to be able to help. It would be wonderful if we could start making the bars by tomorrow at the latest."

"My feelings exactly."

Aribon had lunch ready for everyone and called them to come and eat. The people staying at the inn were happy to come and eat. Aribon was such a good cook, every meal was something to look forward to.

Aribon served ham sandwiches on his famous sour dough bread and vegetable salad for everyone. There was plenty to eat and well water or ale to drink. When Magg, Donavan, and Jarrone were finished eating, they went to the back of the inn to try the spell Jarrone knew to create bars for the windows of the inn. They wanted to start there because it was close and easy to get to.

Jarrone began the spell and was showing Magg and Donavan what he was doing. They practiced as he showed them what to do. Jarrone explained he needed to call forth the iron in the earth and mold it to his desire. Magg and Donavan were learning quickly. As the spell progressed, it appeared that some metal was joining them. Jarrone started molding it into bars and cast them to the closest window. Magg and Donavan did the same with the next two windows. The bars hit the windows with a bang and stuck to the wood framing deeply. They would not be easily removed or broken.

The three of them laughed and clapped at the results they had created. It could be done and wasn't really hard to do. The magic needed was small, but when they considered how many windows needed to be fixed, it was a significant amount for one person. The three of them would have no problem getting it done.

They agreed to start putting bars on all the windows in the village right away. They needed to decide the best way to do that without having to go outside where the Skreechers might be lurking. Donavan and Jarrone began discussing what they could do.

Jarrone said, "I wonder if we could have most of the villagers stay here at the inn until we can get more bars on the windows. I'm thinking we could cast the bars to the homes from here and as we do so, we could have the villagers move back into their homes. What do you think? I will need your help and Magg's too."

Donavan was thoughtful for a moment, then said, "I think you may be right. But how do we get the villagers to move here for a few hours while we do that?"

Magg added, "I'm wondering if we could invite them to come for dinner and explain what we want to do? We could post an invitation in the window of the store across the street. It shouldn't be terribly dangerous if the three of us stay on the front porch and guard the people as they come in."

"That might work. So when do we want to do this?" Asked Jarrone

Magg said, "How about now? We could start getting the villagers to come in with a quick note at the store. I will write the note and take it to the store now so we can get started. We can't wait any longer. The Skreechers are getting far too dangerous."

"Ok, Jarrone and I will watch you move to the store and protect you in case a Skreecher shows up."

Magg hurriedly wrote a note big enough to attract the attention of the locals. She left the inn and moved quickly across the street and walked into the store.

Toran was surprised to see her and asked, "What brings you here, Magg?"

"I would like to post this sign in your front window." She showed him the sign and he approved it.

She posted the sign and thanked Toran for his help. She also asked Toran to bring attention to the sign and hopefully get more of them to come to the inn. Magg left the store and walked quickly back to the inn. Jarrone and Donavan watched carefully to make sure Magg was safe as she hurried back to the inn.

Magg was a bit out of breath as she said, "I hope we get a lot of the neighbors to show up so we can get the bars started on several of the homes nearby."

As they watched the front of the inn and the store across the street, they noticed that some of the villagers were checking the sign on the window. There were several of them that actually started moving toward the inn.

Jarrone and Donavan moved back out on the porch to protect them as they crossed the street. As they watched, a Skreecher appeared at the end of the street nearest the entrance to Anakik. Jarrone started a spell to stop it from attacking anyone. Suddenly, the Skreecher moved toward the villagers. Jarrone cast the spell that would shatter the monster into pieces. It hit the monster and blew it up. Parts of the monster sprayed the area, but missed the villagers.

The villagers screamed and ran for the inn. Donavan held the door open. They all hurried inside in a state of panic. Magg took them to the kitchen saying, "Come with me. Aribon has some food leftover that will help you feel better. Let's talk about what happened and try to relax. Jarrone has killed the Skreecher and you are here safe and sound. I'm so grateful for all of that. We're going to start putting iron bars on the windows of your homes, if you approve."

Many of the villagers were more than happy to have the bars put on their windows. They knew that the Skreechers had almost gotten inside Karmine's home not long ago. They had been living in fear since then. The idea of bars on the windows made them feel that they would be safe again.

One of the villagers spoke up, "Magg we're so grateful that you are working to help us be safer. We're more than happy to have the bars put on all of the windows in our homes."

Magg was happy to hear it. She said, "I appreciate that. We'll be starting on the bars this afternoon. We are hoping you will want to stay here at the inn until we are finished with the bars on your windows. When we finish, you will be free to go back to your homes."

"We're fine with that, Magg. We'll be so glad to be safer from the Skreechers. It will be well worth whatever it takes. It's so great that we can stay here at the inn until that happens."

At that, Magg went to find Jarrone and Donavan. They needed to start putting the bars in the windows of those who were now in the inn.

Magg found Jarrone and Donavan near the front door of the inn. They were watching for any more people wanting to come and eat dinner there. A few more families came across the street with both men protecting them as they crossed.

Magg welcomed them and sent them to the dining room for dinner. As they moved to the dining room she explained to them the plan to put bars in the windows of their homes. They were all excited to have the bars added so they would be safer from the monsters.

When Magg got back to the front of the inn, she spoke to Jarrone and Donavan about casting the spell that would put bars on the windows nearby.

Donavan said, "Let's get started on the bars. Jarrone do you know how to direct the magic to the right places from here?"

Jarrone smiled, "I sure do. I've been practicing and finally figured it out. I can show you how to do that as we cast the spell together."

Magg and Donavan were ready to start the spell to help Jarrone get bars on all the homes that were vacant at the time. The three of them worked together to cast the spell for the bars. Jarrone lead the spell and Donavan and Magg added their magic to Jarrone's.

Suddenly, the bars began to appear in the homes nearby. The bars were going in nicely and went exactly where they were supposed to go. Jarrone was able to direct everything perfectly. They continued casting the bars into the other windows of the homes currently unoccupied. It was nearly finished when there was a sudden feeling of despair. It was worse than they had experienced before.

Magg yelled for the whistles created for this experience. The people in the inn who knew how to use them grabbed one and started to blow on them.

As the tone got louder, there was a clearing of the horrible feelings generated by the monsters. It took a few moments to clear the air, but it was successful.

As soon as the feelings were cleared, there was a scream from one of the villagers that the monsters were coming. Just then, several Skreechers appeared from the forest.

They moved swiftly toward the inn growling as they ran. This was a major attack and none of them were ready for it. They had been under the mistaken assumption that they had a few more days before the war would be joined. Now they had to face the fact that it was too late for planning.

Fortunately, Karmine and Roslin were watching from their windows at the front of the inn and had noticed the Skreechers moving into town. Karmine got his rifle and put a red flag out the window in the front of the inn to notify the neighbors of the danger. When the Skreechers passed below their window, Karmine moved with his gun and stood there, hoping other people would see him and bring their weapons.

The neighbors had noticed the red flag and the passage of the monsters. They saw Karmine in the window above the door to the inn. They knew it was time to protect what they held dear. They came outside with their fifles and any other thing they could use as a weapon. The villagers were up in arms to protect their village from the evil of the Skreechers. It was time to act.

Chapter 38

It was terrifying to watch the Skreechers moving so swiftly toward the inn. Magg, Donavan, and Jarrone were not ready for the fight that was now here. They had just used a lot of magic in placing the bars on so many windows nearby. They had very little magic in reserve for this situation.

It almost seemed that the Skreechers knew all this and were acting on their weakness. What the Skreechers did not know was that there were villagers heading their way with weapons of their own. It would be more dangerous, but possibly almost as effective in destroying the Skreechers. Only time would tell and that swiftly.

As the villagers opened fire on the Skreechers, they began to fall. Some of the monsters turned to face the new threat. As the fight continued, it appeared that some of the villagers might be in danger of the attack. Magg could see the problem developing in front of her. She called Jarrone and Donavan to her. She was going to use one of the new spells she had learned before.

She asked the men to join her as she cast the spell that would destroy several of the Skreechers at once. Magg waved her hands in the careful preparation of the spell. She began the incantation and with the help of Donavan and Jarrone, she cast the spell to the middle of the attack of the monsters.

As the spell hit them, they were instantly turned to ash. Nearly all of the Skreechers were hit. The few that were left were shot by the villagers coming from the other side of town. Magg had fainted from the use of so much magic, especially in her weakened state. But Donavan and Jarrone added their own magic to hers to increase the effect of the spell. They were prepared for Magg to faint from the use of so much magic and caught her before she could fall. They carried her to the couch just inside the inn. It had taken a toll on all three of them. It was difficult to understand the true effect on them for a few moments. Donavan was held up by Jasmine who was nearby watching. Jarrone was supported by his sisters who were close by also watching Jarrone.

Matton was there at Magg's side as soon as he saw her being carried inside. He said, "Magg you knew this would happen even with the help of Donavan and Jarrone. But I'm so proud of you for doing it anyway. Between you and the rest of the villagers, it looks like the Skreechers are destroyed. It's a happy day indeed."

Magg was just coming around and said, "What happened? Is the war over?"

Those standing nearby started to laugh in happiness. Matton said, "Yes, it's over Magg. You and the villagers have destroyed the Skreechers! It's amazing, Magg. It took all of them and you to get it done. Karmine is here to speak to you."

Karmine stepped up to Magg and said, "Magg, all the planning worked! It didn't seem like it was going to when they attacked with such swiftness and rage. Since we had practiced and prepared for so long, the planning came together just in time. It's good that so many of the villagers were here at the time. It meant that there were fewer people in danger from the monsters. There was a lot less danger of innocent people being hurt. Congratulations, Magg on the fight we won together."

Magg was so overwhelmed by the fact that the war was over that she could hardly grasp the fact. She stammered, "It…it's really over? The Skreechers are no more? Are you sure?"

Jarrone came to her just then, "Magg, it really is over. All the planning and help from everyone has made all the difference. We have beat the Skreechers as a village…together. The best sort of victory."

Aftermath

It was looking like the monsters were finally destroyed. Some of the hunters in the village were out searching the forest to make sure they were truly gone. As time passed, none of the Skreechers were ever found.

The people of the village of Anakik were joyful and ready to celebrate their victory for of a certain it had taken everyone to accomplish so great a task. Now that the monsters were gone, what happens to Anakik and its people?

Raven is still helping Horan heal from the injuries caused by the Skreecher near his home. He is healing nicely now after having problems with infection in his wounds. He has started walking around the inn short distances to regain his strength. Raven has been near him encouraging him to keep working on his health and strength. He will be healed soon.

Raven is also finally able to hunt for the food she requires in the nearby forest without fear of hunters or Skreechers. Her happiness and contentment living in Anakik is almost complete. She is also wondering about her feelings for Aribon. What did it mean?

Greta continues to be an important part of the town. She counsels others when they are under stress and uncertainty. She is an impath and can help them calm and move forward with their lives. This has been especially important in the aftermath of the destruction of the Skreechers. So many of the villagers were suffering from the stress and fear of living with the constant threat of the monsters.

The children were especially vulnerable to nightmares from the trauma of the Skreechers. But they were resilient and were moving forward with their lives fairly quickly. It would take time for everyone to adapt to the fear they had felt for so long, now gone.

Jarrone joined Magg and Donavan in discovering more about their magic and testing the limitations of it. There is much to learn and with the help of Zarcon's Book of Spells, they are learning much more. They are also talking about the prospect of the School of Magic and getting it started soon. There was a need for training those who had magic to find out the abilities they possessed.

Revinia, sister of Jarrone, began creating pretty dresses for the village women. The dresses she created for Raven made her very popular with the younger women.

Magg and Matton decided to finally seal their love with marriage. There is a big celebration planned in the next two weeks to celebrate with them sharing their vows.

In the meantime, a huge victory celebration is being planned. The people of Anakik are excited to finally celebrate the end of the tyranny of the Skreechers.

Aribon is ready to celebrate with food. He is looking forward to a party like the town has never seen. He was secretly holding certain foods in his cool cellar for just such a celebration. He spoke to Magg and the others about what he could do to help them plan the party. It was truly going to be epic.

Aribon secretly loved Raven and has been thinking maybe he would really like to get to know her better as a friend, maybe more. He had been feeling that maybe Raven felt the same way. He would find out soon.

Horan was hoping his wife would come back with his family. He feared that she would not. In another way, he was angry about how she had left him without help when he had been injured by the Skreecher. So his feelings were mixed about her return. He would have liked to have his children back, but he wasn't sure about her. He was thinking about sending word to Synkana to let her know that the Skreechers were gone. Yet he was almost fearful of her reply. He would send the message and find out. He must know for his own peace of mind.

Karmine and Roslin were finally able to get back to their home with their four boys. Both of them felt that they had really contributed to the victory over the Skreechers. The children were happier than they had been in a long, long time.

There were children out playing in the town square and where there was much laughter and singing. The sound was so joyful that some of the adults had tears in their eyes from happiness. These were sounds not heard for so long that to hear them now was such a blessing.

It had been a difficult year for the people of Anakik and they had been victorious over the worst monsters they had ever had to face. Their victory had truly been because the entire village had fought together. There was a new closeness as a result. They knew that they could count on each other when trouble threatened. They couldn't ask for more.

The End?

www.ingramcontent.com/pod-product-compliance
Lightning Source LLC
Chambersburg PA
CBHW021330310726
48971CB00001B/56